MOONLIGHT AND MISTLETOE

December is here and it's time to celebrate the holidays with a romantic collection of contemporary stories from three of Arabesque's most cherished authors. Each of these talented authors will introduce us to a special couple who have discovered the holiday magic of true love blended with undeniable desire. Rejoice in Adrienne Ellis Reeves's tale of Christmas's glad tidings, relish the fruits of Kwanzaa with Bridget Anderson, and delight in Candice Poarch's New Year's Eve story. These three unforgettable novellas will touch your soul and are bound to warm your heart during the chilly winter season.

ENJOY THESE SPECIAL
ARABESQUE HOLIDAY ROMANCES

HOLIDAY CHEER   (0-7860-0210-7, $4.99)
by Rochelle Alers, Angela Benson,
and Shirley Hailstock

A MOTHER'S LOVE   (0-7860-0269-7, $4.99)
by Francine Craft, Bette Ford,
and Mildred Riley

SPIRIT OF THE SEASON   (0-7860-0077-5, $4.99)
by Donna Hill, Francis Ray,
and Margie Walker

A VALENTINE KISS   (0-7860-0237-9, $4.99)
by Carla Fredd, Brenda Jackson,
and Felicia Mason

MOONLIGHT AND MISTLETOE

Bridget Anderson
Candice Poarch
Adrienne Ellis Reeves

P

Pinnacle Books
Kensington Publishing Corp.
http://www.pinnaclebooks.com

PINNACLE BOOKS are published by

Kensington Publishing Corp.
850 Third Avenue
New York, NY 10022

First Printing: November, 1997
10 9 8 7 6 5 4 3 2 1

Printed in the United States of America

CONTENTS

Keepsake

Adrienne Ellis Reeves

With deep appreciation for my keepsake friends BJ, Charlotte, Margaret, Roma and Shirley.

Chapter One

"Watch your side for me, Adam. Let me know if I'm getting too close to that truck," Kimberly Washington said backing her red Toyota Corolla into a tight space between a pickup truck and a large Oldsmobile that was parked several inches over the white demarcation line.

Five-year-old Adam, accustomed to serving as sometime navigator for his mother said, "You're fine, Mom, on this side."

"I don't know why some people are so careless about taking more space than they should," Kimberly grumbled as she brought the car to a decisive stop outside the Jamison Public Library. On this late Monday afternoon before Thanksgiving the small lot was filled. As she and Adam walked around the car to get the boxes of books from the trunk the pickup truck was driven away and a dark blue Buick rolled smoothly into the slot.

The young girl who got out of the car looked across at Kimberly and said, "Hi, Miss Kimberly."

Kimberly, busy with opening the trunk, looked up in surprise.

"Why, Amanda, hello!" Her smile was warm and pleased. "I haven't seen you in a long time. How are you?"

Amanda returned the smile. "I'm fine," she said. She was a tall young girl, her heavy dark hair plaited in many small braids setting off her brown eyes and well-defined eyebrows. The dark-skinned man who'd been driving Amanda and now came up beside her could only be her father, Kimberly thought, because they had the same coloring, the same angular face with its prominent cheekbones, generous mouth, and sharp nose. The man wore his thick hair cut close and he had a small scar near his right eye. His jeans and long-sleeved navy pullover fitted his tall, lean body.

"This is my dad," Amanda said.

"Gary Raeford," the man said extending a large shapely hand.

"Kimberly Washington," she said, shaking his hand. Adam had been standing quietly and she turned to him now hoping he'd remember the manners she'd been drilling into him. "Adam, this is Mr. Raeford and his daughter, Amanda."

Adam said, "Hello, Amanda." She replied, "Hi, Adam." Then Adam held out his right hand to Mr. Raeford and said, "How do you do, sir."

Such good manners, Gary Raeford thought, meeting the serious eyes looking up at him as he shook the boy's hand. "I'm glad to meet you, Adam," he responded gravely.

Adam felt he'd found a friend. Looking up at this new friend he confided, "I'll be six my next birthday. How old will you be?"

Kimberly, surprised and embarrassed, opened her mouth to admonish Adam but Mr. Raeford, returning Adam's confidence said, "I'll be forty-two," before Kimberly could say anything.

Amanda, not wanting to be left out, said, "I'll be fifteen."

Three pairs of eyes turned to Kimberly, who thought that she wasn't going to look childish by refusing to divulge her age, and anyway what difference could it possibly make. She said lightly, "I'll be twenty-seven. Now that we have our vital statistics taken care of,'' she went on with a smile for Mr. Raeford, ''I recall meeting you at the fashion tea Amanda was in last year.''

Gary Raeford had been looking with interest at this long-legged young woman with satiny milk chocolate skin and large hazel eyes. The unusual combination drew attention to the way her eyebrows tilted up at the outside, to her wide expressive mouth and her straight nose. An intriguing face with character, he thought, and could easily see how the combination of her slim, graceful figure and her face made her a good model.

''You were the commentator for the show and I remember thinking how professional you sounded. Do you model full time?'' he asked.

Amanda beckoned to Adam and the two of them began looking at the books Amanda was carrying. Kimberly's eyes were on them as she said, ''Only occasionally. There isn't enough work around Charleston and Jamison or anywhere else in South Carolina to make a full-time modeling career.''

Would you like to? was the next question on the tip of Gary's tongue. If she said no, then he wanted to know what would she like to do. In fact, what was she doing now and where did she live? How and with whom did she and Adam spend their time? Was there a Mr. Washington? He was full of questions that were none of his business and he was keeping her standing when she probably wanted to get on with what she'd come to do. Looking at the boxes of books in the trunk he said, ''May I carry these in for you, Miss Washington?''

''Yes, thanks, and please call me Kimberly.'' she said as he picked up the boxes and closed the trunk with her left hand, which Gary saw with sharp interest was bare of rings.

''If you call me Gary,'' he said, smiling into her eyes. She felt a quickening pulse as she returned his look. Amanda and Adam had already started up the long path to the library door and Gary and Kimberly fell into a matching step as they slowly followed.

''Do you come to the library often?'' Gary asked.

"Adam and I spend a lot of time here. We both love books," Kimberly answered. She was busy trying to recall what she'd heard about Amanda's family last year when she was giving modeling instruction to the Girls' Club for their fashion show. Hadn't there been some reference to Amanda living with her father this year? If so, that indicated a divorce. Or was all of that about one of the other girls? It hadn't mattered at the time, but now Kimberly wished she'd paid more attention.

"I'm surprised Amanda and I haven't run into you before now," Gary said. "Amanda calls this her home away from home."

"Amanda and I have something in common because that's just what I used to call it when I was growing up," Kimberly said with a big smile.

Gary noticed how her delight made her nose crinkle and her hazel eyes light up as she looked at him. He returned the smile involuntarily and in that exchange each experienced a penetrating awareness of the other.

At the library door Gary shifted the books to open the door with his left hand. No wedding band, Kimberly noted, and a secret smile turned up the corners of her mouth.

The library held a quiet hum of low-pitched voices while Mrs. Marshall, the librarian, was busy with two assistants at the main desk. Gary eased the boxes of books down. Kimberly spotted Adam showing Amanda the science books at his favorite shelf in the children's section.

Mrs. Marshall was a thin, erect lady of middle years smartly dressed in a tailored skirt and spotless white blouse. She finished with a group of high schoolers and came over.

"I saw Amanda and Adam come in," she said by way of greeting, "and I knew you had to be close by. Thanks for the books. The collection for the sale is going well." She included them both in her thanks as she put the boxes with a group of others.

Mrs. Marshall looked at them as if she had something on her mind, Kimberly thought, so she wasn't surprised when the librarian asked them to wait a moment. She went over to the far side of the desk and took a folder from the drawer. She brought it back and leaning across the counter confidentially said, "Mr. Raeford, you asked some months ago why the library has no homework program. The subject's come before the library board recently. I'm to bring some ideas to the next meeting. I'm going to ask the two of you to draft a homework plan for me to present. You're both parents. You and your children use the library extensively. I'm sure you both have ideas on the subject and you'll find some reference material in the folder. Will you do this for the library, please?" she asked, looking from one to the other.

Kimberly had not expected this. Her first thought was no. Adam was too young to have homework yet. Second, she was already busy enough. Third, she'd just met Gary Raeford and here Mrs. Marshall wanted them to work together as a team on her project.

Gary had taken the folder Mrs. Marshall handed him. He was not as surprised as Kimberly. He knew that if you ever asked why something wasn't being done you stood a good chance of being asked to do it. He glanced quickly at Kimberly's expressive face and saw she was about to say no to the idea. In the hope of forestalling her rejection he turned to Mrs. Marshall.

"When would you need the material, Mrs. Marshall?" he asked.

"By December twentieth," she said. She, too, had seen the look on Kimberly's face so added, "It needn't be anything elaborate. Some statements about the goals of such a program and basic ideas of how we might implement it, that's all I need right now."

Gary turned to Kimberly. "I think we might be able to do that, don't you? After all we have Amanda and Adam to help us and it shouldn't really take too much of our time." He added, "I'll take the responsibility for it but I'd really appreciate your help."

Kimberly wondered what line of work Gary was in. He'd covered all the bases so well in his appeal for her help that to refuse would seem petty and selfish. She wouldn't be surprised if he turned out to be a lawyer. Knowing she could only accede, she put the best face on it and, looking at Mrs. Marshall, said pleasantly, "If it doesn't take too much time, I think Adam and I can help with this."

Mrs. Marshall looked gratified. "If we had more parents like you, the library could serve the community better. Thank you both."

Adam appeared beside Kimberly. "Mom, look at this book I found on science things you can do at home."

Kimberly bent down to look at the pages Adam wanted her to see. "We can check it out. Is that the only book you want?"

"Yes, ma'am," Adam said, already engrossed in pictures of experiments.

There was a line at the checkout desk and while Kimberly waited she could see Gary and Amanda who were waiting in the lobby a short distance away, their heads bent over the material in Mrs. Marshall's folder. Amanda pointed to something and made a remark to which Gary responded. They seem very comfortable with each other, Kimberly thought, as she and Adam inched forward in the line. She was noticing how well the shape of Gary's haircut suited him when he suddenly raised his head and looked straight across at her before she could drop her eyes.

"Mom," Adam said, "we're next." Kimberly thankfully turned her attention to the clerk and in another few minutes she and Adam were through and joined Gary and Amanda.

"Miss Kimberly," Amanda said as they all started down the walk, "my friend Sandra Blair who was in the fashion show with me, she and I sometimes come to the library to do homework and twice it got so noisy we decided there should be screens or some kind of partition. Do you think that's an idea you and Dad could use?"

As Kimberly answered her a group of five people coming

up the walk made her and Amanda automatically swerve around them leaving Gary and Adam behind. Kimberly glanced back and saw the two were in deep conversation and that Gary had adjusted his long stride to a comfortable pace with Adam.

"Kimberly," Gary said as he and Adam arrived at the cars where she and Amanda were waiting, "would it be possible for us all to get together at our house tomorrow evening? I know that's short notice but Amanda's leaving Wednesday morning to join her mother. It'd be good to get her ideas for this."

Kimberly was trying to digest this suggestion when Gary, looking at her surprised himself by saying persuasively, "Unless you'd rather do it now. We'd be happy to have you and Adam come over now or later this evening if that's more convenient for you."

"Could we, Mom?" Adam said in a whisper clearly heard by Gary and Amanda.

Kimberly looked swiftly at Gary whose glance at Adam was pleased. Amanda, puzzled to hear her father who rarely asked people to the house invite Miss Kimberly over right after meeting her, gave him a questioning look. Kimberly saw the look and it confirmed her own feeling that this was all going too fast. She had just met the man and already had committed herself to working with him on a project. Now he was proposing that she and Adam come to his house. But perhaps she was misjudging him, and his sole interest was in the project. However, when she looked at Gary again there was a warmth in his eyes that no library scheme could engender.

"I'm sorry but tonight I'm busy," Kimberly said.

"Tomorrow then?" Gary replied.

She said, "We can come for a little while but it'll have to be early."

"Any time that's convenient for you," Gary said again.

"Six thirty?"

"Fine. We live at 20 Briar Lane," Gary began.

"I know where that is," Kimberly said cutting him off in

her eagerness to get away. She and Adam said goodbye and by the time Gary and Amanda were putting their seatbelts on, Kimberly was backing out, then turning from the parking lot onto Jamison Road, a busy artery running through the town.

People who didn't know thought of Jamison only as a bedroom community for its famous neighbor Charleston, with its historic houses, and Fort Sumter across the bay, where the first shots of the Civil War were fired. But Jamison, though small, had its own distinctive past, first as a retreat for artists, then for wealthy people escaping the stifling summer heat of Charleston, and later still for people seeking health in the purity of its pine-laden air. Jamison's expansion beyond its original central core was due to developers who bought tracts of land, cut down the pine and oak trees, and built houses.

As she drove home, Kimberly was wondering which development Gary Raeford lived in. She'd told him she knew but that was just to get away. Both Green Pines and The Oaks had opened about four years ago and Briar Lane was in one of them. The Oaks was more upscale with three and four bedrooms, a family room, a fireplace, and large yards. Either place was a far cry from the small two-bedroom subsidized apartment she and Adam had felt fortunate to obtain when she left her parents' home three years earlier.

An hour later at supper Adam put a forkful of macaroni and cheese in his mouth and said, "I like Amanda and her dad. Do you like them, Mom?"

"Don't talk with food in your mouth, Adam," Kimberly said automatically. "Yes, I like them."

"Mr. Raeford asked me did I like electric trains and I said yes and he said he still has one with lots of cars that he got when he was little and he wants to show it to me." Adam's clear brown eyes sparkled with enthusiasm as he related this conversation on one continuous breath.

"And he's got some wooden soldiers that his grandfather gave him," Adam went on, his eyes big. He didn't know anyone who had wooden soldiers. He'd only seen pictures of them. He laid his fork down so he wouldn't put food in his mouth while he asked his mother this very important question.

"Tomorrow when we go to his house can I see the trains and the wooden soldiers, Mom?"

"We're going so Mr. Raeford and I can do some library work but if he said he wants to show you the train and the soldiers I guess we can take a little time for that," Kimberly said. "Finish your supper, Adam. It's almost bath time."

Adam, usually a slow eater, finished his supper quickly. After his bath, he took his book of trains to bed with him but fell asleep after looking at a few pages. Kimberly turned out his bedside lamp and as she did every night said a little prayer for Adam's well-being before she left his room.

In the kitchen she washed the dishes and put away the rest of the macaroni and cheese for another meal. A small package of hamburger came down from the freezer section into the bottom of the refrigerator to begin thawing for tomorrow. She wondered who did the cooking in Gary's house. Did he do most of it or was Amanda the cook? How long had he and his wife been separated or were they divorced? No wedding band on Gary could mean anything. After all, she didn't wear one either.

Kimberly straightened up the living room then this being Monday she gave her bedroom a thorough cleaning. Usually these routine chores were accompanied by thoughts of her bookstore job or how to stretch her paycheck, or how she could complete her college degree. But tonight she kept seeing the image of Gary Raeford as he smiled at her and asked her to call him Gary, as he walked beside her from the car into the library, and as he stood beside her talking to the librarian and skilfully drawing Kimberly into working on the project with him. He was not a handsome man, but he had a vital presence and assurance that was more powerful than mere physical attractiveness.

He probably had several girlfriends, a man like that, Kimberly mused as she stripped her bed of its blue and white striped sheets and remade it with her favorite ones of scattered butterflies on sunshine yellow. She noticed the sheets were thin with wear; she'd have to watch for linen sales.

Gary might even have a live-in girlfriend, her thoughts ran on. So many people seem to think that's all right these days. But no, he couldn't because he would not have been so quick to invite her and Adam over.

Kimberly picked up a pillow, held it between her teeth, and pulled on the pillow slip. She fluffed the pillow and placed it on the bed. As she picked up the second pillow she saw herself smiling up at Gary after saying how she shared with Amanda a love for libraries. He'd returned the smile and as their eyes met Kimberly felt she knew the person that was Gary Raeford although she'd just met him.

It wasn't the kind of knowledge that gave her access to information about his life, but it did create an instantaneous connection, a pull that she now resisted mentally. She put the second pillow on the bed and began vacuuming the rug. With each thrust of the machine Kimberly thought of a reason to keep her involvement with Gary Raeford businesslike and minimal. First, he was too old, fifteen years older than she was. Her own mother was only nineteen years older than Kimberly.

There was an even more important difference between them to which Kimberly was very sensitive. She stated it to herself bluntly: he had money and she didn't. She'd looked up Briar Lane and found it was in The Oaks, which meant Gary Raeford could afford to buy a large, expensive house, while she barely made it from month to month. She'd noticed his Buick was the top of the line while her old Toyota was kept running by the frequent attention of her brother Willie's wizardry with automobiles.

She knew nothing about his education but she'd bet a nickel he had at least a master's degree, while she was still struggling to get beyond two years at Trident Tech.

What it all amounted to, Kimberly concluded, as she gave the vacuum one final thrust before unplugging it, was that she had no relish for a cinderella role with Mr. Gary Raeford as the benevolent prince. She could continue to do well enough on her own, thank you very much. Tomorrow's meeting would be strictly business. She would see to that.

On Briar Lane, Amanda Raeford was sitting in front of the bookcase in the living room. She counted the number of books and frowned. "Dad," she called, "what should I do about my books?"

Gary came in from the kitchen where he had been putting away the food and cleaning up. "What did you say?" he asked, sitting down on a couch next to where Amanda was pulling out the books.

Amanda gestured toward the books. "I want to take these with me but there's too many to put in my suitcases. I've counted thirty-three here and there's a few more scattered around." She began stacking them, one by one, according to their size.

Watching her Gary felt again the wave of sorrow that had swept over him when Amanda's mother Charlotte had called from California to say she and her husband had returned from his military duty abroad and to please send Amanda back to San Diego.

He and Amanda had done well this year after she'd decided to enjoy her stay in South Carolina. She'd found her father easy to talk to about everything even when a boy named Jamal asked her to go out. "He's okay," she'd said, "but I don't like him that much. How do I say no without hurting his feelings?"

Gary had been touched by Amanda's confidence and pleased to not have to enforce his strong feeling against his fourteen-year-old daughter going out on dates. In their conversations, he'd appreciated her quick mind and the readiness she'd developed for a solid father-daughter closeness. Her presence in the house had banished the loneliness he'd felt since the divorce.

Now as Gary answered her question about the books his mind was on how much he was going to miss his daughter's companionship.

"Dad," Amanda said resting against his knees and looking up at him, "I want to see Mom and my friends, but I hate to leave you. I wish you lived closer so we could see each other a lot."

"So do I," Gary said, leaning forward and stroking her hair affectionately. "I'm thankful we had this year together." He sighed. "The house won't be the same without you, honey."

Later as Gary packed the books in two boxes he thought of the boxes he'd carried a few hours earlier for Kimberly Washington and how she'd smiled at him on the way into the library. She was very attractive but that wasn't his strongest memory. Their eyes had met and Gary felt a link, a bond of some kind between them that was new in his experience. It made him eager to learn all about her, about Adam and Adam's father. Where was he and was he still a part of Kimberly's life?

He began to tape the boxes. How old did she say she was? Twenty-six? That meant there was fifteen years difference between them. She was still in elementary school when he was getting married. Gary looked at the boxes unseeingly, a frown creasing his forehead. Did he want to become involved with a woman who was so much younger and whose experience was so different from his?

He addressed the books to his ex-wife's home in San Diego and remembered how that relationship, which had begun with such promise, had ended in disaster. He put the boxes in the trunk of the car and turned out the garage light. He decided to be wary of Kimberly Washington. He'd see that their meeting tomorrow stayed on a friendly but businesslike basis.

Chapter Two

Kimberly was late leaving The Bookshelf where she was the assistant manager. A large order had been misplaced by one of the temporaries hired for the holiday season. Kimberly had finally found it filed under old orders, then dashed to her mother's house to pick up Adam.

A hurried supper was followed by a hurried freshening up. Now feeling nervous and tense Kimberly, with an excited Adam beside her, pulled up in the driveway of 20 Briar Lane. Just as she'd expected, Gary lived in a large two-story brick house. The driveway curved in a semicircle bisecting a smooth lawn outlined with well-trimmed shrubbery.

Gary and Amanda appeared on the porch as Kimberly turned off the ignition. Adam was out of the car immediately saying "Hi, Mr. Raeford."

Amanda said, "Hi, Miss Washington," across the car, then took Adam's hand and they disappeared into the house.

"Kimberly, I'm so glad you could come," Gary said with a warm smile.

"Sorry to be so late," Kimberly said, "but I got held up at

work at the last minute, and it made me very late getting home. I've been rushing ever since.'' Kimberly felt like she was babbling but she couldn't stop herself as they walked up the steps and across the porch.

''It doesn't matter,'' Gary said, ''the point is you're here.'' He held the door open for her. ''Welcome to our house.''

The foyer had a curving staircase leading to the second floor. There was a parquet floor, an oval mirror above a marble-topped table, and a graceful chair with petit point cushions. To the right, Kimberly glimpsed a formal dining room.

''We'll go this way to the family room,'' Gary said, leading her left through a sitting room with brocade couches and chairs into a large family room with a big fireplace on one end. There was a full-size leather couch with a matching chair, two red and black plaid chairs, several tables of different sizes, and wooden chairs scattered around. Books and magazines were everywhere on top of tables and filling numerous shelves. The walls were adorned with some photographs as well as prints. A number of lamps spilled their light on a wine red rug and matching draperies enhanced the warm feeling of the room.

''What a lovely room!'' Kimberly exclaimed. ''It's so comfortable and inviting.'' The words came out with a heartfelt sincerity, then she felt like biting her tongue because she'd vowed to herself not to rhapsodize over Gary's house no matter what it was like. But she was struck by the room's combination of light, color, and style.

Gary was pleased. ''I'm glad you like it, Kimberly, it's my favorite place in the house and I spend most of my time here.''

Kimberly seated herself in one of the plaid chairs and picked up a Maya Angelou book from the nearby table. ''Do you like Angelou's writing?'' she asked, glancing at Gary who was sitting on the other side of the table.

''Very much, especially after I heard her in person several years ago. How about you?''

''Yes. In the bookstore where I work we can't keep her books on the shelf.''

Kimberly turned a few pages of the book avoiding Gary's eyes. She had not yet looked at him directly. She looked at his eyebrows, his nose, his ears when she spoke to him or he to her, but somehow she felt unready for direct eye contact. Despite her conversation with herself last night about Gary now that she was in his presence she didn't know what her reaction would be if she really looked at him.

While they talked of Maya Angelou, Gary thought that Kimberly looked cool and smart in her taupe stirrup pants and tan shirt topped by a long russet cardigan sweater, the collar turned up so that it drew your eyes to the proud way she held her head with its weight of dark hair brushed straight back and secured with a narrow russet scarf. *Those lovely hazel eyes have looked everywhere except into mine,* he thought, and decided to change that immediately.

But before he could speak Kimberly glanced at his nose again and asked, ''Where did Adam disappear to?''

''Amanda is showing him some toy soldiers my grandfather made for me. We'll go up and see them in a minute but first I have something special I want to show you,'' he said going over to a small cabinet in a corner of the room.

Now that his back was turned Kimberly looked at Gary. The faded jeans he wore with a blue and brown striped sweater shirt fitted him so well that she wondered if he worked out to keep himself looking so good. *He's the most attractive man I've seen in a long time despite his age,* she decided as she watched him unlock the cabinet and take something from it.

Gary came back to Kimberly and seated himself on a hassock in front of her. He deliberately kept the item from the cabinet concealed in his hands so she wouldn't be able to focus on it. He wanted her to look at him.

''What I want to show you, Kimberly, is a part of our family history,'' he began. Kimberly's eyes were on his hands. ''My great grandmother Selina Graham became secretly engaged to my great grandfather Thomas Raeford when she was sixteen and he was eighteen. But she had two older sisters who were supposed to be married first while Thomas had to help raise his younger brothers and sisters and help support them before he could afford to marry and have his own family.''

The great hazel eyes met his at last with sympathy and candid interest. Gary felt her look hit him in his solar plexus making him lose the thread of what he was saying until Kimberly asked, ''When did they finally marry?''

The poignant drama of Gary's ancestors had drawn Kimberly to look into the eyes of the storyteller. His dark gaze drew her and held her and he found himself telling the familiar story with unusual eloquence and feeling.

''It took seven years before Thomas could leave his family. Selina was very pretty and had offers of marriage but Thomas was her only love. By the fifth year, Thomas was feeling very discouraged. He and his father had a bad year on their farm, Selina's parents were urging her to marry a prosperous young blacksmith and Thomas was frustrated at not having as his wife the girl he'd been loving for five long years. Selina had a gift for needlework and on that fifth Christmas she gave Thomas a bookmark she made for his Bible.''

Gary showed Kimberly the black velvet case he'd been holding. He pressed the latch and it opened with a little click. Kimberly instinctively leaned forward to look at it. Gary moved closer, holding the case out to her. She extended her hands to take it. Gary took her hands gently in his so that the case rested in the palms of their joined hands. He felt very daring but he so wanted to touch Kimberly despite his decision last night to keep his distance. Her presence affected him strongly. Her hands, warm and supple in his, made him want to cover them with kisses.

Kimberly felt a shock of surprise then excitement at Gary's touch. She kept her gaze on the case afraid to raise her eyes with Gary's face so close she could feel his breath on the tendrils of her hair.

''Selina earned her living with her needlework,'' Gary said

quietly, "and you can see from this bookmark the exceptional quality of her work."

The bookmark was made of sturdy muslin with blended-in fragments of pale silks. Down its center were the embroidered words, LOVE IS TRUE LOVE CONQUERS ALL. Graceful embroidered flowers in bright colors interspersed with an angel, two hearts, and two doves bordered the words on four sides. An unbroken green curving vine ran throughout, unifying the whole. Selina's vision was rendered with consummate artistry through her design, color, and exquisite handiwork.

"It is so expressive," Kimberly said in awe. "The angel is on such a small scale, yet every detail is clear and you get the feeling of an angelic presence hovering over the two hearts," she said thoughtfully.

"Yes," Gary said, marveling that Kimberly was saying what he had always felt, "and reminding them that if their love is true, it will overcome the obstacles between them."

"I see roses, pansies, irises, marigolds, daisies, and bluebells among her flowers," Kimberly said. "How could she get them so distinct that I can instantly recognize them? The blending of the colors is . . . is . . . I don't know how to say it—" She stopped in frustration.

"Like she's used the colors on a palette, only instead of a painter's brush, Selina used thread," Gary said.

"That's it, exactly," Kimberly acknowledged. "I wonder what kind of vine that's supposed to be?"

"I'm not sure," Gary said. "But a vine is an important symbol. An unbroken vine of any kind meant the love and the marriage will be unbroken."

Kimberly digested this in silence, still feasting her gaze and her heart on this treasure. Finally, she raised her eyes to Gary. "May I ask you a question?"

"Anything," he said, his eyes intent on her.

"Why isn't this in a museum?"

"Several have asked for it but it's our keepsake and very precious to us." Gary's voice softened. "Selina made it around

1830, and since then it has passed from eldest son to eldest son.'' The look in his eyes deepened and Kimberly felt a tremor. She tried to look away but couldn't.

Gary held her hands closer to him. ''The eldest son presents it to his true love,'' he said, his voice scarcely above a whisper. He didn't understand why he felt himself irresistibly drawn to this cool hazel-eyed girl. He had listed to himself very good and sensible reasons why he shouldn't become involved with her. So what was happening here?

Kimberly was trying to assimilate what Gary had said but became mesmerized by the intensity of his look. Just as she wondered what was going to happen, she heard Adam call, ''Mom, where're you?''

''In here, Adam,'' Gary said, moving toward the door and in another moment Adam appeared flushed and enthusiastic.

''Your toy soldiers are neat, Mr. Raeford,'' he said. ''I brought some to show Mom.'' He went across the room to Kimberly.

Kimberly as mother of Adam had grown accustomed to rapid change, but being jolted from a story of true love to a demand to admire toy soldiers was definitely unusual. She listened as Adam explained how the fat soldiers had been whittled from wood then painted in these bright colors with their uniforms and hats.

''See, Mom, this one's saluting,'' Adam said, handing her one that had an arm stiffly held up to his forehead.

Gary stood watching Kimberly's and Adam's heads bent together over his soldiers. He thought how he nearly didn't go to the library yesterday, and look at what he would have missed!

At that moment Adam looked up, came over, and putting his hand confidingly in Gary's said, ''Can I see the train now, Mr. Raeford?''

Gary looked inquiringly at Kimberly. She remembered that she'd promised this time to Adam and besides it would give her time to regain her calculated distance from Gary. She looked at her watch. ''Remember, Adam, not too long,'' she said.

The train, its tracks, and buildings were laid out on the floor of one of the four upstairs rooms. With all its lights and switches turned on, Gary and Adam were soon moving the train up and down the track. Adam's excitement grew as Gary showed him how to switch the train from one track to another then let him do it on his own. It was hard for Kimberly to cut this short, but after a while she said, "We're going to have to go home soon, Adam." Adam's face clouded.

Gary turned the train off. "You can come another time, Adam, just to play with the train," he promised.

As they came downstairs Kimberly said, "Gary, I'm sorry but we only have another twenty minutes at the most. Adam has to go to bed because we get up so early."

"I understand," he said. "Amanda, would you and Adam please get the tray we fixed from the kitchen and I'll get the table ready."

In the family room Gary pulled up a straight chair to the library table that was placed at one end of the room. Kimberly began to help him. "We'll be up early, too," he said. "Amanda's plane leaves at six forty-five."

"Where is it she's going?" Kimberly asked.

"To San Diego, where her mother lives."

"How long will she be gone?" Kimberly pulled up the fourth chair and sat down in it."

Gary sat opposite her. "She's going back home to live with her mother," he said.

Kimberly's eyes widened. "Oh, I thought she was just going for Thanksgiving."

Gary began to say something when Amanda and Adam came in with a tray of glasses with ice, cans of soda and a plate of chocolate chip cookies.

"What we can do now," Gary said as the soda and cookies were passed around, "is just make a list of ideas, any ideas anyone has. We'll begin with Amanda because she and Sandra Blair have already discussed it." He opened his folder and looked expectantly at Amanda.

"It gets noisy when you're trying to study so there should be partitions or screens," Amanda said. "Another thing we thought about was they need more space. The space they're using now gets too crowded."

"Partitions or screens, too crowded," Gary repeated as he wrote. "Anything else, honey?" Amanda shook her head and he turned to Kimberly.

"If it gets too crowded why don't we recommend that the homework program take place in that all-purpose room they have?" Kimberly said.

"It isn't very large," Gary said. "I was in it for a meeting. They store equipment there and I think it had only two tables."

"Couldn't they use both?" Amanda said. "Maybe one space for upper grades and one for elementary students."

"That's a good idea to work on," Gary said, writing quickly, "and see what we can come up with."

Adam had been eating his cookies and drinking his soda but looking from one to the other as each spoke. Now he turned to his mother.

"Can I say something?" he asked.

"Of course you can."

"When I go to school and get homework can my teacher come to the library and help me?"

Gary said, "No, your teacher wouldn't be there but someone else could be there to help you. A person called a tutor. That's a good idea, Adam," he said as he wrote.

Kimberly looked at her watch and stood up. "We really do have to go." She wrote quickly on a piece of paper and handed it to Gary. "Here's our number. Call me about the next meeting." She turned to Amanda. "Somehow I didn't realize you're going back to stay, Amanda. Adam and I were looking forward to seeing more of you."

Amanda smiled shyly as she came around the table to Kimberly. "That would have been nice," she said. "Adam and I get along so well." Kimberly hugged her then stepped aside as Adam grabbed Amanda's hand and pulled her out of the room.

"Walk, Adam. Don't run," Kimberly said. Adam and Amanda were laughing as they slowed down and walked ahead through the hall, the sitting room, and into the foyer. Their gaiety echoed in the open spaces and Kimberly suddenly thought how silent and lonely the house would be with Amanda gone.

Impulsively she stopped and looking at Gary said, "Our church is having a Thanksgiving eve dinner tomorrow evening. Would you like to come?"

"Yes, I would," Gary said almost before she finished speaking. "Thank you so much, Kimberly. I was just feeling how empty the house will be this time tomorrow." He looked at her with gratitude.

"Dinner's at seven at the First A. M. E. church on Middle Road," she said.

Gary held the front door open and as they walked across the porch said, "May I pick you and Adam up?"

Kimberly started to say she'd meet him there but felt that would be ungracious. "Thanks. We'll be ready at six thirty. Our address is 65 Spring Street, apartment 10."

"I know where that is," Gary said, as they reached the car. Amanda bent down to hug Adam. "Don't forget what I told you," she said.

"I won't," he promised, as Kimberly started the car and everyone waved a goodbye.

Twenty minutes later Adam was being hustled out of his clothes and into his pajamas. It was already an hour past his bedtime, but he was still keyed up and talking. "Mom, you know what Amanda told me?"

"Adam, I'm going to listen to just this one more thing then the light goes out," Kimberly said firmly.

"She told me to come see her dad 'cause he's going to be

so alone.'' Adam interrupted himself with a big yawn as he got into bed. His eyelids fluttered and in another minute he was asleep.

Making her preparations for the next day, Kimberly assessed the evening's events. Why had her resolve about Gary been so hard to keep? Apparently there was something about his mere presence that had an effect on her and she wasn't used to that.

She stepped into the shower and turned it on full force. Keeping men at a distance had not been a problem to her since her husband, Walter Davis, had been killed in the Gulf War five years earlier. For Kimberly those years had been filled with grieving, raising Walter's son, Adam, going to school, and working to keep herself independent. Her social life was limited to family affairs and occasional church events. Men in the community and men coming into the bookstore had often tried to date her. She'd tried going out several times but with no lasting interest. Yet this man whom she'd only seen twice made her feel trembly inside and had been within a hairbreadth of kissing her.

Then she'd been foolish enough to invite him to the church dinner tomorrow. Kimberly got out of the shower and toweled herself vigorously. She thought of Amanda and her face softened. Such a nice person, Amanda. She and Adam had hit it off immediately. There was no doubt that Gary would feel her absence severely, therefore inviting him to the dinner tomorrow had been the right thing to do, she concluded.

She wondered what her mother and stepfather would think when she appeared with Gary, not to mention Walter's mother and father who would be there also. *But the most important thing,* she decided as she turned off the light, *is what will my feelings be?*

Chapter Three

"How're you coming with the Christmas display design, Kimberly?" Mrs. Carstairs, the manager of The Bookshelf, stood in the doorway of the cubbyhole that was Kimberly's office, looking at the sheets spread out on the desk.

"Slowly," Kimberly replied, "because they're always calling me to the front. But they'll be ready for Friday's staff meeting."

Kimberly could never understand how the manager could look so together on the outside from her sleek pumps to her coiffed purple-tinted hair and polished nails and be so disorganized in her work. Everyone knows the Christmas shopping season begins the day after Thanksgiving and their display should be going up tonight to entice Friday's customers. But Mrs. Carstairs had vacillated in her usual way with the planning and ordering. Kimberly fussed and fumed inwardly as she worked steadily, sidestepping the manager diplomatically and finishing the display as much as possible.

Driving home she tried to clear her mind of work so she could enjoy Thanksgiving. Her mother had Adam waiting to run and jump into the car. He immediately announced, "Gramma said to tell you I've had my bath. I helped Gramma make some pies for tomorrow. Gramma said we're all going to eat at the church tonight. Are we, Mom?"

"Ummm," Kimberly assented, negotiating a sharp turn carefully. "Mr. Raeford's going, too, and he'll pick us up."

"Do I have to dress up?" Adam screwed his face up in disgust.

"If by dress up you mean you can't wear jeans, the answer is yes," Kimberly said at the same time deciding that she'd wear the emerald knit with its long sleeves and subtle shaping. That dress always lifted her spirits.

When Gary arrived home from work his house felt so cold and empty that he stayed in it only long enough to freshen up and change the white shirt he'd worn to work for a pale blue one.

Then he went to the florist where he selected a large arrangement of bronze mums, red leaves, and yellow daisies for Kimberly. It was still too early, so he drove all around Kimberly's neighborhood seeing its elementary school, modest homes, a small park, and two churches. Spring Street where Kimberly lived was only two blocks long with a combination of small duplexes and apartments. Gary knew this was subsidized housing and assumed that Kimberly qualified for tenancy as a single parent.

Her apartment was up one flight and two doors down the walkway. The light above the door shown on Gary as he rang the bell promptly at six thirty.

Adam opened the door wide with Kimberly standing behind him. Adam's cheerful, "Hi, Mr. Raeford," and Kimberly's "Please come in," made him feel welcome as he stepped inside and returned their greetings.

"For you," he told Kimberly, extending the flowers in their brown ceramic bowl. She looked stunning in her green dress that clung where it should and flowed where it should. Tonight she'd clasped her shining dark hair with a rhinestone class matched by delicate rhinestone earrings. Her hazel eyes were warm and friendly as she smiled and thanked him for the flowers.

Gary couldn't take his eyes from her as she took the flowers from him and, asking him to please sit down, excused herself for a moment.

"This is a good chair," Adam said, leading Gary to the single upholstered chair that matched the brown tweed couch. A coffee table, a corner table with a television on it, two lamps, and a cushioned rocker completed the furnishings of the small living room. Color and liveliness had been added by a pile of bright pillows in a corner, several area rugs, and a skillfully draped flow of scarlet cloth across the top of the double window with its white mini blinds. A Romare Bearden print of a quilting scene had the place of honor on the largest wall. On the other wall, a black mother, father, and child depiction hung beside a sketch of a group of children hunkered down in a yard listening to one of the group telling a story. The room, Gary thought, was practical but touched with a need for something beyond the mundane.

Adam brought a photograph over to Gary. "This is my father, Walter," he said. The young man in a soldier's uniform looked to Gary like a grown up Adam. "He died before I was born," Adam went on, matter-of-factly.

"I'm so sorry, Adam," Gary said. Adam leaned against him and Gary put his arm around the boy as they looked at the picture and Gary told Adam how he looked like his daddy.

Kimberly came in and saw their heads bent over the photograph. Gary stood as Kimberly brought the flowers over to the coffee table.

"Adam was showing me his father's picture," he said. "Was he killed in combat?" Gary's voice and eyes expressed his sympathetic interest.

"Yes, in the Gulf War," Kimberly said.

Gary, touched by the loss mother, son, and father had suffered said simply, "I'm very sorry, Kimberly."

Kimberly looked at Gary then acknowledged his sincerity with a quiet "Thank you." She turned to Adam. "Get your jacket on, honey. We're going."

When the three of them arrived at the church the hall was filled with people and cheerful conversation. Long tables covered with white paper were decorated with real pumpkins and construction paper colored leaves the children's classes had made. Garlands of green, orange, and brown crepe paper crisscrossed the ceiling. A fragrance of roasting turkey wafted through the air, transporting Gary instantly to his mother's kitchen where he'd been permitted to baste the turkey for the wonderful holiday dinners they always had. Years had passed since he'd been home for Thanksgiving, but he suddenly felt that here tonight with Kimberly and Adam he could regain some of that feeling.

Kimberly, looking for her family's table, finally saw it and turned to tell Gary just as he turned to her with such a compelling look that she said, "What is it, Gary?"

His hand touched hers and she responded at once by putting her hand in his. "You can't know, Kimberly, how glad I am you asked me to come tonight with you and Adam," he said softly. "One day I'll find a way to thank you properly."

"I'm happy you could come, Gary," Kimberly said. Her heart was beating faster as their glances held and he pressed her hand in his tighter.

"I see Gramma and Grampa," Adam said, pulling on Kimberly from the other side. "Let's go over where they are, Mom."

"We're going, Adam, but walk, don't run," Kimberly said, as she gently released her hand from Gary's. The three of them made their way to the middle of the room, stopping to speak to people on the way. Gary knew an occasional person and was introduced to others.

As they neared their table, Adam broke away from Kimberly's light hold and ran to a smiling woman who gathered him in her arms.

"My mother would spoil Adam rotten if I let her," Kimberly told Gary with an indulgent smile.

"Adam's lucky," Gary said and a few moments later met Kimberly's mother, Ethel Baker, whose warmth and unaffected manner made him feel instantly welcome. She was a plump brown-eyed woman whose short haircut showed off a well-shaped head. Her long gold earrings swung back and forth as she talked.

"I'm so glad to meet you, Gary, and this is my husband, Nelson Baker, and our daughter, Clarice Baker," she said indicating the cinnamon brown man with a square face, moustache and graying hair sitting at the head of the table and the pretty young woman sitting beside her mother.

Kimberly, sure that her mother, a generous, gregarious person, would like Gary watched now to see the reaction of her reserved and cautious stepfather. Nelson stood, shook hands with Gary, gave him a searching look and said, "Raeford. Nice to meet you. Have a seat."

Kimberly and her mother exchanged a quick look acknowledging that Nelson's tacit approval of Gary had been given by the terse invitation to sit. Gary said a thank you, seated Kimberly next to Nelson, and sat himself on her other side across from Clarice.

Kimberly turned to another couple who had been talking to the next table and now resumed their seats beside Clarice. "Nana and Papa, I'd like you to meet Gary Raeford. Gary, meet Marie and Walter Davis, Adam's other grandparents."

Again she watched to see how Walter's parents would treat the first man she'd ever introduced to the family. Marie's cool, formal greeting was not unexpected. When Walter and Gary shook hands Gary said, "Don't I know you from the plant, Mr. Davis?"

Walter's long face creased in a smile. "You sure do, Mr. Raeford. When you first came I was on second shift but now

I'm on first shift." He explained to the table, "Mr. Raeford's the new personnel director at the plant, been there about a year."

No wonder he was able to get me to work with him, Kimberly told herself. I thought he might be a lawyer but the personnel director of that large aluminum plant where Papa Davis works would have to be just as skillful and competent in dealing with people as any lawyer in a court room.

Gary, aware that his employment had not yet come up anytime he was with Kimberly turned to her and with a gleam in his eye, murmured, "Surprised?"

The hazel eyes met his. "Not really," she answered before turning to hear what her stepfather was saying. Nelson Baker had married Kimberly's mother three years after Emmett Washington had died when Kimberly was six. Nelson was not the lighthearted laughing man Emmett had been, but he and Kimberly grew to understand and appreciate each other. He'd made no difference between Kimberly and Clarice, the daughter he and Ethel had two years after their marriage.

"Excuse me, Dad, what did you say," Kimberly asked.

"I was wondering how you and Raeford met," Nelson said.

"At the library."

"Does he have family?" was the next question.

With Gary talking to the Davises and Ethel about work and the high noise level surrounding them in the hall, Kimberly was able to answer all of Nelson's questions about Gary as if they were alone. What he learned he'd tell his wife so Kimberly knew she'd only have to tell it once.

A loud chord sounded through the conversation and the hall quieted. A group of choir members stood beside the piano as Mrs. Riley, the church organist, announced through the microphone, "The choir's going to help us sing the hymn we always use to celebrate this occasion. So please stand up. You know the hymn, 'We Gather Together to Ask the Lord's Blessings.'" She played the song through with a flourish as people pushed their chairs back and stood.

Kimberly had no idea what Gary's religious background was or if he knew this hymn that was so familiar to her and tied as inextricably with Thanksgiving as "Silent Night, Holy Night" was with Christmas. She knew all three verses and as the voices in the hall rang out following Mrs. Riley's strong lead, Kimberly was surprised to hear Gary harmonizing in an assured baritone with her clear soprano and singing all the words. She felt him move a step closer to her and as they sang the second verse he took her hand in his.

"Softly, now," Mrs. Riley commanded for the third verse. Kimberly felt Gary's voice following hers, supporting hers as they wove in and out of the melody beautiful in its simplicity. In the music they two were as one, their hands tightly clasped. Kimberly, her eyes closed, felt her heart swell with the joy of the music and of the harmony she felt with this man beside her.

As the last chord faded into silence the minister said a short prayer and Gary and Kimberly stood with bowed heads and hands still clasped as blessings were supplicated and thanksgiving offered. There was a moment of silence as the prayer ended, then the noise of chairs scraping as people sat again and began to talk. Gary pulled back Kimberly's chair, and as he seated her his hands lightly brushed her shoulders.

Serving carts of plates filled with turkey, dressing, candied yams, and green beans were brought to each table followed by rolls, gravy, and cranberry relish.

Gary said how good the food tasted and Ethel said the church community had some good cooks. Conversation became general as stories of cooking and Thanksgiving memories were told.

"Mama, remember the first time I tried to make a pumpkin pie?" Kimberly asked. "The crust was like cardboard and I forgot to put the sugar in the pumpkin."

"I helped Gramma make a pie this morning, didn't I, Gramma?" Adam said.

"You did and we're going to eat it tomorrow for our dinner,"

Ethel said. She looked across the table. "Where are you having dinner tomorrow, Gary?"

"With the Blairs," he said. "Their daughter Sandra and my daughter, Amanda, are good friends. They took pity on me since they knew Amanda left this morning for San Diego to live with her mother and stepfather." Gary had been waiting for an opportunity to give Kimberly's family that information so there would be no doubt about his marital status.

"I knew an Elizabeth Blair at school. Would that be an older sister?" Clarice asked.

"Yes, that's the family," Gary said.

"I know the Blairs," Marie Davis said and embarked on a story about the time she and Mrs. Blair worked together in an office.

Kimberly listened with half of her attention. Although joining in the conversation, she hadn't looked at Gary since dinner had begun. Her intense awareness of him during the singing and the prayer made her shy. In some mysterious way that experience had brought them to a closeness beyond superficialities. She didn't know how to deal with it. She was certain Gary felt the same. Under the cover of a burst of laughter from the table next to them she felt Gary turn to her.

"Did you ever learn to make a pumpkin pie?" he asked softly.

"Yes, I did," she said.

"Will you make one for me, sometime?"

She knew he wanted her to look at him but that would have to wait. "Yes," she promised softly.

"Thank you, Kimberly," he said, his voice caressing her name.

The dinner plates were removed to the serving carts and replaced with pumpkin pie and coffee. After dessert the minister thanked all of the people who prepared the meal then said the benediction.

Adam had grown quiet with sleepiness. "Let's get you home to bed," Kimberly told him as she helped him put on his jacket and cap. Goodbyes were said and Nelson told Gary, "Drop by, Raeford."

"Thanks, I will," Gary said.

In the quiet of Gary's car Adam fell asleep at once, stretched out on the back seat. Kimberly turned in her seat so she could watch him. Gary drove slowly so as not to disturb Adam and began talking to Kimberly, sorting out his thoughts as he went along.

"I know you invited me tonight out of the kindness of your heart, Kimberly," he began quietly, "because of Amanda's leaving. I was glad to accept for the same reason and because I could be with you." He stopped at a traffic signal and she saw the profile of his angular face with its prominent cheekbones and full lips. He stared straight ahead at the light.

"At your apartment I saw Walter's picture and that answered the question I had about Adam's father." He put the car in motion as the light changed. "When we got to the church hall so many things about the people and the place carried me back to my childhood experiences in Jackson, Mississippi. I met your family and the Davises and they made me feel welcome. I appreciate their attitude and I enjoyed their company."

On this Thanksgiving eve the traffic was light. The night sky was clear and after the hubbub of many voices in the church hall the quiet atmosphere outside and inside the car was soothing to Kimberly as she listened to Gary describe his feelings.

They came to the traffic light around the corner from Spring Street. It had just turned red. Gary looked at Kimberly for the first time.

"It's been a very good evening," he said, "but there was a special time that was greater than all the rest." Kimberly held her breath. She'd been wondering if he'd mention how he felt in the singing. The light changed, he turned the corner into her street. "Do you know what I'm talking about, Kimberly?" he asked looking at her and slowing the car until it was barely moving.

"What are you talking about, Gary?" she asked softly, not wanting to commit herself.

Gary brought the car to a stop in front of the apartment building. He turned himself fully to look at Kimberly and taking her hand in his stroked it caressingly.

"When we were singing I felt there was a closeness between us. We came together somehow." His voice softened as he leaned closer. "It's hard to put into words but you felt it, too, didn't you?"

There was such assurance in his question that Kimberly, who had been wondering if she could deny the experience in order to slow down whatever was happening between them, found it impossible to do anything but give an assenting nod as they looked at each other.

"Perhaps I shouldn't be telling you this, Kimberly, but with things as they are there's no point in my being anything but open with you from the jump." He spoke slowly still sorting out his feelings. "The experience I had tonight with you was new to me. I've never felt that before."

But you were married for years, Kimberly thought. "Not even with Charlotte?" she asked hesitantly.

"Not with anyone," Gary said with emphasis. He leaned closer and took her face in his hands. One finger stroked her cheek. "Your skin is so soft," he breathed. "May I kiss you, Kimberly?"

She closed her eyes and waited. His lips were full and firm, his kiss tender. A tremble began in the pit of her stomach and traveled upward as Kimberly felt her own lips soften and respond to Gary. She tried to control the tremble unsuccessfully.

Gary felt it and ending the kiss put his arms around her and held her until it subsided.

Kimberly, embarrassed for reacting like she was fifteen, said, "I have to take Adam in."

Gary reluctantly released her. "Why don't you open the door and let me carry him in."

"Adam's pretty heavy to carry up the steps," she warned.

"I'm pretty strong." Gary smiled.

Adam didn't stir as Gary lifted him from the seat and carried him up the steps into the apartment and put him down on his bed.

"You're right, he's heavy," he said. "I hope you don't try to carry him. Do you?"

"Not any more," Kimberly said, leading Gary back through the living room to the door.

Gary had hoped for an invitation to sit since it was only nine thirty but Kimberly just stood, her hazel eyes thoughtful and a little wary. "I'll call you tomorrow," he said, "and thanks again for the evening." He saw the wariness leave her eyes and she relaxed now that she saw he was not going to ask to stay.

"I'm glad you were with us," she said.

I can't kiss her, Gary thought, but I want to touch her. He took her hands and in the palm of each one he pressed a kiss then folded her fingers over. "These are for you," he whispered and saw a faint blush redden her face. "Goodnight, dear Kimberly."

Kimberly closed the door and stood against it looking at her palms. With a bemused expression she put her lips where his had been and closed her eyes. Then she gave her head a shake and said out loud, "Girl, you better get hold of yourself." But there was a satisfied smile on her face as she went in to put Adam to bed.

Chapter Four

Kimberly awakened to a cloudy Thanksgiving day and gave herself the indulgence of an extra hour in bed. She breezed through her morning tasks with energy, laughing and playing with Adam in between baking a sweet potato casserole and rolls as her contribution to the afternoon's dinner.

When the telephone rang at eleven she realized she'd been subconsciously waiting to hear Gary's voice.

"Kimberly, good morning. This is Gary Raeford." His voice was low and rich on the phone.

Kimberly leaned back against the kitchen counter holding the phone in one hand and looking at the palm of her other hand as she said, "How are you and happy Thanksgiving to you."

"Thanks, and the same to you. It would be happier for me if I were seeing you, but I guess I'll have to be satisfied with last night."

"Your flowers look lovely this morning, Gary, and I can use the ceramic bowl they came in for other things. Thanks again for bringing them."

"I'm glad they please you. What're you doing? Cooking?"

"Making rolls and a sweet potato casserole to take to the family dinner later."

"Sounds wonderful. Do you enjoy cooking?"

"When I have time. Do you cook, Gary?"

"Actually I do. Got interested as a little boy and began to watch and help out in my mother's kitchen. I taught Amanda to make beef stew from scratch and a few other dishes this year. By the way, she called just before I called you."

"She got home all right?"

"Yes. She said to tell you and Adam hello. Kimberly, do you work at the bookstore on Saturdays?"

"Every other Saturday, usually. Why?"

"May I take you to lunch Saturday? If you're working I'll meet you there. If not, even better because we won't have to hurry."

"Saturday will be a hectic day at work, Gary. I won't be good company at all."

"Let me be the judge of that. Just name a time, please," he said persuasively.

Kimberly made a rapid calculation and judged that if she let everyone else go first, she'd have no problem getting away. "Two o'clock is the time I can be sure of, but that's probably too late for you," she said.

"Kimberly, I have the whole day. No time is too early or too late. Which bookstore is it?"

"The Bookshelf in Fairview Mall."

"I've taken Amanda there often," he said in surprise. "I wonder why we haven't seen you there?"

"I don't work evenings because of Adam and that's probably when you went."

"Yes, we did," Gary said. Then he said with a little chuckle in his voice, "Well, I tell you what, Kimberly Washington. I've met you now. It's taken a while, but I don't intend to lose sight of you from now on."

Kimberly, caught up despite herself in this delightful conversation, parried his statement. "You mean there's no place I can hide?"

"No place I won't find you, Kimberly, I promise." His voice deepened and the laughter was gone.

There was a moment of silence along the phone line. Then Kimberly, in full retreat, said, "I have to go look at the rolls."

"I'll see you Saturday, Kimberly, at two o'clock."

All through the rest of the day with the family dinner and the sitting around afterward visiting and laughing, images of Gary and snatches of her conversation with him were in and out of Kimberly's consciousness. Friday was the same and she was thankful to have something pleasant in her mind to counteract the chaos at work as everyone rushed around getting the Christmas display up as they tried to serve customers. On Saturday, the store was crowded with shoppers and by the time two o'clock came Kimberly was tired and had a tension headache.

Gary was waiting outside the store and his face lit up with a smile when she appeared. Her knee-length skirt in a purple and gold geometric print had a matching one-button jacket over a gold top. Her lustrous hair was put up in a French roll set off with gold beaded drop earrings. She wore brown pumps and to Gary she looked delectable. He longed to kiss her but contented himself with saying, "How are you, Kimberly. You look wonderful." He drew her arm through his as they began walking.

Kimberly was surprised at how just seeing Gary made her begin to relax. She was pleased to see that although they were not going anyplace special he was wearing a shirt and tie with dark brown slacks and a tweed jacket.

"The Italian restaurant okay?" he asked.

"That's fine, I like Italian food."

"How long do you have?"

"Until three."

"The restaurant shouldn't be crowded now so we should get fast service," Gary said.

At the restaurant a few other people were having a late lunch also but the hostess seated them at a secluded table and said Dino would be with them immediately. As Dino brought bread sticks and water, took their orders for lasagna and cannellonni and returned with their salad, Gary and Kimberly exchanged comments about their Thanksgiving. Then Gary said, "Tell me what you do at The Bookshelf, Kimberly."

"Mrs. Carstairs is the manager and I've been assistant manager for the past year. What that means is I do a little bit of everything except the hiring and firing. That is entirely her responsibility."

The entrees arrived and when Dion had gone with the salad plates Gary said, "Is it hard work?"

"There's a lot of detail," Kimberly said, "but it isn't hard in itself." She swallowed the lasagna on her fork. "What makes the job so difficult sometimes is Mrs. Carstair's method of managing."

Gary listened intently as Kimberly explained the problem from her point of view and gave as an example the lateness of the Christmas display, which then made needless complications for several days. Gary had never seen Kimberly so animated nor had she been directly across the table focusing her conversation on him. The hazel eyes that so enchanted him seemed to darken when she was excited as she was now, and she used her hands expressively.

"This morning," she said, "people were waiting when the doors opened. Some of the books they wanted hadn't even been unpacked because yesterday was so busy. All of this should have been done by the close of business Wednesday." She took a sip of her ice tea and another forkful of lasagna.

Gary's cannellonni had quickly disappeared but he was so enthralled by Kimberly he hadn't tasted what he was eating. He pushed his plate aside and leaned toward her.

"How long have you been at The Bookshelf?"

"Three and a half years. I began as a part-time clerk when I was in college."

"Do you like working with books particularly?"

Kimberly finished her lasagna. Dino appeared at once to remove the plates and offer dessert which was refused. He served them coffee and left.

"I love books and working in a bookstore sure beats waitressing, cleaning houses, day care work, and the other jobs I've had in making a living for Adam and me," she said lightly.

She looked at Gary with a warm smile. "It really helped to blow off that steam. Thanks, Gary, for listening. I think I can go back and face the rest of the day now."

Gary took her hand and raised it to his lips, his eyes never leaving hers. "I'm happy to listen anytime, Kimberly. But maybe I can do more than listen."

"What do you mean?" she asked, curiosity in her voice and a wariness in her eyes that Gary did not see as he took from his wallet a card and wrote on it before laying it in front of her. Kimberly could see it was his business card with his name, title as director of personnel at the aluminum plant, and his phone number. On it he had written, "Priority Appointment." Kimberly looked at him questioningly without touching the card.

"We have some openings at the plant, Kimberly, and I'm certain we could find something of interest for you. Come see me when you can get some time off. That card will guarantee you an appointment," Gary told her.

The hazel eyes that had been warm and friendly grew cool and distant again. "No thank you, Gary," Kimberly said, handing the card back to him. "I'm staying on at The Bookshelf until I decide to leave. When I do I'll find another job on my own."

Gary took the card wondering what had happened. He was saved from having to make an immediate response by Dino presenting the bill. Gary paid with cash then looked at his watch and said, "Seven minutes to three. Time to go." He was still smarting under her rebuff but made civil conversation about the mall itself as they walked back, keeping a careful distance between them. Kimberly, upset with both Gary and herself, tried to respond.

When they reached the bookstore she said, "Thanks for lunch, Gary."

"It was my pleasure, Kimberly," Gary said politely with an impersonal look.

Kimberly waited a moment then with head held high said, "Bye, Gary," and went into the store.

As she dealt with customers and later at home with Adam she thought about Gary. Each time she'd seen him or talked with him she'd felt a little more relaxed and the instinctive nearness experienced during the singing had made her more open to him.

His kiss had been sweet and exciting. When he'd called Thanksgiving day and said now that he'd found her he didn't intend to lose sight of her, she'd felt a little glow of anticipation. She'd let herself think that despite her initial misgivings she and Gary could be friends.

Then at lunch he'd done exactly what she'd been afraid of, played Lord Bountiful! All she did in being glad to see him was to talk freely about her job when he asked about it. All jobs have ups and downs and in talking about hers she wasn't implying that she wanted him to give her a better one. He'd pulled out his little card, wrote the magic password on it and said, in effect, come to me and I'll give you a job. She didn't want Gary or anyone else to give her anything, she could take care of Adam and herself!

At first Kimberly felt offended and resentful. Then she began to feel sad. She and Gary had been doing so well. They'd only met six days ago but it seemed she'd known him a long time because they'd seen each other on four of those six days. In some ways she felt very close to him, although there was much she still didn't know about him. She had been getting very comfortable with him and now this! By the time she went to bed she was ready to cry but refused to do so.

* * *

Gary left the mall and arriving home changed into old clothes and went to get rid of his frustration in yard work. What had he done wrong? Kimberly had been friendlier and more spontaneous in her manner and conversation than ever before. All he'd done was give her his undivided attention and ask a few questions because he was genuinely interested in what she did. She hadn't minded and in fact had thanked him for listening. So why did she turn cold later? What did he say wrong?

He cleaned out the beds around the house and raked the leaves as he thought of Kimberly describing her job and how he'd automatically catalogued her experience and skills. Those skills would be valuable in several of his own job openings, so he'd told her about them. In his job, he had some idea of the area wage scale and he was certain the plant would not only give her a better salary and benefits package but also superior advancement possibilities. No matter how he thought about it, Gary could find no reason for Kimberly's attitude. His inner agitation drove him to do the yard work more energetically than usual. He finished it, took a shower, lit the fire already laid in the family room, and sat down in his leather chair in front of it.

With the lamps lit and the fire going Gary thought how inviting and comfortable the room looked and how lonely he felt sitting in it by himself. His hazel-eyed girl he was so attracted to should be sitting here with him. He leaned back in the chair and closed his eyes seeing Kimberly's animated face across from him a few hours ago. He heard her again describing how busy the store was and how she'd been there three and a half years and how much she liked books. She said how that job beat the other ones she'd had in earning a living for herself and Adam, like waitressing, cleaning houses, and day care.

Gary's eyes flew open and he sat upright. What a dumbbell he was not to have seen the clue earlier. Kimberly was a young woman clearly capable of taking care of herself and she probably saw his offer as a blow at that capability, an implication that she needed his help. What had she said? That she'd decide if and when to leave the bookstore and when she did she'd find another job on her own.

On her own. Kimberly had worked at a variety of jobs, gone to college as and when she could, left the security of her parents' home, and put herself and Adam in their own place. It was obvious that her independence was important to her. Therefore when she complained about the poor management on her job and he'd handed her his card for an appointment that most certainly would have ended in a job offer given his position, her pride had been offended. She might even have the mistaken idea that he thought she'd been hinting for a job when all she was doing as she explained was blowing off steam. No wonder she'd been resentful and turned cold. *In her place, I'd have felt the same way,* Gary thought.

Now that he felt he knew the problem, he could apply himself to a solution. The first thing was to apologize to Kimberly. He got to his feet reenergized and hopeful. With a smile on his face he went to the telephone but stopped as he was picking up the receiver. He had a better idea. In the kitchen, he turned on the Saturday night jazz program and began cooking.

The Sunday after Thanksgiving was clear and sunny but the temperature had fallen to an uncharacteristically low forty degrees for the Lowcountry. The weather lifted Kimberly's spirit as she and Adam got ready for church. She enjoyed wearing the smarter looking clothes suited for cool weather and this morning put on a brown woolen skirt with a cranberry sweater topped with a blazer of tan, cranberry, and black checks.

At church she and Adam sat with her mother and Clarice. After the sermon as they stood to sing the closing hymn, Adam, who'd been fidgeting and looking around, pulled on his mother's arm. When she looked at him he whispered, ''I see Mr. Raeford, Mom.''

Kimberly's heart skipped a beat. Gary was here. Despite their unspoken quarrel yesterday, she felt certain he'd come here today hoping to see her. Adam disappeared as soon as the benediction was over.

Kimberly stepped out into the aisle along with her mother and Clarice and moved slowly with the stream of people who'd filled the church for the traditional sermon ushering in the Christmas season. She looked ahead and saw Gary waiting by the door his head bent in conversation with Adam. Already Gary looked so sweetly familiar to her and she knew at that moment that she wanted to listen to what he'd come to say and to move beyond the incident.

The three women reached the door and exchanged greetings and small talk with Gary as they moved out into the sunlight. After a few minutes Ethel and Clarice went on their way. Gary had been courteous to them but his whole mind was focused on Kimberly and he'd taken heart from the way her hazel eyes had met his in friendliness.

Adam had found some children to play with so Gary very gently put his hand under Kimberly's elbow and guided her away from the people still coming out.

"Kimberly," he said, his voice soft and intense, "will you please let me take you some place where I can apologize and where we can talk awhile?"

"I'd like that, Gary," she began, then hesitated.

"But what? You already have plans for this afternoon?" he asked, disappointment in his face and voice.

"You know that huge tree called Angel Oak?" she asked. He nodded. "Adam saw a picture of it at the library and I promised to take him and a friend of his out there this afternoon. Would you like to come with us?" she offered.

"I'd love to," Gary said, a smile replacing the disappointment. He took her hand and held it lightly. "I'll go to Angel Oak with you if you'll have dinner at my house afterward. I want to show off my beef stew," he said, the gaiety in his voice contrasting with the weight of his look as his eyes held hers.

"I've always liked beef stew," Kimberly said with a full dazzling smile that gave Gary a rush of happiness. For a moment the two stood just smiling at each other and people nearby who knew Kimberly asked each other who in the world was that attractive man paying her so much attention.

"I'll pick you up in an hour," Gary said and with a final pressure of her hand, turned and left.

Chapter Five

On the long drive from Jamison to Johns Island, Gary and Kimberly's conversation was general. They were glad to be together again and although the apology was on Gary's mind he knew this wasn't the time, not with Adam and his friend Jerome active in the conversation.

They drove through Charleston to Johns Island, which was separated from the mainland before the bridges were built, Kimberly said. Now it was a part of the city of Charleston but still referred to by its original name.

"It's much more rural than Charleston," Gary observed.

"Yes and folks don't want it to get citified," Kimberly said.

At the sign ANGEL OAK they turned into a narrow bumpy dirt road that provided the only access to the site. After a few minutes they turned right into the plot that was nearly filled with cars on this beautiful afternoon. Gary found a space at the end of the parking lot then, they walked back and stood with others looking at the tree.

At first sight its extraordinary size kept even Adam silent. His eyes grew wide as he looked at the sprawled and twisted limbs extending out. The largest was nearly a foot thick and some ninety feet long.

"It's so big!" he exclaimed. He bent his head back trying to see the top of the tree. "How tall is it, Mom?"

"Sixty-five feet."

"I've never seen anything like it," Gary murmured in wonder. The giant tree had five immense limbs that touched the ground and had supports under them as they spread out. The central trunk of the tree, although large, did not seem sufficient to have generated the vastness of the tree.

"Do you know what the total spread is?" Gary asked.

"When it was measured in 1981 it covered seventeen thousand square feet," Kimberly said.

As they walked slowly around looking at how the tree had metal supports in some of the higher branches and how ferns grew on the thicker ones, Jerome said, "How come there're no branches on that one side?"

"A hurricane blew them off almost eighty years ago."

"I wonder how old it is," Gary mused.

"During the hurricane, a limb close to the trunk was blown off and they counted the rings," Kimberly replied. "It's over one thousand four hundred and fifty years old. That means it was already one hundred years old when Columbus discovered America."

Adam and Jerome began going from limb to limb playing at how to measure them. Gary and Kimberly found chairs set out in a small grove of trees on the side of Angel Oak where there were no limbs.

"Have you ever seen any other living thing this old?" asked Kimberly.

"Only the giant redwood trees in California and they're breathtaking, just like this. When Amanda was here," Gary went on, "we talked about coming to see this tree, but we never got around to it." His voice was full of regret.

"There'll be another time, Gary," Kimberly said sympathetically.

Gary looked at her gratefully. He clasped her hand and turned so he could see what her eyes would tell him about his apology.

"Kimberly, this isn't the ideal place for talking," he began.

"Mom," Adam yelled running toward them from behind the trunk of the tree.

"What is it, Adam?" She was on her feet at once.

"Look what I found. See, it's a turtle shell. Can I keep it?" Adam was nearly dancing with excitement as he held out the fawn colored shell the size of his hand. "What kind is it, Mom?"

As Kimberly talked to Adam, Gary looked around for Jerome and not seeing him started toward the place where Adam had been. He found Jerome there looking for another turtle shell.

"Come look on this side, Jerome," Gary said, "and I'll help you. We need to be where we can see each other."

Adam came running back to help Jerome. "Sorry for the interruption," Gary said as Kimberly joined him and they stood watching the boys.

"It's all right, Gary. We can talk later at your house where there'll be more privacy," Kimberly said softly as a noisy party of four standing nearby exploded in laughter.

Gary, needing a commitment that he would have the opportunity to lay his case before Kimberly, said in a tone that only she could hear. "Is that a promise, Kimberly?"

"It's a promise," she replied, her eyes steady. "After all there may be a thing or two I want to talk about also," she added. Her hazel eyes had a little sparkle.

"Good! I'm anxious to hear anything you have to say." Gary was thrilled that Kimberly had something to say to him. If she was ready to talk about herself and her feelings surely that meant she cared something about the relationship.

"Supposing what I want to say isn't good news?" Kimberly said, her eyes now on the boys who were jumping over one of the lower branches of the tree.

"News can't be good all of the time so you can tell me anything at all," Gary said. "With one exception."

"What exception?" Kimberly looked at him in surprise.

"That you don't tell me to go away." He held her hand tightly in his and looked at her in a way that shut out everything else around them. "You're not going to tell me to go away." It was not a question. It was a statement. "Are you?" he whispered, his eyes so intense she could not look away.

"No, I'm not," she answered, and in that acknowledgement knew that a breach had been made in the wall of her defenses against permitting Gary Raeford to come close to her.

"Good," he whispered, "because I'm not going." His words, though whispered, were clear and emphatic as they looked at each other. He drew her arm firmly through his and covered her hand with his own. They stood quietly watching the boys, who were now chasing each other around one part of the tree.

Kimberly was thankful for the support; her legs had suddenly felt weak when Gary said he was not going away. *No matter what I say he's still there firm and determined,* she thought. Her intention had been just to see how he apologized. Then she'd told him she might have something to say as well, and more teasing than anything else, she had added it might be bad news. She thought now that subconsciously she'd been doing two things: deciding to straighten out her misgivings about him, and also pushing to see if he'd meant it when he said she couldn't hide from him now that he'd found her.

She wouldn't need to hide if she could be certain of his integrity and strength. She had long ago vowed not to waste time or to put herself and Adam in close contact with a man who was not strong and dependable. Now it seemed Gary might turn out to be that kind of man.

Gary knew he'd won the first big battle. He'd refused to be vanquished after his mistake at lunch (was that only yesterday, he thought) and now his hazel-eyed girl was not only coming to his house for the evening but was ready to talk about her feelings. And she'd acknowledged that she wasn't going to send him away! For a moment Gary wished he could be like Adam and Jerome and run for sheer exuberance.

The conversation on the way back to Gary's house was about the wonders of Angel Oak and Gary told the boys about the giant redwood trees in California. But underneath his attention to driving and conversation, Gary's thoughts were on why Kimberly held such a strong attraction for him. She was laughing at something Adam had said and Gary admired her satiny skin, her gleaming dark hair, her generous mouth, and her clear hazel eyes, now seeming to be a transparent brown. She was certainly good to look at, but he remembered when he first arrived in Jamison he'd gone out with a woman both he and Kimberly knew named Glennette Percy. Glennette was a stunning woman and he'd liked her very much but she fell in love with someone else.

Yet Glennette for all her qualities had never touched him in the way Kimberly had from their first meeting at the library. It was then in the look that passed between them that he had made the first contact with the inner person that was Kimberly; it happened again at the church hall when they were singing and a chord was touched that brought them into a sense of harmony with each other. He knew that Kimberly's independent spirit might not let her give these experiences the weight that he was willing to give them. He was still going to have to get past her biases and the defenses she'd erected over the years, but he looked forward to the challenge. He smiled to himself inwardly for one of the things that stood out about Kimberly was her tendency to hold people at arm's length. That was fine with him. He wanted to be the one to make the advances and the victory would be all the more precious.

"You're being very quiet," Kimberly said as they took the Jamison exit off the highway.

"Just wondering if you and the boys would prefer cornbread or biscuits for your dinner," Gary said.

"The boys love cornbread and so do I," Kimberly said

thinking how lucky she was to have met a man who cooked as a matter of course.

"That makes four of us then," Gary smiled.

"Can me and Jerome play with the toy soldiers, Mr. Gary?" Adam said as soon as the four of them entered Gary's house.

"Not so fast, Adam," Kimberly said. "I think Mr. Gary wants us to have dinner first and maybe we can help." Her inquiring look encouraged Gary to invite them all into the kitchen with him.

Kimberly was interested to see that Gary's kitchen had windows looking out into the back yard, ample counter space with cupboards above, and in a corner a round blond table with four chairs. The walls and appliances were white. There was a door leading to the service porch and another to the dining room. It's half again as large as mine and better arranged, she thought. No wonder he enjoys working in it.

"What can we do," she asked Gary who had turned on the oven and was getting out a mixing bowl and measuring spoons.

"You and the boys can get the table ready while I get the cornbread in the oven. You'll find everything you need over there." He indicated a set of drawers and a cupboad. "Please make yourselves at home." Gary's pleasure at having Kimberly and the boys with him expressed itself so strongly in his warm smile and his own sense of ease that any feelings of strangeness on their part were soon gone.

Kimberly opened a drawer with a number of table coverings and the boys chose one with black and white checks. This went onto the dining room table, then silverware and dishes. Gary stirred his beef stew and listened to the boys getting a lesson in table setting interspersed with a lot of laughter.

"We're through, Mr. Gary," Adam reported coming over to the stove. "Sure smells good. Is it ready yet?"

"Let's look at the cornbread and see." Gary opened the oven door.

"Looks done to me," Adam said.

Kimberly, putting ice in glasses for Jerome to carry to the

table, was relaxing in the comfortable atmosphere with Gary and not thinking beyond each moment as it came.

"We're about ready to sit down," Gary announced. He gave Jerome the butter, Adam the relish dish, and Kimberly the apple salad while he brought the tureen of stew and last, a basket of cornbread. He pulled out a chair for Kimberly at one end of the table and seated himself opposite her at the other end with the boys on either side. He asked Kimberly to bless the table then he said, "Adam, do you know what a toast is?"

Adam looked puzzled. "You mean like I have at breakfast?"

"No, I mean this kind of toast. We all raise our glasses like this." Gary held his up and the other three did the same. "Then someone says something that we all would like to have like good health good cheer, or better days. We touch our glasses together if we want to and then we take a drink." He looked across the table. "Would you give us a toast, Kimberly?"

Kimberly extended her glass to touch Gary's as she smiled at him. "To friendship." The four glasses clinked, then the boys, watching the adults, imitated them and took a sip of their water.

Gary served bowls of stew with its tender chunks of flavorful beef surrounded by potatoes, carrots, peas, and onions in dark, rich gravy. Generous pieces of cornbread were used enthusiastically to help sop up the gravy. The boys declined the apple salad but pitched into the ice cream and chocolate cake Gary had purchased almost as an afterthought.

"Now can we play with the train and the soldiers, please?" Adam gulped the last spoonful of ice cream down and looked at Gary.

While Gary took the boys upstairs, Kimberly cleared the table and stacked the dishes. She was in the family room looking at books when Gary returned. The sight of her in his firelit room kindled in Gary a deep happiness. It felt so right that she was here in his house.

Kimberly felt his presence. Their eyes met and held as he came to her. "I'm so glad you're here." Gary wished he could take her in his arms but knew this was not the time. He seated her in one of the plaid chairs and pulled the other around so he could look directly at her.

"Kimberly, before anything else I want to apologize for my insensitivity yesterday at lunch. You were describing part of your job and as you said, blowing off steam. As I listened I saw what a valuable person you were and without further thought gave you my card. It honestly didn't occur to me until last night that you might interpret my response as meaning that I don't recognize or appreciate your ability to secure employment on your own. I didn't mean to hurt your feelings."

All of Gary's body language expressed his sincerity as he tried to put his feelings into the right words.

Kimberly was so pleasantly surprised at his honesty and insight that she was moved to match it. "I'm sure you didn't, Gary, and I'm sorry I reacted like I did, but I tend to do that if I think my independence is threatened in any way."

"I'll bear that in mind," Gary said, glad that hurdle was over. "You made a toast to friendship and as friends we need to get to know one another. So what may I tell you about myself?"

"A thumbnail sketch of your life will do for now," she said, ready to hear whatever this man who was attracting her more and more had to say.

"You already know I'm forty-one and was born in Hartford, Connecticut, but I lived the early part of my life in Jackson, Mississippi, where my parents tried to make a go of my father's family farm. Jeff and Paul, my brothers, were born there. We moved back to Hartford after six years, where daddy eventually got a job in one of the insurance companies. He retired from it last year. Mama worked for years as a teacher's aide and she retired. I went to California after finishing at the University of Connecticut, helping a college friend to drive a car there. I'd always wanted to go and once I got there, my degree in business administration got me a job in a small company called Personnel Resources. It grew and I began to travel for the company. I was transferred to Boston after some years. Then about three years ago, this plant here with which we'd done business offered me the job of personnel director. I took it so I could settle in one place, I was tired of traveling.''

Gary paused and sat looking at the fire. *How different his life's been from mine,* Kimberly thought. *He wanted to leave home and did. He's traveled all over, seen many places and people. He's had big responsibilities and done well, so I wonder why his marriage wasn't a success?*

Gary looked away from the fire and leaned forward a little. ''I want to tell you about my marriage, Kimberly,'' he said, his eyes seeking hers. ''Charlotte's family were San Diego natives. We met, dated for a year, then married. She taught first grade until Amanda was three, but she really liked accounting so she went back to school. Then I was transferred to Boston. Charlotte was very reluctant to leave California but she did and finished her accounting in Boston. She felt better for a while after she got a good job in her field. But our differences seemed to get larger. We got farther and farther apart. We went to counseling but all it did was to make us see clearly that the marriage had ended.'' He paused and looked at Kimberly. He waited to see what she would ask.

''Was there any one thing or one main problem?'' she said.

Gary shook his head slowly. ''No, not really. It was a lot of little things, nothing big. The conclusion I've come to is that I didn't know myself well or what I truly wanted, so I made a lot of mistakes. Charlotte and I both thought it was true love when we met, but it wasn't. We made it as easy as possible for Amanda. We have shared custody and we never fight about her so she can feel comfortable with both of us.'' His face clouded. ''I want to watch Amanda grow up. I miss seeing her every day. But that's what happens in a divorce, and it's not Amanda's fault.''

''May I ask you something else,'' Kimberly said.

''Of course.''

''You and Charlotte couldn't find a way to stay together for

Amanda's sake?" She kept her tone nonjudgmental but it was important to know what kind of effort Gary had made in his marriage.

"We asked ourselves that same question," Gary said, "and we decided we could do it. So we tried for nearly two years, but we ended up as strangers and that wasn't a good situation for Amanda or for us. So four years ago we divorced. Charlotte and Amanda moved back to San Diego where Charlotte met her present husband. They've been married a little over two years and she seems to be happy."

"How has Amanda adjusted?"

"She likes him all right. His name is Bruce Allen and she feels comfortable with him. But she won't call him Dad," he said with a hint of satisfaction in his voice. He looked at Kimberly as if he expected her to remonstrate with him.

"Naturally not. She already has a dad, alive and well and in touch," Kimberly said.

There was an easy silence between them as they gazed at the fire. "It was different for me when my mother married Nelson Baker," Kimberly went on. "Emmett Washington, my father, died when I was six. Mama got married three years later, so he was the only male parent I really knew and I called him Dad. You've met Mama and Clarice. I have two older brothers, Ted and Willie who live here. I was born in Jamison and have lived here all of my twenty-six years."

Gary waited to hear about the place Walter Davis held in her life. Was she still emotionally attached to him? Would she talk about him or skirt around it? All he wanted was to know, to hear from her own lips about Adam's father. He could deal with whatever it was, but he needed to know.

I've never discussed Walter with any other man, Kimberly thought. She looked down trying to decide if she could speak openly to Gary. Could she trust him? Would he understand? If he didn't, it would be the end of any relationship between them. So why should she take that chance? Because friendship had to be based on honesty and openness. She looked up at

Gary. He was sitting, relaxed and waiting for whatever she had to say with a look of such warmth and kindness that all apprehension left her.

"I first met Walter when I was a junior in high school," she began. "He was a senior and in ROTC. He went to a military school for a year then into the army, but we'd see each other whenever he came home. I began college and we were to be married when I finished the two-year course. Then in December 1990 he found out his unit was going to the Gulf War." Kimberly paused, seeing again Walter's face thin and tense with unfulfilled longing when he told her the news.

"Mama and Dad had talked to all of us very openly and in detail about having sex before marriage and why it wasn't the right or wise thing to do no matter how we felt at the moment. So Walter and I had never been lovers, but when I knew he was going to war there was only one thing to do. My minister married us in his front room and we had three days together before he left. That's when Adam was conceived."

"Did Walter know about Adam?" Gary asked quietly.

"Yes, I wrote him as soon as I knew in late January."

"Good. I certainly would have wanted to know."

"Walter wrote back immediately. He was so happy to know we had a child on the way. His letter was full of plans about what we would do and telling me please to take care of myself. We told our parents, so I had a lot of support." Her expression changed from one of calmly looking back to one of remembered tragedy. Her eyes grew shadowed and Gary moved in his chair knowing this would be the hard part of the telling.

"Three days after I got his letter, I got the news that he had been killed. I couldn't take it in that he wasn't coming back, that we weren't going to have the life together we'd been planning so long. The worst thing was that Walter and his child would never know each other because I hadn't had the wisdom or the courage to marry him earlier when he asked." She looked at Gary and saw in his eyes only acceptance and compassion. "I felt so guilty."

Kimberly's voice began to shake. "They thought I'd lose the child, but I thought I'd lose my sanity. It was terrible," she said, rocking herself and crying deep sobs.

Gary was by her side in an instant. He perched himself on her chair so that he could put his arms around her and hold her to him.

Kimberly had thought she had no tears left to shed for Walter after those nightmare months that had left a great emptiness in her. Adam's arrival had filled a large part of that emptiness. Now she realized some of it was still there, ignored in the daily need of making a life for Adam. She was crying now because as she unfolded the past to Gary the memory of the bitter pain and guilt had reasserted itself.

Gary looked at Kimberly's head on his chest and wished with all of his heart that he could comfort her. Her story had been revealing. For one thing, he hadn't realized she was a widow. She wore no wedding band and Walter had been referred to as Adam's father rather than as her husband. But more significantly he was aware of the burden she'd carried all these years of pain and loneliness compounded with guilt for depriving Walter of marriage and family. No wonder she was prickly and protective of the life she'd worked hard to provide for Adam and herself. She'd had to become strong and focused, and he admired her for it. When the worst of her crying was over he put his clean handkerchief in her hand. Kimberly took it and began to dry her eyes, thinking how kind Gary was. Resting against his strong body with his arms around her felt so good that she found herself reluctant to leave this unaccustomed shelter. Her way had always been to rely on herself, so this experience of Gary's perceptive support presented a new factor for her consideration. She made a small movement preparatory to sitting up and Gary moved his arms from around her.

As Kimberly dabbed at her eyes she told Gary the final part of her story. "There's one other thing," she said, and Gary braced himself for whatever that might be. "Walter was always

Walter to me for so long and husband for only three short days that went by like a dream then were followed by a nightmare." She looked down at her bare hands and said reflectively. "We didn't even have rings. We were going to get them together when he came back."

So that's why no ring and no reference to "my husband" from her, Gary thought. It might not be usual but if that was the way Kimberly had coped with it, he could respect that. At that moment Kimberly looked at him with some apprehension. "I understand, Kimberly," he reassured her, and her face cleared.

There was a little silence as Gary waited to see where she would lead them next.

"I'm so surprised at myself," Kimberly said unself-consciously, her clear hazel eyes looking at Gary as if she were speaking of someone else. "I'd no idea all of that was coming."

"Maybe it needed to come out," Gary said. "May I get you something to drink?"

"Water would be fine. I'm going to wash my face."

When they were back in their chairs sipping the water, Kimberly said, "There isn't much more to my thumbnail sketch. I lived at home after Adam came while going to college full time to finish the associate degree, then we moved to the apartment. I took all kinds of jobs to support us and I still work some weekends for a friend who has a catering service. I'll be going back to finish college as soon as I can." She stopped. "Any questions?"

Are you involved with anyone? was the one question Gary had. He knew better than to ask it outright. "No social life?"

"It took me a long time to get over Walter," Kimberly said. "Then all of my interest was in Adam and work. I did eventually go out a few times, but it hardly seemed worth the effort."

Gary, pleased with her answer, said, "I know what you mean. I've felt that way myself. I go out very little."

That answered the question in Kimberly's mind and she smiled to herself in pleasure. Gary saw the smile and found her increasingly enchanting to him with her independence and this newly revealed vulnerability. An attractive combination!

"We'd better look at the boys," Kimberly said, getting to her feet. "They've been up there a long time and they're very quiet." She gave a little stretch then stood looking at the fire. Gary looked at his watch. "Actually it's only been half an hour."

The hazel eyes widened. "Is that all? It seems much longer than that."

Gary stood close to her. "That's because we've come such a long way," he said softly.

"Yes, I think you're right," she murmured.

Gary spoke her name caressingly, "Kimberly?"

She turned to look at him and Gary knew that the moment was his to make a further step. He took her gently in his arms and held her close with his cheek against hers. Kimberly stood quiescently in the embrace she'd wanted, assessing her feelings of contentment and confidence in this man. In one way, she was surprised to find herself where she now stood, but in another, she realized that an emotional dam inside her had given way when she told Gary about Walter.

"My dear, Kimberly," Gary whispered as he tightened his embrace. Kimberly felt a shiver go through her. "Kimberly," his caressing voice said her name again. "I want to see your face."

Kimberly raised her face to his, her eyes downcast at first until a stern inner voice commanded her to look into Gary's eyes. She saw tenderness and a question. "We're not going back now that we've come such a long way, are we?" he asked soberly.

"Oh, no, I don't want to go back." She was startled at the idea.

"Good! Then we go forward. Together." He said each phrase deliberately and saw in her eyes the meaning registering.

"We go forward together and see how it works out." She added the codicil as her own statement of independence.

"Then let's seal the bargain." Gary bent his mouth to hers and took the draught for which he'd been waiting so long. Her lips, soft and sweet, yielded to him for a prolonged kiss that became so intimate Kimberly knew she could never think of Gary in the same way again. He had penetrated too far into her emotions.

On Monday while Kimberly and Adam were eating dinner there was a knock at the door. It was a delivery from a florist. "What's that, Mom?" Adam asked as she brought the long white box to the table and began to open it.

"Flowers." She pulled back the green tissue to show Adam the six long-stemmed red roses. "Aren't they lovely?"

"They smell good," he said.

She found the card tucked under the flowers. *Lovely flowers for my lovely Kimberly, Gary.* Flowers coming to the house was a new experience for Adam. "Who brought the roses?" he asked.

"The man from the place where they sell the flowers."

Adam was puzzled. "Why?"

"Because Mr. Gary called him on the phone or stopped by and ordered them. You know like we order pizza sometimes?"

"But why?"

"People send other people flowers because they like them and they think the flowers will please them, make them feel good."

"Mr. Gary sent you the flowers because he likes you?"

"Yes."

Adam digested this. "Are you going to send him flowers?"

"I don't think so."

"Why not? Don't you like him? I like him a lot. Why can't we send him some flowers, Mom?" Adam was enthusiastic about this idea.

"Women don't usually send flowers to men, Adam."

"But I want to, Mom. I like him. Why can't I send him

some?'' Adam was getting the stubborn look Kimberly dreaded because it meant he had a very firm hold of an idea and it would be hard to shake it away. ''Why, Mom?'' Adam was prepared to keep asking the question, as she knew from past experience.

There's no reason except convention to keep them from sending flowers to Gary she thought as she put the roses in water. ''Okay, Adam, we'll send Mr. Gary some flowers,'' she said. Adam's face broke into a big smile.

''I bet he'll like that,'' Adam said.

At nine o'clock when Kimberly was laying out clothes for the next day Gary called. ''Thanks so much for the lovely roses,'' she said.

''Did they arrive after you got home? I specified the time.''

''Yes, they came as we were having dinner.''

''I'm glad you like them. How was your day?''

Kimberly told him about a customer who insisted on finding a book by a nonexistent author and Gary told her about an argument between two secretaries. They found a lot to talk about and laugh about. ''How's my friend Adam?'' Gary asked.

''Fine. When he came home last night he kept saying how much he likes you, Gary.''

''I'm glad because I really like him. He's interesting and you've done so well with him. Would you trust me to borrow him sometime?''

''Yes, I would,'' Kimberly said unhesitatingly. ''I know Adam would love it.''

''We'll arrange something. I'd love to take him around with me and we'd just hang out together.''

''You two men together, huh?'' Kimberly said, not bothering to suppress the smile in her voice.

''Don't knock it, girl, that's important.''

''I know,'' she said laughingly.

''Adam said he likes Mr. Gary. How about his mother? Does she like Mr. Gary?'' His voice had become soft and intimate.

Still filled with laughter she said, "I don't know, but I'll check with her and find out."

"That'll give me something to look forward to tomorrow."

As she hung up, Kimberly thought of how she'd flirted with Gary so easily and enjoyably. Now what would she tell him tomorrow? At work the next day she thought of the effect of her talk and tears with Gary. It must have been a kind of catharsis she hadn't known she needed. Now she had truly let go of her grieving and she felt free and unburdened. She was free to take risks, and she saw now that in the previous years she had so structured her life that no risks were involved. Her heart was now impelling her to take a risk in letting Gary Raeford come close to her.

That night she hurried through her chores so she could sit in her big chair and be totally relaxed when Gary called. He said, "Is it all right to call you this late? I figured Adam would be asleep by now. I admit to being selfish and wanting your undivided attention."

"You have it, Gary. Tell me how your day went." The two secretaries had gotten together and caused some agitation for a third, he reported. He and Kimberly laughed at the absurdity of it then discussed it from a management point of view. She said how a lady had interrupted her as she stood daydreaming with books in her hand and how the lady had ended up buying ten books, Kimberly's biggest sale of the day.

"That must have been a potent daydream. Dare I ask about it?"

"Be brave, Gary. Dare to ask."

"What or who were you daydreaming about, Kimberly?" In his chair in front of the fire Gary leaned back and closed his eyes, picturing his hazel-eyed girl in her chair talking to him.

"Actually I was thinking of you. That is, I was doing a

close check with Adam's mom on your behalf as promised last night.''

''And?'' Gary's voice deepened. This was the first time he'd risked asking her if she liked him. He clutched the phone tightly.

Kimberly took a deep breath. ''Adam's mom said she liked you very much, that the longer she knows you the more the liking grows.'' Her boldness surprised her, but she realized it was true.

Kimberly heard Gary give a sound as if he'd been holding his breath, then she heard a sound like ''Ahhhhh!'' expressing satisfaction.

''Kimberly?'' Again he caressed her name. ''I have a message for Adam's mom. Will you give it to her, please?''

''Of course.''

Gary felt he could begin to express more of himself now that he knew Kimberly liked him and this device they were using of Mr. Gary and Adam's mom made it easier also. ''Please tell her that Mr. Gary likes her very much. In fact, thinking over the past years he finds he likes her more than any other woman he's known. Will you be sure she gets that information?'' His voice was quiet but intense.

Kimberly began to tremble as she took in the implication of his words and the intensity of his voice. She was thankful Gary couldn't see her. ''Is Mr. Gary sure?'' she asked, and this time there was no laughter in her voice. ''I wouldn't want Adam's mom to get any wrong information.''

''Believe me, my dear Kimberly,'' Gary said in the same intense voice, ''Mr. Gary is very sure.''

''Then I will tell her,'' Kimberly promised. The next night she said only that Adam's mom had received the message and was taking it under advisement. The following night, a Thursday, Mr. Gary asked to take Adam's mom out on Friday but she had to decline because of a commitment for catering jobs not only on Friday but also Saturday and Sunday. ''I'm really sorry, Gary, but this is the busiest season of the year for my friend and when she counts on me the most. Also the wages are very good and I count on that.''

Gary bit his tongue in order not to express his frustration. After all, wasn't her spirit and her independence part of what he loved about her? Of course, he hadn't envisioned it keeping him from seeing her when he wanted to. "I miss seeing you and seeing Adam," he said, 'so don't mind me if I sound disappointed. I realize you have to do what you have to do.''

"Thank you for being understanding, Gary," Kimberly said.

"Don't thank me, girl. I'm sitting here chomping at the bit, but what can I do? When do you think you'll be free?''

"Perhaps Sunday evening, if I get home early.''

"Will you call me, please, when you do get home?''

"I don't want you spending your evening sitting by the phone.''

"There's nothing I'd rather do if it means I may see you, my dear. One more thing before you go, any message from Adam's mom?''

"She said she'll be ready to tell you Sunday if she sees you," she said softly, having decided just that moment what to tell him.

"Dearest Kimberly, please work fast Sunday," he said and she felt his voice in the pit of her stomach when he said "dearest.''

On Friday Kimberly went to a florist in the mall and together she and Adam selected a flower arrangement of mums, carnations, and greenery that looked sufficiently appropriate for a man. She wrote on the card, "We like you a lot, Mr. Gary. Adam and Adam's mom.''

Gary called early Saturday morning. "I got some flowers yesterday from Adam and his mom. Do you know it's the first time in my whole life I personally have received flowers?'' The elation he felt was evident in his voice and it lifted her spirits.

"When your roses arrived, Adam wanted to know why people sent flowers and after I explained he wanted us to send you some."

"Is he there?" Kimberly handed the phone to Adam.

After he thanked Adam for the flowers Gary said, "Your mom said I could come by and get you sometime and we'll do something together. Okay?"

After that conversation Adam spent most of breakfast talking about going somewhere with Mr. Gary and where it might be and what they might do. "When can I go with him?"

"We'll arrange something soon," she promised and urged him to hurry so she could get to work.

"Am I glad to see you!" Leah Givens said when Kimberly walked into her catering place. Leah, dark brown with smooth skin, a round face, and brilliant dark eyes, was peeling potatoes at a furious rate. "Nancy has the flu so she won't be here today or tomorrow, and I haven't been able to reach Bernice yet."

"What's on for tomorrow?" Kimberly asked, getting a paring knife and beginning on the potatoes.

"It's the Manigault wedding, remember? Ceremony's supposed to be at two which means about two fifteen, then the photographs, then getting to the hall for the sit-down dinner, which ought to be around four-fifteen."

Kimberly did a rapid calculation. "So that means we should be finished by eight at the latest."

"I should hope so. I'll see to it that you'll be home in time to get Adam in bed," Leah said.

Saturday's work was hectic and tiring and Kimberly was glad she'd arranged for Adam to stay the night at her parents' house. Sunday she was up at eight and in the shower when the telephone rang. Wrapped in a towel she answered it. "It's just me," Gary said. "How does it look for tonight?"

"It looks like I'll be home by eight."

"You've made my day! Just one more thing. Could I have

Adam today?'' Arrangements were made for him to pick Adam up after she called her mother to let her know. Throughout the busy day Kimberly wondered what Gary and Adam were doing and always in the back of her mind was a feeling of anticipation.

She had been home only five minutes when Gary called to see if she were home and to say he and Adam would be there in half an hour. ''Give you time to catch your breath.''

Time to get the shower I'm dying for, Kimberly thought stripping off her clothes as she walked. Then minutes later feeling fresh and clean again she put on a silky lavender jumpsuit that made her feel very feminine. She brushed her hair until it shone and applied her makeup. Silver earrings and a silver chain completed her toilette. She had thrust her feet into black slip-ons when the bell rang. With her heart thumping she opened the door.

''Hi, Mom, we're home,'' Adam said, running in and throwing his arms around her as she bent to greet him.

She stood up to greet Gary who was waiting his turn. As their eyes met she felt a jolt. ''As Adam said we're home,'' Gary said, wishing he could embrace her as Adam had done. ''You look lovely.''

Kimberly felt impelled to touch Gary. She put her hands in his and saw the pleasure in his eyes as he grasped them. ''So do you, Mr. Gary,'' she said. She felt as though she hadn't seen him in a very long time. How good he looked in his charcoal slacks, white turtleneck, and gray sweater. ''Come sit down and tell me what you two found to do,'' Kimberly said leading the way to the sofa.

Adam inserted himself between them as they sat down. ''We went to the Fun Park, Mom, and we rode in the cars and then Mr. Gary showed me how to play golf there. I could hit the ball, couldn't I, Mr. Gary?'' Gary assured Kimberly this was so. ''Then we had some pizza and then we went to a movie.''

Gary said, ''I took him where they show old movies to see

'Beauty and the Beast.' He said he'd never seen it and had always wanted to."

"This is the way they danced," Adam said sliding off the sofa and giving them his version of a waltz, turning giddily until he fell on the floor in a heap and they all dissolved in laughter.

"I can see you enjoyed your day," Kimberly said, "but now it's bedtime."

Adam flung himself at Gary. "I want Mr. Gary to carry me to bed," he said. Gary put his arms around him as Adam nestled close. Kimberly saw the unguarded look of tenderness in Gary's face before he looked at her seeking permission to carry the boy. She nodded and led the way down the hall to Adam's room. Adam put his arms around Gary's neck and Gary held him tightly until he put him down on the bed.

"Thanks for going with me today, Adam. We'll do it again as soon as we can," he said. "I had a nice time."

"Night, Mr. Gary," Adam said.

"I'll be with you in a few minutes, Gary," Kimberly said.

Gary was too stirred up to sit while he waited for Kimberly. He stood looking out of the window at the empty street. He knew he was well on his way to falling irrevocably in love with Kimberly. As for Adam, he'd liked the boy from their first conversation at the library, but today Adam had felt like a son, the son he'd wanted since before his marriage had ended. He heard a slight sound and turned to find that Kimberly was standing looking at him.

Kimberly was surprised to see the agitation in his face. She took a step closer. "What's the matter, Gary," she asked.

Gary opened his arms and Kimberly walked into them. "I need to hold you," he said. Kimberly linked her arms loosely around his waist and laid her head on his chest. She could feel his rapid breathing gradually becoming smooth and rhythmic again. After a while she lifted her head and smiled up at him. "Better?" she said softly.

Gary's dark eyes looked into hers. He bent his head and kissed her softly, lingeringly. "Now I'm better," he said.

"Come and tell me what you were thinking," Kimberly said. Again they sat on the sofa facing each other.

"That evening we first met at the library," Gary began, "I thought about you a lot after I got home. I wanted to know about Adam and his father and if the man was still a part of your life. I thought of the differences in our ages. Fifteen years between us and did I want to become involved with a woman who was so much younger and whose experience was so different from mine. You were still in elementary school when I was getting married. I thought of how promising my relationship with Charlotte had begun and how badly it ended." He looked at her with a wry smile. "On the basis of all of that, I decided to keep our relationship on a businesslike basis. Then you and Adam came over the next evening." He paused and Kimberly, enthralled by these revelations, waited breathlessly for him to continue.

"I looked at you and all of these sensible reasons went up in smoke. I told you about the keepsake and held your hands. All I could think about was how much I wanted to kiss you, how right it felt for you to be in my house. The next night in the church hall we sang together and there was a joining between us. Last Sunday we talked and agreed to go forward in our relationship together. Then Mr. Gary sent Adam's mom a message that he likes her more than any other woman he's known. Now he wants to change that message."

Kimberly was startled. She'd been carried along by Gary's recital and thinking of what she'd say of her original thoughts about him. She felt a little coldness in her stomach and its reflection in her face. He had met someone else or returned to his first rationale. Maybe that's why he'd looked so upset.

Gary, seeing the dismay on her face, knew she'd misconstrued the change in the message. He took her hands in his and kissed them. "Mr. Gary now wants Adam's mom to know that he's falling in love with her," he said simply, his eyes intent to see her reaction.

Kimberly thought her heart had stopped beating for a moment. Then she felt a blush cover her face and neck. She tried to look away but couldn't. Gary's dark eyes were telling her that what he said was true and he needed to hear her answer. The anxiety in his face touched her. "Adam's mom," she began, and then had to swallow and start again. "Adam's mom is surprised at the change in the message."

"Before you go any farther just tell me, is the change good or bad?" Gary's voice was roughened with emotion.

At least she could give him that assurance, Kimberly thought. She touched his face in a brief caress. "She finds the change to be a pleasant surprise." Gary expelled a breath and he settled back to listen to Kimberly.

"When Adam's mom first met Mr. Gary she wondered if he was separated or divorced. She thought he probably had several girlfriends. Although she felt a connection to him, she resisted it. There was quite a difference in age and a difference also in their education and financial status. Adam's mom had no intention of being in a Cinderella role. So she decided to be on a strictly business basis with him."

Gary was listening with all of his senses because his knowledge of this woman was crucial to his future happiness. He hadn't realized she felt anything about their education and their economic status. He was glad she'd mentioned it. Kimberly's characteristic directness was a source of attraction for him, it could be hard to bear but he always knew what she was thinking and where he stood.

"She was touched by his keepsake story and the feeling he had about it," Kimberly continued. "She also knew he wanted to kiss her. He upset her at lunch in the mall but she was glad to see him next day at church." Now it was Kimberly's turn to pause as she came to their talk about Walter. "Adam's mom thought she was risking a lot when she told Mr. Gary about Walter because she didn't know how he would feel, but he turned out to be understanding. She thinks now that she went through a catharsis and is free from the past.'' Looking at Gary she ended quickly because she was finding it hard to keep her composure. ''When he kissed her in front of the fireplace she realized he had entered deeply into her emotions. So she and Adam sent him flowers.''

Gary moved closer and tenderly cupped her face in his hands. ''Kimberly, is Adam's mom falling in love with Mr. Gary?'' His eyes searched hers intently.

Kimberly gave the only answer she could. ''It's been so long since she's had any such feelings that she can't be sure. But maybe,'' she whispered, her gaze lost in his, her senses spinning from the buildup of emotion. She felt a hunger now to have his lips on hers and his arms around her.

Gary, thrilled by the implication of her answer and the desire in her eyes, bent his mouth to hers in a gentle kiss. The taste of her and her readiness for his embrace inflamed him. He pulled back from the kiss to look at her. ''Put your arms around me and kiss me,'' he whispered.

Kimberly heard the request and as if in a dream she put her arms around Gary's neck and closing her eyes kissed him gently. His lips were firm and warm and felt so good. She made a little sound and caressing the back of his head, moved closer to him. Gary had been receiving the gentle kiss and trying to keep his response in the same range but when he heard her sound and felt her caress he began to kiss her with the passion that was pouring through his body.

Kimberly, unable to breathe or think, made a little movement of protest that registered itself with Gary. ''I'm sorry, sweetheart,'' he began but Kimberly laid her hand against his lips. ''It's all right,'' she said. ''Excuse me a moment.''

Gary was grateful to have time to compose himself. He was rapidly learning that Kimberly had an effect upon him unlike that of any other woman he'd known. She touched him at the core of his being without effort, just by being herself. When she returned with glasses and a pitcher of fruit juice she said in her candid way, "I don't know about you but I need to cool off." She offered him a glass and with hers went to sit in her chair.

She looked adorable to Gary with her flushed face and sparkling eyes and he thought she was wise to sit away from him. He raised his glass to her. "To Adam's mom and Mr. Gary."

"I'll drink to that," she said with a happy smile. She felt a little shy now and wasn't sure what to do with the conversation. She was thankful when Gary, leaning back in a corner of the sofa, his legs crossed, said, "Adam and I saw Christmas decorations everywhere today. He talked about Christmas trees. When do you put yours up?"

"No special time, usually whenever I can get around to it."

"Then how about you and Adam and I going together to find one for your house and one for mine?"

"I'd like that, Gary. Then we can have tree-trimming parties," she said. She smiled at Gary. "They're so much fun, aren't they?"

"I've only been to a few," he answered, "and for one reason or another they weren't so enjoyable. You know, Kimberly, for years the holidays have been a very lonely time for me."

"I know," she said, her face sobering as she looked at Gary. "Even with my family around and friends there's a personal loneliness."

"That's what I mean." Gary said. "You know one of the reasons I like you so much? You always understand what I mean."

"Kimberly, I have to go." Gary drained his glass and stood.

Kimberly stood, also, looking puzzled. "Is it that late?" she asked as they walked to the door.

"It's not that late." Gary stood by the door but not touching her. "You know why I'm going, Kimberly." It was a statement, not a question. The color rose in her face. "You sat there in that luscious outfit looking so ravishing and speaking so wisely how could I not want to hold you and smother you with kisses. But that isn't what you want, is it?"

They stood utterly still looking at each other. *Not yet*, she thought.

"Not yet, Kimberly?" Gary said quietly.

"Not yet," she echoed softly.

"I'll call you tomorrow, sweetheart," he said, and the door closed behind him.

In the week that followed, busy though she was, Kimberly found herself sustained by what was taking place inside herself, for the emptiness from which she had suffered almost subconsciously for the past years was gradually disappearing. In its place was a growing sense of what life could be like. The vision of fulfillment gave her joy. Each night on the phone, she and Gary, hungry to know about each other, told stories of their families, growing up, ideas, hopes. She said how she wanted to finish college; he said he thought of establishing his own personnel business.

She discovered Gary was a pragmatist whose realistic view of life and people was underlaid by a keen sense of fairness. He found that Kimberly, despite her own ups and downs, tended to be idealistic in a broad sense and was swayed by her own loyalties. Their differences enhanced their interest in each other. When Kimberly went to work on Friday she was frustrated at only telephone contact with Gary and she intended to find at least an hour on the weekend when they could see each other.

She waited on a customer and then hurried over to the new fiction section to finish putting books on the shelves. Someone called her name and she looked around.

"Glennette! I'm so glad to see you," Kimberly said. Kimberly had used her modeling knowledge to help Glennette put on the show that Amanda Raeford had been in. Later when Glennette married James Ellington, Kimberly had been in the wedding and thought Glennette was the most beautiful bride she had ever seen.

"We never seem to see each other lately," Glennette complained. She was glowing with happiness and well-being.

"How's James?" Kimberly asked.

"Working hours on end setting up his law practice and helping me to get my counseling practice off the ground. You know I left the school system and have a private practice."

"How's it working out?"

"I've got more clients than I'd hoped for. What's new with you?"

Here was someone she could speak to about Gary, Kimberly thought because Glennette had met the parents of all the girls who had been in the show. "Do you remember a girl named Amanda Raeford who was in the show?" she asked.

"Of course. She brought her friend, Sandra Blair."

"I met Amanda and her dad, Gary Raeford, recently."

Glennette pricked up her ears. Gary Raeford had taken her out a few times. She had found him extremely attractive and might have become seriously interested in him except that she discovered it was James Ellington with whom she was in love. "How is Amanda?"

"She's gone back to San Diego to live with her mother."

"Is her dad still at the aluminum plant?"

"Yes. We've been seeing quite a bit of each other." The hazel eyes looked at Glennette candidly as the telltale color came into her face.

Glennette knew about Walter and Adam and had tried a time or two to get Kimberly to be more social. "That's wonderful, Kimberly." Then in a confidential tone. "What do you think of him?" she asked.

"As far as I can tell he's a fine person. I think he's a man I can trust," Kimberly said.

Glennette could see there was more to it than that, so she asked directly. "Do you like him, Kimberly?"

"Very much," Kimberly said.

"I don't have the idea that he's a person for casual affairs, Kimberly, and I know you aren't, so if the two of you are spending time together and liking each other, I think that's fine," she said affectionately.

A harried customer said, "Miss, do you have anything by Stephen King?"

"Yes, ma'am, right over here," Kimberly said, showing her the books in the adjoining section.

"I'd better move on," Glennette said, "but I want to tell you something first, Kimberly. When you know what it is you want you have to be brave and grasp it."

She looked at Kimberly until Kimberly said. "I understand, Glennette."

That night on the phone Kimberly told Gary. "You know who came into the store today? Glennette, the girl who did the show Amanda was in."

"Glennette Percy?" Gary said.

"She's Glennette Ellington now. She looks so happy and even more beautiful than before."

Gary was glad to find that he could hear about Glennette without any feeling of regret. Once upon a time he'd begun to think that she was the woman he wanted, but that was before he knew Kimberly. Kimberly awoke in him emotions he'd never experienced before and he was profoundly thankful now that nothing had developed with Glennette. "She certainly is a stunning woman," he said, "but there's a certain hazel-eyed woman I know who is infinitely more beautiful to me."

There was silence on Kimberly's end of the line. She felt a glow of pleasure at Gary's words but she didn't know what to say.

"Did you hear me, sweetheart?"

"Yes, Gary, I heard you," she said, "and that is a great compliment."

"The heart sees more than the eye observes and my heart carries an image of you that grows more precious every day."

Gary's words, quiet and intimate, described a situation so familiar to Kimberly that without thinking she said, "I know exactly what you mean!"

Now there was silence on Gary's end. *What have I said?* she thought, but it was too late to retract the confession of how dear Gary was becoming to her. When Gary spoke again she could hear the emotion he was trying to control. "Sweetheart, can you possibly mean that Adam's mom is thinking that way of Mr. Gary?"

"Adam's mom says yes, that's what she means."

"Please tell Adam's mom how happy that makes Mr. Gary and he wants to know when can he see her so he can tell her in person?"

Kimberly, more at ease now that Adam's mom and Mr. Gary had appeared, smiled dreamily at what that in-person telling would be like. "She has to work tomorrow but she'll call you as soon as she gets home."

"Good! What's Adam doing tomorrow? If there's no other plan can he be with me?"

"I'm sure he'd like that. Same arrangement?"

"Yes, I'll pick him up at your parents' house and bring him home when you call."

Glennette's words stayed in Kimberly's mind as she worked and tried to sort out her feelings. Did she know what she wanted? There was no doubt that she was falling in love with Gary. But what did he want ultimately? When she took a late lunch she bought a sandwich and sat by herself on a bench in the mall. Christmas decorations of red, green, gold, and silver were everywhere, and Christmas songs played through speakers filled the air. On this second Saturday before Christmas the mall was packed with shoppers, but Kimberly concentrated on her self-analysis. *What do you want, Kimberly?* she asked. She tried to empty herself and without thought sat still, certain the answer would come. From her deepest subconscious the answer rose to her conscious mind: to love and be loved. Kimberly was flooded with a joyous certainty. The other part of the advice Glennette had given was to be brave and grasp what it is you want. *I understand, but am I ready to be that brave,* she wondered. This had all happened so fast.

* * *

In the bookstore that afternoon the rush of customers and the demands on her from the other staff members were so constant that it wasn't until she was on her way home at seven that she had time to think of anything personal. Her immediate thought was that she was so tired. Then what should she do about dinner? Did she have the energy to see Gary? In the apartment, she called Gary to find out if Adam had eaten.

"I know you must be worn out," he said, "so why don't you relax until Adam and I get there. We're bringing dinner with us. Okay?"

Kimberly, with a sigh of relief, said, "Fine. See you soon." In two minutes she was stretched out on the sofa, asleep under the warm afghan. When the doorbell awakened her she turned on the lamps and opened the door.

"We're home," Gary and Adam said in unison as they stood with bags of food in their hands, smiling.

"Please come in, gentlemen." Kimberly said with a smile. In the kitchen they carefully put down their bags. "Something smells good," Kimberly said.

"We've been cooking all afternoon, me and Mr. Gary," Adam said proudly as he vanished down the hall toward his room.

"Please come and tell the cook hello," Gary said, standing against the counter, his eyes never leaving Kimberly. "It seems like months since I've seen you, sweetheart," he whispered as he took her in his arms. She laid against him and he held her close. He shut his eyes for a long moment. When he opened them he saw Adam looking at them from the doorway, his eyes wide. "Here's Adam," he whispered to Kimberly and held out his hand to the boy.

Adam came running over. Gary and Kimberly bent down so the three of them could hug each other. The spontaneous gesture lit a tiny flame in Kimberly, for as she embraced Adam and Gary, the designation, "my son and my love," unbidden made itself known in her heart. Adam's little arms held tight then he said. "I'm hungry, Mom. I bet you're hungry, too."

Gary heard the cue but couldn't bring himself to relinquish Kimberly. He kept his arm around her waist. "Adam and I are going to put the dinner on the table. He can tell me where things are if you don't mind and you can rest some more. You've had a busy day and we haven't. So let me escort you back to your sofa and we'll let you know when dinner's ready. Okay?"

Kimberly felt like she was floating as they moved wordlessly from the kitchen to the living room sofa. At the sofa he took up the afghan and as she laid down, spread it over her. He carefully tucked it around her back and feet. They still had not spoken as he made sure the cover was around her neck. When he completed his self-appointed task he laid his hand on her cheek. She took his hand and pressed a kiss in its palm.

In the kitchen with Adam, Gary felt the kiss and dreamed of what he thought he saw in Kimberly's eyes. They warmed the chili, corn muffins, the drumsticks, especially made for Adam, and put the Jell-O banana salad, another of Adam's favorites, on plates. Adam brought his mother to the table. She complimented the cooks as she ate a little of each dish. She was too filled with emotion to eat properly. She was so aware of Gary that she was torn between wanting to look at him all of the time and not being able to meet his eyes. The air was electric between them and each was glad Adam was in his usual loquacious mood. Gary longed for the meal to be over and Adam put to bed. The strength of his feeling for Kimberly continued to surprise him.

Adam saw his mom glance at the wall clock. "Do I have to go to bed now? I want to stay up."

"I know you'd like to, honey, but it's already past nine." She knew how hard it would be to get him up in the morning.

Tears popped out in Adam's eyes. With a mutinous look and his voice a decibel higher he wailed, "But I want to stay up with you and Mr. Gary. I want to!"

"I know you do, Adam, and you'll get to stay up with us another time, but not tonight." Adam heard the firmness in his mother's voice and decided to settle for what he might be able to get. "I want Mr. Gary to put me to bed," he said climbing into Gary's lap and curling up against him.

Gary held him and looked over his head at Kimberly for her response. This is sheer blackmail from both of them, she thought. Adam must feel warm and safe like I do when Gary holds me. "Mr. Gary can put you to bed and I'll clear up in here," she said.

"Thanks, honey," Gary said. He stood up and shifted Adam to hold him more comfortably.

"He can walk, you know," she said mildly.

"Yes, but for now both of us need this," Gary said.

Ten minutes later as she was wiping off the counter Gary came in. "Adam wants to tell you good night." Kimberly dried her hands. As she came near where Gary was standing they moved toward each other as if an invisible tie was pulling them. He held her tightly, his cheek against her hair. With a small sigh she released herself. "I'll be right back," she promised. Adam was already half asleep. She kissed him and turned on his nightlight.

As Gary waited for her in the living room it was clear to him that he had reached another place with Kimberly and he desperately hoped she had also, for he could no longer restrain himself from telling and showing her how he felt. When she came into the room she walked into his embrace, stood on tiptoes to put her arms around his neck, and offered him her lips.

Their kiss, withheld so long, was tentative at first. Then Kimberly felt a shock wave running through her. She put her hands on Gary's head and pulled him to her almost fiercely. Gary responded with a long fiery kiss and caress into which he tried to put all of his love and longing. Kimberly began to feel a weakness in her legs and she clung to Gary for support. Through a daze of emotion Gary felt the difference in her and ended the kiss. He seated himself in a corner of the sofa with Kimberly beside him resting her head on his shoulder and his arms holding her tenderly.

Kimberly's only love affair had been with Walter beginning in high school as an immature girl. For only three nights had they been lovers with Adam as the result. Her knowledge of motherhood was much more extensive than that of being in love and being loved. She was in turmoil now with so many unfamiliar feelings.

Gary was trying to calm himself so he could talk to Kimberly without losing control. He cleared his throat of its huskiness. "Kimberly, yesterday I told you that my heart carries an image of you that grows dearer each day. I came in tonight and saw you. Then I held you. Adam came in and I held you both," Gary stopped. The words wouldn't come out. He was overwhelmed by the surge of love rising in him. He took Kimberly's hands and held them against his heart.

Kimberly felt like she was drowning in what Gary's eyes were telling her. When he put her hands against his heart she could feel its message through her fingertips.

"I have to tell you I love you, Kimberly. I love you so much." The words finally emerged from Gary in a voice whose raspiness neither of them noticed.

Kimberly could not bear to see the painful yearning in his face as he waited for her response. She cradled his head against her. She caressed him and laid her cheek against his hair. "Adam's mom wants you to know that she's in love with Mr. Gary," she whispered, not yet ready to say "I love you, Gary" for a reason she couldn't define.

Gary raised his head, his face transfigured. "Is she sure?"

"She's sure," Kimberly said with certainty.

"Oh, my darling, my dearest love," Gary said, gathering Kimberly in a full and passionate embrace.

"Mom, I'm sick," a small voice said. Kimberly and Gary

came out of their own world to see Adam standing in the doorway with his hands on his stomach. "I'm going to throw up," he announced.

Kimberly got him halfway to the bathroom when the eruption came splattering the hall floor and part of the baseboard. Gary, watching, berated himself for letting Adam eat the french fries, the potato chips, the ice cream, and the cookies.

"I threw up a lot, didn't I?" Adam said proudly as he got back in bed, clean and in clean pajamas.

"You certainly did, but don't eat so much junk next time," Kimberly said knowing her words would soon be forgotten but she had to say them anyway.

When she went to clean up the hallway she found Gary on his knees, his pants protected by newspaper, finishing up the job. "I found a pail and rags under your sink," he said, as he carefully wiped the baseboard clean. "Is it clean enough?"

"As clean as you can get it," she said.

After she deodorized the carpet and they were in the kitchen he asked how Adam was feeling and apologized for letting him eat the wrong food.

"I should have warned you. He never could eat all day long like he probably did with you," she said. She smiled, the hazel eyes alight with amusement. "Welcome to the real world." And then to her embarrassment, she yawned. "Excuse me," she said.

"This is the real world I want," Gary said putting his arms around her.

"A part of the real world we both seem to have forgotten is the library project. When are we going to work on it?"

"Why don't you and Adam come over for breakfast around nine and we can finish it," Gary suggested. Kimberly yawned again. "Am I boring you?" Gary said with an exaggerated hurt look.

"Sorry, it's been a long day and, yes, breakfast sounds good," she said and kissed him good night.

* * *

As the three of them sat down to biscuits, ham, eggs, and grits the next morning, Gary thought of how his life had changed and how blessed he was to have at his table the woman and her son who he prayed would soon become his new family. Adam went up to the toy soldiers and the train. Gary took Kimberly in his arms. The softness of her body, her natural fragrance, even the way her breathing moved the fine hairs on his face captivated his senses as he kissed her. "Good morning, beloved," he whispered.

"Good morning, dear one," she answered. For a long moment they stayed looking and lost in each other. Then Kimberly sighed. "We'd better get to work, Gary, before the morning disappears."

They agreed on a statement of goals relative to promoting learning by encouraging consistent and successful completion of homework assignments and providing multiple resources toward that end. They developed implementation ideas including tutors, reference materials, quiet spaces, and training in the use of the electronic card file. At the end of an hour they had enough for what Mrs. Marshall wanted. "I'll complete it and deliver it for us," Gary said. "I was thinking that if you still have time, why don't we go out and get the Christmas trees?"

"I still have three hours, so let's go."

"I need a large one for the family room," Gary said later as they walked up and down the lot in Ridgeville, which had the greatest variety of trees.

"I like this one for my apartment," Kimberly said looking at a tree she could see would fit in the corner of her living room. Trees were getting more expensive every year, she thought, as she looked at the thirty dollar price tag but she knew she could afford this one from her catering jobs.

"Look at this one, Kimberly. Will it do for my family room?" Gary asked pointing to a ten-footer that was perfectly proportioned and stately in its symmetry.

"It's the best I've seen," she said noting its price tag.

Gary went to get the clerk and when he returned with him, the clerk took the large tree and Gary took the smaller one to the pickup truck. "But I haven't paid for it," Kimberly told Gary as they walked to the lot. "Don't worry, honey, it's taken care of," he said.

I don't want it taken care of, was her instinctive reaction. It's my tree and I have my money to pay for it. He didn't ask, he went ahead and paid. He has no right to do that. All the way home while Adam asked Gary about Christmas trees Kimberly was quiet and Gary, thinking she was concerned about getting to work on time, increased his speed. In the apartment they put the tree in the corner and it did fit perfectly. Gary put his arm around Kimberly's shoulder. "It looks fine. When do you want to decorate it?"

"Depends on how late I have to work this week," she said. "Here's the thirty dollars for my tree, Gary." She held out the bills.

Gary looked at her but made no gesture to take the money. "I don't want you to pay me back," he said with a puzzled look.

"But I want to pay you back. I had the money in my pocket ready to pay the man for the tree. So please take it."

It's that blasted pride of hers again, Gary thought. How will we ever get around it. He took the bills. "Thank you, Kimberly. I'd better go so you can get to work," he said quietly and was gone.

The look on Gary's face and the way he left without any kind of goodbye stayed in Kimberly's head while she was at work. She knew she'd hurt his feelings by insisting he take the money, but he'd hurt hers by paying without even asking. Then he'd told her not to worry, it was taken care of as if she couldn't take care of her affairs. She fumed inside and was miserable. By the time she got home at ten she was glad it was too late for him to call and she crawled into bed tired and unhappy. Monday was no better. When she went to get Adam, her dad was watching him build a fort with plastic sections. Her mother had gone to the beauty shop. She dropped down into a chair and answered Adam in monosyllables while she tried to summon the energy to take him home and face the evening chores. Nelson went into the kitchen and in a few minutes called her.

"Sit, Kimberly," he said. She sat and he poured fresh coffee for both of them. He sat opposite her. "Problem?" Her weariness and unhappiness made her vulnerable to the loving concern she heard in that single word. Her eyes filled with tears. Her dad as always went straight to the point. "Raeford?" She nodded, brushing the tears away. "What?" Nelson asked. Kimberly knew her dad had a good opinion of Gary and she didn't want to denigrate him but she did want her point of view to be clear. She related their first run-in over the job then told him about the Christmas tree. She stopped but Nelson waited, knowing there was more. She found herself telling him her earliest misgivings about Gary. Finally she'd said it all and she fell silent.

"Raeford love you?" her dad asked.

The tears came again. "He says he does."

"Believe him?"

She thought about this, going back over Gary's actions as well as his avowals from the time they'd first met. "Yes, I believe him," she said.

"You love Raeford?"

"Yes."

"Sure?"

"I'm sure, dad."

"Marriage?"

"We didn't get that far. Adam got sick." Her description of that episode elicited a broad smile from Nelson. "I told him welcome to the real world," Kimberly finished.

"Man who'll do that must love you and Adam," he said, still smiling but making a point.

Nelson had been watching Kimberly grow up and grow older with no one to love. He had seen her develop a strong pride in caring for herself and Adam and had always known this could be a hindrance to her acceptance of love and marriage. Breaking through that pride would take a secure man who loved her enough to persist.

"Kimberly," he said, elbows on the table, looking across at her. "Raeford loves you. Wants to take care of you, give you everything. That's what love is. Man's supposed to do that. Right?"

He waited. She nodded her head yes.

"Trust Raeford. He'll give you room to be independent, have your pride. But remember, he has his, too. Part of it is doing for you. And about the Christmas tree—he'll learn how to balance his generosity. You'll learn how to accept his generosity."

That's the problem, she thought. *Why can't I accept things from Gary? What am I afraid of?*

Nelson had a final point. "Kimberly, in love and marriage, both give, both receive."

These final words coming after her dad's explanation of how a man like Gary felt seemed to erase the resentment and unhappiness she'd carried for two days. We both give, we both receive. She would keep that as a mantra instead of putting her pride and her independence first. "Thanks, dad." She kissed him on the forehead ready now to go home.

"Better?"

"Much, much better."

When the phone rang promptly at nine, she picked it up on the first ring. "Hello."

"Hi, sweetheart," Gary said. "You must have been right at the phone." His voice was low and unchanged and Kimberly, who'd been afraid he might still feel offended, felt her heart turn over with thankfulness and love. "Oh, Gary, I'm so glad to hear your voice and I was sitting right here in case you called."

"In case I called?" He sounded surprised. "I always call

you at nine. Last night I called at nine and again at nine-thirty. Your party was late, wasn't it?''

"I didn't get home until after ten. Gary, I'm sorry for my attitude about the tree and I apologize if I hurt your feelings.''

"It's not so much that my feelings were hurt, sweetheart. I don't want anything between us that makes you or me uncomfortable or unhappy. I knew you had to be at work in a little while and there wasn't time to talk it out so I left.''

"I've been thinking about us and there are some things we need to talk about,'' she said.

"Good things?''

"Of course good things,'' she said gaily. Then she said, "I can understand why you'd ask.''

"Listen, dear heart. Good things or bad, you must always remember what I told you. Now that I've found you at last, nothing will drive me away.'' His voice, deep and husky, sent waves of feeling through Kimberly's body. "When may I see you, dearest? May I come over now?''

Kimberly cleared her throat. "No, sweetheart, it's too late. Tomorrow I have to work late but why don't you come to dinner Wednesday and you, Adam, and I will have our own tree-trimming party?''

"I like the sound of that very much,'' he said. "What about my tree? Let's have a big party for that. Are you working Saturday night?''

"I'm supposed to, but I'll tell Leah I can't.''

"Bless you, my darling, let's have your family, the Blairs, and anyone else we can think of. Eight o'clock okay?''

"Yes and we'll plan the food when you come on Wednesday.''

At The Bookshelf the next day the busy hours flew by. When she got home Kimberly made a pumpkin pie, then got out the tree lights and boxes of ornaments. Gary called her early Wednesday morning to ask if he could bring the dinner, please.

Yes, she said, except for dessert. At home that evening she took a fast shower and put on a white knit pantsuit she'd bought because of its fit. With it she wore a delicate green necklace and earrings and soft green suede slippers. Her heart was beating erratically when she followed Adam to the door to let Gary in. How wonderful he looked, tall and strong, his brown face glowing, his eyes lively and vital.

"Hi, Adam's mom." She was even more beautiful than ever, her lovely hazel eyes luminous tonight, her skin like satin, her mouth delectable.

"Now we all have to hug each other," Adam announced from his secure position with an arm around Gary's neck and leaning to put one around Kimberly. Gary and Kimberly cooperated and after a second Adam said. "Mom said you were bringing dinner but I don't see any food, Mr. Gary."

"Go get your coat and you can help me bring it in from the car," Gary said as he set Adam down. As Adam disappeared Gary said, "Kiss me, sweetheart, before I starve to death for you."

They came together fiercely, each eager for the taste and touch of the other. They clung until they heard Adam coming back. "Come with us to the car," Gary said not wanting to let her out of his sight.

The three went chattering and laughing to get the food. Their gay mood lasted throughout the meal of baked ham, macaroni, and green beans. Kimberly cleared the table and set the pumpkin pie in front of Gary. "The pie you said you'd make for me! I was sure you'd forgotten," he said delightedly.

"You might wish I had. Better taste it." Gary took a big forkful and ate it critically while she watched.

"It's very good! Flaky crust and a smooth, rich custard. Do you by any chance sew, Kimberly?"

She was puzzled by the change in conversation. "Yes."

"You can cook, sew, decorate, perform several different types of jobs competently, you're a model, a college student, you know catering, you've raised a fine son. What an outstanding woman you are, Kimberly!''

Gary looked at Kimberly with such genuine admiration and respect it made her blush. She'd never thought of herself in that light. She did what had to be done as it came along to make a suitable life for herself and her son. ''Thank you, Gary, but you have to admit you're not exactly unbiased.''

''True,'' he agreed, ''but in some ways I can see you more objectively than you see yourself, and I stand by my assessment,'' he said seriously.

Adam, who'd been excused from the table, came in with a pile of tree lights. ''These're all messed up, Mom.''

''Lay them out on the floor and we'll be in in a minute to help you,'' she said.

Gary rose quickly and going to Kimberly's chair pulled it out so that when she stood up she was in his arms. ''I haven't told you yet how beautiful you are tonight in your white and green,'' he whispered. ''You look delicious.'' His words ended in a fervent kiss. When it was over they stood embraced until, reluctantly, they separated and joined Adam in the living room.

They strung the lights and decorated the branches with colored glass balls, candy canes, glass stars, and angels. There was a box of ornaments gathered over the years. ''What a nice rocking horse,'' Gary said taking it from the box and turning it over. It had a red saddle, red rockers, and a braided tail.

''It's like the one I had when I was little,'' Adam said. ''I'm almost six now so last year we gave it to a family with little kids. Did you have one, Mr. Gary?''

''No, but I'll tell you what I did have. When I was eight, I spent Christmas with some cousins in Ohio. There was lots of snow and they let me use a sled that was just right for me.'' His voice was nostalgic and Kimberly stopped what she was doing to listen. ''We played in the snow every day I was there having snowball fights, building snowmen, and going down a long hill on our sleds. My sled was a Red Flyer and sometimes

I still dream about flying down that hill on it. It was the best Christmas I ever had.''

"I've never played in snow," Adam said.

Adam found a gingerbread boy ornament to hang on the tree. They threw icicles on it here and there then sprinkled it with snow. Gary lifted Adam so he could put the golden angel on the very top.

Adam ran around the room turning off all the lights then he turned the tree lights on. They twinkled off and on lighting up the tree with its many colors and textures. "It's so pretty!" Adam said.

"Not a bad job," Gary agreed his arm around Kimberly's shoulder. Adam put his hand in Gary's.

"We always sing when we light our tree."

"What do we sing?" Gary asked.

"Let's sing 'Away in a Manger,' " Adam said.

Kimberly began the carol softly with Adam's clear treble joining in and Gary providing a baritone harmony. Adam only knew the first verse. As Kimberly and Gary sang the other two each felt again the special unity that occurred when they sang. It's happened again, she marveled. We belong together, he thought, it's meant to be.

After Adam went to bed Kimberly and Gary planned his party while clearing up the kitchen then went back to the sofa. "I need to tell you what I've been thinking about, Gary, so I'll sit here and you sit there, please." She indicated the other end of the sofa.

"These are the good things you mentioned on the phone?"

"Yes."

"Then I'll be glad to sit here miles away from you. For now." He laid one arm on the back of the sofa and turned his body toward her. "You have all of my attention."

"When you paid for the tree, my thought was about the hurt I felt to my ability to do things for myself. I didn't think about it from your point of view. I could see later that I'd hurt your feeling when I insisted on giving you the money and I was miserable. I see now that my ability to do for myself and Adam can no longer be the only important thing. I have to learn to be more flexible and especially to be more accepting. Do you understand, Gary?"

The tension in Gary relaxed. "I do understand and I can see how this is hard for you because you've depended only on yourself for so long. But sweetheart, I want to give you and Adam so much." Gary moved closer to Kimberly unconsciously. "But it's only because I love you, not to impress you. I've been wanting to send you little things like flowers and candy and jewelry I think you'd like and something for Adam every day because its a way to express how I feel and because it makes me happy to do it. I haven't because I've been afraid you'd object." He was sitting close to her now and took her hands in his. "Can't you see my point of view, sweetheart?"

"I can now, Gary." She repeated her new mantra. "In love each one gives and each one receives."

Gary had told himself not to rush Kimberly, to take matters one slow step at a time but the force of his emotions overcame his judgment. "In love and in marriage. Sweetheart, I love you so much. Will you marry me, Kimberly?" Gary held her hands tightly, his eyes dark, his face drawn. "Will you entrust yourself and Adam to me for the rest of your lives?" His voice was urgent, husky.

Kimberly took a deep breath. "Adam's mom says yes."

The yes resounded in Gary through the coursing of his blood. His kisses poured in a shower over Kimberly's face, mouth, hair as he murmured her name again and again. She responded in a daze of feeling that left her breathless and overwhelmed. She leaned against him and took deep breaths in and out to calm herself. Gary held her against him, wordlessly letting the tumult of emotion subside.

Thought and reason began to emerge. What had Kimberly said? "Adam's mom says yes." He thought of the implication of her choice of words. To him they meant she wasn't yet ready or able to give her full assent, some inner part was holding back. He didn't know why, perhaps she didn't either, but it wasn't enough. They would have to wait until she could fully acknowledge their love. But how to tell her? "Time for me to go, sweetheart, come walk me to the door," he said. They walked silently, arms around each other.

Kimberly sensed the anxiety in him and at the door said, "What is it, Gary?"

He put his arms around her loosely. "You must know, love, how dear Adam is to me. He's like the son I never had and I do love him. You're his mother. Sweetheart, what I'm trying to say is that it's Kimberly I love. Adam's mom is a lady I admire and respect as a fine person. But if there wasn't an Adam in the picture I'd still have fallen in love with Kimberly." He held her close and gently bent her head back as if he would drink from her lips "It's you I dream of, Kimberly, not Adam's mom. It's you I love; everything about you captivates me. It's you I want more than I've ever wanted anything in life." His voic ended in a whisper as he laid is mouth on hers. "It's Kimberly I'll marry, not Adam's mom. So I'll wait until you can tell me it's Kimberly who loves me and Kimberly who'll marry me. Do you understand?"

"I do now," she said, her eyes wide. After he'd gone she went through the apartment turning off lights and thinking of what Gary had revealed to her about herself. It stayed with her the next day and when he called she assured him she hadn't forgotten.

When she hung up from Gary the phone rang again. It was Glennette saying she and James would be at the party and how were things going. When Kimberly described the present state of affairs between herself and Gary, Glennette said, "What is it you're afraid of, Kimberly? That's what you need to think about. There's something you're afraid of losing or something you're afraid of happening or experiencing. If you haven't been able to figure it out by the time I see you Saturday, let me know. But I predict you'll know by then."

"Do you know?" Kimberly asked curiously.

"Yes, but it's better for you to discover it for yourself," Glennette said.

In the morning it was rainy and cold. Adam was grumbly and slow. When she got to work one clerk was absent and an important delivery of books hadn't arrived. Kimberly had to spend an hour on the phone to track it. Despite the rain, shoppers poured into the store and all of the staff were kept busy. She did some hurried shopping on her lunch hour then rushed home to get ready for the catering job, thankful that her mother had called to suggest Adam spending the night there instead of coming out in the cold rain. As she changed into her work clothes for the catering job, the doorbell rang and a delivery man gave her a floral box. Inside were six perfect roses, two red, two white, and two yellow. She inhaled their lovely perfume and read the card: *Darling, You'll have to forgive me sending these but since I can't be near you myself, these will tell you of my love, Gary.*

Kimberly looked at the card and wept. She put the flowers in water still crying and drove to the job sniffing occasionally. I'm so tired and frustrated that a sweet gesture of love sends me into tears, she thought. I'm going to call Gary when I get home. But the job wasn't over until nearly midnight. Her apartment felt empty, cold, and lonely to Kimberly for the first time. Always before she had been glad to enter it as a haven, a sanctuary she had created that was her very own. Tonight it was just a set of pleasant rooms devoid of the warmth of love. The tree lights blinked on and off but she felt only loneliness and isolation. She looked at the roses and suddenly she was pierced with a longing for Gary's presence, a need that was overwhelming and that left her shaken and afraid. Always before she had been self-sufficient, but now there was an inadequacy. Gary was the other half to make a wholeness. She knew with certainty that this was the source of her fear. She was afraid of giving herself totally to the strong emotions he stirred within her that would sweep her from familiar moorings. The self-control she valued would be endangered. Yet if she didn't commit herself wholly to their love, she would be incomplete. If she rejected him, she'd do irreparable damage to herself. Glennette had said when you know what you want then you have to be brave enough to grasp it. Now she knew, but was she brave enough?

Kimberly slept deeply and dreamlessly. Her eyes flew open at five thirty and despite the fact she'd only had five hours of sleep she felt energetic and rested. Now she at least knew the question that had been elusive for so long, and she knew the answer would come. Meanwhile she had a vegetable tray to prepare for tonight and after that a trifle-like dessert in a punch-bowl with layers of cake, pudding, bananas, strawberries, and topped with whipped cream. Gary was doing meat balls with crusty rolls, barbecue, potato salad, dips with chips, and beverages.

She called Gary on her lunch hour. "I loved the flowers, dear. I wanted to call you last night but it was past midnight when I got home."

"Sweetheart," Gary said, "you really must get it in your head that you can call me any time in the twenty-four hours. There's no time that's too early or too late. Can't you understand that, Kimberly?" There was almost a note of pleading in his voice.

"I'm trying to understand it, but this is all so new to me. Be patient with me, please."

"I know, dearest." Gary's voice, warm and caressing, enveloped Kimberly as if in an embrace.

She was seized with a vehement longing to see him, to touch his face, to look into his eyes, to be held in his arms. The longing had to be expressed somehow. "Gary." She stopped not knowing what else to say.

"Yes, sweetheart, what is it?"

"Gary."

"Please, dearest," Gary could feel Kimberly's effort to communicate something important. "What do you want to tell me?"

"I have such a longing to see you, to touch your face, and to feel your arms around me." The words poured out of Kimberly in a rush.

"Oh, sweetheart, if only I could be with you now. How soon will you be here this evening?"

"As soon as I can be, around six thirty, maybe earlier."

"I'll be waiting, dearest."

During the afternoon Kimberly decided on which of two outfits to wear and when she got home she was so hyper she felt like she could vibrate like a plucked string. After her shower she put on the long golden tunic over a matching asymmetrical skirt with a slit up one side. Her earrings, hose, and heels were a complementary chocolate brown. The skirt swung as she moved. She left the house at six fifteen and at six thirty drove into Gary's driveway. She was surprised to see him standing on the porch. He opened her door. "Let's go in," he said.

"What about the food?"

"Later." He walked her up the steps across the porch and into the house.

In an instant they were in each other's arms. Gary put his hands under her coat and pulled her as close as he could. *This is where I belong,* she thought as she put her arms around him and met his kiss with her own.

Behind them the doorbell rang. Gary opened the door to Adam whose headlong entrance ended in a hug from Kimberly and Gary then, they greeted the rest of Kimberly's family.

"We came early to help," her mother said. "Ted and Muriel'll be here later and Willie said to tell you he can't make it."

"Let me show you the house," Gary said. By the time the tour was over and Adam had proudly shown how he could run the train, the doorbell rang again bringing the Blairs and after them Walter and Marie Davis.

Ted and Muriel Washington arrived later followed by a group of Gary's friends. Gary introduced them to Kimberly coming last to a dark-skinned man of medium height whose shaved head, well-trimmed mustache, and goatee combined with a diamond stud in one ear gave him a distinctive appearance. "Kimberly, this is Cy Brewster. We work together. You have to watch him. He can't be trusted around lovely women."

"Don't believe a word he says, Kimberly," Cy said.

Kimberly was glad to meet the man Gary had often spoken about and she gave him her warmest smile as they shook hands. "Hello, Cy."

No wonder the women can't get his attention, Cy thought, looking at her admiringly.

"You wouldn't have a sister, would you?" he asked with a smile.

"Actually I have."

"But Clarice is out of your age group, Cy, so go on in the family room and behave yourself," Gary said, as the doorbell rang again.

"Hello, Gary," Glennette Ellington said.

"I'm so glad you could come, Glennette," Gary said, pressing her hand warmly.

"I don't think you've met my husband, James Ellington."

Gary had wondered how he'd feel when he saw Glennette but as he said hello and shook hands with her tall, attractive husband, he was glad they'd found each other. They had the kind of happiness about them that he wanted for Kimberly and himself. He watched Kimberly talking to Glennette. Each woman had a very special beauty but his heart and soul responded only to Kimberly.

James had been intensely jealous of Raeford when he was taking Glennette out but now he saw he could be friends with him because it was clear that Raeford's only interest was Kimberly. James wished him well and they made easy conversation together as the women excused themselves to go upstairs.

"I can see you've figured it out," Glennette said, "so tell me quickly."

"If I give myself wholly to our love, I'm afraid of what

will happen to the Kimberly I've always known. Who will I become?''

''You're afraid of losing control?''

''That's part of it.''

''I had to ask myself the same question. Do you think I've gained or lost through my marriage to James?''

''Gained.''

''Believe me I have, more than I can ever say. Thank goodness I'm not the same Glennette I was when you first met me. What you'll become will be a complete person in so many ways. You'll be happy, loving and loved.''

Kimberly, listening intently, knew that what Glennette was saying was true.

''Kimberly, it's a matter of trust. Can't you trust yourself and Gary with your love?''

''Yes,'' Kimberly said. Then with a feeling of utter conviction, ''Yes, I can.''

''Our men will be up here after us if we don't go down,'' Glennette said.

Gary and James were engrossed in conversation and didn't hear them until they were halfway down the stairs. James saw them first and lost the thread of what he was saying. Gary turned and as soon as he looked at Kimberly he knew something in her had changed. He moved toward her and took her hand. ''Are you all right, dearest?'' he asked softly.

''Yes. I have something to tell you later when everyone's gone,'' she said. Gary looked around for James and Glennette but they had disappeared.

''Give me a kiss to carry me through until then.'' She kissed him briefly.

''Now we have a party to give,'' she said.

From the noise that greeted them from the family room and the kitchen the party hadn't waited for them. Gary had hung green garlands with red berries all around the room. The majestic tree stood at the end of the room farthest from the fireplace. Two tables were piled with painted glass balls, stars, angels of all sorts, Santas, teddy bears, candy canes, icicles, snowmen, toy ornaments, sleighs, houses, and tiny red bows. Clarice and the two Blair sisters, Elizabeth and Sandra, had already begun the trimming. Cy Brewster was helping them and gradually everyone joined in with much laughing discussion of what looked best where. Nelson and Walter as the oldest persons present were appealed to when there were differences of opinion.

"Where's the popcorn? We must have popcorn strings for good fortune," someone said. Corn was popped and strung while the food was being warmed up and set out. Gary had found a black angel at a crafts fair and he affixed it on the top with Cy holding the ladder for him. Then Gary said, "Adam, it's ready." Kimberly turned off all of the lights and Gary showed Adam where the switches were for the tree. Adam clicked them on one after another and the tall tree sprang to life.

There was a moment of silent appreciation of the magic then applause and cheers. Kimberly, standing at the door from the hall, looked at the beautiful tree and felt the sting of tears. Then Gary was behind her holding her against him, his arms around her waist. "Our first tree," he whispered. He kissed her on her neck and she shivered. Someone turned on the lights and Gary moved away.

Food was served and for another hour people ate and talked. In the wide waxed hallway and in the front room music was played and people began to dance. James and Glennette danced together dreamily. "Has Kimberly found her love?" he asked.

"I'm sure she has," Glennette said.

"I hope so, she deserves to be happy."

In the kitchen Kimberly was refilling a dish of chips. "Will you dance, Madam?" Gary said, putting the dish down and taking her in his arms. As they danced into the hall he said, "You know I've never had the chance to take you out at all, not even to a restaurant, much less for dancing."

"The holidays will be over soon and my weekends will be

free,'' she promised. She looked at him a little self-consciously. ''I'm surprised I can even dance, it's been so long.''

Ethel and Nelson danced up to them. ''Change partners,'' Ethel said dancing away with Gary and leaving Kimberly to her dad.

As they moved slowly around the hall Nelson said, ''Things better?''

''Yes, dad, thanks to you,'' Kimberly said.

''Good man,'' Nelson said, looking pleased. ''Good party.''

People gradually returned to the family room, content to snack on the food and look at the tree. Gary whispered to Elizabeth Blair and she began to play softly on the keyboard she'd brought over earlier. She played ''Away in a Manger'' through then started the singing.

Everyone gathered in the large room. From chairs, from cushions on the floor, and from the sofa they looked at the glowing fire and at the beautiful Christmas tree shimmering and sparkling with its multitude of tiny lights and ornaments. In soft sopranos, altos, and basses they blended their voices in celebration. Elizabeth went from one familiar carol to another: ''Hark the Herald Angels Sing,'' ''O Little Town of Bethlehem,'' ''We Three Kings of Orient Are,'' ''Deck the Halls,'' ''Joy to the World,'' and ending with ''Silent Night, Holy Night.''

Kimberly thought her heart would overflow with joy as she sat between Gary and Adam, singing. Then Elizabeth struck a chord and began ''O Holy Night.'' Her voice, high and true, filled the room with beauty and a sense of awe. As the last echo of the song died away and the plangent note of the instrument faded there was utter silence.

Then little by little there was movement and people got up to go home.

''It's the best party we've been to,'' Glennette and James said. Cy echoed this. ''It was great. I'm having one on New Year's Eve and expect to see you both there.'' Gary and Kimberly said they'd be there, thanked Elizabeth for the music as the Blairs left and closed the door behind Kimberly's family, the last to leave. Gary took a sleepy Adam upstairs to lie down and found Kimberly picking up cups and glasses when he returned.

"It was such a good party, Gary. You could see people were enjoying themselves," she said as she took the glasses into the kitchen. She returned with a tray and began to fill it. Now that they were alone she became increasingly nervous about talking to Gary, who was standing quietly, hands in pockets, waiting on her.

Finally she stopped handling the dishes and stood behind a chair, facing Gary. "Are you going to tell me now?" he asked.

"I'm going to try. When I was in love with Walter I was young and immature. I knew very little about the kinds of feelings I have for you."

Gary had vowed to himself he would not stand near her, he would not touch her. Whatever she had to say, she had to say on her own. He had gone as far as he could to meet her. She would have to come the rest of the way by herself, of her own volition.

"When we are apart," Kimberly said, "I feel you close to me. When I am near you, sometimes I feel like the fire will burn me up. I've been afraid, Gary, afraid of losing self-control, afraid of such an overwhelming force. Do you see?" She looked at him for understanding.

Gary said, "I do see, Kimberly." *My sweet love, you do feel like I do, you do love me,* he was thinking. His hands were clenched inside his pockets to keep himself from going to her.

"But if I give in to fear, I'll lose the chance to be complete because I'll lose you. It became a question of trust. Can I trust myself and you with my love. I finally realized that I can." Kimberly stopped but Gary didn't move. Does he still think this is Adam's mom talking, she wondered. She left the chair and came to him.

"Dearest Gary, what I'm trying to tell you is that I love you."

Gary still made no move. His eyes were so dark, his look so intense and fixed that Kimberly felt he was searching her innermost self. "You must be certain, Kimberly," he finally said. "No second thoughts, no turning back. It has to be all or nothing!"

"I know," Kimberly said. She moved closer and put her hands on his shoulders. "This is not Adam's mom," she said emphatically. "This is me, Kimberly. I want to be your wife, dearest." She put her arms around his neck. "I want to be everything to you," she whispered and closing her eyes kissed him. With all of her being she told him of her love.

Gary began to tremble. His hands came out of his pockets and he took Kimberly in his arms. They stood embraced oblivious to the world as heart spoke to heart through their kiss.

"I didn't know what you were going to say at first," Gary said as they sat on the couch. "You kept avoiding it, playing with the dishes and it made me nervous."

"I was nervous, too, that's why I was playing with the dishes."

"You really do love me?" he asked, disbelieving.

"Truly I do."

"Show me," Gary whispered, his voice hoarse, his face filled with a deep longing.

His words and the look on his face set off a spark in Kimberly. She responded with a hunger that moved like electricity throughout her body. Pulling his head down to hers and pressing herself as close to him as she could, she kissed his mouth, his face, his neck. Then they were both engulfed in the whirlwind, caressing and kissing and saying each other's names trying to appease their passion.

Breathless and shaken they separated at last. When she could speak Kimberly said, "This is the fire I was afraid of."

"I know, it's been burning me for a long time," Gary said. "I want you so much, more than I can ever tell you." He kissed her fiercely over and over. "You intoxicate me so, Kimberly, and I am carried away before I know it."

"I know," she said, her voice low and thrilling. Her face was flushed, her eyes brilliant and her lips full and plump from kisses.

"Do you, sweetheart?" His voice was both eager and hopeful.

"I feel the same way you do, Gary, so for both our sakes I'm going."

He held her again but gently this time. "I don't want to let you out of my arms but you're right," he said.

Sunday and Monday were a blur to Kimberly. She was too happy to try to hide it and she went about her work with a smile. When she picked Adam up after work on Monday they went to the florist and selected a plant for Gary. They delivered the plant to Gary and his look of surprise and pleasure at their impromptu gift stayed with her. They arranged to spend the next evening, Christmas Eve, together.

Kimberly finished her Christmas shopping on her lunch hour Tuesday and left work promptly at five for the first time in two weeks. Gary brought Adam from her mother's house and they had supper together at her apartment. Then they went to church for a Christmas Eve service. They smiled at each other over Adam's head and shared the hymnal as the carols were sung. After the service, they stood and talked with Kimberly's family and the Davises.

"Coming by?" Nelson asked Gary.

"Not tonight," Gary said.

"Other business?" Nelson said quietly.

"Yes," Gary said and asked, "All right?"

"Yes." Nelson said. "Good luck, Raeford." Nelson offered his hand and Gary knew he'd given his permission.

On the way to Gary's house Kimberly said, "I saw you and Dad talking and then you shook hands. What was that about?"

"He gave us his blessing," Gary said.

"You told him about us?"

"Not in so many words, he just seemed to know."

"That's the way he is," Kimberly said fondly. "I'm glad he agrees."

"What about your mother?"

"Dad's already told her, I'm sure. They operate as a team always."

"So will we," Gary promised.

The house was warm and cozy. Gary built up the fire and turned on music while Adam looked at the many presents under the tree. Gary had cider and cookies ready and after that Adam tried to put off going to bed by declaring he was still hungry. Kimberly said he could have one more cookie then bed. She and Gary went up with Adam. After he was tucked in she sat on one side of the bed, Gary on the other.

"When you wake up, Adam, it'll be Christmas and you'll have a big surprise. You'll only have a little while to sleep because it's already after eleven."

"So go right to sleep," Gary added.

Downstairs Gary sat on the couch and held Kimberly in his arms. "I never get to see enough of you, when do you have to go back to work?"

"Not until the day after New Year's, I'm taking a few days off." She looked at him to see his reaction.

"You mean we're actually going to be able to spend some real time together? I can't believe it!" Gary said.

"I thought that if we're going to be married we need to see more of each other than we have." She wrinkled her nose at him. "After all, when we've been shopping together you might change your mind."

"Or you might change yours when you see me after I've worked on the car and can't find out what's wrong or when we've tried working in the yard together."

"It's exciting," she mused looking at Gary reflectively, "there's so much still to discover about each other."

"The most urgent thing I want to discover is how you're going to look as a bride," Gary said kissing her tenderly but briefly. Without saying it in words each knew the other was trying to keep emotions dampened down. Their fire was too volatile, too near the surface to be played with.

Before Kimberly could reply the clock on the mantel struck midnight. Gary pulled a black velvet case from his pocket and gave it to Kimberly. "Merry Christmas, dear heart."

Kimberly recognized the case. She pressed the latch to open it. Inside was the exquisite bookmark Gary had shown her the first time she'd come to this house.

"Oh, Gary, I can't take this," she protested. "It's such a treasure!"

"It is mine as the eldest son to give on Christmas to his true love," he said firmly. "I want to tell you something about this, Kimberly. It may not make me look very good, but I want you to know. I never gave this to Charlotte. We'd been married nearly a year when our first Christmas came but I never told her about it. But the first time you came into my house I felt impelled to show it to you and tell you its history and meaning. My heart knew then that you were my true love."

"I will cherish it always," Kimberly said. She kissed him on the lips and whispered, "I'll keep it in trust for our eldest son."

"One more thing, sweetheart," Gary said. He took from his pocket a ring box, opened it, and put a circlet of gold with four sparkling diamonds on the third finger of Kimberly's left hand.

"It's so beautiful!" Kimberly said.

"You will marry me, Kimberly?"

"Yes, Gary, I will marry you."

"When?" He asked.

"As soon as we can arrange it," she said.

"Two weeks, three, when? I must know." Gary was insistent.

"As soon as we can get your folks and Amanda here, say three weeks.

"We'll use the week you're off to work on it," he said. His breathing was getting ragged. "Sweetheart, I've been so good tonight. Please give me one real kiss," he said.

Kimberly, equally filled with yearning, put her arms around

his neck and gave herself up to the fever of his kisses and caresses. When he finally lifted his head he leaned back against the sofa to let his breathing quiet and his pulses subside. Kimberly stirred and slipped out of his arms. "Don't leave me," he protested.

"I'll be right back," she promised and returned in a moment with a gold box with a green satin bow. "Merry Christmas, dearest," she said.

Kimberly had wondered what to give Gary, a man who had everything he needed. She purchased a handsome pair of fine leather gloves and two books he'd mentioned. These gifts were wrapped and under her tree for him but she wanted something special, something that couldn't be bought in a store. When they were trimming her tree he'd spoken about a particular Christmas in Ohio with his cousins. That gave her an idea. She watched him now as he opened it hoping he would like her idea.

Gary lifted from the box a small sled. His eyes widened in delight as he examined it. It was exquisitely carved with a high gloss on it and the name, Red Flyer, printed on it in clear scarlet letters. "Every detail is just as I remember it, even the runners," he marveled. "Where in the world did you find it?"

"I didn't," Kimberly said, thrilled that Gary liked it. "I asked Mr. Jethro to make it. He lives near here in Sweet River. He's been carving all of his life."

"But how did he know how the Red Flyer looks?"

"He found a picture in one of his catalogs. He said he remembered making one years ago for a tourist who wanted it for his little boy."

"Is it Christmas yet, Mom?" came from the doorway and they looked up to see Adam rubbing his eyes sleepily.

"It's Christmas, baby. Come on over here with us," Kimberly said. Adam nestled himself between them and looked at the tree.

"I don't see it," he said.

"See what?" Kimberly asked.

"I don't see my great big surprise under the tree. There's just the same things that were there when I went to bed."

"It's not under the tree," Kimberly said.

"Where is it?" Adam looked around the room.

"Listen and I'll tell you." Adam turned to look at her. "Adam, you're going to have a daddy, that's your surprise. I'm going to marry Mr. Gary and that will make him your daddy."

Adam's eyes grew wide. Kimberly and Gary watched him anxiously. Then with all the savoir-faire of the almost-six male child, he said, "That's okay, Mom. I like Mr. Gary."

Gary, aware of the dignity involved here said, "I'm glad you approve, Adam," and held out his hand. He and Adam shook hands gravely.

Kimberly, watching with tender amusement and respect saw in the gesture a foretaste of a future she'd never even fantasized, and in her heart she said a special prayer of gratitude on this Christmas morning.

Imani

Bridget Anderson

Chapter One

Natalie picked up her heavy suit bag and threw it in the trunk of her car. She had enough clothes to last her two weeks. She'd give anything to see the look on Kevin's face when he wouldn't have her to unwrap this Christmas. Two weeks ago she ended a three-year-old relationship that was going nowhere. Men were at the bottom of her list for a while. The last thing she wanted to do was spend her holiday with one.

Her car was gassed up and she had on her comfortable riding jeans. Two weeks in Hopkinsville, Kentucky, should relieve all her stress. Her Aunt Polly had invited her to spend the holidays with relatives in Hopkinsville. Since her mother and stepfather were in Germany visiting Natalie's brother for the holidays, she took her aunt up on the offer. She looked forward to spending the Christmas holiday with relatives, then learning about Kwanzaa immediately following, while helping her cousin prepare for the celebration.

Natalie couldn't wait to get out of Atlanta. She sped down the highway in her little Honda wanting to put as much distance between herself and Kevin as possible.

Seven hours later, Natalie pulled into her aunt's driveway honking her car horn. The cute little two-story white house hadn't changed much over the years. Natalie remembered the green window shutters now trimmed with white Christmas lights. A grin as big as a Kentucky cornfield spread across Natalie's face when her aunt, Pauline Williams, stepped out onto the front porch. She'd always be Aunt Polly to Natalie. The name she called her in her youth. One look at her Aunt Polly and Natalie realized how much she'd missed being around her family. Ever since Natalie's mother remarried and moved to Minnesota, Hopkinsville, Kentucky, had become her surrogate home. Most of her relatives lived here.

"Well look at you!" Pauline stood holding the door open for her niece. "Don't you look good."

Natalie walked up the steps lugging her suit bag on one shoulder and a duffle bag on the other. "Hi, Aunt Polly, you're looking pretty good yourself." She kissed her aunt on the cheek as she passed her going inside.

"Honey, I'm so glad you could make it." After closing the door Pauline walked over and gave her niece a big hug.

"So am I, Aunt Polly. I'm glad you invited me." She dropped her bags with a thump, and returned her aunt's hug. The smell coming from her aunt's kitchen made her stomach growl. She'd only stopped once during the seven-hour drive down, for a chicken sandwich.

"Here, let me take your coat." Pauline helped Natalie out of her coat. "You can put your bags in the back bedroom. Wanda should be here any minute now. I told her you were on your way." Pauline hung Natalie's coat in the hall closet.

Natalie quickly went into the back bedroom, dropped her bags on the floor and glanced around the room. She immediately felt at home. The guest bedroom had a country, sit-yourself-down feel to it. Everything was yellow and blue, from the stripped wallpaper to the floral pillows. She closed the door and returned to the living room with her aunt. "How is Wanda? I haven't seen her in so long."

"Oh she's fine. Getting big as a house though. She sits over there cooking for them kids every night, but you can't tell it. One look at her and you'd swear she's eating all the food."

Natalie laughed at her aunt's description of her daughter. Pauline had put on a few pounds also, Natalie noticed. She was a statuesque woman with distinguished features and a stylish, short haircut. However, because of her height, the weight was hardly noticeable. Natalie thought the haircut made her aunt look ten years younger.

Pauline stood across the room with her hands on her hips staring at her niece. "Honey, you'll never gain any weight will you? You look like you're still in high school. You're such a cute little thing."

"Auntie, you've gotta remember, Mama's small, so I'm probably going to be small like her." Natalie looked down at herself. To her, she'd been cursed with not much of a body at all. Everything was small, from her feet to her hands. "I didn't inherit any of the hips in the family. But speaking of gaining weight, I think I smell something that could help." She raised her chin to get a better whiff of the aroma coming from the kitchen.

"Then you come right in here and let me feed you. Honey, if a good wind comes though, it'll blow you away." Pauline led the way into the kitchen.

After both women loaded their plates and sat at the kitchen table, Pauline cut to the chase, "Okay, what's that young man done now?"

Natalie looked surprised. "What makes you think Kevin's done anything?"

"You're spending your two weeks vacation here in Hopkinsville instead of in Atlanta with that good-looking gentleman of yours. Don't get me wrong, we're glad to have you, but you've never spent that much time here before."

Natalie looked into her aunt's all too wise eyes. There was no fooling her Aunt Polly. "We broke up two weeks ago."

"Are you going to be all right?" Pauline asked, before she began eating.

"Yeah, I'll be fine. Our relationship had been on the rocks for months anyway. I just wanted to spend some time with you guys and get away from men for a while. If I don't see another man for a long time, it'll be too soon." Natalie jabbed her fork into her sweet potato.

"Is he the reason for the bags under your eyes? You look like you could use some rest."

"No, that's work. I think they're trying to drive me crazy. Sometimes I ask myself if it's worth it. I needed a mental health break from that place, that's another reason why I came." She continued eating.

"Well, you be sure to try and squeeze in some rest while you're here. Between the shop and my grandchildren, I haven't had much rest lately. I've been feeling a little under the weather. Wanda's working on the Kwanzaa celebration for the family and I know she wants you to help."

"Sure, but I don't know much about Kwanzaa."

"Don't worry, Wanda will tell you everything you need to know. We've celebrated Kwanzaa for the past two years. Believe me, you'll enjoy it. It'll be the most delightful learning experience you've ever had."

"Boy, I should learn a lot this vacation, between working with you in the shop and helping Wanda. Two things I know nothing about." She shrugged her shoulders and smiled at the challenges.

After they finished eating, Pauline stood up to empty the plates and put them in the sink. "You'll love working in the shop. It's my little home away from home, and I love it. It'll be some of the easiest work you'll ever do."

"Well, I'm yours for the next two weeks and I'm sure I'll enjoy myself."

"That's the spirit."

* * *

It was Monday morning and time for Pauline's Antiques & Crafts to open its doors. However, Pauline got the chills Saturday night, which turned into a sore throat Sunday. By Monday morning she couldn't get out of bed. Natalie had assured her aunt she could run the shop for one day. *How hard could it be?* she asked herself. If she could handle all the stress of running a retail clothing store in Atlanta, a one-woman antique shop should be a cinch. All she needed was for Wanda to open up and get her started. Wanda picked her up at 8:30 A.M. and drove in town to the antique shop that reminded Natalie of a little gingerbread house.

Natalie had a pleasant morning dusting off old furniture and knick knacks. Things were peaceful until she heard the bell over the door jingle, and knew she had her first customer. Within minutes so many people were in the shop she couldn't keep her eyes on everything. *Where had all these people come from?* she wondered. Her problems had just begun.

She couldn't find any small bags or tissue paper to wrap delicate items in. Whenever she looked up the line was still growing. After the fifth sale, she needed change. All she had under the register drawer were large bills. Now she'd told her aunt she could handle the day, and already things were falling apart.

Suddenly, the bell over the door jingled loudly several times like someone was playing with the door. She looked up and noticed a man backing in the door. From behind he had the body of a perfectly built basketball player. His broad back and shoulders filled the doorway. That tightly muscled behind was covered in a pair of close fitting jeans. Those long legs stopped at a pair of brown cowboy boots. Natalie's eyes traveled back up to his backside as he nudged his way in with a large box in his arms. *My God, who is that?*

As the door closed, he turned around and repositioned the

box in his arms. The change dropped from Natalie's hand
back into the register. Her customer cleared her throat as she
impatiently tapped her fingernails on the counter.

"Sorry, ma'am." She picked up the last of her change and
finished the transaction. As the next customer set a small antique
lamp on the counter, Natalie's eyes traveled across the room
following the Black cowboy as he walked by. He walked back
toward her aunt's office.

"Excuse me. Can I help you with something?" she asked,
wondering who this hunk was.

"Nope, I've got it. Besides, it looks like you've already got
your hands full." He motioned toward the line, which grew
longer.

She rang up the next purchase and glanced at him over her
shoulder as he walked into her aunt's office. The height, the
build, the deep voice, the tight jeans—oh, what a man he was!

Natalie shook her head and groaned inwardly, as she continued working. *Why did such a gorgeous-looking man have to
walk into this shop on this very day?* She looked away,
reminding herself he was the enemy. *You came here to get
away from men, repeat it until you hear it,* she said to herself.
Turning, she forced a smile at the next customer, who had been
watching her watch HIM.

He walked over and stood next to the counter as Natalie
opened the register and realized she had no more small bills,
or change. "Excuse me ladies," he said to the women in line.
He pushed his cap back a few inches and looked down at
Natalie. "You can tell Pauline her lamp parts are here. You
must be Natalie? I'm . . ."

As he talked, Natalie eyeballed him a moment, then decided
he looked honest enough. She cut him off. "Yes, I'm Natalie
and I need change." She grabbed two hundred dollar bills
from under the register drawer and shoved them into his hand.
"Quick, small bills and change." Whoever he was, she needed
his help. They could trade introductions later.

In less than five minutes he returned with her change. She was delighted and grateful. He found bags and tissue paper in the back room. He threw his jacket on the couch, and helped customers with selections and purchases as if he worked there. For all she knew, maybe he did. But her aunt hadn't mentioned him.

Every chance she got she watched him move around the shop. He had the tall and tight build of a basketball player. Her favorite body type. Every time he picked up something, the muscles in his arms contracted and she could imagine them around her. She shook her head to clear her senses and got back to work. When she finally came up for air the shop was empty. After a long sigh of relief, she walked from behind the counter and flopped down on a couch. He joined her.

"Boy," she sighed. "Do they come in droves like that often?"

"Every now and then. Those were charter buses from Louisville. Hopkinsville is sort of the antique capital of Kentucky, and Pauline's is in the middle of Antique Row. Lucky for your aunt you were here today. Normally, if she's not feeling well, she closes shop."

Natalie sat up as she realized she had no idea who this man was. "I'm sorry. Here I've been working you to death, and I don't even know your name."

"Roderick Taylor, but everybody calls me Rod."

They shook hands and Natalie noticed how his huge hands swallowed hers. He was gorgeous. His huge brown eyes seemed to be pulling her in. His smile was warm and inviting, but he seemed to be holding most of it back. To her, his look was more of an inspection of her.

"So, Rod, how do you know my name?" She pulled herself out of his entrancing gaze and relaxed back onto the couch.

"Your aunt's been talking about you for weeks now," he said with a drawl.

"I hauled that box over from Webster Lamps for her. She

said her niece from Atlanta was coming in for the holidays. So, I figured the new face in the shop must be Natalie.''

In all her twenty-seven years she'd never met a real country boy before, but here he was in the flesh. He sounded like *he* was from Georgia, instead of her. He stretched his long legs out, resting the heels of his boots on the wood floor. Suddenly, she had a vision of those legs wrapped around her body. It had obviously been too long since she'd been with a man. She broke up with Kevin two weeks ago, but hadn't been intimate with him for over three months.

''Do you work for my aunt?'' she asked, wondering why he picked up the box and pitched in to help her.

''No, I guess you could say I do her favors from time to time. The box was too heavy for her and Webster's doesn't deliver.'' He shifted himself to the edge of the couch. ''Is this your first time in Hopkinsville?'' he asked.

''No, I spent a little time here when I was younger. Holiday visits with my parents. But, I don't remember much about the town.''

''Then you'll have to let me give you a tour of our little town before you leave. Of course, it doesn't compare to Atlanta, but it's nice.''

Natalie noticed how he cocked his head, and said Atlanta like it was a dirty word. ''Sure, I'd like that,'' she replied. She wondered what he had against Atlanta.

The bell over the door jingled as another customer walked in. Rising from the couch with ease, Rod stood over Natalie smiling down at her.

''Well, I better be going. I've got to get back to work.''

Natalie sat there awestruck, looking up at him. She reminded herself that he wasn't anything out of the ordinary—just all male. He walked toward the door adjusting his cap forward on his head again. He stopped in the doorway and looked back at her.

''I'll catch you later.'' He nodded his head and walked out the door.

All she could manage was a slight nod of the head. She couldn't help but follow him to the door to see if he was getting into a truck, or on a horse. He pulled away in a huge black pickup truck.

Chapter Two

"Girl, my kids enjoy celebrating Kwanzaa, but we still celebrate Christmas. If they woke up Christmas morning and there weren't any toys under that tree, I'd have three devastated little monsters on my hands."

Natalie helped Wanda wrap gifts for her children. She had two little boys and a little girl named Grachel that Natalie had fallen in love with. The kids were at their grandmother's house for the moment.

Wanda lived in a comfortable two-story brick house in a quiet subdivision of new homes. White Christmas lights and rich green garland gave the house a festive holiday air.

Natalie envied her cousin for all she had. Wanda was blessed with a loving husband, a family, and status within the community. Everyone in Hopkinsville knew who she was. She worked on local town parades, and every type of African-American celebration to be had. Natalie was surprised that Wanda knew as much about Kwanzaa as she did.

"So, Wanda, when did you learn so much about Kwanzaa?" Natalie asked, after wrapping her last gift. She watched her cousin put the finishing touches on a beautiful bow, while she helped herself to more popcorn.

"Believe it or not, it all started with one of Brian's homework assignments."

"You're kidding? He's in elementary school."

"I know, but his teacher sent home a story for him to read and do a book report on. He asked me what Kwanzaa was, and I couldn't answer him. I helped him read the little story and write the report. But after he went to bed, I pulled the book back out and read it again." She took a breather and grabbed a handful of popcorn to munch on.

"Natalie, that little story was so touching. I want my children to know about their African roots. But going to all-white Taylor County School isn't going to cut it. That's the only assignment any of my children have ever had about African-Americans. If we lived closer in town they could go to the city schools. That's where all of the black children in the county go to school. They also have a few black teachers. But Arthur and I wanted to move out here. We need to teach the children ourselves—their family. And I thought I had. I mean, they know who Dr. Martin Luther King is, and Jessie Jackson, but that's about the extent of it. Girl, they thought Africa was one big jungle where Tarzan lived." Wanda shook her head as both women broke out into laughter.

"We're laughing, but so did I until I got into junior high school. I couldn't imagine walking around downtown Zimbabwe, and having it look almost like downtown Atlanta."

"Well, growing up in Atlanta, I'm sure you were exposed to more of your culture than we were here in Hopkinsville. Mama should have moved with your mom after high school."

"I don't know about that, Wanda. Hopkinsville's nice."

"It's okay." She shrugged her shoulders and gave a half smile. "Well, after reading that book I went to the library and checked out everything I could about Kwanzaa, which consisted of two books and one was more like a pamphlet. So, I went to the bookstore and ordered more books by and about African-

Americans. I borrowed Brian's teacher's idea, and now my children read a book a month about or by African-Americans. And I make them give me a report.''

"A book a month! Wow, where do you find the books?''

"There's plenty out there now, but if it's a big book, I let them take two months with it. I don't want that to interfere with their school work.''

"Wanda, that sounds great. So they must know a lot about Kwanzaa?''

"They learn a little more each year. What I think they like best is making gifts. Girl, wait till you see some of the stuff they come up with.''

"I can't wait.'' Natalie smiled at the thought and couldn't wait to help the children with their gifts.

"Girl, thanks for helping me wrap all these gifts. The kids will be so excited when they come in here tonight and see these presents under the tree.''

"Your tree is beautiful.''

"Thanks, Arthur and the kids picked it out. And I guess you can tell they decorated it.''

Natalie thought the multitude of ornaments on the tree looked good. It definitely had the children's touch. For a moment she felt sad. She wanted a good husband like Arthur, and beautiful, well-behaved children like Wanda's. Kevin's image flashed through her mind. She couldn't have any of those things with him. What she needed was a new man who didn't feel like the world owed him everything. Someone who could focus on something other than himself for a moment.

"Nat, you all right?'' Wanda peered at her cousin from across the room.

Natalie looked up realizing Wanda had been talking to her while she stared into the tree. "Yeah, I'm sorry. What did you say?''

"I said, Mama told me you met Rod yesterday.''

Natalie fought hard to stop the huge smile from breaking through, but couldn't, and it lit up her face. "Yeah, he came by the shop and helped me out of a rough spot.'' She tried her best to pull that smile off her face. For the life of her she couldn't figure out what she was smiling about anyway. He was just a man.

"I'm sorry you got stuck in there by yourself on your first day. But at least you had something good to look at."

The two women looked at each other smiling. "Girl, admit it. That man is fine. I shake my head myself every time I look at him. It don't make no sense for God to make a man look that good. He should have *temptation* written on his forehead."

"He is good looking." Natalie walked over and sat on the couch, tucking her stockinged feet underneath her. "Shoot, I almost forgot I had customers in line when he walked in. Talk about a distraction."

"And believe it or not, he's single."

"Single! A man that good looking doesn't have a woman?"

"Nope."

"What's wrong with him?" Not that she was interested, she told herself.

"Nothing, honey. I don't think there's a woman good enough in this town for him. He used to date this girl who lived in Greensburg for a while. But she moved to Atlanta, and that was the end of that relationship. That boy's not leaving Hopkinsville for anybody."

"Huh, he was a nice little surprise for the day."

"So you like him, huh?"

"I didn't say I liked him," Natalie huffed. "I just met him."

"Yeah, I know. But, I saw the way you smiled when I mentioned his name. He has that effect on women. But not many have an effect on him."

"So what do I care." Natalie shrugged her shoulders.

"He called Mama this morning talking about you."

Natalie sat up, shocked. He was good looking, but she didn't want to be involved with any men right now in her life. She could care less if he looked good enough a blind woman could see. "What did he say?"

"Well he called pretending to be asking about something else. But Mama said he really wanted to know about you."

"He wanted to know what?" He stomach began to flutter. *What could he have been asking about her?*

"Things like how long you were planning to be in town, if you were working all week, and were you participating in the Kwanzaa celebration."

"He asked Aunt Polly all that?"

"Probably not, but she volunteered the information. You know how Mama is. And let me tell you right now, she's crazy about Rod." Wanda walked over and joined Natalie on the couch.

"What are you looking so scared for? Rod's cute."

"I'm not scared of anything. I just don't want to get involved with anyone right now, that's all. Especially not some country boy who thinks he's God's gift."

"Girl, he doesn't think that. It's the women around here who think it. And they all want a piece of him." Wanda pulled her papers out of a folder and laid them on the cocktail table.

"Well, come on, let me fill you in on all the Kwanzaa happenings. We're going to have a great time, and Rod will be participating."

"Wanda." Natalie said her name in a whining tone. She hoped her family wasn't about to start playing matchmaking for the two weeks she'd planned on being in town. When she said she didn't want to be involved with a man right now, she meant it. Especially a man that made her weak in the knees.

It was two days before Christmas and Natalie felt wonderful. The laid-back life in Hopkinsville suited her fine. Everything about the town was so cute and quaint to her. Absent was the stress that came along with a big city, and she appreciated that. She picked up gifts for all her relatives, and couldn't wait for Christmas to be over with, and Kwanzaa to begin. Wanda had loaned her a book to read on the subject. The celebration was being held at the Armory. Wanda had a speaker coming into town, and activities planned for every night. Several church members were helping with the Kwanzaa *Karamu* feast on the thirty-first.

Natalie went to the shop early to help her Aunt Polly. She was relieved that her aunt felt better, though she knew nothing could keep her aunt down for long.

"Well, good morning, little lady."

"Morning, Aunt Polly." Natalie looked at her watch. "How long have you been here?" She walked into the back room to put up her purse and coat, then returned.

"Oh, I came in around seven o'clock this morning. Tomorrow is Christmas Eve, and I've got lots to do."

"Well, I'm just glad you're feeling better."

"It must of been some type of bug, because I feel much better today. Besides, I'm too busy to be sick."

"Yeah, those last minute gifts and all."

"Yes, and there's deliveries to be made." Pauline busied herself behind the counter. After a moment she said, "Honey, could you take this sheet and mark down those angel ornaments in the basket over there." She pointed to several baskets sitting at the foot of the shop's Christmas tree.

"Time to start slashing prices. I remember Mama used to love those Christmas sales."

"And I'm sure she still does. Don't bet for one minute she doesn't have them taking her somewhere over in Germany looking for sales." She walked over to Natalie with a red pen.

"Yeah, I hope she's enjoying herself." The one thing Natalie missed most about Christmas was spending it with her parents. Since her parents' divorce, she only saw either of them once or twice a year. Everyone seemed to be living their own lives, ones that didn't include family anymore.

"She is, honey, and so will you. Here . . . mark everything fifty percent off. I hope to move all this stuff before my new shipment comes in. This isn't Macy's so it takes a little longer."

"Aunt Polly, I really love your shop. It's great. I like how you've mixed all these antiques with the locals' crafts."

"Thank you." Pauline looked down at her watch slyly. "Oh, Natalie, I just remembered something. In a few minutes Rod's coming by to make a delivery for me. I wonder if you can ride with him and bring back some pies I ordered for the Kwanzaa celebration?"

Natalie thought for a moment. This was just her aunt's way of matchmaking. She remembered what Wanda had said about her aunt liking Rod. But how was she going to get out of the trip?

"Aunt Polly, I thought Kwanzaa was all about making your own things?"

"It's also about cooperative economics. I buy pies from Mrs. Pennick because she has her own baking business. She's an African-American woman, so I'm within the seven principles of Kwanzaa." Pauline stood with her arms crossed, smiling at her niece.

"Well, Ms. Thing, I see you know your stuff. So, I guess I'm going to pick up pies." Natalie rested her hands on her hips as she cocked her head, laughing at her aunt.

"I sure do." Pauline turned and walked back behind the counter. "Rod should be here any minute."

Natalie shrugged her shoulders and got back to work. What harm could a little ride do? She didn't want to have anything to do with men, including Mr. Taylor. After her disastrous relationship with Kevin, she vowed to lay off men. Still, she figured doing this favor for her aunt couldn't hurt her vows.

An hour later, as she climbed into the truck with Rod she asked, "Just how far is Bardstown anyway?" He held her hand as he helped her into the truck.

"It's right up the road a piece." He pointed ahead of her.

"That tells me a lot." Her aunt had forgotten to mention that little bit of information. All along, Natalie thought Mrs.

Pennick lived right there in Hopkinsville, and the ride wouldn't take long. Now she wanted to know how long she had to be confined in the truck with this man.

"I'll have you back before supper, I promise." He started the engine and pulled off. When he noticed her shiver from the cold, he turned the heat up.

The half smile he gave Natalie was just enough to call a smile. Again, she told herself, *I'm only along because Aunt Polly asked me. It has nothing to do with Rod.* She tried to glance at him without him noticing. In his worn leather bomber jacked and cowboy boots, he looked like a rough and tough country boy who probably didn't know how to treat a woman in the first place, she told herself. However, minutes into the ride she was surprised to find she enjoyed his company.

"So, how do you like our little town so far?" he asked.

"I like it, I always have. It's so Mayberryish. Have you lived here all your life?" Feeling a little warmer, she took off her gloves and eased out of her coat.

"Yep, but after high school most people leave."

"Why's that?"

He gave a raised brow grin and said, "This ain't the big city, you know. Not one night club in the whole county. Most of the young people around here don't have much responsibility. Nothing to keep them tied to this place. They can't wait to get out of school, and Hopkinsville."

"So what's keeping you tied here?" Wanda had told her a little about his parents' tragic death, but she didn't know if he'd share that with her or not.

He looked out the window in the direction of the cornfields. She waited for a response, but he didn't seem to want to give one. She was about to repeat the question, wondering if he'd heard her, when finally he answered.

"I've got responsibilities. About forty acres worth." He leaned forward and turned on the radio. The truck picked up some hiss and crackle, then finally the music of an R&B station from Louisville.

They rode on listening to the DJ's version of a mix of Prince music. Natalie gazed out the window and thought about all the stress she had to put up with in Atlanta. Her life hadn't been stressful until Kevin entered it, pretending to be something he wasn't. A loving, kind, gentle man is what she had wanted, and thought he was. Instead, she got an aggressive, quick-tempered, dictating womanizer. She looked over at Rod who intrigued her. How come such a good-looking man wasn't married? And not only was he handsome, but she could tell he was a good Christian man. He seemed like a man with a good head on his shoulders. The real boy next door type. She finally broke the silence.

"Hopkinsville is absolutely beautiful. Everywhere you look there are fields of luscious green grass, partially covered in snow. It seems so peaceful and quaint. Almost like another world, compared to Atlanta."

"Yeah, I wouldn't dream of living anywhere else. If you want more out of life, the airport's only an hour and a half away. You can take your fancy trip, and return to a nice, peaceful surrounding. I like that." He shook his head as if he were agreeing with what he'd just said. "How long do you plan on staying in town?"

"I'm not sure. Until the first of January or longer."

"You must have plenty of vacation time."

"I took two weeks vacation, but if I stay longer I can call it a leave of absence. My boss knows how stressed I am. She even suggested I take a leave before I left for vacation."

"A leave from Atlanta? The big city where everything's happening?" His surprise came though in his voice.

Natalie ignored his crack on the big city. She'd already gotten an understanding that he didn't like big cities, and especially Atlanta. "No, a leave from being the manager of a retail clothing store. The pressure is unbelievable, besides I needed to get away for a while. My ex-boyfriend went ballistic when I ended our relationship. Somebody had to put some distance between us."

"I'm sorry."

"Oh, don't be. I'm happy. It worked out for the best."

"Ending a relationship can be hard, but you're right, sometimes it's for the best."

Rod made a pit stop at a gas station. Or, rather a gas/bus station/restaurant. A Greyhound sign hung in the window. The house where they made the deliveries was only ten minutes from the gas station.

After stopping at Mrs. Pennick's to pick up the pies, they headed back. Natalie watched how Rod waved at practically every car passing on the two lane road. She wondered if he knew all those people, or if it was a country thing. Whatever it was she decided it was fun, and even waved at a few cars herself.

Back at her aunt's shop Rod helped her inside with the pies. Pauline walked around the shop passing out holiday cookies to her customers. She stopped when she saw the couple come in the door.

"Natalie, dear, you had a call this morning."

Natalie stopped in her tracks. Who would be calling her here? "Who was it?"

Her aunt walked up to her and whispered in her ear. "It was Kevin. He wanted to speak to you, but I told him you were out."

"If he calls back I don't want to speak to him. Did he say how he got the number? I know I didn't give it to him."

"No, and I didn't ask him."

After not talking to Kevin for over two weeks, she wondered why he'd gone through all the trouble to track her down. Whatever he wanted, he'd have to wait until she got back into town. She wasn't going to return his call, and she hoped he wouldn't call back.

As Pauline walked away to greet the next customer with cookies, Natalie hoped Kevin would leave her alone while she was on vacation. Lately, every time she talked to him she developed an upset stomach. Just the sound of his voice made her sick. She could see him lying in the bed with his coworker every time she spoke to him. That wasn't the first women he'd been with, but she was the last straw. Natalie didn't need a man like that in her life, and she had sense enough to leave him alone.

"Hey, everything okay?" Rod raised his brows in concern.

Natalie hadn't even heard him approach her. "Yes, just fine." She forced a smile trying to perk herself up.

"Then how come you look like you're upset about something?" He reached out and gently touched Natalie's chin raising her eyes to meet his.

She gazed into his eyes feeling a little embarrassed. For a moment she started to spill her guts and tell him all about her problems, but she came to her senses. *He's a man,* she told herself. Just like any other man. He's no different from the rest of them. Do what I say, like what I like, build your world around me!

"I'm okay, believe me. I couldn't be better." With authority she put her hands down on the counter and told herself, *No man is going to get the best of me. I'll live my life as I chose and do what I want to do.*

He let go of her chin after several women walked past the counter. "Okay, if you say so. Thanks for going to Bardstown with me, I enjoyed the company."

"So did I," she confessed, then instantly scolded herself. *So what!* she thought. *I had a good time. Nothing's wrong with that. It's not like I'm saying I like him or anything.*

"Well, I'll catch you later. Tell your aunt I left the signed delivery slip on the register."

"I will."

He stood there staring at Natalie for what seemed like an eternity. She looked back at him, not sure what to say. He finally rubbed his hands together and let out a sigh.

"Have a Merry Christmas if I don't see you till Kwanzaa."

"Oh, you, too. Merry Christmas."

The minute he walked out of the shop she missed him. Natalie had a comfortable feeling riding around with him most of the day. He let her be herself. He didn't put on airs, or pretend to be somebody he wasn't. The fact that every man she had met in Atlanta lied about who he was, or where he worked, had gotten on her nerves.

With a renewed vigor and spirit, Natalie began walking around greeting customers and helping them make decisions. Wanda even came into the shop to help out. The evening turned out to be a busy one for the shop. Most of the shelves were half empty. She'd sold two pieces of furniture herself today. At closing time she began cleaning up around the counter when the phone rang.

Pauline was with a customer and Wanda had closed herself up in the office counting receipts. Natalie answered the phone.

"Hello, Pauline's Antiques and Crafts."

"So that's where you ran off to."

The familiar sound of a man's voice came over the phone. Natalie felt a constricting knot in her throat as she tried to speak. How in the hell had he found her? And what did he want? She felt her body start to shake.

"How did you get this number?"

"Don't worry about that. When you coming home?" he asked in a stern voice.

"Why?"

"Because I want to see you. We need to talk things over."

"Kevin, I don't have anything to say to you!" She shielded her mouth with her hand, trying to keep her aunt from overhearing her conversation.

"Then I have something to say to you. Baby, I'm sorry. You know how I can't control myself sometimes. I didn't mean to—"

Natalie cut him off. She'd heard that song and dance too many times. "Kevin you did what you did, and I don't want to talk about it. You obviously have a problem, and I think you need to check yourself out."

"What you mean check myself out? Nothing's wrong with me. You just tick me off sometimes, that's all."

Silence filled the next few seconds. Natalie heard him clear his throat into the phone. She wanted to let him listen to the dial tone, but she knew he'd only call back. Somehow she had to get him off the phone without upsetting him.

"Kevin, I don't want to talk about this while I'm on my Christmas vacation. We can talk when I get home."

"And that's another thing. Why in the hell would you pick Christmas to leave me alone? You know we always spend Christmas together."

"Kevin we broke up two weeks ago. I haven't heard from you once, until today."

"I couldn't find you until today. Look, Nat, we need to talk about this breakup thing. I'm not sure it's what I want to do."

What he wanted to do! She never asked Kevin if he wanted to break up. The day she ended their relationship she'd caught him in bed with another woman. What on earth gave him the right to say he wasn't sure if he wanted it to end. She'd decided for him.

"Kevin, it's done. We don't need to talk about anything. You've got you another woman. I don't know why you're calling me anyway." Natalie yelled into the phone forgetting about anyone hearing her at this point. He had her about to rupture a vein she was so upset. He still wanted to control her life, tell her what to do, and when to do it.

"She's not my woman—you are." He lowered his voice and tried to sound sexy.

"Not any longer." To Natalie, he sounded like the sleazy, good-for-nothing, pimp-daddy he thought he was.

"You wanna bet. This isn't over until I say it's over. That's what's wrong with you—"

The moment she heard his voice raise, she decided it was time for him to listen to the dial tone. Click—end of that conversation.

Chapter Three

Okay, so she appears to be interested in me—maybe. Rod drove back to his house after he dropped Natalie off at her aunt's shop. He hadn't stopped thinking about her all evening. She was as cute as a button in his book. So small and feminine. Natalie with the honey-brown skin, big brown eyes, and a permanent address in Atlanta. What did Atlanta have anyway? Why did all the good-looking women have to live there?

He still hated Pam for leaving him and moving to Atlanta. If she'd really loved him, she would have stayed in Hopkinsville. They had planned to marry and start a family. He wanted his children to go to school in Hopkinsville like he did, not in Atlanta with all the drug and gang problems.

"So maybe I should forget asking Ms. Natalie to the New Year's Eve dance?" *She's not the woman for you, so forget her. What you need is a nice country girl. Someone who's content living the country life. Someone like—who?* He hadn't met a woman who turned him on like Natalie in a long time. The minute he saw her standing behind that counter, he felt a charge run through his body.

When she looked up at him with her shoulder length curls swirling around framing her face, he was instantly attracted. Her body was little and firm. He bet she worked out in one of those Atlanta gyms all the time. When she walked across the room her body screamed, sexy. He'd found it hard to keep his eyes off her most of the day. She had a very attractive, sexy look, but he wondered if she knew it.

After pulling into his driveway, he sat in the car. His eyes were fixed on his house. Another lonely Christmas. His little brother Brandon was spending the holiday at his girlfriend's. So, Thursday he'd probably have Christmas dinner with his uncle's family. They were always kind enough to invite him over whenever he didn't have any plans. He'd have to wait until the first day of Kwanzaa to see Natalie again.

As Natalie helped her aunt cook Christmas dinner, she wondered where Rod would be eating since he lived alone. This was the first Christmas in a long time that she felt as if she'd come home. Plenty of cousins were around and Christmas music filled the air.

"Nat, how many bags of beans did you get out of the deep freezer?" her aunt asked, as she looked into a large pot on the stove.

"Two, I think. Why?"

"Girl, there's not enough beans in here for anybody. Go back downstairs and grab two more bags. That's how you stay so skinny, eating like a bird."

Natalie put down the knife and the sweet potato she was peeling and walked over to the stove. "It looked like enough to me." She peeked into the pot while her aunt had the lid up.

"Enough for whom? You and me maybe. Honey, we'll have an army over here for dinner tomorrow. Wanda and all her children can eat two bags of beans alone." Pauline replaced the lid.

Natalie wondered if Rod would be part of that army. She

didn't want to ask her aunt and get her started, so she let it go. She went back down to the basement and returned with two large bags of frozen green beans. After giving them to her aunt, she continued peeling potatoes.

"Aunt Polly, I can't remember the last time I had a holiday like this. It really feels like Christmas here. Like it used to when I was a little girl, before Mama and Daddy separated."

"Once you kids grew up, your mama never did like to cook Christmas dinner, did she?"

"No, we always went out. We always decorated the house, but then left town until New Year's. Last year I met them in Bermuda. It was nice, but it didn't seem like Christmas."

"Honey, consider yourself welcome here every year."

Natalie looked up when she heard the back door opening.

"Em, em, it smells good in here." Wanda walked through the kitchen with her daughter in tow, and a shopping bag in her hand.

"You need to put that bag down and help." Pauline turned with a tea towel in hand, surveying her daughter.

Wanda ignored her mother and turned to Natalie. "Nat, thanks so much for helping out. Girl, I don't know what I'd have done if you hadn't come in town." She walked past them into the dining room.

"I'm enjoying myself. Never mind that you guys are putting me to work, but I don't mind." She peeled her last sweet potato and walked over to the sink to rinse them off.

"But don't you love all this hustle and bustle at Christmas time? I know I do." Wanda stood in the doorway taking off her coat. Her daughter Grachel ran in past her straight to Natalie.

"I haven't had a Christmas like this in a long time. Aunt Polly and I were just talking about that." She dried her hands and leaned down to give Grachel a hug.

"Aunt Natalie, Mama said you could come live with us if you wanted to. Don't you want to?" Grachel stared up at Natalie with her doe-like eyes.

"Oh, thank you, honey, but I have to go back to Atlanta."

Natalie kissed her little cousin, who insisted on calling her aunt.

"For what?" Pauline asked.

Natalie looked up at her aunt, surprised. "Because I live and work there. What do you mean, anyway?"

"You don't like Atlanta, and I know you don't want to keep seeing that old boyfriend of yours. You don't have any family there, and I bet you work all day and read all night."

Pauline was too perceptive for Natalie. "No I don't. I get out from time to time. I'm a homebody, I like staying home for the most part. Besides, what's wrong with that?" She walked over to the kitchen table and sat across from Wanda, with Grachel on her lap.

"Nothing if you've got a good man to be a homebody with," Wanda interjected. "But you don't want to sit around the house weekend after weekend alone. Unless, you're waiting for Kevin to come back into your life." Wanda raised her brows as she took the wrapper off a piece of Christmas candy and ate it.

"He's the last thing I want in my life right now. Believe it or not, I really don't mind my time alone. I work so much that when I get home all I want to do is relax and read a good book." She knew she was also trying to convince herself.

"Yeah, well, it wouldn't hurt to do a little cuddling next to a good man, instead of a good book. Especially on a cold night like tonight. Y'all know it looks like it's going to snow tonight."

Natalie had a vision of her and Rod laying back on a couch cuddling and watching television. They would rent a good movie and buy some microwave popcorn. Maybe after the movie and popcorn they could get a little closer.

"All right you two, help me get these potatoes in the oven and let's start on the Kwanzaa preparations." Pauline walked over to the table with baking dish in hand. "Here, Wanda, work something other than your jaws. Butter these pans up."

Natalie laughed at the interaction between her aunt and cousin. Grachel ran off to watch television while the women finished cooking.

* * *

Later that evening Natalie helped Wanda go through her Kwanzaa items. "So what's this?" Natalie held up an old ceramic looking mug.

"That's the *Kikombe cha umoja.*" Wanda responded, taking the cup from her.

"The what?"

"It's a communal unity cup. What you're supposed to do is pour *Tambiko* in the direction of the four winds, you know, north, south, east, and west. That's in remembrance of the ancestors. Then, you pass it around and drink from it as a sign of solidarity. However, we don't actually drink out of it. We use paper cups instead."

"So you somewhat modified things a bit?" Natalie looked over the items sitting on the table.

"Well Kwanzaa's a personal holiday. You can celebrate it however your family wants. Even single people can celebrate Kwanzaa, of course, they modify it differently than someone with children. Like the day after tomorrow, we have sort of a kick off celebration for *Umoja,* the first principle. Then for the next four days we celebrate quietly in our own homes. On the fifth day of *Kuumboa* we all come together and feast. And on the last day, called *Imani* we go back to our homes. But, that's just the way we've decided to do it here. It varies from family to family."

"I think I'm really going to like this." Natalie was beginning to feel a part of something, and she felt better than she had in years.

"I know you will. I'm surprised that living in Atlanta you don't already celebrate Kwanzaa. Especially with such a large African-American population there."

"I know a lot of people who celebrate it, but I've never attended any of the celebrations. To tell the truth, about the only thing I know about Kwanzaa is what I learned on a made-for-television movie. At first, I thought you celebrated Kwanzaa instead of Christmas, until I learned better.''

''I think a lot of people get that first impression. But it's really an African-American holiday that pays tribute to the rich cultural roots of Americans of African ancestry. It's not as commercialized as Christmas either.''

''Okay, Wanda. Here's the two statues I bought in Saint Thomas last year.'' Pauline walked into the room with two black wood carved statues of a man and woman embracing. She reluctantly held them out to Wanda. ''And let me tell you now, if you let them kids damage my statues—''

Wanda cut her off. ''Mama, don't get started. You know I won't let them touch your statues, let alone break them. I'll set them up on the mantel, where the kids can't reach them.'' She placed the status in the shopping bag with her other items.

''Well you better not. I love my grandkids, but if they break my statues, their mama's going to Saint Thomas to get me another one.''

Wanda smiled at Natalie shaking her head. ''She just had to get that in, did you see that?'' Grabbing her mother by the shoulders, she quickly reached over and kissed her on the cheek. ''I'll guard them with my life.''

''Oh, I know you will. I don't know about you ladies but when I finish dinner, I'm going to bed. Wanda, you need to take Grachel home. It's Christmas Eve. That child should be in bed.''

Wanda looked at her watch. ''Mama, it's eight o'clock and she's on vacation. She's my little helper tonight. Don't worry, I'll have her in bed before Santa comes.''

Natalie's head was like a ping pong ball, from Wanda to her Aunt Polly. She wished she had that kind of rapport with her mother. They hadn't spent much time together in the last couple of years, since her mother's second marriage. She missed her mother just as much as she missed traditional family gatherings.

Whenever she didn't meet her family somewhere for Christmas, she'd spent it with a boyfriend. Her Christmases with

Kevin weren't traditional, to say the least. All he ever wanted to do was exchange gifts and party with his friends. She was glad she wouldn't be doing that again this year.

Christmas morning came and moved along in a flash. Natalie exchanged gifts with the few relatives she'd purchased them for. She'd brought her Aunt Polly a hat from a hat shop in Atlanta. Knowing how Pauline liked wearing hats to church, the gift was more than well received. She had so much fun helping her little cousins play with their new toys. Her brother had been in Germany for two years with a little niece she'd only seen pictures of. She loved children, but never had the opportunity to be around any. Maybe one day she'd have some of her own, she thought.

One thing she noticed and liked about Wanda and her husband, Arthur, was they didn't shower their children with too many gifts. She'd heard Wanda complain about the commercialization of Christmas, and guessed that was why Kwanzaa had become such an important part of their holiday celebration. Each child received an appropriate number of toys and clothes.

Around 4:00 P.M. everyone started showing up at her aunt's house for dinner. They danced around the house to the Temptation's Christmas songs. Dinner would be served at 5:00 P.M. sharp, her aunt warned them more than once. Several of her young male cousins kept popping in and out of the house all morning.

Natalie helped set the three tables for dinner. She counted out the children's places, but wondered who all the adults seats were for.

"There's more seats here than we've got people, why?" she asked Wanda.

Wanda never looked up from positioning the silverware on the table. "I don't know, Mama said set some extras. I think she invited a few friends. You know how that woman is, always opening her home up for hungry people.'' Wanda smiled up at Natalie and kept working.

Deep down Natalie had hoped she'd say Rod was coming by. She kept telling herself to stop thinking about the man, but she couldn't. Finally, she came to the conclusion that some lucky country girl had probably invited him to dinner.

Minutes later, more guests arrived. More aunts, uncles, and friends filled the house. Everyone brought a dish with them, some even brought gifts.

Wanda found Natalie standing off to the side of the room with her arms crossed smiling.

''What you smiling about?'' Wanda asked her.

''Oh, nothing. This is fun, that's all. I haven't seen some of these people since elementary school, but I remember them.'' This was like coming home again. Home to a familiar little town she once knew and loved.

''You've been here since then, Natalie, I remember.''

''Yes, I have, but I don't remember seeing Uncle Otis the last time I was here, or his children.''

''That's because he and Mama weren't on speaking terms for a long time. Something that went back to when they were younger. After we held our first Kwanzaa celebration, Mama picked up the phone and called him.'' Wanda snapped her fingers, ''and just like that they patched things up.''

''Really?''

''Yeah, Kwanzaa really helps to bring families together. In a small town like this you want all your family together, loving and blessing one another. We need each other. No man can do anything by himself.''

Natalie gave Wanda a tilted head grin. ''And how did you get so wise, honey?'' She uncrossed her arms and placed them on her hips.

''Reading, honey. When I find the time, I read everything I can get my hands on. Of course, I don't have to turn in a book report, but I make myself read a book a month also. Hopefully, I get something from them.''

"Believe me, you're getting a lot from them." Natalie looked up to her cousin. Wanda was a role model if she'd ever seen one. She only hoped she could be that much of an inspiration for her children when she had them.

"Okay." Pauline walked into the family room banging a spoon on a pot. "It's time to eat, everyone wash up and sit down."

Natalie was the last person to get into the bathroom to wash her hands. She heard the doorbell ring as she walked out of the washroom. Everyone was in the kitchen hovered over the food and didn't hear the bell. She walked over to answer the door wondering who was left, everybody seemed to be there.

When she opened the door, she blinked twice—hard. Rod stood there in a gray cashmere overcoat, with a huge smile on his face. Under his arm were two wrapped boxes.

"Merry Christmas," he said in a deep sexy voice.

This man looked good enough to serve for dinner, she thought. And he had dimples! She'd never noticed his dimples before. *Close your mouth girl, and let the man in.*

"You think I can come in? It's kind of cold out here."

"I'm sorry. Yes, Merry Christmas and come on in." She stood aside as he walked in. So her aunt had invited him. As she closed the door she thought, *Damn, he smells good, too.*

"I'll take your coat." She held out her hands for his coat.

He set his packages on the hall table, then took off his coat. "Thank you." He handed her his coat.

He had on a crew neck sweater in the most beautiful shades of brown. Underneath he wore a cream turtleneck. He had brown slacks and loafers to match. Natalie nodded her approval, biting her bottom lip. This man knew how to dress, which only made matters worse. She liked nothing better than a well-dressed man.

"This is for Pauline." He pointed to the small package. "And this one," he pointed to the larger of the two, "is for you."

"Rod! You didn't have to do that."

"I know, but I wanted to."

"Well, thank you and I'll give this to Aunt Polly. I guess you can go on in and help yourself, they've started." She stood there waiting for him to walk away so she could sneak another peek at him. But he didn't move.

"Are you enjoying your vacation?" he asked.

"Yes, I am. It's one of the best ones I've had in years."

"No kidding?" He looked surprised.

"It really is."

"Well I'm glad you could come to such a small town like ours and enjoy yourself so much."

"Rod, come on in here and get yourself something to eat." Pauline called him for the kitchen doorway. "I'm glad you could make it."

"I'm on my way." He looked down at Natalie again. "Well, I'm glad you're enjoying yourself. I still want to take you on that tour, if you haven't gone already?"

"No, I haven't. They've kept me fairly busy around here."

"Good, then we've got a date?"

A date! She smiled at him thinking, *I didn't come down here to go on dates. I'm here to relax and get away from men.* "Yeah, we've got a date." *What else could she say?* she wondered. As he walked away, she watched him. He had a body like a model she'd seen in so many magazines—Tyson. She hadn't seen a gym since coming to town, so those muscles must be from hard work. He said he had forty acres of responsibility, he must live on a farm.

When Natalie looked down she realized she was holding onto his coat like it was him. She took the gifts in the living room and placed them under the tree. She'd open hers after dinner. After hanging up his coat, she joined everyone else in the kitchen.

Natalie wasn't sure where to sit. The dining room table was reserved for the elders, she remembered that much. She went into the family room to join Wanda with the children. The card table was full with Wanda's three children and two other children. So, she went back into the kitchen and found a spot at the kitchen table.

Before anyone could eat, her Uncle Otis had to say the blessing. Right before he started, a plate was placed next to her. She looked up to see Rod smiling down at her.

"Mind if I sit here?"

"Ah . . . sure. I mean, no, I don't mind." She stumbled over her words. Why did he make her do that? When he looked at her she got tongue tied. She became speechless, and felt dumb. No matter what, she had to fight her attraction to him. Especially once she noticed the way her cousin, Deborah, perked up once he sat down. That girl definitely had her eyes on Rod. Too bad he hadn't seemed to notice her.

Two more teenaged cousins joined them at the circular table for five. Dinner conversation consisted mainly of chitchat, until Rod turned his attention to Natalie.

"Did you help cook any of this?" He pointed to his plate.

"I helped with a few things, but that's about it."

"You mean to tell me you're not a great cook?"

"I wish. I cook, but I can't touch Aunt Polly in that department."

"Oh, you're being modest. I bet you cook really well."

What she wanted to say, she didn't dare say. *I'll have to show you sometime.* Instead she laughed and said, "I make a mean microwave popcorn."

He laughed and replied, "I hope you don't consider that cooking?"

"I'm a woman of the nineties. The microwave is just another oven to me. And anytime you put food in the oven, you're cooking."

They shared a laugh and returned to their meals. Natalie listen as the men at the table talked about everything from cars to sports. She was surprised they didn't get up from the table to find a television.

"Natalie, are you a sports fan?" Rod asked.

"I like basketball. That's about all I can stand to watch on television." She noticed how Rod kept bringing her into the conversation. He didn't seem to be interested in talking to anyone else.

"Well, we have something in common. I can't stand to watch a baseball game on television, and I catch a football game every now and then, but I love to watch basketball. Who's your favorite team?"

Natalie had to think for a moment. She only watched during the NBA playoffs. "I'd have to say the Bulls."

"Why?"

"I like to see Michael Jordan play."

"Have you ever been to one of their games?"

"No, television is about as close as I've been. How about you?"

"Yeah, I've been to a few. I've got a buddy who lives in Chicago. He has season tickets."

"Boy, it must be nice to have friends in high places."

"He's just a guy who got lucky, that's all. I think he waited for about two to three years on the list for season tickets. We went to college together. He lets me know in advance when he can't make a game."

"Have you ever been to a Hawks game?" Natalie asked him.

"No, I can't say that I have. I've never been to Atlanta either."

"Oh, you have to visit sometime. It's a nice vacation spot."

"Maybe I will, once I have someone to visit."

Natalie looked up at Rod shaking her head. Did he mean her? Did he want to come to Atlanta and visit her? The man was fine, but she wasn't getting into the web again.

Her cousins sitting at the table ended their conversation and Deborah pulled Rod into a conversation with her. She pulled her chair close to his and leaned suggestively on the table.

"So, Rod, tell me something. What did Santa bring you for Christmas?"

Chapter Four

Deborah ate and flirted with Rod at the same time. He didn't seem interested. Natalie felt bad for him, considering his efforts to be congenial. Deborah was obviously too young for him. At first, Natalie thought it was cute, but she soon grew tired of her cousin. She kept telling herself she wasn't interested in him, but at the same time she wanted Deborah to shut up so he could continue talking to her.

Finally, one of Deborah's girlfriends arrived.

"Oh, that's my girl Rhonda. Well gang it's been real, but I've got to run." Deborah dabbed her mouth with a napkin. "We're making our rounds today, you know. My relatives' houses, then hers."

"Well, Deborah, we're going to miss you," Natalie said, hoping the whole table got the joke.

"Sure you will." Deborah gave a sexy smile in Rod's direction as she got up. "Rod, maybe I'll see you around later."

He almost choked on his food as he shook his head trying not to laugh.

"Natalie, it was nice to meet you. Now that I know I have a cuz in Atlanta, you'll have to invite me down."

"Yeah, you bet, maybe over the summer." Once her younger relatives found out she lived in Atlanta, everyone wanted to come for a visit. *Thank God, I only have a one-bedroom apartment.*

"Ew, that sounds fun. You can take us to all the clubs."

"You bet!" Natalie smiled at her cousin, trying to remember the last time she'd set foot in a nightclub.

"Bye, everybody." Deborah switched her way out of the kitchen waving back over her shoulder.

After Deborah left, Rod took a drink of water and started laughing. "Man, she's not bashful is she?"

"Just ignore her. She's one of the hottest things around town. I'm surprised it doesn't warm up the minute she walks outside," Marvin said.

"Rod, you better watch out, that girl wants you," James, another cousin, commented.

"Man, she's too young for me. How old is Deborah anyway—sixteen?"

"Fifteen, going on twenty-five if you ask me," Marvin said. "Something better slow that girl down."

"You guys are terrible. Talking about your cousin like that." Natalie had to admit her cousin was a big flirt, but she liked Deborah. The girl just needed to tone down the makeup and perfume a bit.

"Hey, we love her, too, but like Prince says in his song, 'she's a Hot Thing.' " Marvin leaned back in his chair as all the men at the table laughed, except Rod.

Natalie noticed Rod had finished his meal, and was staring at her. Feeling uncomfortable, she reached over for Deborah's plate. "I'm going to clean off the table if you guys are through. Any one ready for dessert?"

"You know I am." Marvin spoke up.

"Here, Natalie, let me help you." They grasped Deborah's

plate at the same time from opposite ends. For a moment Rod captured her gaze with his eyes.

"That's okay, I've got it." She carried both paper plates over to the garbage can and threw them in.

"Here, I'll get this one." Rod threw his plate in behind hers.

"So much for all those fancy plates, huh," he commented, while looking at the stack of Christmas plates that lined the can.

"Yeah, well it keeps Aunt Polly from washing dishes all evening long."

Marvin and James grabbed their desserts and left the table. Probably to catch some sporting event on television, she thought. Rod remained at the table looking comfortable and content. Before Natalie knew it, the house was almost empty.

Pauline breezed into the kitchen carrying her coat. "Natalie, we're going to run over to Mrs. Hattie May's house and take her a plate. You two relax and enjoy yourselves." Pauline rushed out of the kitchen, winking at Natalie as she left.

Natalie wanted to run after her. *No, don't leave me here alone with him! I'm afraid of what I'll do or say.* All she could do was look up and watch as her aunt left the room. Too late.

"What do you say we grab some dessert and take it into the family room?" Rod stood up.

Natalie looked up at him with a questioning look on her face.

"I want to check out your aunt's Christmas tree."

"Oh, yeah, let's do that." Maybe she was reading too much into this, she thought. Her aunt probably invited him to dinner all the time. He seemed right at home. He appeared to know all her relatives, and was enjoying himself.

Natalie cut Rod a piece of her aunt's red velvet cake. She cut a piece of pecan pie for herself. In the living room, she sat in an easy chair across from the tree. Her nerves were on edge. When she looked over at the tree, she saw his gift sitting there. "Oh, I didn't open your gift yet."

"It's something I saw, and immediately thought of you. I

hope it's not too personal. Go ahead and open it." He set his cake on the coffee table, and crossed his legs.

Natalie put her pie on the coffee table and reached for the small package. She loved surprises, and tore into the paper. Pulling open the box, she found inside a silver pin with her initial, N, on it.

"Rod, this is nice, but you shouldn't have."

"But I wanted to."

"Well, thank you. I'll pin it on my coat."

He stood up and walked around looking at the tree, touching some of the ornaments.

"See this ornament here?" He pointed to an ornament on the other side of the tree.

Natalie had to get up and walk around the tree to see what he pointed at. It was a little black angel on a sleigh. "Yes, that's a nice ornament."

"My mother gave it to her."

"She did! That makes it even more special."

"She made it. They were best friends, you know. I've got a few at home, too. She was into crafts and stuff. Every year I come by here, and your aunt has this little angel on her tree. It makes me think of my mother."

Natalie suddenly felt sad. Rod smiled at her and returned to the couch. He seemed to have come to grips with his parents' death very well. She'd never met anyone who'd lost both parents before, and didn't know if he wanted to talk about it or not.

"Your aunt always has a great tree." He picked up his cake and finished it off.

Natalie returned to her chair and finished off her pie. A few moments of silence fell over the room as they ate.

"So, how's Mrs. Pennick's pie?"

"What?"

"The pie. Isn't that one you brought back from Bardstown?"

"I'd forgotten about that, yes, it's great." She sat there at a loss for words. He looked so handsome sitting back on the couch with his legs crossed. His arms were stretched out along the back of the couch.

"How many days before you head back to Atlanta?"

"Six. I've decided to leave New Year's Day."

"It's probably a little too slow around here for you. No concerts or clubs to go to."

"No, not at all. I'm not into nightclubing anyway."

"So, you'll be here on New Year's Eve?"

"Yes, I plan to."

"I can't believe a beautiful little thing like you wouldn't have New Year's Eve plans in Atlanta."

Natalie crossed her arms and smiled at Rod. "Well, I can't believe a man as handsome as you doesn't have a date for New Year's Eve."

"I never said I didn't have a date."

Natalie felt like a fool. Maybe he already had a date for New Year's Eve. If so, why did he ask her if she would be in town? "No, you didn't, did you?"

"No, I didn't."

Friday morning Natalie helped her aunt mark down more inventory. Pauline ran her after Christmas sale just like all the other stores in town. Natalie was glad to have something to keep her mind on. She didn't want to spend her day thinking about Rod. Last night she'd enjoyed his company very much. They talked well into the night about everything from their college days to who sang the best, Whitney Houston or Mariah Carey.

He even helped her clean the kitchen, to surprise her aunt when she returned. Around ten thirty he decided it was time for him to leave. On one hand, she hated to see him leave, but on the other, she wished he hadn't come in the first place. She liked Rod and she knew she had to fight her attraction to him. Several times during the evening, she'd wished he'd pull her into his arms and kiss her.

The bell over the door jingled and she looked up to see several women walking in. She went back to her work once she realized it wasn't Rod. *Now,* she told herself, *forget that man. He lives here in Hopkinsville and you're in Atlanta.* Besides, he could be another Kevin. She didn't really know him. Maybe his country charm was a front, and he was as jealous and unfaithful as the next man. As she thought the words, she didn't believe them for a minute. For the short amount of time she'd spent with him, she could tell he was a good man.

Besides, if her Aunt Polly was crazy about him, he couldn't be all bad. Her relatives seemed to like him. Too bad he didn't live in Atlanta, she thought. She told herself not to let her attraction go any further than it had last night. She'd be better off forgetting about him. The less she saw of Rod the better. He didn't walk into the shop all day.

Her aunt closed shop early for the first day of Kwanzaa. Natalie went by Wanda's to help prepare for the opening celebration.

When Natalie walked into Wanda's house she couldn't believe her eyes. Wanda had redecorated for the celebration. Everything was in the black, red, and green color scheme. The colors of Kwanzaa.

The floral paintings that hung on the walls several days before were replaced with African art. The mantel over the fireplace displayed several carved African statues, including her Aunt Polly's. As she glanced around the room she noticed other things she hadn't seen before. A throw had been placed on the back of the couch. She picked it up to examine it.

"That's beautiful isn't it?"

A man's voice came from behind her. She turned to see Brother Johnson, one of the young ministers at First Baptist.

"Yes, it is. I'm trying to see what's on it." She spread the throw along the back of the couch for a better look.

"It's called 'Breaking Bread.' It's a family during their Kwanzaa feast. See that's the child there." He pointed to a figure at the bottom of the throw. Then, he moved to the other end of the couch and held up the throw to give her a better look.

Natalie raised her end also. "Oh, yes, I see it better now. This is beautiful! I wonder where she got this?"

"My sister sent it to her from D.C. A woman in her church makes them."

"I'd love to have one. Could you get me one?" She looked up at him with wide eyes, hoping he'd say yes.

"Sure. I like to practice *Ujima* whenever I can."

"*Ujima,* wait, that's . . . ?" She had to think for a minute. She'd heard her aunt say it. "Oh, I know." She snapped her finger when she came up with the answer. "That's cooperative economics."

"Yes it is. Is this something you practice in Atlanta?"

Natalie thought for a moment, she couldn't remember the last time she purchased something from an African-American, or lent her support in any way. "No, I can't say that I do. You see, I live on the north side of town, and I'm afraid most of the African-American shop owners are on the south side, or downtown."

He nodded his head and smiled at her. "There aren't any African-American shop owners here in Hopkinsville. But we lend our support to all of the out-of-state shops that we know of. I'll call my sister tomorrow and have her order you one. Just give Wanda your mailing information." He put the throw down, shook her hand, and excused himself.

Still holding her end of the throw in the air, she realized something—he was right. She lived in a town with many African-American shops. And not once had she even checked to see if there were any on her side of town. I've got to do better. *If it was my shop I'd want support,* she told herself.

Now that he'd made her feel like she had so much more to learn, she was eager for the ceremony to begin. She'd only skimmed through the books Wanda loaned her. A picture slowly formed in her mind that Kwanzaa was more than saying affirmations and eating.

She was on her way into the dining room to check out the centerpiece when Grachel ran up to her.

"Aunt Natalie, you gonna come live with us?" the child asked as she grabbed Natalie by the leg and held on for dear life.

"No, honey, but I'm not getting ready to go home yet. We've got a few more days together." She reached down for Grachel's hand.

"You wanna see my room?" Grachel pulled her in the direction of the stairs.

"Yes, I'd love to see your room." Off they went up the stairs.

"Liz, give me your hand." Rod tried to help his great-aunt down the stairs.

"I don't need your help. Hell, I can make it down these stairs by myself. How do you think I get the mail every damn day?" She held onto the rail walking down the front stairs of her one-story house.

Rod worried about his great-aunt. A stroke a few years ago had damaged the right side of her body. But with her white hair pulled into a bun atop her head, she didn't let that stop her. Liz acted like a young woman instead of a senior citizen.

"I'm going to have the mail box moved up to the front porch so you don't have to risk walking down these stairs. What if it's icy out here one morning after a snow storm. How will you get your mail then?"

"I'll call you over to get it for me. I might be old, but I'm not stupid. I know better than to walk out here on ice. And you leave my mailbox where it is. My walk in the morning does me good. I like to get out and see what's going on in the neighborhood."

"You like to meddle, that's all."

"I don't meddle. I see things. Like that young lady that moved into the house on the corner. I don't believe she's married. Not once have I seen a man walk through those doors." She completed her trip down the five steps and held Rod's arm as they walked out to his car.

He could see his great-aunt now walking out to the mail box in her robe, casually looking up and down the street for something interesting. "You know it's not a sin to be single."

"But you've been single for too long. Don't you want a wife and a family? Your mother would want you to be married by now."

"Aunt Liz, when I find the right woman I'll marry her. Now come on, I'm going to be late."

"The damn thing doesn't start until six o'clock and it's only five now."

"I know but once I drop you off I've got to get the truck and swing by the Armory for some chairs. Wanda asked me to bring a few over. She invited more people than she had room for."

"Okay, then help me in the car. Where's that little brother of yours anyway."

"I told you he's spending the holidays in Louisville with his girl's family."

"Oh, yes, I keep forgetting that."

When Rod walked his aunt to Wanda's door, he wondered if Natalie was inside. He started to go in and ask her to ride with him, but decided she was probably helping Wanda. He drove back to his house and exchanged his car for the truck. Driving out to the Armory he couldn't get Natalie off his mind. His great aunt wanted him married so bad, and he'd found the perfect woman. There was only one problem; he didn't know how she felt about him. She was single and didn't have a man, that much he knew. But, she also lived hundreds of miles away. Would a long-distance relationship work? Would she even consider one?

He pulled into Wanda's driveway and hurried inside with a few chairs. As he placed the chairs around the room he looked for Natalie, but didn't see her.

"Oh, Rod, thank you so much for bringing the chairs. Is that it?" Wanda asked.

"No, there's a few more. I'll get them."

"Thanks, Arthur would help you, but he's not here yet. He went to pick up his mother."

"No problem, I've got it." He walked back out to the truck wondering if Natalie had arrived. At least he was sure she'd be here. A quick glance at the cars lined up outside Wanda's house didn't include Pauline's or Natalie's car. Maybe they hadn't arrived yet?

After grabbing the chairs from the cab of his truck, he set them down, an took a deep breath. *Relax, boy, she's just a woman. Something you haven't had in a long time.* But she wasn't just *any* women. Natalie was special to him. Her innocent looking smile turned him on. Especially the way he could tell she wanted to reach out and touch him, but dared not to, excited him. She was attracted to him and he knew it, but he didn't want her to sense it, or she'd probably run the other way.

He picked up the chairs and walked back into the house. The cold air cleared his head, and settled his nerves. He only hoped he could remember his Kwanzaa speech once she showed up.

"Natalie, come here, I've got some people I want you to meet." Wanda stood at the bottom of the stairs as Natalie came down with Grachel in tow.

"We're on our way." She held Grachel's hand as the child hopped down the stairs.

Wanda had invited all of their relatives, and a few friends. She introduced Natalie to two of her girlfriends, then they walked over to an elderly woman sitting next to their Uncle Otis.

Wanda touched the woman on the shoulder to get her attention. "Mis Liz, I want you to meet my cousin Natalie. She's visiting us for the holidays."

"Hello, it's a pleasure meeting you." Natalie shook the woman's frail hand. Her silver hair reminded Natalie of her grandmother.

"It's nice to meet you, too, honey." She smiled up at Natalie.

"Mis Liz used to be Mama's high school teacher," Wanda interjected.

"Now you done gone and told this child how old I am." She rolled her eyes and waved her hand at Wanda. All three women laughed.

"Natalie did you come up with your family for the holidays?"

"No ma'am, I'm single, so I came by myself."

"Well, honey, have a seat for a moment and let's talk before your aunt gets here. You know once she arrives she'll take over and nobody will get a word in edgewise."

Natalie laughed at Mis Liz's description of her aunt, as she sat next to her. She obviously knew Pauline well.

"So, how are you enjoying your visit?"

"I'm having a wonderful time. I think this is the best vacation I've ever been on."

"Now that's really nice. You know"—she paused and looked around as if she had something private to say—"I know just about everybody in this town. I remember when most of the people in this room were born."

"Yes, ma'am." Natalie wasn't too sure what to say to that, so she let the woman talk and nodded her head.

"Do you know my nephew, Rod?"

"Rod Taylor?"

"Yes, that's him."

Natalie wanted to ask, "Is he here?" She wanted to stand up and look around the room for him, but she controlled herself and kept her seat.

"Yes, ma'am, I've met him."

"Now that's a nice single young man for you. You young people stay alone too long for me. When I was his age I was married with two children. Every woman needs a man, honey, remember that." She smiled as she patted Natalie on the leg.

Not if he's an unfaithful one, Natalie thought. But Mis Liz wasn't talking about Kevin. She was talking about her nephew, Rod.

"You're right, she does. And as soon as I find the right man I'll marry him." *But until then, I'll watch television alone, and listen to my music alone.* She'd have to settle for the men in her romance novels for right now.

Mis Liz leaned over to whisper something to Natalie. She lowered her head to hear what she was about to say.

"Is this old woman bothering you?" Rod's deep sexy voice interrupted them.

Natalie and Mis Liz looked up to see him standing in front of them. Natalie noticed how Mis Liz straightened up and pulled her hand back.

"No, we were having a very good conversation if you have to know." Natalie smiled up at him and noticed something different about him. He'd gotten his hair cut and trimmed his mustache down to a shadow. How could he possibly look any more attractive than when she first laid eyes on him? But he did.

"Who you calling an old lady anyway? You know you're not too old for me to throw you over my knee." She rolled her eyes at him, then turned to converse with Otis.

Rod let out a thunderous deep laugh and pulled a chair up next to Natalie. "I see you've met my great-aunt."

"Yes, Wanda introduced me."

"She's a character isn't she?" He shook his head and peeked past Natalie at his great-aunt. "Look at her . . . she's forgotten all about us and started another conversation."

"I like her." Natalie smiled at him.

Rod looked at her and she felt his eyes staring deep into hers. Here he was, the man she'd been looking for all her life, and she wanted to run from him. Now wasn't the right time, and this wasn't the right place. Why did he have to live in Hopkinsville?

He finally looked away when someone called his name.

"Excuse me, I'll be right back."

Natalie nodded her head as he walked away. She decided to walk around the house herself. Before she got very far, Wanda announced they were ready to begin. She looked back at her seat and someone else had taken it. She also noticed her aunt had joined the celebration, dressed in traditional African clothing. Natalie thought she looked wonderful in her headwrap.

"Habari gani," Wanda said opening the celebration.

"Umoja," everyone said in unison.

Wanda struck a match and lit the black candle in the center of the *Kinara*. "The first Principle of Kwanzaa is *Umoja*. To strive for and maintain unity in the family, community, nation, and race."

Natalie listened to Wanda talk about *Umoja* as she looked around the room for Rod. Had he left the ceremony? She looked back over her shoulder and his great-aunt was still there. Well, he hadn't left to take her home. Where could he have gone, she wondered.

"Now we will have Brother Johnson deliver the Libation Statement." Wanda moved to the side of the fireplace and took a seat.

Brother Johnson lifted the communal cup and poured in the direction of the four winds. Because they were inside, he poured into a large bowl, instead of on the ground. As everyone drank from their cups, he read the Libation Statement.

"For the Motherland cradle of civilization.

"For the ancestors and their indomitable spirit.

"For the elders from whom we can learn much.

"For our youth who represent the promise for tomorrow.

"For our people the original people.

"For our struggle and in remembrance of those who have struggled on our behalf.

"For *Umoja* the principle of unity which should guide us in all that we do.

"For the creator who provides all things great and small."

Natalie drank her punch from the cup. Wanda had told her that no one actually drinks from the unity cup. However, they still passed the cup through the crowd.

Brother Johnson moved on to salute the ancestors as the cup was passed. He started with Marcus Garvey and threw in a few local leaders from Hopkinsville.

Natalie caught a glimpse of Rod standing in the kitchen doorway. He held a book in his hand and appeared to be reading. She realized he was part of the ceremony and had probably been preparing as she looked for him. The butterflies in her stomach began to flutter when he glanced back at her. She wanted to smile, but knew someone in the room would know how she felt about him if she did. Instead, she lowered her head, then crossed her legs as she looked around the room, before settling her eyes back on him.

Finally, Brother Johnson stepped aside and Rod moved in front of the fireplace.

"We are one, our cause is one, and we must help each other, if we are to succeed." He read a quote first spoken by Frederick Douglass. "Tonight I'd like to read to you an excerpt from *Climbing Jacob's Ladder* by Andrew Billingsley."

Natalie sat in awe as she listened to Rod read. He had the gift of a storyteller. There was so much more to this country boy than she thought. So he wasn't some jock who thought he was God's gift to women. He was a genuinely nice, sweet man. Why couldn't she have someone like him? Someone who lived in Atlanta?

After Rod finished his reading he gestured for the person closest to him to stand and express what *Umoja* means to them.

Get **4 FREE** Arabesque Contemporary Romances Delivered to Your Doorstep and Join the Only New Book Club That Delivers These Bestselling African American Romances Directly to You Each Month!

No Obligation!

WE INVITE YOU TO JOIN THE ONLY BOOK CLUB THAT DELIVERS HEARTFELT ROMANCE FEATURING AFRICAN AMERICAN HEROES AND HEROINES IN STORIES THAT ARE RICH IN PASSION AND CULTURAL SPICE...

And Your First 4 Books Are FREE!

Arabesque is the newest contemporary romance line offered by Pinnacle Books. Arabesque has been so successful that our readers have asked us about direct home delivery. We responded to your requests. You can start receiving four bestselling Arabesque novels a month delivered right to your door. Subscribe now and you'll get:

- ❖ 4 FREE Arabesque romances as our introductory gift—a value of almost $20! (pay only $1 to help cover postage & handling)
- ❖ 4 BRAND-NEW Arabesque romances delivered to your doorstep each month thereafter (usually arriving before they're available in bookstores!)
- ❖ 20% off each title—a savings of almost $4.00 each month
- ❖ FREE home delivery
- ❖ A FREE monthly newsletter, *Zebra/Pinnacle Romance News* that features author profiles, book previews and more
- ❖ No risks or obligations...in other words, you can cancel whenever you wish with no questions asked

So subscribe to Arabesque today and see why these books are winning awards and readers' hearts.

After you've enjoyed our FREE gift of 4 Arabesques, you'll begin to receive monthly shipments of the newest Arabesque titles. Each shipment will be yours to examine for 10 days. If you decide to keep the books, you'll pay the preferred subscriber's price of just $4.00 per title. That's $16 for all 4 books with FREE home delivery! And if you want us to stop sending books, just say the word...it's that simple.

See why reviewers are raving about ARABESQUE and order your FREE books today!

WE HAVE 4 FREE BOOKS FOR YOU!

ARABESQUE

(If the certificate is missing below, write to: Zebra Home Subscription Service, Inc., 120 Brighton Road, P.O. Box 5214, Clifton, New Jersey 07015-5214)

FREE BOOK CERTIFICATE

Yes! Please send me 4 *Arabesque* Contemporary Romances without cost or obligation, billing me just $1 to help cover postage and handling. I understand that each month, I will be able to preview 4 brand-new *Arabesque* Contemporary Romances FREE for 10 days. Then, if I decide to keep them, I will pay the money-saving preferred subscriber's price of just $16.00 for all 4...that's a savings of almost $4 off the publisher's price with no additional charge for shipping and handling. I may return any shipment within 10 days and owe nothing, and I may cancel this subscription at any time. My 4 FREE books will be mine to keep in any case.

Name _____

Address _____ Apt. _____

City _____ State _____ Zip _____

Telephone ( ) _____

Signature _____ ARHM97
(If under 18, parent or guardian must sign.)

Terms and prices subject to change. Orders subject to acceptance by Zebra Home Subscription Service, Inc. .
Zebra Home Subscription Service, Inc. reserves the right to reject or cancel any subscription.

Everyone in the room stood and said something. When it was Natalie's turn, she stood and expressed what *Umoja* meant to her. She hadn't quite gotten the flow of things yet, so she felt uncomfortable speaking.

"*Umoja* means peace within the family to me. Living harmoniously with your parents, brothers, and sisters. When there's peace in the homes, I believe it's possible to have peace in the community."

She kept her eyes on Rod the whole time she spoke. They locked eyes and she spoke as if she were speaking only to him.

Chapter Five

Rod grabbed an armful of firewood from the stack beside the barn, and proceeded toward the house. He didn't know when he'd light the fireplace, but he wanted dry wood inside when he decided to. His dog, Paso, ran circles around his legs barking at him.

"Okay, boy, I know, you're hungry. Let me get inside and I'll fix your dinner." Paso stared at the door rapidly wagging his tail, as Rod opened the door to let him inside. He dropped the wood by the fireplace then went to feed his dog. Paso sat by his food bowl following Rod's every move with his eyes.

"You need me, don't you, boy?" Rod rubbed the top of Paso's head as he passed him. His dog was all he had to keep him company. After opening two cans of dog food and watching Paso chow down, Rod went to get dressed.

He'd already showered for the day, but he needed to shave. Knowing he was going by Pauline's this morning, caused him to pay close attention to his looks. He'd gotten a haircut yesterday after work, but he liked to trim his own face.

Paso appeared in the doorway watching him shave.

"Hey, boy, you want to go by Pauline's with me this morning? Natalie will be there." He lathered his face and turned back to the mirror to shave. "And you know how much I like looking at Mis Natalie. But dig this!" He pointed his razor at the dog. "She likes looking at me, too."

He began shaving the left side of his face, occasionally pointing his razor at the mirror as he talked. "I can see it in her eyes, I know she wants me. Probably about as much as I want her. But what do I do about it? She lives in Atlanta, miles away from here." He rinsed his razor out in the sink, then started on the other side.

"I wonder how she feels about long-distance relationships? We could make it work, if we really wanted to. Yeah, I could visit Atlanta every now and then. It's not like I'd have to live there." He cleaned out his razor and wiped off his face. Paso sat in the doorway with his head tilted, looking at Rod.

Rod tossed his towel in the dirty clothes hamper and started laughing. He looked down at Paso and said, "Damn, I must be lonely—I'm talking to you like you understand me. Let me got out of here and over to Pauline's."

He changed into a clean pair of jeans and a sweatshirt before leaving.

When Rod walked into the shop, Natalie kept her head down going over her figures a second time. She knew they were right, but it was her way of not making eye contact with Rod.

"So, how's Mis Natalie this morning?" he asked, leaning on the counter.

"I'm fine," she said without looking up.

"Um, hum." He stood there tapping his fingers on the counter looking down at her figures.

Natalie looked up with a straight face. "I'm sorry, did you want something?"

Rod stood straight up from the counter. "No!" He stared at

her for a moment. Then he leaned back on the counter smiling. "I'm waiting for Pauline."

"She might be out all morning, she had some personal business to take care of. But I'll tell her you stopped by." She tried her best to smile. Being rude and obnoxious wasn't her intent, but she had to put some distance between them.

"No need." He turned around and walked over to the couch across from the counter. "I'll wait for her right here." He eased back onto the couch crossing his legs and spreading both arms across the back of the couch.

Natalie tapped her pencil eraser on the counter as she looked at him. "Do what you like, but you might be sitting there all morning."

He merely shook his head, pouting his bottom lip. He kept staring at her and she knew why. Unable to take his stares any longer, she stacked her papers neatly on the side of the counter and turned her back to him. *Where was a customer when you needed one?* she wondered. Pretending to sort Christmas ornaments in a box, she kept her back turned.

After about five minutes of silence the bell over the door jingled. Natalie's first thought, "Oh good, a customer." But when she turned around, her Aunt Polly strolled in carrying a shopping bag. Natalie looked over at Rod who hadn't taken his eyes off her.

"All morning, huh?" He lowered his arms from the back of the couch as he winked at Natalie.

Natalie crossed her arms and slightly shook her head. Why had her aunt returned so soon? She was supposed to be doing some after-Christmas shopping for her grandchildren.

"I'm telling you, everywhere you go it's so crowded. I didn't even bother to go into Belks." She stopped when she saw Rod.

"Hi, Ms. Pauline, doing a little after-Christmas shopping?"

"Rod! Yes. Honey, I'd forgotten I asked you by this morning." She put her bag behind the counter.

"That's okay, Natalie here was keeping me company." He

winked at Natalie, then turned back to Pauline. "Did you want me to run out to Shady Grove for you?"

Natalie wanted to explode. She hadn't said but a few words to him. While her aunt looked through her delivery book, Natalie picked up her box of ornaments and walked into the back office. She made sure to stay there until Rod left.

That evening, Wanda let Grachel light the first green candle as they observed *Kujichagulia*. Wanda relit the black candle. The second principle of Kwanzaa stood for self-determination. Wanda and her husband Arthur discussed how self-determination and persistence helps you to acquire and maintain your identity. The relatives gathered today were fewer than the day before. Only the immediate family was in attendance. After Natalie listened to everyone express what *Kujichagulia* meant to them, she read Nikki Giovanni's poem "Choices." She wished Rod was there to hear her read.

Sunday morning she saw Rod again at Church. Avoiding him there was easy. He sat on one side and she sat on the other. As soon as morning service ended, she slipped out the door and left. She spent her Sunday afternoon thinking about Rod, even though she tried not to.

That evening the family had another quite observance of the third principle of Kwanzaa. *Ujima,* collective work and responsibility. Natalie had been exposed to one aspect of this principle, but she sat back to learn more. Again tonight she noticed Rod hadn't joined them.

Natalie didn't get into the shop Monday until around eleven o'clock that morning. Life in Hopkinsville was so relaxed and laid-back, she didn't have to be in a hurry to do anything. No stress. Only peaceful living. She helped her aunt with new inventory.

Business was slow, so they had time to price and put out

new pieces. "So, tell me what you're wearing to the New Year's Eve dance?" Pauline asked.

"I'm not going." Natalie replied.

"Why not?"

"Nobody asked me. I'm not going to a New Year's Eve dance by myself."

"Honey, you're in Hopkinsville, not Atlanta. It's okay to go dancing stag here. If you wait for one of these guys to ask you out, you might never leave the house."

"Well, I don't know." Natalie sighed.

"If you'd quit treating Rod like he has the plague, he might ask you."

"I don't want to go with him anyway. I didn't come up here to find a man." It was about time she let her aunt know she didn't want to be matched up with Rod.

"Maybe you didn't. But one found you. And I don't believe in coincidences, it was fate that brought you here." Pauline put down the antique ash tray she was about to price. "Natalie, I can see in your eyes that you're searching for something. I know it's not just your family that you miss. You're a lot like your mother. You need somebody to love you. I know you kids were surprised when you mother finally remarried. But, I understood her. She needs love and companionship all the time. Everybody can't handle being alone. She was alone long enough. I see a lot of your mother in you. Don't push men away. It's not true what they say, you know. All men aren't alike."

"I know it. I guess once you get burned it's hard to put your hand back in the fire."

"Don't run from love, honey. It's all in His master plan, and if it's meant to be—it will be."

Natalie thought about what her aunt said once Pauline left for the day. Tonight they were celebrating *Ujamaa,* which meant cooperative economics. Pauline and a few other business owners in town were speaking to a women's group at the

community center. Her aunt believed in giving back to the
community whenever she could.

Fifteen minutes before closing two women walked into the
shop. One explained she'd had her eye on an armoire and
needed another look. Natalie showed them the piece of furniture
she'd dusted and polished earlier that morning. The cherry
armoire was beautiful. As she opened the cabinet doors displaying the inside to the women, she heard the front door open.

Another customer! Man, I'll never get out of here tonight.
When she looked past the ladies she almost fell out. It was
Kevin! He stood in the doorway in his black leather wrap coat
grinning at her. The women turned to see who Natalie had
stopped to look at. One lady cleared her throat to get Natalie's
attention.

"Excuse me." Natalie shook her head and told herself he
wasn't there. He hadn't driven over four hundred miles to
intimidate her. She returned to the armoire and explained their
delivery process to the customer.

"I really want this armoire. I think I'll bring my husband
by over the weekend to have a look at it. Could you ask Pauline
to put my name on it, and not to sell it until I can get George
over here?"

"Yes, ma'am." Natalie looked back toward the door, but
Kevin wasn't there. "If you'll give me your name I'll write it
down for her."

The women followed Natalie over to the counter and gave
her a name and phone number. "Pauline knows me very well.
Just tell her Mrs. Riley wants that armoire."

Natalie walked behind the counter and gabbed a pen and
some paper. With shaking hands she took down the information.
"I've got it. And thank you ladies for coming in today."

She followed the women to the front door, then flipped over
the closed sign.

"Say, your aunt's got a lot of high-priced junk in here."

Her knees shook as she followed his voice. She found Kevin

sitting on the couch across from the counter. Fear swept through her as she thought about their last argument.

"What do you want?" she asked in a harsh tone, with her arms crossed.

"What! No hello, hi, Kevin, how you doing? I figured you'd be glad to see me. After all, we missed spending Christmas together, and you know I hate spending Christmas alone."

He sat back on the couch with his legs crossed and his expensive crocodile boot dangling in the air. Dressed in a pair of expensive wool slacks and one of his two-hundred-dollar camel hair sweaters, he made her sick. He looked like every woman's fantasy. She hated the way he made himself at home.

"What's wrong, baby, you're not glad to see me?"

"How did you find me?"

He stood up and walked over to the counter. She backed up as he approached. Slithering like a snake, he leaned across the counter in his coat. "You weren't trying to hide from me, were you?"

"Kevin, I ended our relationship weeks ago. It should be obvious that I don't want to see you again. How did you find me?" she asked again in a harsh tone.

"Look, Natalie, I came up here to talk to you about this breakup thing. I'm not ready to end our relationship. I know I messed up, but . . ."

"Is that what you call it? I call it messing around, and you seem to be addicted to it."

He banged his fist on the counter with a loud sound that Natalie thought would break the glass. "Damnit! I explained that to you. Don't keep bringing that up. I said I was sorry." He abruptly walked away from the counter and around the shop.

"So you left me for Hopkinsville. What in the world are you doing in this little nothing of a town anyway? You need to get your stuff and come back with me."

"I'm not going anywhere with you."

He returned to the counter. "What do you think I drove all

the way up here for? My health? You need to close this little dump and go get your clothes. We can talk about it on the way back.''

Natalie shook her head and began to laugh. God, had she actually been that naive when she met him? Had he always told her what to do?

''What's so funny?''

''You, if you think I'm leaving with you. I don't know why you came up here, but you shouldn't have. Kevin, you don't own me, nor do you run my life. You can't waltz in here and tell me I'm going home. I'll leave when I get good and ready.''

He rested both elbows on the counter. ''Look, baby, you know how much I miss you. I had to spend Christmas by myself and everything. I didn't know where you were until I called your boss. Do you know how many messages I left on your recorder?''

There he goes, trying to disguise himself as prince charming. ''I doubt that you spent Christmas alone, nor do I care.'' She looked down at her watch, it was after five o'clock. Somehow she had to get him out of here and get to Wanda's for the observance of Kwanzaa.

''What are you looking at your watch for? It's time to leave all right. Time to leave this town. Come on now, let's go get your bags. We won't get home before one in the morning as it is.''

Natalie grabbed her purse from under the counter. ''I'm leaving all right, but I'm not going with you. It's time to close shop.'' She turned off things preparing to close down.

Kevin paced the floor around the counter in silence. He pulled the belt on his leather coat tighter, and turned up the collar.

Natalie walked toward the front door, hoping he'd leave as easily as he'd come. ''Well you'd better leave, I have to lock up.'' She'd put on her short black scarf coat.

Kevin walked toward the door behind her. ''Natalie, I'm

asking you one more time. Are you coming home with me or not?''

"Kevin, I told you I'm not going anywhere with you." She pulled her purse strap on her shoulder and backed closer to the door. "After what you put me through, how dare you ask me to come back with you. For what, so I can find you in bed with another woman next week?"

He rubbed his chin as he stood staring down at her. "I've gotten all that out of my system now. I'm a changed man, you'll see."

"Changed how Kevin? Maybe you'll be a little more discreet this time?"

"Hey, I said I've changed!"

"Kevin, I don't want to fight with you about women. I don't want to fight with you about anything."

"Don't try to lay the fight on me. You started the fight that night. I was trying to keep you off me."

She turned and reached for the door knob, when he grabbed her arm and spun her around.

"Natalie, you're going back with me tonight and I mean it. I don't want to discuss it any more, you're mine."

"I don't belong to you ... get off me." She struggled to free her arm from his grip.

Rod drove down through town after work out of sheer curiosity. It was almost five thirty and he knew Pauline's would be closed, but he had to ride by anyway. Natalie hadn't talked to him at church yesterday, and he'd thought about her at work all day. Every since Saturday morning she'd given him the cold shoulder treatment. He took the hint and backed off, but he hadn't wanted to.

During the first night of Kwanzaa they shared something special. He gave his words to her and she gave hers to him. There may have been a room full of people, but when he spoke about *Umoja*, he spoke to her. Even the time they spent later that night talking meant something special to him. Natalie was someone special to him, and he wanted to spend more time with her.

As he got closer to Pauline's he noticed the light was still on. He decided to pull up and see why they were working so late. When he parked his truck by the front door, he saw people standing inside the door. As he turned off the motor, he saw Natalie look out the door at him. Then he saw a tall, dark-complected man dressed in all black standing behind her. He got out of the truck slowly, not sure who this man was to Natalie. He didn't want to be walking in on anything he shouldn't. But, when he saw Natalie jerk her arm from the man, he quickened his step.

When he opened the door Natalie seemed to reach out to him. He wanted to grab her and protect her from whoever was harming her.

"Hey, what's going on here?" he asked touching her hand.

"Hi, Rod."

"Sorry, man, but we're closed. You'll have to come back some other time." Kevin let go of Natalie's arm.

Rod ignored Kevin and walked up to Natalie. "Natalie, are you all right?"

"Yeah, she's fine. What's it to you?" Kevin stepped closer to Natalie, pulling her close to him.

"He's leaving." She turned to Kevin and hoped he would leave now that Rod was here. But he didn't move. He pulled her closer to him as he slid his arm around her waist.

"Get off me, Kevin. I told you I'm not going anywhere with you."

Rod was about to explode. This was Natalie's ex-boyfriend she'd told him about. The one who hurt her.

"Look man, I think you'd better let her go and leave— now."

Kevin struggled to hold onto Natalie as she pushed away from him. "This is none of your business, country boy, so I suggest you get your butt back in your pickup and leave."

Now Rod was angry. It looked like he was going to have to teach this city boy a lesson. "Natalie, do you want me to leave?"

"No, you don't have to go anywhere."

That was all he needed to hear. He rushed up to Kevin, causing him to let go of Natalie. If they weren't in Pauline's, he'd pick Kevin up and throw him across the room, but he didn't want to mess up Pauline's shop.

Kevin backed up a few steps as Rod drew closer. "So what you gonna do, country boy? Fight me for her?"

Rod reached out and pushed Kevin. His arm swung out sending a lamp crashing to the floor, before he followed it. That was the last straw, for Rod.

"Man, you've got one minute to get your butt out of here. Natalie's not going anywhere with you."

When Kevin stood up, Rod pushed him again. Rod stood about three inches taller than Kevin, and outweighed him by about fifty pounds. Rod considered himself too old to fight another man, but if Kevin didn't leave quick he'd reconsider that.

"What are you, her new boyfriend or something? Man, you can't force me to do anything." He stood there straightening his coat and pulling the belt tighter.

"I'll tell you what, pretty boy. If you don't leave maybe I'll beat you to a pulp, then throw you way back in the woods somewhere where nobody will find you for days. If they find you at all." Rod rushed up and grabbed Kevin by the collar of his coat spinning him around.

Kevin fought to push him off. "Man, get your hands off me."

Rod let him go and pointed his finger in his face. "If you don't leave in the next few seconds, you'll loose some teeth, I promise you." He kept advancing toward Kevin shoving him backward.

"Get off me." Kevin swatted at his hand. "I'm leaving." He turned and walked toward the door, then stopped once his hand was on the knob. "Natalie, I'll see you when you get back in town. You have to come back to me some time." He flipped up the collar on his coat and walked out, slamming the door.

Rod rushed to the door after him, but Natalie stopped him. "Don't, Rod, let him go. I'm just glad he's gone."

Rod watched him get into a convertible BMW and drive off. He banged the door frame with a balled fist. Man, he wanted to hit that guy so bad. When he turned around Natalie was sitting in one of the high back chairs with her head down.

He kneeled down to her. "Hey, baby, you okay?"

She looked up with tears in her eyes, and it broke his heart. Without saying a word, he pulled her into his arms and held her as she cried.

Minutes later, she sat up and began wiping her tears away. He helped her.

"Don't worry, everything will be okay." He tried to comfort her.

"Until I go back to Atlanta anyway. Sooner or later I'll have to deal with him."

"I thought you two had broken up?" He got up and sat in the chair next to hers.

"We did! I broke up with him two weeks before I came to Hopkinsville. Believe me, I had no idea he'd come walking in here today. I was stunned . . . I'm still stunned."

Rod sat back and thought about what could have happened if he hadn't driven by. He leaned forward, resting his elbows on his knees. Kevin wasn't a very big guy, but he still could have hurt Natalie.

"Thank you, Rod."

He reached over and rubbed her knee. "No need to thank me, I'm just glad I happened to ride by."

She closed her eyes and leaned her head back against the chair. "I can't go to Wanda's like this. I'm a nervous wreck." She looked down at her watch. "It's almost time for the Kwanzaa observance."

"Want me to call her for you?"

"And tell her what?"

"That you're taking a ride with me. We can go on that little tour I promised you. That should settle your nerves."

"I don't know."

"Natalie, I'm not about to leave you alone right now. Do you think he'll come back?"

"No, he's probably gone. Kevin doesn't have much heart. Once he realizes how determined you are, he'll go home. Besides, he probably has some woman waiting for him at home."

"I can't believe he drove all the way up here if he doesn't care."

"It's a pride thing with him. It's okay for him to leave me, but not for me to leave him."

"Man, that's silly."

"That's Kevin. I don't know how I ever fell for him in the first place. God, I must have been stupid." She slapped her forehead and closed her eyes.

"Don't blame yourself. That guy dresses nice, probably talks a good game, and from that convertible BMW, I'd say he has money to burn. You were a couple years younger when you met him, so the material things probably caught your eye."

"Yeah, I guess so."

"Let me call Wanda right quick, and we'll get out of here."

The tour through town was quick. There wasn't much to see, and it was getting dark. Rod filled Natalie in on a little Hopkinsville history as they rode. With the heat on in his truck she'd relaxed enough to take off her coat.

"Well, that's the city, but I know a perfect place to watch the sunset. Unless you're ready to go home?"

"No, I'm not ready to go home if you don't mind. But I am a little hungry." Right now she felt safe with him, and didn't want to leave him.

"I'm hungry, too. Let's grab something to eat, then we'll watch the sun set."

"Sounds good to me."

After a quick dinner they rode out into the countryside. Natalie wondered where he was going, but didn't ask. She sat back and enjoyed the ride, trying her best to get Kevin off her mind.

"See that over there," he pointed out her side of the truck.

Natalie looked out at the orange glow of the sun setting. "Yes, and it's beautiful."

He turned into a long driveway, at the end of which a white house sat back off the road. She looked out the window wondering again where they were going.

"This is my forty acres of responsibility I told you about."

Natalie looked out the window at the fields of trees, grapevines, and the huge barn that sat behind the house. The house was nice. It wasn't grand, only one floor, but it had a quaint elegance about it. It was perfect. She turned to look at Rod, as he smiled at her.

He pulled into a graveled parking spot in front of the house and cut the motor off. When he got out of the truck, he walked around to open the door for her.

He took her hand to help her out of the truck. "This is my house, what do you think?"

"Well, it's not your typical bachelor's pad."

Chapter Six

Rod picked up a wicker basket sitting in the white rocker on his front porch. He read the note attached and stuck it in the basket.

"They're from my neighbor. Cookies. Want one?" He offered the basket to Natalie.

"Sure, I'll try one. She bakes you cookies all the time?" Natalie imagined a man this handsome had women trying to get his attention all the time.

Rod opened the front door and motioned for her to go in. "No. A couple weeks ago we had a bad storm. I picked up a lot of tree limbs from her yard, because at seventy-two she can't do it herself. Besides, I don't mind. Every time I do something for her, she bakes me cookies."

"Oh," was all Natalie could say after what she'd been thinking. Stepping into the living room she was impressed. The forest-green walls topped with a floral border, definitely had a woman's touch. The sofa, chairs, and tables didn't look like they matched, but had been collected over time, because they meant something to someone. She wondered if everything had once belonged to his mother. The room had a warm comfortable feel to it.

At his invitation she followed him into the kitchen. He set the basket on the table and reached into the refrigerator.

"Would you like something to drink?"

"No thank you." Natalie walked over and looked out the back window. She saw a basketball goal, and land stretching as far as the eye could see.

Rod walked over and stood next to her drinking a glass of milk. He didn't touch her, but she felt him. She could imagine what it felt like to have his hands running up her arms, and his breath on her neck as he bent to kiss her. But, it was all in her imagination.

"Nothing like this in Atlanta, huh?"

"What?" she asked. When she turned she realized he was standing entirely too close for comfort. *He's a man, girl, remember that.*

"That." He pointed out the window. "Fields of green grass even in the winter time. I love it here."

She looked back out the window, nodding her head in agreement with him. "So, I see you made yourself a basketball court. You any good?"

"I used to be. I'm still good enough to beat Brandon when he comes home."

"Who's Brandon?"

"My little brother. He thinks he's a basketball star. He plays for Western University. When he comes home from school, I have to put him in his place real quick."

They stood gazing out the back window while Rod told her all about Brandon and their parents' death. "You know, you never think your parents will leave you. At least not until you're much older. My parents were hit by a drunk driver at three o'clock in the afternoon, believe it or not. I was away at college and Brandon was in school." He took another swallow of milk, and a deep breath before continuing. "When my aunt called I was numb. I don't even remember flying home. And because

I didn't get a grant or anything, that was the end of college for me. Besides, somebody had to take care of Brandon and the house.''

"What about your aunt?"

"She wanted us to move in with her, but I knew we'd loose the house and all this land if we did. My dad worked too hard to get this place for me to let them sell it. So, I dropped out of school and got a job."

"Rod, that must of been so hard?"

"It was. But I've managed to keep the house and get Brandon in college. I don't regret a minute of it."

"Man, I know your parents are smiling down on you. That was such a mature decision to take on all that responsibility."

"Come here, I want to show you something."

He took Natalie's hand and led her down the hallway into the den. She stepped into the county-style room literally oozing with put-your-feet-up comfort. The huge stripped soft looked like something she could sink into. Several lamps gave the room a soft warm feeling. This room looked really lived in, with newspaper and throw pillows on the floor. She assumed he spent most of his time in here.

The bookshelves were crammed with books and pictures of his family. He pointed everyone out to her. He and Brandon were the only children.

She picked up the picture. "Your little brother's cute. I bet he's a lot like you."

"Believe me, he's nothing like me. Stick around long enough and you'll meet him." He walked over to the stereo and put on some music.

"I had planned to leave on the third of January, but now I think I'll stay until New Year's Day. I only wish I didn't have to deal with Kevin once I get back." For the life of her, she didn't know why she brought him up again.

Rod stepped closer, taking the picture from her hand. "I wish you didn't have to go back at all. He didn't hit you, did he?'' he asked, looking into her eyes with genuine concern in his.

For a moment her breath caught in her throat. With his hand he pushed her hair back, around her ear. His touch was so gentle and tender.

''No, but I bet he wants to. He's so mad at me right now. And tonight only made things worse.'' The tears wanted to spill down her cheeks, but she wouldn't let them. She needed to talk to someone, but she'd be damned if she'd cry over Kevin.

''I hope I didn't make things worse for you?''

''No, not at all. You helped me more than you'll ever know.''

''You want to talk about it?'' He motioned for her to have a seat on the couch.

When Natalie sat on the couch, she felt his hand on her shoulder, giving her permission to open up.

''Several months ago I had to attend a conference in Orlando for my job. Kevin called my hotel practically ever hour. When I wasn't in my room, he accused me of messing around with a coworker. I ignored him, but it happened again a few weeks later.

''I finally got tired of his jealous behavior and decided to end our relationship. When I went by his house to talk to him, I found him and one of his coworkers in bed together.'' She heard her voice shaking as she spoke. Rod put his arm around her shoulders. She fought the tears that were moments away.

''Some men are stupid.''

''He slapped me in front of her and said if I could sleep around, then so could he. But not once had I ever cheated on him, it was all in his head.''

''Natalie, it's not safe for you in Atlanta. He's got serious problems. He doesn't follow you around or anything, does he?''

''No. I made it clear that our relationship was over, and I never wanted to see him again. And I hadn't seen him until today. Actually, his job keeps him away for weeks at a time, and I hadn't seen him for three months, until I went by to break up with him." God, she didn't want to cry in front of this man again. But, she couldn't hold it back any longer. She had to release the tension shed through her tears.

Rod must have sensed how intense her pain was, because he pulled her into his arms just as the downpour began. She tried to stop but couldn't. At first, he let her cry, then she felt his hands caressing her back. He gently caressed her until she stopped crying.

He whispered ever so softly in her ear. "It'll be okay, you'll see."

She eased back from his embrace and looked up into his eyes. He had the eyes of a storyteller. She remembered his reading the first night of Kwanzaa. He looked so serious standing before everyone in that room, just as he did now. Why had she told this man all her business? How did she know he wasn't another Kevin? He reached up and wiped the tears from her face, rubbing his huge hand gently across her face. She shivered at his touch.

He grabbed a tissue from a box on the end table and offered it to her. "Are you okay?"

"Yes, thank you." She knew her eye makeup was all over her face, and she probably looked a mess. With the tissue she made an attempt to restore her looks.

"Sometimes it helps to cry."

He said it like he'd experienced it, and somehow she was sure he had, even though he looked too tough and masculine for her to picture him crying about anything.

She smiled at him through her tears and realized she had pressed her hand against the wet spot on his shirt.

"I'm sorry I cried all over you." She rubbed the spot with her hand.

He took her hand into his and raised it to his lips, kissing her knuckles. Caught off guard she didn't quite know what to do. Watching him kiss her hand, she sat there in shock and couldn't move. He pressed her hand against his chest and moved in to kiss her on the lips.

Natalie's whole body tingled with delight. She smelled the outdoorsy smell of his aftershave lotion and closed her eyes. In spite of all her resolutions, she wanted him to kiss her. If only for a moment, she wanted to be held and kissed passionately.

Their kisses grew from gentle to ravishing. Her whole body was on fire with desire. She wanted this man in the worst way. She wanted his strong arms wrapped around her. Her back arched at the feel of his hands caressing her breast. His kisses moved from her lips down her neck.

Natalie knew she was losing her head. But God, how she wanted to lose her head right now. She responded to his every touch, wanting more. He unbuttoned her blouse and opened the front clasp of her bra. At that very moment she wanted all her clothes off. She wanted nothing more than to feel his skin against hers. She nearly exploded when she felt his mouth against her breast. Minutes later, he released her breast and raised his lips to her ear.

"Natalie," he whispered. "I want you."

She wanted him, too, but something inside her head went off and she froze in her seat. *My God, you're doing it again! You're getting involved. This is not what you're here for.*

He looked down at Natalie, startled by the change in her behavior. She no longer responded to his touch.

"Are you okay?" His hand was still on her breast.

"No, I'm not." She repositioned herself on the couch as he pulled away from her. *How had she gotten so carried away in the first place?* Her hands shook as she tried to button up her blouse.

"Here, let me get it. I'm sorry." He finished buttoning up her blouse and sat back on the couch.

"Rod, I'm sorry. I didn't mean to lead you on. Right now I'm just confused and real tired."

"Don't apologize, it's my fault. After what happened today, I had no right to come on to you like this. I know you're only in town for a short time and you don't want to get involved. I can understand that.'' He got up and changed the music in the CD player, then left the room.

Natalie didn't respond to him. He was right. She didn't want to get involved. Or at least, she didn't think she wanted to. She got up and tucked her blouse back into her pants. Walking over to the bookshelf, she scanned his family pictures lined up on various shelves. She heard him clear his throat behind her. When she turned he stood in the doorway holding the basket of cookies.

''They're not so hard now, want another one?''

''No, thank you. I think I'd better leave before Aunt Polly gets worried.''

On the ride back into town they were both quiet. Natalie couldn't believe what she had almost allowed to happen. She wondered what he was thinking? Hopefully, he wasn't thinking bad of her. She told herself, *after tonight I can't see this man anymore.* There was no need in her teasing him, knowing she couldn't give herself to him. In a couple of weeks, he'd be nothing more than a fond memory. He deserved someone who would appreciate him for the strong, yet gentle man he was. Someone around on a daily basis.

Rod finally broke the silence. ''So, do you have any plans for New Year's Eve?''

''The Kwanzaa feast at the community center, why?''

''I thought you might like to go to the New Year's Eve dance with me at the armory.''

''I'm not really up to partying. I'm sorry.''

''Sure, don't worry about it, you're not missing anything. Just a bunch of small town folks dressed up and pretending they're going somewhere. Nothing like the fancy dances in Atlanta, I'm sure.''

He pulled the car to a stop in front of her aunts' house, and killed the engine.

"I wouldn't know. I don't go out in Atlanta. I'm not a party girl, believe it or not. I'm more of a homebody."

Rod got out to walk her to the front door. The temperature had dropped with the night air. Natalie pulled her coat tighter around her. Rod stood on the porch with his hands in his jacket pocket as Natalie rang the bell.

"Look, I'm sorry about my behavior tonight. I didn't mean to—"

She cut him off. "Don't apologize. I needed your help tonight and you were there for me. I enjoyed the tour and your company. We both got a little carried away that's all."

He smiled at her and shook his head as the front door came flying open.

"Natalie, I've been worried to death about you." Her aunt pushed open the screen door for them. "You two get in here."

"Mis Pauline, I'll let Natalie explain everything to you, I've got to run. Good night, Natalie."

"Good night, and thanks again."

Midway down the stairs he stopped and smiled up at her. "Sure, anytime."

For some reason she didn't think they were referring to the same thing. She stood in the doorway and watched him pull off into the night.

Rod banged his hand against the steering wheel. "Damn, how could you have done that." He pushed her too fast, and his timing was off. Tonight was not the night to make a move on Natalie. She needed comforting and consoling. He'd tried to be there for her, until she got too close to him. Holding her in his arms like he was, made him want her.

Next time maybe they'd watch a movie, something safe. After he'd gotten a taste of her, he knew there'd be a next time. That is if she wasn't mad at him about tonight. He hadn't wanted a woman like he wanted Natalie in a long time. At first he didn't know if it was all hormones or not, because he hadn't

been with a woman in a while. But tonight, he knew that wasn't
it. He wanted her to be his, and he wanted to be hers. If only
she didn't have to return to Atlanta.

Instead of taking the left turn out Route 1, he kept straight
to his buddy Terry's house. Terry and Rod played basketball
together in high school. He and Terry were the only ones on
the team to stay in Hopkinsville. He had to talk to somebody
about this woman. He didn't want to give up on her, but he
wasn't sure what his next move should be. The last thing he
wanted to do was mess up again like he did tonight. Terry was
his closest friend, he knew he could talk to him.

"Habari gani!" Wanda addressed the small circle of relatives in her living room.

"Nia!" they responded.

"This afternoon we celebrate the fifth principle of Kwanzaa,
Nia, which stands for purpose. To make our collective vocation
the building and developing of our community."

Tonight Natalie got to light the first red candle. Wanda's
family relit the green candles, and the black one. Arthur led
the discussion on how we use our purpose to build and develop
our communities.

Natalie felt so grateful and appreciative to have family around
her right now. She thanked God for sending her to Hopkinsville
for the holidays. She hadn't known what she was going to do
for the holidays before her aunt called. Germany was out of
the question, but staying in town meant dealing with Kevin. It
had to be divine intervention that led her here, she thought.

While listening to Arthur speak she wondered what her life
direction was? Purpose—did her life have any? Since breaking
up with Kevin she'd promised herself to make some definite
choices in her life.

For one, she hated her job. The pay was good, but the stress
was unbearable. Kevin had told her she'd be a fool to quit.

But, she didn't care what Kevin thought any longer. Time had come for Natalie to make decisions for Natalie, and choose her path in life. What she dreamed of was being self-employed. She wanted her own clothing boutique, and one day she would have it. For years she'd saved up enough money to start a business, but hadn't dared to take that plunge.

Natalie listened as Arthur talked about how serving others was his purpose in life. He worked with the youth at his church. Her thoughts drifted away as she pondered over he life. She went to church periodically, but wasn't very involved. However, she did feel good about the volunteer work she did through her job. Plus, she felt good about her school visits for Junior Achievement.

When Wanda stood up to talk about Clara Hale, the woman who started Hale House, Natalie thought about Rod. He helped her Aunt Polly by making deliveries and pickups all for free. She didn't pay him, nor barter with him in any way. Everything he did for her was out of the kindness of his heart. She also liked the way he helped his elderly neighbor just because she needed it.

When it was Natalie's turn to express what *Nia* meant to her she was ready. It was time for her to make some important decisions in her life, and now she felt like she could do so. She told everyone how she planned to give her life more of a purpose, and to stop living from day to day.

After dinner Tuesday night Natalie sat down to watch a movie with her little cousin Grachel. The child worshiped the ground she walked on. When Natalie sat on the couch with a huge bowl of popcorn, Grachel scooted closer to her. Natalie put her arm around her little cousin while they watched *The Lion King*. A few minutes after the movie started Wanda's son Richard joined them.

* * *

Wednesday morning was New Year's Eve. Natalie felt sad knowing she had to leave the next day. For the past week and a half her days were filled with family and fun. The thought of her lonely apartment depressed her.

She couldn't bring herself to go into her aunt's shop this morning. Memories of Kevin were still there. Instead, she spent the morning with Wanda, preparing the Community Center for the Kwanzaa feast.

Wanda read over the program while Natalie drove to the grocery store. "Man, we've got a full program this evening. I hope we don't run over."

"Why? Do we have to be out of the center at a certain time?" Natalie asked.

"No, but whoever's not going to church tonight will be trying to get to the New Year's Dance. Did Rod ask you to go?"

"Ah . . . yeah. He asked me yesterday, but I'm not going."

"Why not! I thought you wanted to go?"

"I thought I did, too, but I don't want to keep leading him on. If I go to the dance with him, he might get the wrong idea."

"What idea? You're leaving town in a couple of days. What idea could he get, other than you enjoy his company."

Natalie shrugged her shoulder. She really did want to go to that dance. She'd brought a dress with her just in case she found somewhere to go on New Year's Eve.

"Natalie I know he likes you, and I can tell you like him. Girl, I would, too, especially after he sent Kevin running back to Atlanta for you."

Natalie gave her cousin a quick look. She should have known her aunt tell Wanda about the incident. "So she told you?"

"You know she did. I'm telling you, Rod cares about you. He was ready to kick Kevin's butt for you. I don't even know Kevin, but I don't like him."

"Well, I'll either stay home and watch Dick Clark, or I'll go to church with aunt Polly."

"Honey, don't sit around and watch Dick Clark whatever you do. Go with Mama to church if you don't change your mind about the dance."

"I'll do something." Natalie had second thoughts about the dance now. She really didn't want to spend the night watching the never-aging Dick Clark again. In the past, she always had her girlfriends to go out with if she didn't have a date.

After the grocery both women went to the Community Center to start decorating. Wanda pulled most of the items she'd used at her house to use at the center. Natalie had on a pair of jeans and a sweatshirt, ready to work. When they walked in several people were draping cloths over the tables, and blowing up balloons.

"Hey, Natalie, I'm glad you could make it. Come help me with this centerpiece." Wanda's friend Angela waved Natalie over to help.

Natalie worked with Angela. They placed the large straw place mat known as *Mkeka* in the center of the table. Angela set a basket of corn on top of the mat.

"How many ears of corn are in there?" Natalie asked.

"I'm not sure. Wanda said to just fill it up. We're not sure how many children will be here tonight."

Natalie remembered reading that an ear of corn was placed in the centerpiece for each child in the family. She reached in Wanda's bag and pulled out the *Kinara* and the seven candles. After inserting each candle into its appropriate place, black in the center, red to the left, and green to the right, she placed it in the center of the mat.

Angela sat the *Kikombe cha umoja,* the unity cup, on the table. Next to it, she sit a stack of plastic cups. Beside them was a large *Mazao* bowl, full of fruits, nuts, and vegetables. Natalie had to help her with this one. Other trimmings were added to the table for color.

"Where'd you get these?" Natalie picked up the red, black, and green linen napkins.

"Some friend of Wanda's made them."

"I didn't know they went with the centerpiece."

"I can tell you've been reading those Kwanzaa books. You can add whatever you like to the centerpiece. Remember *Kuumba* is all about creativity, talent, and imagination. We can set this centerpiece up however we like. Just use your imagination to make it pleasing."

"Okay, yeah." Natalie thought the centerpiece looked beautiful like it was. She didn't change a thing.

"Could you help me hang that banner over by the door?"

"Sure. You know I'm going to be ready for this feast tonight. Especially after I work up an appetite."

They stood on ladders on both sides of the doors. Angela pulled her end higher, causing Natalie's to slip from her hand.

"Hey."

"I'm sorry." With a hand over her mouth, she looked down to see who she'd hit with her end of the banner.

Rod looked up at her as a passing woman pulled the banner out of his box. "Don't worry about it, I know you were trying to get my attention." He winked at her and walked over to set his box on a table.

"If I wanted your attention, I would have called your name." She took a few steps down the ladder and grabbed the banner from the woman. "Thank you." She stepped back up the ladder and finished helping Angela.

Natalie walked around the center helping wherever she could. She managed to avoid Rod most of the time. She noticed him setting up stereo equipment with some other men and wondered why he wasn't at work. Actually, she was still embarrassed about the incident at his house.

"Hello."

Natalie jumped at the sound of his voice. Rod startled her when he walked up to her. "Hi."

"Sorry, I didn't mean to startle you."

"That's okay. I guess I'm still a little jumpy. What are you doing here anyway? I thought you'd be at work."

"I took a long lunch break. I've got to run back in a few." With his hands in his back pockets Rod stood talking to Natalie.

"Say, uh, you haven't changed your mind about the dance tonight have you?"

Natalie thought for a few minutes. She did want to go now. Everyone would be there, but her.

Rod looked down at her moving his head from side to side. "She's thinking about it, and the answer is . . . ?"

"Okay, I'll go."

"Great. I'm glad you changed your mind. I really didn't want to go alone. I kind of had my mind set on going with you."

"Oh you did, huh?"

"Yes, I did. If you hadn't changed your mind, I probably would have had to sit through another Dick Clark rocking New Year's Eve party."

"That's what I usually do."

They both laughed.

"Yeah, but they're no fun alone."

"You've got that right."

"Well, I better get back to work. I'll see you later."

"Okay, don't work too hard."

"I never do." He winked at her and left.

Natalie blushed when he winked at her. She stood there grinning as she watched him walk away.

Minutes later Angela walked up to her. "What kind of gift do you think Rod will give you tomorrow?"

"What makes you think he'll give me something?" Natalie was surprised Angela asked her this.

"Girl, I saw the way that man looked at you when he walked in here. Besides I hear you two have been seeing each other."

Natalie wondered how Angela could have concluded that from her conversating with Rod. Even thought nothing was going on, somebody was talking about them. "Who told you that?"

"You know how small this town is. Gossip travels fast. I heard you and Rod have been seeing each other."

"Well we're not seeing each other. He comes by and helps my aunt in the shop that's all." She couldn't believe what she was hearing.

"Girl, don't sweat it. Rod's a nice guy. Half the women in this town have been trying to land him. I can't think of one who's ever been invited out to his house."

Natalie looked at Angela with her mouth wide open. How did she know she'd been out to Rod's house last night?

Angela finished positioning the items on the table, then looked up at Natalie. "Hey, like I said, it's a small town."

Chapter Seven

"Habari gani?"

"Kuumba," the audience responded.

Natalie looked around at the crowd of people in the center. All her relatives were there and many people she'd seen at church on Sunday. The table was decorated beautifully with fresh flowers, candles, and colorful appetizers. Everything from sauteed pecans to stuffed red snapper had been prepared. Everyone brought a dish or something to compliment the meal. After all the work she'd done earlier, Natalie couldn't wait to start feasting.

After Wanda's welcome, it was time to light the candles and pour the liation. Everyone sat at one long table that spanned the length of the center. Wanda sat at the head of the table, surrounded by numerous children. The crowd stood for the lighting ceremony. Richard lit the first candle, with Wanda's help. Then all the other candles but one were lit by the remaining children.

Mis Liz picked up the Unity cup and poured the libation. Natalie looked in her direction, but she was actually looking at the man sitting next to her. Rod sat beside his great-aunt sipping from his cup in observance of the libation. As he put the cup down, he smiled at Natalie.

She tried not to look at him, or think about him. But now that she'd accepted his invitation to the dance, she couldn't keep her eyes off him. She wondered what the night would be like? Every time she was in his company she had a good time. Tonight shouldn't be any different, she told herself, except tonight they'd be dressed for the occasion. She couldn't wait to put on her new dress.

Her cousin Marvin picked up his program and read the introductory remarks. He acknowledged the seven principles of Kwanzaa, and gave a definition of each. Natalie picked up her program and read everything in an attempt to keep her eyes off Rod. Marvin recognized the guest and elders at the table. Natalie thought he did his job very well. She'd been told that the sixth day of Kwanzaa was hosted by the children. Wanda's children had been practicing a song for the ceremony all week.

She wondered if Rod would be speaking today? When she looked up at him, she noticed him looking down the table and shaking his head. Her eyes followed his until she saw Deborah smiling and giving him the eye. *That girl's crazy.* Here they were at a table full of people cerebrating, and Deborah had found a way to flirt with Rod. When she looked back at Rod, he smiled at her then lowered his head. She'd have to have a talk with her cousin. The girl was embarrassing herself.

Natalie sat beside her aunt looking at the food spread before them hardly being able to contain herself. She wanted to reach out and grab something to eat. After working all morning, and only having breakfast, she was starved. However, she couldn't eat too much. She didn't want her stomach sticking out in her form-fitting dress tonight. All she needed was a little something to stop the hunger pangs.

After several toasts were performed to recognize certain elders, it was time for the children to perform. The church piano player was there to play for the children. Grachel stood up front and sang louder than all the other children. Pauline grabbed Natalie's hand laughing.

"My God, that girl's just like her mother. She can't sing and she wants everybody to know it."

"But she's so cute." Natalie felt like a proud parent watching her little cousin out sing all the other children. The day had all the makings of a family reunion, Natalie thought. She had that same nostalgic feeling she'd had during her father's family reunion a year ago.

When all the ceremonies were over it was finally time to eat, Natalie filled her plate with a little fish, red beans and rice, and a sampling of fruits. She skipped dessert since she was going out later that night. Finally, she sat down next to her aunt to eat.

"Is that all you're eating?" Pauline asked.

"Yes. I don't want to fill up too much."

"Why not?"

"I'm going to the New Year's dance tonight with Rod."

"I know." Pauline smiled at her niece, pleased.

"Why am I not surprised about that?" Like Angela said, news travels fast in small towns.

"I'm just glad you have somewhere to go. I hate to see all the young people going out, and you sitting at home watching television."

"Yeah, well, you don't have to worry about that now. I've got a date." A date! Had she actually said that? Here she was going out on a date, when a man was the last thing she wanted to be bothered with only weeks ago.

"Good evening ladies, enjoying yourself?" Rod sat across the table from Natalie and Pauline.

"Rod, honey, it's nice to see you. You've finished eating already?"

"Yes, ma'am. I was pretty hungry, it didn't take me long to finish off my plate."

"Where is Mis Liz?" Pauline looked around. "I need to talk to her."

"She's sitting over by the kitchen."

"Well, I need to talk to her a minute. Excuse me you two."

"Aunt Polly you're not even finished eating," Natalie pointed out.

"Oh, yes I am. I always put too much food on my plate. But, I'll take this in the kitchen to wrap up my leftovers. You know how I get hungry late at night." She picked up her plate and walked off. "Now where is that Liz?"

Natalie shook her head. "She's something else."

Before either of them could say anything else, Deborah took a seat next to Rod.

"Hi, Rod, I've been trying to catch up with you all night. Hi, Natalie." She gave a quick wave toward Natalie.

Natalie tried her best not to laugh as she spoke and continues eating. "Hi, Deborah."

"Hello Deborah, what can I do for you?" Rod let out a sigh and looked at the young girl.

"Oh, don't ask me that. At least, not in here." She leaned forward displaying her cleavage. Her sweater appeared to be about two sizes too small.

"Deborah, stop it. Don't you have any self-respect?" Natalie chastised. She couldn't help herself. Somebody had to tell this girl about herself. As good looking and fully developed as she was, some men would take advantage of her.

"What did I do?" She sat back in her chair and raised both hands palms out. "I just came by to ask Rod something."

Rod tried not looking down at her breasts, but it was impossible. This young girl was too much. She had the body of a fully-developed thirty-year-old woman. He'd spent the last six months avoiding her. Every chance she got she seemed to be pressing something up against him. She was lucky he wasn't like some of the men in this town. He could resist her no matter how great the temptation.

"What did you want to ask me?" He had to treat her like the child that she was.

"Are you going to the New Year's dance tonight?"

"Yes, I am."

"You'll save a dance for me, won't you? A slow one."

Rod thought Natalie would explode. She'd pushed her plate away and eyed her cousin like she wanted to wring her neck. The whole thing was funny to him, but he noticed she didn't share his opinion.

He turned and leaned his elbow on the table to face Deborah. "I will if my date doesn't mind."

"Your date?" She turned up her lip, looking surprised.

"Yes."

Deborah pushed away from the table and stood up. "Well, I'm sure your date won't mind. So, I'll see you later tonight." She walked away without saying another word.

"That girl's unbelievable." He shook his head watching her switch away.

"Isn't she though."

"I wanted to tell her you were my date, but she didn't give me a chance."

"Oh, she'll find out soon enough. Maybe that will get her off your back. Or maybe she'll meet a nice boy at the dance."

"Natalie, she's met all the nice boys in the county. I don't think she wants a nice boy. Deborah's looking for a man. But it won't be this man. I can handle her."

Rod checked his watch. He was ready to leave and get dressed for the dance. He couldn't wait to go out with Natalie tonight. What a way to start the new year. A date with a beautiful woman who turned him on.

"What time is it?" she asked.

"Eight thirty. What time are you leaving?"

"I'm not sure, whenever Aunt Polly gets ready. What time are you picking me up?"

"Well." He looked at his watch again. "The dance starts

at nine o'clock. Let's say I pick you up around nine forty-five, we'll be there at ten. How's that sound?''

''That sounds good.''

With the swirl of people mingling about in the room Rod didn't notice anyone but Natalie. He sat there talking to her for a few more minutes, not wanting to leave her company. Every time he made her laugh and smile he felt good. Tonight they would have a great time, he knew it.

Natalie ran around the bedroom feeling like a sixteen-year-old on her first date. From the minute they walked into the house she had one hour to get ready. Her aunt had left to pick up a friend before church. She must have looked out the window three times before he arrived. Finally, the door bell rang.

She slipped on her shoes and stood before the cheval mirror one more time before answering the door. Her long black dress hugged her body without the stomach bulge. She breathed a sigh of relief then went to answer the door.

''Well, well, don't you look all spiffy tonight.'' Rod grinned at her shaking his head. There was definite approval in his gaze.

''Spiffy! I hope I look a little better than that,'' she teased him.

''Oh, I'm sorry. Mama, you look so fine.'' He stroked his chin and cocked his head like a character in a hip-hop video.

Natalie gave him a quick punch in the arm. ''You know what I mean.'' After he walked in, she closed the front door behind him.

''I'm just kidding. You look absolutely beautiful. You city girls sure do clean up good.'' This time he ducked out of the way before she swung at him.

''You look very handsome yourself.'' Delicious was more like it, she thought. No baseball cap, tight jeans, or cowboy boots tonight. Tonight he had on a taupe and brown striped suit, complete with tie and pocket handkerchief. He definitely didn't buy that suit in Hopkinsville; it looked too expensive.

"Thanks. Hey, spin around and let me see that dress."

Natalie did a little spin for him. She knew he wanted to check out how the open back laced up. When she turned to face him again he bit his bottom lip and winked at her.

"Perfection."

"Well thank you."

"Where's Pauline?"

"She went by Mrs. Clark's before midnight service at church. Let me get my coat, and we can leave."

Once inside the Armory, Natalie saw women dressed in just about everything. Just as they walked inside she saw a woman in jeans, and wondered if her slinky black dress wasn't overkill. It definitely wasn't too much for Rod; he couldn't take his eyes off her. Silver and white streamers hung from the ceiling. Balloons were everywhere. A net full of balloons hung securely over the dance floor. Party favorites trimmed every table.

Every head turned as they walked across the floor. Natalie recognized a few faces from the shop. Almost everyone spoke to Rod, and a few spoke to her as well. She thought about what Angela said about this being such a small town. There was no telling what stories would be circulated after tonight. Eventually, she saw a few more women come in dressed for the occasion, which made her feel a little better.

After a drink, Rod was ready to dance. He wasn't Fred Astaire, and Natalie wasn't Ginger Rogers, but they burned up the floor despite that. Then a slow song came on, and Rod held her close to him. She didn't know if she could take it. The spicy scent of his cologne and the warmth of his body totally relaxed her and titillated her at the same time.

"That's my favorite song," he said, as he sang "Spend the Night" by The Isley Brothers softly into her ear.

The night was turning out so romantic to Natalie. He caressed her back and held her close to him. Their bodies met and moved to the rhythm of the soft music. She closed her eyes and let herself be carried away. They could have been the only two people in the room as far as she was concerned. Being there in his arms felt marvelous.

"Hey, man, don't hold her so tight, you'll break her."

Natalie opened her eyes and saw a young man standing behind Rod. They could have been twins. Rod loosened his embrace and turned around to hug the young man.

"Natalie, I want you to meet my little brother . . ."

"Little! I'm his younger brother, Brandon."

She shook his hand and noticed Brandon had Rod's eyes and smile. They had the same full lips and full eyebrows as their father in the picture he'd shown her. Two very handsome men. They left the dance floor and returned to the table. Brandon and his girlfriend had arrived in town right before the dance. Moments later, his girlfriend made her way to the table and Brandon introduced her. They made a really cute couple. Natalie loved her long auburn hair and how it matched her dress.

Natalie noticed how well the two brothers got along. They appeared to be best friends. They talked non-stop and relished in each other's company. Minutes later, Brandon and his date stood to leave.

"Natalie, it was nice to meet you. I'm glad you got Rod away from the house. The old boy doesn't get out much these days."

"It was more like he got me out. But, we're having a great time. It was nice to meet you, also."

"Cool, we'll catch you guys later. I see a few people I'd like to introduce Mia to." He patted Rod on the back and walked toward a group that had gathered across the room.

"He seems like a nice guy," Natalie said, as she watched them walk across the floor. She also noticed how crowded the room had gotten. Everyone in town must have come in since they did.

"He is a nice guy. I'm really proud of him. My parents would have been, too." He looked across the room.

The sadness in his eyes hurt Natalie. Rod was such a nice, decent, and honest man. He was the man she'd been looking for when she ran into Kevin. When he turned and looked at her, she sensed he knew what she was thinking. He winked at her and reached across the table for her hand.

"I'm a nice guy, too," he said, as he kissed the palm of her hand.

"I know, and I'm having a wonderful time tonight."

More might have come from the conversation, but suddenly people started coming from everywhere to their table. All the men wanted Rod to introduce them to Natalie. He did, but held her hand possessively, as if they were in love. When everyone left he turned and said, "What do you say we get out of here?"

"And go where?" She asked.

"I know where there's an after-party. Come on, it's getting a little too crowded in here."

It wasn't twelve o'clock yet, but she didn't mind. As they walked across the floor, she wondered what type of after-party they had in such a small town. Rod excused himself and ran into the kitchen for a minute. He walked out with a paper bag in his hand.

When Rod made a turn onto Route 1, she knew what type of after-party he had in mind. He turned into his driveway, killed the engine and smiled at her.

"Believe me, this party will be better than the one we just left."

He walked around to help her out of the car, and held her hand as they walked up the stairs and into the house. She didn't mind at all. She thought his maneuver was so cute; it made her feel like his girl. He didn't like all the attention they were getting at the party, he wanted her all to himself.

In the den, he turned on a lamp with a soft light, and took her coat. Before leaving the room he grabbed the remote and turned on the stereo. Soft music filled the air.

"Can I get you anything?" he asked.

"No, I'm fine."

He left to hang her coat up and returned with a bottle of champagne and two champagne flutes.

"I hope you don't mind me wanting you all to myself tonight?" he asked, as he walked into the room closing the distance between them.

"No, not at all." She wanted to be with him, but was still a little afraid. Did she really want to get involved again? Not with the wrong man, but Rod was the right man.

He set the champagne and glasses on the den table and turned to her. "Then may I have this dance?"

"Yes you may." She blushed and smiled at him.

He pulled her into his arms and they slow danced on his makeshift dance floor.

"Now this is the type of party I like. Just you and me. I don't want to share you with anyone else."

"So why didn't you just invite me out here for a party?"

"Would you have come?" He held her at arms length and looked down into her eyes.

"I don't know, maybe not."

He stood there gazing into her eyes. The music played softly in the background. She wanted him to kiss her, then pick her up and carry her into his bedroom, just like in the movies.

"You're so beautiful," he whispered in her ear. "Nat, I want you so bad."

Nat! He's already using my nickname. I've known this man for such a short time, but I want him. Before she could respond he pressed his lips over hers. She felt the heat from his tongue, and her knees gave way. He held on to her until she steadied herself.

"Rod, I know this is crazy, but I need you."

"There's nothing crazy about it. I'm here for you, baby. I'll always be here for you. Just don't leave me, because I need you to be here with me."

Natalie looked up into those big, beautiful eyes, speechless.

He was a wonderful man. The man of her dreams. But could she be happy in Hopkinsville? On the other hand, did she have any reason to stay in Atlanta?

He pulled her back into his arms and kissed her again. This time his kiss was one of intense hunger. He wanted her as much as she wanted him. They stood there in the middle of the room, ready to rip each others clothes off. He pulled back, and looked down into her eyes.

"Promise me you'll think about it?"

She couldn't say no. "I promise." Almost breathless she managed to get the words out. She threw her arms around his neck as he lifted her into his arms. It felt as if they floated down the hall and into his bedroom. Once inside, he turned her around to untie her dress. Her body tensed from memories of her earlier fears. He sensed it, because he turned her around to face him.

He kissed her neck and shoulders as he helped her out of the dress. "Relax, Natalie. I'll never hurt you." He kissed the top of her forehead and the tip of her nose.

"I know you won't." She reached up and helped him unbutton his shirt. Once his chest was exposed, she ran her hand across his hairy chest. That was one of her biggest turn-ons, a hairy chest. He moaned and grabbed her hand moving it down to his pants. She helped him out of his pants.

They discarded everything in a pile on the floor. He took her hand and led her to the bed. The slightest touch from him made her body shiver.

"Oh, Nat, you're so beautiful." His voice was heavy with emotion as he lowered himself to the bed. He pulled her close between his legs and caressed her breast.

For such a big man with huge hands, his touch was so gentle. His kisses were like feathers exploring every inch of her body. Natalie wanted to be nowhere more than she wanted to be here with him at this very moment. Rod brushed his lips past her breast and down her stomach. He stopped at her navel and licked.

Natalie wanted to pull her hair out from the roots, his touch was driving her insane. He raised his head and pulled her down on top of him. They rolled around and tangled themselves up in the covers; lost in the moment of desire for one another. At the feel of his hands gently sliding between her legs, Natalie spread them eagerly. She wanted him inside of her, to fill her with his love. She needed him.

Rod's breathing grew heavier as he rolled on top of her and slowly entered her. They moved to a slow rhythm and together picked up the pace. Natalie wrapped her legs and arms around his body and closed her eyes, as they rocked into a peaceful space. She gave her body to him as he gave every ounce of himself to her.

Later, she lay beside him feeling happy, giddy, even silly. No man had ever made her feel the way Rod had. She wanted to burst she felt so good inside. She questioned herself, *Is this what love feels like? If so, if feels so good.*

Suddenly, Rod raised up and looked at the clock on his night stand. "What time is it?" He threw back the covers and jumped out of bed.

Natalie sat up wondering what the hell was going on. "Rod, what is it?"

"Look at the time!" He grabbed his robe and left the room.

Natalie turned to look at the clock, it was five minutes till twelve. A few seconds later Rod walked back into the room. He had the bottle of champagne in one hand and the glasses in the other.

"I almost forgot about the champagne." He held the bottle up smiling at her as he walked across the room.

Natalie sat up in bed pulling the covers up over her chest. The chill in the air gave her goose bumps. Rod sat on the edge of the bed next to her. He placed the bottle and glasses on the night stand and reached for the remote control.

"Now we can catch Dick Clark." After turning the television

on he took a bottle opener out of his robe pocket and laid it on the table. Climbing out of his robe, he eased in bed next to Natalie.

"Are you cold?" He put his arm around her.

"Only my shoulders, it's a little chilly in here."

"Then let me warm you up."

He pulled the covers up around her, then wrapped her in his arms, running his hands up and down her arms and shoulders. Her body began to warm to his touch.

"Hold on, baby, we've got to toast in the new year." He grabbed the two champagne flutes and gave them to Natalie. "Hold these for me."

"Okay." She held the flutes and watched him open the bottle of champagne. If someone had told her she'd be spending her New Year's Eve in bed with a handsome man, she wouldn't have believed it. Here she was in bed about to share a New Year's toast with a man she'd met ten days ago, but she felt as if she'd known him forever.

He filled their glasses and turned up the volume for the countdown. They held their glasses up and stared into each others eyes. "Four, three, two, one, Happy New Year's!"

He cupped her cheek in his hand as they shared a special kiss. Then they drank their champagne. Natalie sipped from her glass, not really being a champagne lover.

"Nat, I've got something serious to ask you." Rod refilled his glass and turned to look down at her. His eyes had a sincere look in them.

Suddenly she felt scared. "Yes," she whispered.

"Do you think you could give me and Hopkinsville a chance? I'd really like to get to know you better. I think we're good together, and I don't want to lose you."

"Rod, I want to get to know you better, too." she answered with an uncertain smile. Then she asked herself, *What am I returning to Atlanta for anyway?* This time she answered herself—nothing. She didn't have any family there, only a job she hated and a man she was afraid of.

"Rod, I don't want to rush into anything, so can we take it slow?"

He bent down and gave her a soft kiss on the forehead. "I understand. We can take it as slow as you want, as long as I don't lose you in the process."

"You won't. We've shared a New Year's toast and kiss, don't you know how special that is?"

The next morning Natalie awoke slowly and looked around the room. Where was she? This wasn't her aunt's guest room with the flowery wallpaper. She rolled over and saw Rod laying next to her. Yes, now she remembered!

My God, what will Aunt Polly think? she asked herself. She's probably worried to death about me.

Rod stretched and rolled over looking into Natalie's eyes. "Good morning."

"Good morning." She smiled at him, feeling completely satisfied for the first time in a long time.

"You know I hadn't planned on staying the night."

"I wondered about that when the phone rang around three this morning. Wanda wanted to make sure you were here."

"She wanted to make sure I was here!"

"Yeah, so I told her to relax. I'd bring you home some time today." He grinned at Natalie.

"Oh, yeah, so now I have to walk into the house in the gown I wore last night."

"Yes. But, that won't be the only thing you'll be wearing."

"What do you mean?"

"You'll also be wearing that beautiful warm glow you woke up with this morning."

"Thanks to you." She blushed and kissed him.

Rod reached out and pulled Natalie into his arms. She forgot about being anywhere this morning other than where she was— out on Route 1.

Chapter Eight

"Habari gani?"

"Imani," everyone responded.

Tonight was the last night of Kwanzaa. They were observing *Imani*. The seventh principle of Kwanzaa stood for faith. Wanda stood before the small crowd of people gathered in her living room and read the observance.

"To believe with all our heart in our people, our parents, our teachers, our leaders, and the righteousness and victory of our struggle. To care for each other and control our destiny." Wanda motioned for Arthur to join her in front of the fireplace. She handed him the unity cup as he proceeded with the libation.

Tonight Natalie's Aunt Polly lit the last red candle. Wanda's family relit all the other candles.

Natalie sat on the couch with her shopping bag before her hardly able to contain herself. She wanted all the ceremonies to be over so she could hand out her gifts. In the ten days she'd been in Hopkinsville, she'd learned a lot about Kwanzaa. She used several of the principles studies throughout the week to come up with her *Zawadi* (gifts).

Pauline closed the ceremony by remembering their ancestors. She talked about relatives Natalie knew nothing about. Since her mother left Hopkinsville as a teenager, they hadn't visited much. Natalie didn't know much about her grandparents, but was learning some on this trip.

When time came to exchange *Zawadi*, the fun began.

"Aunt Natalie, I made this for you." Grachel handed Natalie a piece of construction paper with a drawing on it.

Natalie held up the very colorful painting the child had made herself. "Grachel, this is beautiful, did you make this?"

She nodded her head. "Uh, huh, all by myself. You know what it is?"

"Well, let's see."

"It's a lady." She pointed at the figure in the middle of the picture.

"Oh, I see. Yes, and she's beautiful."

"She's a black queen, Mama said."

"Grachel this is the best gift." Natalie set the picture on the couch and reached into her shopping bag. "And I've got a little something for you." She pulled a video tape out of her bag. "Now your Mommie told me you didn't have this one."

Grachel took the tape and looked at the cover.

"It's *Jirimpimbira: An African Folk Tale.* You can have your Mommie play it for you tonight."

"Thank you, Aunt Natalie, I don't have a whole lot of video tapes." She leaned forward and kissed Natalie on the cheek. "Mommie, Mommie, look what I got." Off she ran to find Wanda.

Natalie reached in her bag for her aunt's gift. She had searched and searched for the perfect gift for her. Pauline had given Natalie these two weeks that she'd never forget. Her life changed over this vacation. She found Pauline in the den helping Richard tie up his shoes.

"Aunt Polly, I've got something for you." She handed her a book, *In The Spirit,* by Susan Taylor. "I know you already have everything by Maya Angelou but I didn't see this one on your shelf.''

Pauline set Richard down and took the book. She stood to hug Natalie. "Oh, honey, thank you very much.''

"It's a very inspirational book. I've got a copy of it at home.''

"Natalie, this is from me and Arthur.'' Wanda handed Natalie a rather large box.

Natalie set the box on the table. "Man, what could this be.'' She began opening the box.

The doorbell rang and Arthur opened the door. The women in the kitchen could hear him talking to someone.

Natalie pulled a *Kinara* out of the box. Her eyes widened in surprise.

"Now you can start celebrating Kwanzaa yourself. You've learned a lot these seven days. And I can tell you enjoyed it.''

All Natalie could do was hug her cousin. "Wanda this is a great gift. I am going to celebrate Kwanzaa next year. And every year from here on out. Let me go get yours, it's in my bag.''

When Natalie walked into the living room she found Arthur and Rod sitting on the couch talking. Her heart skipped a beat. She hadn't planned on seeing him so soon in the day, but she was glad to see him. She'd been thankful Wanda or her aunt hadn't teased her about staying all night at his house. But, now she could be assured they'd bring it up.

Both men looked up when she walked into the room. Rod smiled and stood up when she approached.

"Hi.''

"Hello, I didn't expect to see you so soon.''

"I wanted to bring my *Zawadi* gifts by. I meant to be here sooner, but Aunt Liz needed me this morning.''

Arthur made an excuse and left the room to let them talk. Rod pulled Natalie into his arms and kissed her. They stood there kissing until Wanda walked in clearing her throat.

"Are we trying to repeat last night?'' she whispered.

Natalie pulled away from Rod and started laughing.

"Hi, Wanda." Rod still had his arm around Natalie when she walked into the room.

"Hi, Rod."

"Wanda, here let me give you the gift I have for you and Arthur." Natalie walked over to her bag and pulled out their gift. She walked over and handed it to Wanda. Arthur walked back into the room.

"What's that?" he asked.

"It's Natalie's gift to us." Wanda looked at the box while Natalie went to sit on the couch with Rod.

"It's a game. 'Journey to the Motherland,' Natalie where did you find this?" Wanda and Arthur opened the box and looked at the game.

"I saw it in a magazine, so I called and had it overnighted here. I knew you'd like it."

"It's a board game of African-American trivia. I didn't even know they made things like that," Arthur said. "You know this will be good for the kids to learn on also." He looked up at Natalie shaking his head.

"Well, I guess we can say you learned what Kwanzaa means this holiday season."

"I did. And I enjoyed myself tremendously." She turned her head to Rod when she said that.

Wanda and Arthur left the room to show Pauline their gift.

"Well, Kwanzaa's officially over today." Rod scooted closer to Natalie on the couch.

"Yeah, but you know you're supposed to observe these principles every day. I read how you can incorporate the seven principles into your everyday life."

"But how can a single person celebrate Kwanzaa? It's not the same as when you have family members around."

"I know the books say you can, but I agree it's not the same. Wanda gave me a *Kinara*, so I can start celebrating Kwanzaa in Atlanta."

Rod slouched down on the couch. "Don't remind me about

your going back to Atlanta. I don't want to think about it right now."

Natalie leaned her head against his shoulder and thought for a moment. She didn't want to go back to Atlanta either. She'd fallen in love with Rod and wanted to spend more time with him, not leave him. What were the chances of him coming to Atlanta to see her, or her returning to Hopkinsville anyway soon? Besides, she didn't want a long-distance relationship. For one, she wasn't a believer in them.

"I'm going to miss you. But I'll do my best to make it down in a couple of weeks. That is, if you want me to."

Natalie raised up looking at Rod in surprise. "You'll come to Atlanta to visit me?"

"Of course I will."

"But, I thought you hated Atlanta?"

"I don't hate it. I've never been there. What I hate is that the last woman I dated deserted me for Atlanta. After one visit to her cousin's in Atlanta, she wanted to be a city girl so bad. She wanted to spend life in the fast lane. All the nightclubs and concerts Atlanta had to offer enticed her. Hopkinsville can't compete with that."

"It shouldn't have to compete. I like it just the way it is. If you want, I can try to come back sometime soon."

"Like how soon?"

"I don't know, maybe next month."

"Next month!" Rod leaned forward resting his elbows on his knees. "Natalie that's a long time without seeing you. I don't like long-distance relationships, but I don't want to lose you. We need to be spending more time together, not less."

She wrapped her arms around his arm and leaned on his shoulder again. "I know."

"Are you still leaving today?"

"I'm going to leave around six in the morning. I don't like to drive once it gets dark."

"Then I get to spend the evening with you?"

"If you want to."

"I do. I know you need to say goodbye to your family and all, but can I pick you up around six? We can just sit and talk."

"Okay, I'll be ready."

Natalie spent the rest of the morning packing and saying goodbye to her family. Grachel cried as she left Wanda's house. She thanked Wanda and Arthur for everything they'd given her in the last two weeks.

Pauline fixed Natalie a big dinner and they sat down to talk before Rod showed up.

"So I see you've quit treating him like he has the plague."

"Aunt Polly I never treated him like that. I was just scared he'd turn out like Kevin. But, like you said, all men aren't alike. Once I realized that and opened my mind to a few things I saw him differently."

"You learned a lot during Kwanzaa didn't you?"

"Yes, I did. And you know when I get back to Atlanta I'm going to take a close look at my life. I need to change a few things. First of all I'm going to examine my purpose in life. I never realized before that I don't have any direction. I've just been living from day to day."

"Honey, everybody needs goals, or a plan in life."

"Well before I thought Kevin and I would get married one day and I'd settle with being a housewife. But, you know, that's not want I want to do. When I get home I'm going to make some definite choices in my life. A family is important to me. My family is so spread apart, it's hard for us to unite the way we should."

"You're not thinking about moving to Minneapolis are you?"

"Are you kidding, I couldn't stand the cold. I know Mama handles it, but not me. However, I am going to focus on my family more. Maybe next year I can get all of us together to celebrate Kwanzaa."

"Now that sounds good."

The doorbell rang and Natalie quickly finished her food while Pauline went to let Rod in.

He took Natalie for dessert and coffee. They spent the next couple of hours talking about how much they'd miss each other, and how long it would be before they met again. Rod expressed his concern for her returning and having to deal with Kevin. He wanted her to call the police if Kevin showed up at her apartment.

Because she had to get up early the next morning, he reluctantly took her back to her aunt's house. They sat in the car for several more minutes, not wanting to leave one another.

"Natalie, call me the minute you get in town. After you call your aunt, of course. And don't forget, if Kevin shows up . . ."

"I know, call the police. Rod, I have no intention of letting him into my house, trust me."

"I know you won't. I'm just so afraid for you that's all. I wish I could go back with you."

A few minutes later, Natalie pulled herself away from him and walked into the house. She stood in the doorway and watched as his truck moved slowly down the street.

Natalie returned to Atlanta and the stress of her job. Every time she picked up the phone she prayed it would be Rod. A couple of times her prayers came true. He called everyday. At night they talked on the phone for hours. She missed him terribly.

Kevin came by, but she pretended she wasn't at home and didn't answer the door. She called the police to report someone lurking around her apartment. Kevin was still outside when the cops showed up. Two weeks later, she hadn't heard a peep from him.

At night when Natalie went to bed she dreamed of Rod. They had one wonderful night together. One very special night. She'd told her girlfriends about him and they all wanted to meet him. He had plans to come to Atlanta at the end of the month, but she didn't think she could wait that long.

After a terrible day at work, Natalie walked into her apartment and slammed the door. She'd had about all she could take. She kicked off her shoes, flopped down on the couch and picked up the phone.

"Hello."

"Hi."

"Natalie?"

"Yeah, it's me."

"What's wrong, baby, you don't sound so good." Rod detected a slight quiver in her voice.

"Remember when you asked me about giving Hopkinsville and you a chance?" *Here goes,* she said to herself.

"Yes."

"Well, I'm ready."

Rod exhaled. "What do you mean, you're ready?"

"I want to be with you. Can you come get me?"

"For how long?"

"For good."

"Baby, I'm as good as there. These have been the hardest three weeks of my life. I need you. We need each other."

Natalie wanted to cry she was so happy. "During my vacation I learned that I need a lot of things. I need my family. I need to take control of my life, and live it as I want to. I also need to do more for others. But most of all, I need you."

Six months later Natalie had her grand opening of Imani's, her specialty clothing boutique in the heart of Hopkinsville's antique district. Rod took her out to celebrate the occasion, and pulled a small blue velvet box from his jacket pocket during dessert.

They were engaged, and Natalie was truly happy with her new life. She had a job she enjoyed, lived in a town she loved, and had the man she'd been looking for all her life.

A New Year, A New Beginning

Candice Poarch

Prologue

As the sun cast its last hour's glow of the day over the cragged formations, Amanda Burns looked into the vast picturesque scene of the Grand Canyon. A sudden sadness, in contrast with the bright colors of orange, red, yellow, and gray, washed over her as the late September day displayed signs of the autumn season.

What should have been tender evenings of relaxing and conversations, sweet kisses and hand holding, that rejuvenation of love she'd planned for years with her husband, had turned into a solitary vacation.

Amanda was not supposed to be here alone. It should have been her first honeymoon with her husband of twenty-two years. She'd pleaded and begged for this trip so many times until he finally gave in. Since that time, five years ago, Brian had postponed it year after year saying he and Adam Somerville needed to work on this project or that one until it was much too late.

She'd grown to have a keen dislike for the unreasonable amount of time Adam had demanded from her marriage. If she heard it once, she'd heard it a thousand times. "Adam thinks they need to do this" or "Adam needs to do that," especially around the time they had made special plans. The man had even called her, asking her not to take her trip alone. As if it were any of his business.

Now, as Amanda stood overlooking the vast beauty of the Grand Canyon, her eyes misted and she unlocked the tight grip she held on her purse strings.

Brian was gone forever. He died in June last year. She'd gone through the "firsts." The first time doing any number of things as half of a pair. The lack of warm, sweet memories to lift her spirits still disturbed her. And worst yet, she considered for the first time, if they were together what would they do? Special intimacies had left their marriage long ago. They had each gravitated to their own little worlds. Their separate worlds. On his deathbed, Brian had gripped her hand and said he loved her. And she wanted to scream, "Don't tell me now." Why didn't he show her all those lonely days and nights when he'd cast her away and she'd had to create a world of her own if only to maintain her sanity. High school dreams of peace and love ever after had been destroyed, dying with Brian's last breath. It was too late now.

As she stood in her little piece of the vast canyon, Amanda tried not to slump into the gloom of why they hadn't shown each other that love while he was here. "Why did your friends mean so much more than your own wife? Why did Adam mean more?" Amanda whispered as warm tears washed a line down her cheeks.

Why weren't we each other's best friends?

As the sun slowly slipped away, the few warm memories she did have seemed a lifetime away.

Shaking her head and trying to clear it, she thought of their son, Josh. He had called just before she came to ask her if he could vacation during the holidays in Montana with his roommate. Trying not to be a clinging mother, she'd responded with a "yes."

With a touch of selfishness, Amanda wondered exactly where that left her? Spending Christmas and New Year's alone. She sighed with the loneliness and the burdens of single parenthood. Brian had handled all the finances in the past but had left nothing for Josh's education. She'd been forced to sell the Land Rover that Brian loved so much to pay for Josh's junior and senior years of college.

Now Josh wanted to go to veterinarian school and she didn't have the money to send him. Brian had willed the insurance money to the business to compensate for the loss of his position. He had built up only a very small savings through the years, since most of the money went back into the business. He'd said over and over that the company needed to keep up with technology to stay on top. Even the house was more a business venture than a comfortable haven. She'd been the perfect corporate wife, entertained more clients, thrown more business New Year's parties, and since many times Brian couldn't make it back from his business trips in time to attend, she had given them alone more times than she cared to think about.

Now she was at loose ends. Adam Somerville, Brian's partner for the last fifteen years, mailed her a monthly check that covered her expenses and small extras, but not enough to cover the enormous fees of veterinarian school.

The volunteer work she did at church was emotionally rewarding but not economically practical right now. At least the senior's center she helped plan and the entertainment drive she'd engineered were successful endeavors. They wouldn't continue to require the enormous hours.

As the last of the sun disappeared into the horizon, Amanda started back to her car. It was time she found her place in life alone. This trip marked the beginning of her new independence, even though it was painful.

Now, she needed to provide for Josh's future.

Chapter 1

"Think positive" was her decree. Amanda looked at her numbered items in her Day Timer. This call was step one. Soon she'd be able to scratch a line through it. Mission accomplished. She took a deep breath before speaking.

"I want to sell my share of the business to you," she told Adam Somerville. Her positive resolve lasted all of five seconds as she listened, tight-lipped through the satellite connection, hating having to go to that man for anything. The Day Timer and lists weren't doing their job the way they were supposed to. Irritated by the prolonged silence that greeted her announcement, she tightened her hand around the phone as she held it to her ear and, with nothing to do with her other hand, drummed her fingertips against the blue tiled kitchen counter top.

"We're in the process of expanding. I don't have the money to buy you out right now." In her mind's eye, she could almost see the creases in his forehead from concentration. He usually gave his undivided attention to the problem at hand. "If you could give me a year or two . . ."

How many times had she heard that line from Brian, *Wait*

a year for this Amanda, or Wait a year for that, Amanda thought as she drowned Adam's voice out. No more waiting. "I need the money now." Life was much too short to wait. If she'd demanded more from Brian, maybe. . . .

"Is something wrong? Can I help you with anything?" came his conciliatory reply.

"No, just buy out my share of the company." She knew she sounded like a shrew, but couldn't stop herself. He made her feel incompetent, like a child begging for an allowance. It was her money after all. He had no right to make her feel this way.

She flipped the Day Timer to another page for the affirmations she'd jotted down to help her day go more smoothly. *Stay calm,* she read.

"As I said . . . ," came his reasonable voice, as if he were soothing a troubled client. It only fueled her temper more.

"Then you can find a buyer. Or I can sell to the Blakes. Joel Blake approached me again a week ago." She wouldn't actually sell to the competition, but he didn't need to know that.

"I hope you won't do that. I can't raise the spare cash right away. I need a little time for this new expansion to take place. If you need money for anything, I can get it for you, but not enough to buy you out. The company is your son's legacy . . ."

Line two of her affirmations said "take calming breaths." She took two. It didn't help. Her hand was cramped by its stranglehold on the phone. He didn't have a twenty-year-old son to worry about.

"He's part of the reason I need the money." Her calm voice belied her inner turmoil. She hadn't meant for that to slip. Adam had a way of rattling her even at the best of times. Amanda sighed. Now that she'd started, she knew she had to finish the thought. "He wants to attend veterinarian school. He isn't interested in satellite communications. Without Brian, there's no reason for me to stay in the business." She wasn't about to elaborate that her husband hadn't provided the funds to cover Josh's continued education. She didn't have the money to send him to vet school. But money was money. The sale of her stock would work just as well. The company had always come first with Brian. Not so with her.

Amanda could imagine Adam's thick black brows furrowing. His hand swiping across his stern, thoroughly masculine face in irritation with her. His tone contained barely leashed annoyance. Even though they rarely saw each other, his dark brown features, sharp eyes, and controlled smile were so imposing they were impossible to forget.

"I can raise the money for his college education. He is Brian's son, after all, and my godson."

"This isn't your concern. If I sold my shares, I'd be able to afford it." She wanted to sever all connections with the past. As Brian's family had done to her. They blamed her for his heart attack and refused to have anything to do with her.

She heard a voice in the background.

"Look, I'm coming there soon. Josh is a junior this year. We have some time to work things out. We'll have the money for his education." He chuckled in a familial way. "We've worked as partners for the last fifteen years . . ."

"You and Brian were partners," she interrupted.

"Same thing. We can work this through. You don't have to want for anything. I'll see to that."

"I'm not your responsibility." Amanda gritted her teeth.

"Look, Brian was my best friend, as well as my partner. I wouldn't be much of a friend if I didn't see that your needs were satisfied. Let's talk about this when I get there. Don't make any hasty decisions." Someone called out. "We'll talk when I get there. I'll see you New Year's."

Contemplating his last statement, Amanda hung up the phone on the kitchen wall. *I'll see you for New Year's.* Brian had made that very same statement year after year when he had to travel to the Ivory Coast just before the holidays. He'd said it before their last Christmas together. Tears misted her eyes with the memory of her past anticipation of his arrival. And she didn't know if the tears were from the loss of him or a loss of her dreams. Dreams she'd hoped would come true once Brian wasn't so busy anymore.

She had nothing to look forward to this year.

Amanda expected the pain to stab as it had before. For some reason, it wasn't quite as sharp as it had been last year, a short few months after his death. Still, the loneliness had worsened. And Christmas was closing in, the worst season of the year for someone alone.

At a glance around the kitchen, she knew she should be counting her blessings instead of wallowing in self-pity. She had a house in an upper middle income neighborhood in Fairfax, Virginia, a short drive from D.C., most women would love to have. And a monthly check arrived to cover the expenses. A check she didn't work for. Still, she craved for more. Those were all material possessions. She needed something—perhaps something for her soul. She needed to accomplish something meaningful for herself.

Arms swinging back and forth, Amanda speed-walked on the neighborhood track, her breath expelling in cloudy puffs.

"Hold up some, will you?" Struggling along to catch up, Lottie Rodgers wore hot pink, form-fitting spandex covered with three layers of sweats on her upper body to keep in the heat. "What're you doing? Trying to win a marathon?"

Amanda slowed her pace and turned while marching in place, not realizing that while so deep in thought, she'd left the woman behind. "Sorry. You're a little slow today, aren't you?"

Finally reaching her, Lottie bent over to catch a breath. "What the hell is wrong with you today?" Air whistling through her teeth, she straightened and they resumed their five-mile walk at a more leisurely pace. "You act like you've got a bee in your bonnet."

"In the name of Adam Somerville," Amanda huffed, barely taking in the brown leaves of the massive oak. She usually enjoyed her commune with nature on these walks.

"What's he done now?" Lottie asked as one who'd heard it all before and then some.

"I called to tell him I wanted to sell my stock last night. With the big expansion, he wants me to hold off. I can't sell anyway for a year. The bylaws say I have to give him that long to purchase before I offer it to someone else." Amanda's teeth gritted. Yesterday at this time she thought it would all be settled by now. Her life would be on the right track with a straight line drawn through item number one.

"Do you really want to sell that stock? It's a great company." It wasn't often that Lottie made sense, this was one of those rare occasions. Under any other circumstances, Amanda would hold on.

"It isn't a matter of choice. I need the money for Josh's education."

"Oh, that's right. He wants to be a vet now," was her dubious reply.

Amanda looked sideways at her friend, suspicious of her tone. "Why did you say it like that?"

"He's a junior. He'll probably change his mind at least a dozen times before he graduates."

"I don't think so. He's so goal-oriented and he's always loved animals." He was the exact opposite of Lottie's two children who'd changed majors with the end of each semester. Poor Henry finally put his foot down and demanded they choose one major or else.

"Still, it would be nice if you can hold onto the company. You did get some insurance money to tide you over after Brian died, didn't you?"

"The insurance went to Worldwide Satellites. Nothing for Josh and me to live off of."

"That worm!" The woman stopped and Amanda had to pull on her arm to get her moving again. Lottie came up with too many reasons for rest stops during their walks. This wasn't going to be one of them.

"I'm looking for a job after the new year, but it's going to take a while for me to work my way up in the company."

"A job!" A particularly big cloud puffed out as Lottie slowed and placed hands on her hips. "Hell, you own half the company, don't you? Just hire yourself on. You couldn't be in a better position. Think up some job you'd like to do and tell that stiff lip what salary you want for the job you decide to hire yourself on as."

Leave it to Lottie to think she could railroad herself into the company. "It's not that easy. Adam's the CEO. I have to go through him."

"Last time I heard, fifty percent means you've got as much say as he does. Lord, child, what the hell would you do without me?" Throwing her arms in the air, Lottie sighed. "This way we can still do the things we enjoy like torturing ourselves three times a week in twenty degree weather so you can stay slim."

"You wouldn't be dieting so much if you didn't eat a box of chocolates after every walk."

"It's my reward for this torture," she sputtered as she plodded on, leading Amanda now. "This way we can continue these idiotic walks."

"I'll be working. It's time I put the degree I got when Josh was a baby to work for me. I won't be able to take off in the middle of the morning to exercise."

"Why not?"

Amanda had forgotten for a moment that Lottie went through jobs the way a child went through cookies. She got a new one at least once a year. And if she was lucky—very lucky—she'd last two weeks. The last time she was fired, Lottie was incensed when her boss had taken exception to what he called her "excessive breaks." She told him that she needed a ten-minute break every half hour. It just wasn't humanly possible to sit behind the desk and answer phones for three-hour stretches without one. He'd kindly told her she could break the entire day from then on.

Fortunate for Lottie, her husband was vice-president of a local brokerage firm. She really didn't need to bring in an income, but felt, with all the women getting into careers, to be a whole woman she needed one, too.

She was still working on the perfect career for herself. Her children had at least completed something, even though they were now working on their doctorates. And Lottie's husband had learned long ago, to have a peaceful household, to let her explore without comment from him.

All in all, they had a wonderful marriage. Henry loved Lottie immensely and she loved him in return. Amanda still didn't understand how a solid man like Henry could be attracted to a scatterbrain like Lottie.

They walked silently for minutes, each in her own thoughts.

"If you didn't get any insurance, how are you taking care of yourself?"

"I get a monthly check from the company."

"Well, what do you need to work for? You're getting money anyway. You're just thinking up problems. Had me thinking you were on the verge of bankruptcy."

"I need some stability, some purpose in my life. Can you understand that?" Frustrated, and holding back tears, Amanda clamped her jaw tight and stared.

"Honey, you've got purpose," Lottie said softly. "You do all that volunteer work at church with Everett. You care about people. You stay busy. There's only one of you." She patted Amanda on the arm, geared up for the last two miles. "My brother has been lucky to have a worker like you in church." Amanda knew that Everett's career as a minister still baffled Lottie, though after all the years, she accepted it and helped him.

"I feel like I'm getting paid for nothing. I'm not working for that check. And I should be."

"It's the least your husband could have left you. You did work for it. All those business dinners. The New Year's party you plan every year. Don't forget you raised your son almost single-handedly. You do plenty.'' The silence stretched a moment. ''I know we don't value what we often do, but that's work, too. It builds up a good rapport with the clients and the employees. You work very hard for that money.''

''I guess.'' Uncertainty cloaked her voice as much as it had cloaked her life this last year.

''There's no guessing about it. Just count yourself lucky that if anything happens, you can fall back on that stock. In the meantime, just be cool, and as my brother would say, 'Count your blessings.' ''

Amanda laughed and shook her head. ''There's still Josh's education.''

''I've already told you the solution for that.''

''There's no need for me to hold onto the company. Josh isn't interested in it. And with selling it, I'll have more than I need for the rest of my life. I don't need that much to live off. I could even sell the house and get something smaller.'' The maintenance and lawn were only a small fraction of the work required to maintain a home. A condo would be less work.

''Sell that beautiful house?''

''It's too big for one person. I've been thinking about it a lot lately.'' She'd miss the neighborhood, the familiar surroundings and people. Change was the most difficult of challenges.

''Now don't go making major decisions when you're down in the dumps. Take small steps at a time. Tell you what. They're having a makeover for women at church tomorrow night. Now that I've lost a few pounds, I'm looking forward to some new makeup and clothes.''

They waved to a neighbor walking his dog on the opposite side of the street.

''My spirits and clothing are just fine, thank you.'' Her closet was filled with serviceable suits and church dresses.

''I know, I know, but it wouldn't hurt to try something different. If for nothing else, think of the charitable cause. It's to help displaced women get on their feet.''

That did the trick. "Well, we could try it out." She could always use a new sweater or something to life her spirits.

Amanda soaked in the Jacuzzi after her walk, then dressed and ambled into the foyer. It was a week after Thanksgiving and time for her to put up Christmas decorations. With a glance at the boxes full of ribbons, bulbs, and garlands for decorating scattered on her living room floor, a bit of nostalgia hit her. This would be the last company New Year's party she would host. In the last week, the cleaning crew had washed every window and dusted every cranny in preparation for the holidays. The company employees, along with their spouses and business acquaintances, would attend. For years, she'd prepared the lavish dinner and cleaned the house herself. Until one year Adam had, on a rare occasion, traveled back with Brian for the holidays and requested that she hire a cleaning crew for the house and a caterer for the food. She'd marveled at how uncharacteristically thoughtful he seemed.

Amanda dug into the box and pulled out a star that Brian topped the tree with each year. That had been the finishing touch. After they'd gathered glasses of wine and Josh a warm cup of hot cider before turning the room lights out and the tree lights on. Brian had laughed and toppled on the unsteady ladder they never seemed to replace. Awash in contentment, they sat back to digest and enjoy the rewards of their loving labor. She relished it so because those occasions were rare.

She untangled a string of bulbs to hang on the twelve-foot tree, which stood in a prominent place in the foyer. It was best to keep busy.

Across the Atlantic Ocean, in the Ivory Coast, Adam shook hands with Gil Macklin and walked him to the office door, wishing he'd dare take the rest of the morning off to enjoy the perfect sunny weather outside. Instead he stalked back to his own office where Sheryl Weber, his office assistant, was rearranging chairs. Expansions didn't happen and business didn't move by shirking his duty.

"All right," she said in a stern voice, hands on hips. "You may as well tell me about it. Something's been worrying you all afternoon." Her colorful mauve dress with delicate needle work reached midcalf. She wore slacks beneath it. He enjoyed the colorful African fashion all the women wore.

Adam dropped into the leather chair behind his desk.

"That bad, hum?" She raised an eyebrow.

"Worse." He sighed. "It's that flighty wife of Brian's."

"What's she done?" With coffee cup in hand, she took the chair across from him.

He leaned forward, elbows on the desk. "Now that I'm practically down to bare bones in finances with the expansion, she wants to sell the company." Beyond disgusted, he rose and stalked to the window, half turned and pounced on Sheryl again. "You'd think she'd have *some* sense of responsibility, some respect for the hard work Brian and I've sweated to make this company what it is today!" His hand sliced the air.

"And *worse,* if I can't buy out her share, which I can't, she wants to sell to the Blake brothers. How long do you think the company will survive then? They're a resale company. They don't care who they hurt when they sell parts of it away. Half the employees would be out of jobs within the year. But do you think she'll worry about that? No, she'll have her fat bank roll put away without giving a care about anyone else. She owns half the business. She can do anything she wants to." He sank into his seat, drawing out a long sigh.

"Oh, Adam, she wouldn't really sell, would she?"

He shook his head. "I don't know. Brian always said she was flighty. Didn't have a head for business. No telling what she'd do." Sheryl had worked for Adam for years and had his complete confidence. He knew anything he said would stay with the two of them.

"You and Brian got along so well together. You wouldn't find a partner like that again."

"I really miss him. His cousin raised me after my parents died."

"Really? You never talked about your family," she said softly.

"No." He opened his mouth as if to say something and changed his mind.

"Don't you think it's time? I've always wondered about that icy veneer of yours."

He grinned that twisted smirk he was famous for. "The original ice man," he knew they called him. But suddenly a warm smile covered his features. "We were very poor and very happy. My dad went from job to job. He was a fun man and he loved his family. My mom," a catch marred his voice, "my mom loved him and me more than anything. Regardless of where we were or what idiotic business venture he got into, she loved him and she believed in him."

"You were fortunate, weren't you?" Her eyes were gentle with understanding.

"I was." He didn't feel fortunate after they died and he had no one. But looking back, he realized he was.

"Adam, Brian always thought too much of himself. Amanda may be a different woman from what you think." She paused as if to weigh her words. "You're going back to the states. You're going to be near her. I have yet to see a better salesman than you. You'll be able to convince her to keep the business. I have complete confidence in you." She rose from her seat and gathered the coffee pot. "I'll bring your mail in."

Adam watched her tall dark graceful form glide out the office and wondered why he wasn't romantically attracted to her.

"Here's the mail." She placed the stack on his desk.

"Thank you, Sheryl. For everything."

"Anytime." She left, closing the door quietly behind her.

The heat was oppressive, but he was glad to be here. Thick emotions clogged his throat. He was going to miss her most of all when he moved back to Virginia where the corporate office was located. Some of the company's most lucrative satellite transmission services accounts were here. His replacement, however, was more than qualified to manage them.

As the CEO, Adam needed to be in the corporate offices. After spending the last ten years here, he was in for a huge readjustment.

He shuffled though business letters and marketing barbs until he recognized a letter from Josh. Putting the others aside, he picked up the silver letter opener to slash the top. A scrap of paper had been hastily scribbled on. He opened it and read.

Hi, Uncle Adam,

Sorry I'm going to miss you for Christmas vacation. I'll be in Montana with my roommate. He lives on a ranch, so I'll get plenty of prevet practice and lots of snow this year.

I'm glad you're coming home so Mom won't be alone. The house is so big and lonely for her and filled with memories. You could stay there until you get your own place. And you can keep her spirits up for the Holiday. Otherwise she'd brood. I'm counting on you. Thanks, Uncle Adam.

Got to study for exams. Talk to you over the Holidays.

Josh

Thoughtfully, Adam folded the paper in half thinking fondly of his only godson. Brian had brought the boy to Africa twice on trips and Amanda joined them once.

Adam could stay at the house—or try to.

Amanda was likely to toss him out on his ears. He stroked his chin as he considered. The house was half his, a point he hadn't brought to her attention and wondered if Brian had. She couldn't sell the stock for a year without his approval. Without angering her, that would give him time to find out what was going on in her life and convince her not to sell the stock at all.

Adam dropped the letter on the ebony desk. He was going to miss this place when he left. Vivid woven cloths and masks hung on the wall. Looking outside at the tropical setting, it scarcely seemed like Christmas.

Ten years had passed since he'd celebrated the holidays in the States. Suddenly, Adam was looking forward to it—no matter what mood Amanda might be in.

Chapter 2

He'd always thought Amanda was pretty, but pretty was too bland for the smile that hit just the right angle, the eyes a spark of sunshine on a dreary day, lips that invited a man's kiss, and rounded curves a man's dream.

Feeling like he'd been kicked in the solar plexus, Adam wondered what bomb had suddenly dropped on him. What happened to the homey plain-looking woman, the wife of his partner? Straight suits and subdued lines. The red form-fitting sweater with huge white petals over the shoulders softened her face, outlined generous breasts.

Adam pulled up short. A man did not think of his best friend's wife's breasts. But what else could he think with her so inappropriately attired? It was all her fault, her unconscious sensuality causing him to have indecent thoughts of her. If she'd dressed as she should have, he wouldn't have these unseemly thoughts. That wasn't quite true. He'd always felt some stirring around her he failed to identify. This stirring always brought on the guilt. It was also the reason he jumped at the opportunity in Africa. He didn't have the safety of Brian and distance now. He did, however, uphold common decency.

The red and her cherry countenance made her appear all Christmasy and bright. Added to the form-fitting blue jeans, she was hot. At least until she noticed him at her door.

"Adam." She greeted him in that sweet husky voice that fired his senses no matter how capricious she was. Looking from his face to the suitcase she managed a barely cordial, "Come in." With raised eyebrows, Adam took her comment more as a question than statement. He let it ride as she stepped back to allow him entrance while continuing to glance at his suitcase as he passed her. Adam still hadn't decided how to handle the sticky situation.

But the suitcase was forgotten completely when the magnificently decorated twelve-foot cypress standing proudly in the huge foyer immediately drew his attention. Strains of "Silent Night" floated in the background. It reminded him of his youth. His parents had always decorated huge trees. And they'd seemed so beautiful with strung paper, popcorn, and tin cutouts. Amanda's was decorated more lavishly, but it still exuded the feeling of warmth and caring. To his surprise, the decorations he'd mailed to her through the years were on the tree. Whenever he traveled, he'd purchase gifts for Brian's family. He always choose hanging decorations for Amanda.

A discrete cough from the living room drew his attention. To his annoyance, he saw that she was entertaining company. Male company. He left his suitcase by the door to shrug out of his newly purchased cashmere coat and handed it to the waiting Amanda. An introduction to the frigid temperature in New York the previous day had induced him to make the hasty purchase. As she hung it in the spacious hall closet, Adam advanced into the living room, decorated in discrete antiques. A man dressed casually in a sweater and slacks sat on a comfortable Queen Anne sofa. Gray hair peppered his temples. Adam had often heard it made women go wild. His lips tightened. Was Amanda going wild over those streaks of gray?

The pleasant smile on the man's face further irritated Adam. "Good afternoon." The man rose as Amanda entered behind Adam.

"Reverend Smart, meet Adam Somerville, Brian's partner. I think I mentioned to you he'd be moving to the area."

"Yes, you did."

Adam relaxed a little at hearing the man's title, but not for long once he noticed the rev's ring finger was bare. Adam threw a tight smile as he shook hands with him. The reverend had no business at his home trying to make passes at his best friend's wife. With an outward affable appearance, Adam extended his hand. "How are you, Reverend Smart?"

"Ah, what's this 'reverend' business among friends? Call me Everett." The man passed a secret grin to Amanda that further annoyed Adam. "Welcome back to the States."

"Thank you."

Amanda took the seat across from Everett, so Adam sat on the delicate love seat beside her. Adam frowned as Amanda leaned over to reach the tea pot, her V-necked sweater cutting a little deeper than he thought appropriate. "We're having tea. Would you like a cup, Adam?"

"Thank you," he responded, almost regretting his answer when he noticed the direction of the rev's eyes. Adam cleared his throat to divert the man's attention.

"How are your parents, Amanda?"

She looked up from her task. "Enjoying Europe," she answered. "I'm glad they finally took the trip. They delayed it long enough."

"And Josh?"

"He'll be out of school in two weeks."

"I'm going to miss him this year."

"So am I," she said quietly. "Sometimes I wish I'd said, no."

Everett reached over and covered her hand. "You did the right thing by letting him go."

"I suppose." A vulnerable smile escaped before she swallowed hard and lifted her chin boldly.

"We'll keep you too busy at church to get lonely." He squeezed her hand and leaned back.

Amanda's smile was more confident this time.

"I won't take up much more of your time. I know you two need to talk." He turned to Adam. "How was you trip, Adam?"

"Long," was Adam's short reply.

She relaxed enough to laugh for the first time. "Oh, yes. Brian often complained about it whenever he traveled so far," she said in the strained atmosphere. The good humor drifted away at the mention of Brian's name, to be replaced with sadness.

Adam wanted the radiance back and could have kicked himself for putting her on the defensive. There was probably a legitimate reason for the pastor's visit, other than his obvious interest in his best friend's widow. A very attractive widow. A very *rich* widow. Adam wondered if the reason Amanda needed the money had anything to do with financing any of the rev's ventures. After all, Amanda was a very wealthy woman, if one considered the value of her stock.

She walked with Everett to the door and the rev used the opportunity to grab her hand and squeeze it before he took his coat from her.

Soft hands, Adam remembered from their shake. Hands that probably never experienced the callouses of manual labor. Adam looked at his own hands. They'd seen many callouses as a teenager, callouses so deeply ingrained they never went away. Those callouses were one of the reasons he'd worked so hard to get into college and again to maintain a 3.9 average once there. Adam swore he'd have a better life. A life that would afford him more than the bare necessities and the many extras for comfort.

Now, all of that was threatened by Amanda's desire to sell her stock. His stomach roiled at the thought of loosing the business after pouring his life's blood into it for the last fifteen years. How could he convince someone who'd never had to lift a finger toward it what the company meant to Brian and him? Adam rubbed his forehead, willing away an impending headache. Perhaps if he increased her monthly allotment, she'd at least hold onto the business long enough for him to raise the money to buy her out. But with the expansion, that could take years. He remembered his father, the failed businesses, the lost jobs. At least his dad had an understanding wife who knew what it was to love and stand by a man. Really love a man. Adam only had his business.

The reverend's voice brought him out of his contemplations.

"It was a pleasure meeting you, Adam. I hope you enjoy living in the States."

"I'm sure I will, thank you."

"We'll meet on Friday to purchase the food for the shelter. I'll pick you up," he said to Amanda.

"I'll be ready," Amanda said before she closed the door against freezing temperatures that hovered in the twenties.

Adam looked around her living room. She had it all. A designer's dream of decorations and furniture. A loving son in college, and money to spare. She didn't want for anything. What more could she possibly desire? She could keep all her money. He'd pay for Josh's education. He owed Brian that much. Since Adam didn't have children of his own, the closest he'd get to a son at forty-five was Josh. At the same time, perhaps it would buy him time with Amanda.

Flustered, Amanda had to force herself not to pat her hair before stepping back into the room. She hadn't expected Adam for a few days yet.

He always looked perfectly put together, perfectly proper, and at six feet, much too tall and attractive for so cynical a man. The suitcase worried her. There was plenty of hotel space in town. Even when Brian was alive, he'd never stayed at her house, always preferring the freedom and privacy of a hotel room. Why would he arrive with suitcase in hand now?

Uneasy, Amanda eyed the suitcase again. Perhaps it was

filled with important papers she needed to see. She had no idea why he didn't bring them in a briefcase as most normal people would have. She would still give him the benefit of doubt. There must be too many papers to fit into a briefcase, she told herself staunchly.

He'd made himself comfortable while she'd seen Everett out. With one arm stretched out across the back of the chair, not even the cable-stitched sweater could conceal the muscled strength in his shoulders and arms. A shiver flashed over her.

She would not be intimidated by him this time. If he thought for one second that she would tolerate his presence under her roof for one night, he had another thought coming. Head held high, she took the seat on the sofa Everett had vacated. Adam's mouth jerked into a half smile. Amanda abhorred being anyone's source of amusement. "So," she said smartly at a loss for words. How did one broach the subject of the suitcase without sounding stupid?

"I must thank you for permitting me to stay here until I find a place of my own." Adam didn't have the same lack of conversational skills.

"Excuse me?" Now, owl-eyed, Amanda looked at him in horror. Unable to close her startled mouth, she knew she must look like a fish. If she was speechless before, she was even moreso now. "You . . . you must be mistaken." She shook her head. "You couldn't possibly . . ."

"Josh's room. He offered it when he wrote to me a week ago. I was sure he got your permission first." Adam leaned forward and scrubbed a hand across tired features. "I was so thankful for the invitation. I've been busy with getting everything in order for the move. And after your call, I moved the date up. It'll also give me a chance to go through Brian's papers. There's so much stored here. It'll save me the time of driving back and forth from a hotel."

"There's one that's not too far from here," came her weak reply.

"You wouldn't want me coming and going, disturbing you

at all times of the day and night. I talked to a real estate agent before I left Africa. They should have something soon after the beginning of the year. That should give me ample time to get Brian's papers in order. Even though I own fifty percent of this house, I've always considered it yours and Brian's. I wouldn't dream of imposing on you.''

Amanda's head swam. ''You own half this house?'' Her voice squeaked. ''What are you talking about?'' If she wasn't already seated, she would have fallen.

''You mean Brian didn't tell you?''

She shook her head no.

''He said you loved it. I was single and didn't need much space. I paid half the down payment and monthly mortgage. After all, we used to have our offices in the basement. Some equipment is still down there, isn't it?''

''Yes . . .''

''Good.'' He stood. ''I'm bushed. If you show me to Josh's room, I think I'll crash for the next twenty hours.''

Before Amanda knew what had hit her, Adam had unpacked the car and his luggage was safely ensconced in the spare bedroom upstairs, at the opposite end of the hall from hers, instead of Josh's room, and she was downstairs in her—their— kitchen wondering what tornado had hit her.

Not only had she not thrown him out, she'd quickly fallen into the role of dutiful hostess as she put fresh sheets on the bed and dusted the furniture as he showered, even though it had already been dusted three days ago. Her critical eye made sure everything was in perfect order for him. He could stay the night, but tomorrow he absolutely had to leave.

As Amanda dumped the remains of the tea into the sink, she wondered how she could tell the half owner of her house that he couldn't stay there until he found other accommodations.

How could Brian do this to her? Her shoulders slumped. She was so unnerved, the situation almost sapped her energy as she allowed herself a quick few moments to wallow in the despair stealing over her. Had her husband just once considered her worthy of knowing about her own home? Did he honestly believe her head was filled with fluff? That she couldn't comprehend something as simple as her own living arrangements? What was she to do? She couldn't demand that Adam leave the home he owned. She couldn't find other accommodations for herself immediately. Without a job and money—a great deal of money—a real estate agent would laugh in her face if she went looking for another house.

She just had to sell her share of the company. She'd approach Adam with it at once. Once the stock was sold, she could afford another home. Nothing as large and elaborate as this one, though she'd grown to love it.

She considered the curtains, furniture, paintings, and wallpaper she'd spent months choosing. The huge kitchen with its egg shell wallpaper with burgundy and blue stripes was a woman's dream. The granite and tiled counter surfaces were so satisfying to work with. The round oak table by the huge bay window overlooking the flowers and trees in the backyard was perfect for relaxing with her family. Often she'd watch the birds and squirrels play as she took a moment to savor a cup of tea with her lunch.

Her neighbors were kind. A sudden sadness stole over her. She'd miss the people she'd come to know, many of them mothers like her, sharing their concerns for their children. They'd conversed many times as they watched their children play.

So much had changed in the last two years. This would only be one of many.

Her thoughts wandered to Everett. What would he think—and the volunteers she worked with? He was a handsome and kind man and she enjoyed his company as a friend. She wondered at the lack of romantic response for him. He'd be an easy man to love. Then she thought of the imposing Adam and the unwanted awareness. She couldn't possibly feel anything for that man. He was Brian's best friend.

As she sat in front of her dressing table, her fingers stilled in the process of spreading the cream over her smooth skin. How many surprises would she encounter before her life was in order again? As hard as she tried not to worry, her thoughts returned to her finances and the house.

This was exactly what happened when women didn't get involved in the family's finances. After Brian died, Adam had taken care of everything for her before returning to the Ivory Coast to train someone so he could transfer back to the States. Exactly as Brian had done during their marriage.

Amanda had been so surprised and devastated by Brian's death, she'd been incapable of taking care of anything. Now that the shock had worn off, she realized she needed to know more about their finances. She'd seen to the personal accounts, but after the day with the lawyer, Adam had taken care of the house and insurance. Half of what he'd said had just melted into grief. Now, she was more determined than ever to start a career and get her life in order. Starting right after the holidays. In the meantime, she'd work on her resume.

The next morning, Adam awakened refreshed to the smell of home-baked cookies and fresh coffee. A quick shower had him descending the stairs in short order. When he reached the kitchen Amanda was bent over, pulling one pan out of the oven and shoving another one in. He snatched up a cookie and munched, fixating on her shapely rear.

"Adam, you're eating cookies before breakfast," she admonished as she placed the hot pan on a rack.

"That's the kid in me," he said and snatched up another one, looking at the mountain of them on the counter tops. "Who's going to eat all of these?" He leaned against a cleared end of the counter.

"They're for the bazaar on Saturday. The proceeds go to

entertainment for the senior citizens.'' Pulling the mitt off, she asked with a tight smile, ''What would you like for breakfast?''

''Anything. I usually eat light.'' Her tone was anything but. It ranked that she disliked him. But why did she? He'd done nothing to warrant that internal hostility under her appearance of cordiality. He turned over backward to ensure her comfort.

''Well, I bought eggs and sausage while I was out this morning. It'll only take a few minutes to fix it.''

''I don't want to put you through any trouble,'' he replied in a mocking tone.

''No trouble at all.'' Her curt response was muffled as she bent to pull open the stove drawer to retrieve the frying pan.

''What can I do to help?'' Adam asked, angry that her acid tone didn't detract from his fascination with her.

Amanda gave him a strange look. She seemed to carry on an inner debate while she glanced at the cookies. Finally, she decided to put him to work. ''If you like, you can stack the cooled cookies into the tin over there.''

''Okay.'' He got up to do as she requested.

''The waxed paper is in that drawer, and layer them with the paper sheets,'' she said as she sliced the sausage into cakes and popped it into the frying pan. ''Put two dozen cookies into each container.'' As the sausage sizzled, Adam felt her scrutiny as he carefully layered cookies into the tins before topping them with the waxed paper and layering them again.

Her brows puckered and her eyes squinted as she surreptitiously watched him. He wondered again at her suspicious nature. So far, Adam realized, he'd done nothing to win her good graces as he'd planned to do.

''You can start in the office downstairs whenever you please. It's all ready for you,'' she said shortly.

''Thank you. I'll start tomorrow morning. My body is still on Ivory Coast time,'' he said easily. ''I've about burned out on work. The earth won't stop if I take one day for myself.''

She looked sharply, her eyes narrowing. ''Well, whenever it suits you,'' she snapped, and turned to flip the sausages.

Now, what had he done? No wonder he never married. "Is something wrong, Amanda?"

"No. How is the new project going?" She cracked eggs in a bowl.

He debated before he decided to let her non-answer ride for now. "One contract we're trying to get is going to keep me busy through the holiday. We should know something by the end of the year, or the beginning of next year." He topped one container and picked up another one. "How are the New Year's party preparations going?"

"Everything's on schedule."

"Between that and your volunteer work, you're quite busy aren't you?" Adam suddenly wondered just how busy the reverend was keeping her.

"Quite."

When she opened the oven door again, another wave of aromas mixed with that of the sausage. What really held Adam's attention was the yellow apron tied around the bright green blouse that accentuated her waistline. A waistline that had maintained its narrowness even after having a child. Not that he would have held it against her if her waist had thickened a bit during the course of nature. What he didn't agree on was all the tummy tucks and face lifts women had to suffer trying to hold onto the last scrap of youthfulness. Until the silver screen celebrated the old as well as the young, plastic surgery would be here to stay.

Then he caught himself. He was as bad as the reverend. Adam Somerville had no business looking at her derriere and waist.

"Adam have you thought about buying my shares of stock yet?" she asked.

Unprepared for the question, Adam was startled for a few heartbeats.

Chapter 3

"I have." Adam put the last filled canister on a pile with the others and decided to come forward with the idea that had been turning in his head for a week. "I need help with some of the contracts. Since you're looking for new directions—a new career so to speak, I thought you might be willing to help out with the company."

"I've never worked on those contracts before," Amanda said, uncertainty in her voice.

Adam filled in the blanks. "You went to night school and have a degree in business, as I recall, even though you never used it. Most of the work is common sense. You'll be working with Joe at first to learn the ropes." He leaned back assessing her. "Give it a try. Let's say, six months before you make a final decision." Thinking that she was spending too much time with the reverend, he added, "Of course, working for the company would cut into your other activities."

Amanda cleared her throat and looked away. "I realize that, with a career, I'd have less time for my volunteer work. I can do that on the weekends and in the evenings."

"Certainly." It was too much to hope she'd stay away from the man altogether.

"Don't worry about Josh," he added. "I can scrounge up enough money for his education. And as a working employee in the company, you'll be get a regular paycheck in addition to what you're getting now." He didn't want her worrying about Josh's education.

It seemed that an immediate weight lifted from Amanda's shoulders. She had no real idea what she could do. Her career aspirations could come down to what she could get in a tight job market. Wasn't this as good as any other? If she didn't jump at this opportunity, at forty she'd have to compete with others who'd been in their careers for years. Who would take a forty-year-old over a twenty-two-year-old when they could train that person at lower wages? And how much would her volunteer work really count with a company? She could say that she managed funds for the food shelter the church provided, or that she managed the senior entertainment program for a small retirement home run by the church or that she was PTA president for six years. But would they recognize those as legitimate skills when they could get a forty-year-old who has been in the job market for twenty years?

It didn't take her very long to reach a decision after all.

"I'll try it out." She set the plate of warmed, home-made apple sauce, sausage, eggs, and buttered toast in front of Adam, filled a glass with orange juice, and topped his coffee. She had tried not to think about how pleased she was, once again, watching a man eat, even if he wasn't involved with her, and with his affability, he was making it difficult for her to hold onto her acrimony. In the early days of her marriage, Brian and she had enjoyed many companionable mornings together, lingering over coffee to make the intimacy last.

Kitchen work certainly didn't detract from Adam's masculinity, Amanda thought. Her nerves were a tangled glob. Anger was easier than the treacherous desire racing through her.

This might be the longest six months of her life. She only

hoped she didn't live to regret this decision. She needed to remember that he was responsible for keeping Brian away from his family. Even though Brian ran the offices in the States, Adam was the leader.

"I think we'll work well together," Adam said as he sliced a piece of the sausage. The phone rang and with Amanda in the process of taking another batch of cookies out the oven, Adam answered it for her.

"Hello?" He listened a moment. "All rested from my trip. She's right here."

Amanda placed the hot pan on a trivet and picked up the phone. "Everett, hi." A smile that touched an unwelcome cord in Adam spread over her face when she discovered the caller's identity.

"No, no. They're almost done. You can pick them up tonight, but you really don't need to. I can see to it." She smiled at something he said. "Really, I'll bring them over. They aren't too much for me." She smiled and blushed again. "All right, I'll see you at church at . . ."—she looked at her watch—"let's see—three-thirty? Sure. Goodbye." Still smiling, she put the phone back on the hook.

"I can help you with the cookies," Adam said shortly. "You're going to have enough for an army." Why was her response so friendly to Everett and cold to him? That rankled. The smile still lingered on her face, the sparkle still lit her eyes. All that put together made her breathtaking when she was happy.

The stab of jealousy that racked Adam was so staggering and unwanted it shook him. She was Brian's wife. His best friend. He shouldn't have designs on her and she shouldn't have sweet smiles for Everett. It was too soon for her to even consider dating again.

"It's not that bad really," she said. "I'll welcome the help, though. But you should be resting. Everett volunteered to pick them up, but his hands are full with other preparations. He really gets involved with everything that happens at the church. We're so lucky to have him.''

That was more than she'd offered of her personal life since his arrival. Perhaps it was an indication that he'd done something right. Adam picked up the ball and ran with it.

''Um, I've already had plenty of practice boxing them. I'm a pro now,'' Adam responded. He'd reserve judgment on Everett.

They worked companionably for another two hours.

Later that day they loaded up the packages of cookies and took them to church. Adam's system still hadn't acclimated to the freezing temperatures and he shivered in his newly-purchased coat. A manger display featuring African-American characters and surrounded by soft lights was arranged prominently on the front lawn of the huge brick church that dated back to the late eighteen hundreds.

Adam only took a moment to enjoy the scene before he made quick work of unpacking the car. The church basement was noisy with the chatter of what seemed like more than a hundred volunteers and filled with the colorful lights of Christmas decorations and cheerful spirits. Before they could barely clear the door, Everett was hot on Amanda's heels.

''Amanda,'' he said, coming to a smiling halt. ''You made it.'' He glanced at Adam. ''And you bought Adam. Good of you to help our Amanda out.'' His tone was filled with possession. ''The seniors drive this year is a resounding success. Indeed, God has truly blessed us.''

Everett evidently took pride in a plan well-executed. There were enough boxes of cookies stacked in the place to feed a small town. That was all well and good, Adam thought, but the possessive note in the man's voice rankled.

''You actually expect to sell all these cookies?'' Adam asked, not believing enough people were around to purchase them.

''Last year we received over one thousand mail orders. This year that number tripled. Between the mail orders and what we'll make from the bazaar tomorrow morning, I don't think we have enough, though we've quadrupled our supply this year.

The cookies are becoming more and more popular. Lots of wonderful family recipes.''

With a myriad of conversations, one stood out above the others. "Keep your hands off my cookies, Harry," came a sharp voice.

Adam turned toward the harsh reprimand. A gentleman, every bit of ninety, was gingerly trying to snitch a box of cookies from the woman's pile.

The woman was at least five-ten and as spare as she was tall.

"One little box won't hurt, Mary. Give me just one box. You got a hundred here."

Stern, she stared him down with her hands on her hips. Poor Harry bent under the war of wills and slid the box with one arthritic finger back on the pile, his spare shoulders drooping. After winning the battle, Mary reached into her oversized purse, pulled out a huge plastic bag of cookies, and handed them to Harry.

"Ah," Harry groaned, a half smile showing half his teeth were missing, touched his face. "Thank you. You're all heart, Mary, to think of an old man."

"Uh-huh. Now go on back home before dark."

Harry got up with his cane in one hand and his bag of cookies in the other and slowly tottered his way out the door while the crowd looked on. The woman clearly had a soft spot for him.

"Brother Cox lives next to the church," Everett explained. "He's lived in this neighborhood all his life. Just loves Sister Mary's cookies though," Everett said. "They go through this every year."

Adam couldn't blame the man. He'd snitched a few of Amanda's while they packed, and made sure she saved a few for him. She promised to make him more. He would hold her to that promise, although she looked as though she regretted the impulse as soon as the words were spoken.

"So, are you all settled in and over the jet leg?"

"I am." Adam focused on the officious minister.

"I hope you were able to find good accommodations." It was a question. He must have noticed the suitcase.

"I was." Adam replied, but offered no more.

"Is it some place nearby?" Everett's brows furrowed.

"I'm staying with Amanda." May as well nip that little tryst in the bud right now.

Everett cast a quick look at Amanda who wouldn't meet his eyes.

"Reverend Smart?" someone called out.

"Excuse me. Yes?" He turned toward the voice.

"We can't get this cash register to work." The puzzled man was clearly at a loss.

"Well," Everett said, as he walked over to the machine, "I'm not an electronic wizard, but let's see."

"Did you have to tell him that?" Amanda snapped once Everett was out of hearing range.

"He asked." Adam shrugged and decided to help the hapless Everett out. After all, his spirits had elevated immensely.

Smarting, Amanda went over to her own cookies and started to pack her boxes into the shipping crates. They now sold almost as many by mail as they did from on-site sales.

Everything was well-coordinated. Volunteers printed out the addresses and labeled shipping boxes for the cookies. She merely had to stack hers into the boxes and someone would seal them tonight and ship them off. By tomorrow morning, the room would be set up and readied for Christmas shoppers. She had stuck her pack of cookies into a box and shoved packing paper over it when she felt a hand on her shoulder.

"Amanda, could you help me with something in my office, please?" Everett asked.

"Of course." She knew what he was about to say to her. Wearily, she followed him down the corridor to his spacious office, arranged as a combination sitting room and office. He spent so much time with counseling people that the committee felt he should have appropriate accommodations. The church was lucky to have someone who was willing to work as hard as he was. He'd engineered so many wonderful programs for the needy. The seniors entertainment project was just one of many. He had a true sense of the needs of people. An inner sense of their problems.

He closed the door slowly after they entered as if he needed time to pull his thoughts together.

Amanda geared herself for a lecture on inappropriate behavior in living arrangements. She decided to forestall it by explaining first.

"I know what you're going to say, Everett, but I didn't have a choice. He owns half the house. I can't very well refuse him." The arrangement warred with her conscience and what she thought was appropriate. She had a son to consider.

"I thought it belonged to you and Brian," he stated, perplexed.

"So did I." Amanda sighed and rubbed her brow.

"Come on and sit down." He grasped her hand and led her to the chair in front of his tidy desk Mary, as church secretary, always kept in order. He sat on the one next to her. "You know there's space at the senior's home. You can stay there until you can resolve this problem. He can't expect to live in that house with you."

"He's in the process of finding other accommodations. In the meantime, he's working through a lot of Brian's papers. Adam has been overseas for the last ten years. He's back to expand and take over this part of the business. He shouldn't be at my house for more than a month."

"I hate to see you so upset." His hand touched her brow then ran down her arm.

"It's just that I'm finding out things little by little. I should have been more involved in the details hanging over my life, Everett." Too agitated to sit, she rose and began to pace. Everett stood and leaned against his desk.

"Things happen for a reason. God will see you through this. And you know I'm here to help you if you need it."

She paced over to him and grasped his hand to covered it

with her own. "I don't know what I would have done this last year without you. Now that my grief is beginning to abate, it's time I get my life in order." She took a quick breath and sent him a fleeting troubled smile. "He's offered me a job with the company. We'll see how that works."

"It is your business, too. You should be an active participant. We will miss your work here."

"Not entirely, I hope. I plan to continue some of my volunteer work." She offered a uncertain smile.

"Good." He looked at her a good long time.

"Well," she said, uneasy with his scrutiny. "I have to get back to packing or I'll be here all night." She got up in her usual brisk manner and left the room.

Everett sat where he was for a long time, contemplating as background voices mixed with Christmas music filtered into his office. Amanda was a beautiful woman. She was free and finally getting over Brian. And he was growing to love her immensely. He needed someone like her in his life. A wonderful volunteer in the church, she'd fit perfectly into his life. Even though he was constantly surrounded by people, at night he longed for something more. He was the sounding board and advice-giver for many people. He lived his life according to the vows he'd taken twenty years ago. Just as with Brian, his wife passed away five years ago. She'd been a kind woman, older than he. He never once considered breaking his commitment with God or his vows.

Now, he was ready for love, for a special someone to share his life. Amanda would make the perfect preacher's wife.

Chapter 4

Lottie Rogers, vibrant and effervescent, glided into the house. "So, you're Amanda's friend." Stopping short and sliding the gloves off her delicate hands, she looked Adam up and down, making no attempt at trying to hide her frank perusal.

"I'm Adam Somerville," he said in a no nonsense voice that could cause his worst adversary to tremble in his shoes. He extended a hand.

She raised an well-arched eyebrow, clearly not intimidated. "Uh-huh," reaching out, she barely touched his hand with the tips of her manicured fingers. Obviously she had all the time in the world.

Adam cleared his throat, amused by her frank appraisal. God bless the man strong enough to handle the bold woman.

"Oh, Lottie!" Amanda rounded the corner, rescuing him in the process. "I'm glad you stopped by. I've prepared one of your favorite dinners."

The woman immediately came out of her trance and seemingly forgot Adam was even present.

"Hi, yourself, girl. I'm here to take you out before the madness of the season hits."

Amanda looked down at her jeans and sky-blue angora sweater. "I hadn't planned . . . I'm not dressed . . ."

"You look just fine," she assured Amanda, with a cursory glance. "We're just going dancing anyway. Doesn't she look beautiful, Adam?" She remembered he was there after all.

"Ye . . ."

He obviously spoke too slowly for the tornado who blew in.

"Besides, certain men—better known as my husband and brother—are just about to drive me crazy." The woman dropped her purse beside the sofa and carelessly draped her coat on the sofa arm. "I will not return home until I've burned off some energy. I left them in the kitchen, Everett lamenting about you and the hunk here," she said, raising an eyebrow, "and Henry about God knows what. I learned to tune him out years ago."

"By your tone, nobody could tell you're madly in love with Henry," Amanda said, rolling her eyes and shaking her head at the woman.

"These nights out with you and the girls keep me sane and in love with him." She headed to the kitchen. "What's that smell?"

"Just some barbecued ribs."

"We've got time to eat before we leave." Lottie picked up the phone and dialed. "Glenda, Mandy and I'll be a little late tonight, but we'll be there." A pause, then, "Uh-huh. Yes. Got to go, girl." After hanging up, she flew to the powder room, where Adam heard through the open door, water running. "My diet just flew to hell, girlfriend. Why you ever baked those ribs, I don't know. Everyone can't eat that greasy food and stay slim like you."

"I wonder who's forcing you?" came Amanda's dry reply as she handed china to Adam. In another minute, Lottie joined them. The three of them worked companionably together to ready the meal.

"You always fix too much." Lottie forked ribs on her plate. "So you're the one who has Everett so nervous. He thinks he's in love with girlfriend, here," she said to Adam.

"Don't be silly, Lottie. He's not in love with me." Mortified, Amanda kicked Lottie's ankle. It had no effect on the woman's tongue.

"Of course he thinks he is. But you need someone like the hunk here and Everett needs someone . . . well, he hasn't met her yet." She narrowed her eyes at Amanda as she reached under the table, obviously to rub her smarting ankle.

"Thank you, friend," was Amanda's rueful reply. "You know how to lift a woman's spirits, don't you?"

"Don't start spouting that junk with me. You wouldn't want me to lie, would you?"

Adam knew Lottie and he would be fast friends.

"He sees you as the perfect little preacher's wife, what with all the volunteer work and all. Thinks it goes well with his post. But you don't love him. You'll just make yourselves miserable." She waved a saucy rib in the air. "So I'm kinda glad the hunk moved in here. Without him, you two probably would have talked yourselves into marrying. And that would have been a disaster." She bit into one of the homemade rolls.

Lottie monopolized the conversation during the meal and, knowing Lottie was on his side, Adam had no qualms with Amanda spending the evening with her friends. Not that she actually asked him, or needed to.

"What kept you away so long? And why is someone like you still single?"

"Work. And never settled down long enough." He shrugged. "Unlucky, I guess."

"Um, it's a good thing you stayed single long enough for Mandy here."

"Lottie, he didn't stay single for my benefit."

Since she sat between Adam and Amanda, Lottie's neck swiveled to talk with both of them.

"Fate, Mandy. Don't you believe in fate?"

"No."

They finally completed the meal as Lottie continued to dominate the conversation, as usual. Amanda couldn't leave fast enough. She hastily put her dishes in the dishwasher and wiped down the kitchen.

"So, what time will you all be in?" Adam threw in.

All commotion stopped.

"When we get in, sweetheart," came Lottie's sassy reply. "We haven't been on curfew in years." She patted his hand and rose to stack her dishes in the dishwasher.

Amanda dashed upstairs to change, leaving Lottie and Adam on their own.

Amanda returned home around eleven and she had finally snuggled into bed, exhausted from the dancing, when Josh called.

"Hi, honey," Amanda yawned.

Hearing it, he said, "Oh, Mom, I forgot the time difference."

"It's okay, sweetheart. I just got in."

"Where did you go?"

"Out with Lottie." Amanda plumped her pillow and sat up to lean against the headboard.

"Is Adam back in the States yet?" he asked, with more enthusiasm than Amanda cared for.

"Yes, and in the spare bedroom." She decided not to berate him for his part in that fiasco. He was so protective of her.

"Good. I don't like your being alone in that big house."

"His stay is only temporary. Then I'll be alone again."

"But at least he'll be close by if you need help."

"Honey, I don't want you to worry about me. I can take care of myself." Silence greeted her.

"He offered me a job with the company. I start tomorrow."

"That's great!"

"I'm a little nervous about my first job."

"But you've always worked, Mom. You just didn't get paid for it."

"I know, but still . . ."

"Where's that confidence you always poured into me? You're very capable, Mom. You'll do a fantastic job. Don't worry."

"Thanks, honey. I think I needed to hear that."

"I'm sorry I'm out west and left you alone to face this."

"Oh, don't worry about me. How do you like it there?"

"It's great, Mom. All the animals. Something's always going on."

"I'm so glad you like it there."

"It's great experience. Well, I'll let you get to bed, Mom. Tell Adam I said hi, okay?"

"Sure."

Amanda placed the phone on the hook feeling better about tomorrow. Josh loved it in Montana. At least that was one worry off her chest. She snuggled under the covers and it wasn't long before she was nodding off.

Amanda's first day on her new job started with a burst of energy and with more than a little trepidation. Determined to do the very best she could, she rose at five to dress and eat and opened her first folder for her first contract by five forty-five. Joe had written details for organizing the files in a way she could use it. First, he explained what the company did. She knew they provided video, data, and voice satellite transmission services, but she wasn't aware they offered terrestrial lines as well in some remote locations. They were a satellite resale company and did not actually own any satellites. They purchased huge blocks of space from satellite owners and resold time to smaller companies.

Joe was coming by around nine to spend the day training her. Actually, he was taking part of his day every day this week to train her.

She had read through three folders by the time she heard the shower go off at seven and got up from her work to start Adam's breakfast. Slicing potatoes into the frying pan, she wondered how he looked undressed. It must be the masculine aroma in the house making her so aware of him. That didn't explain why she never had those feelings for Everett.

The potatoes were done and she was pouring the beaten eggs for the omelet into the pan when he came downstairs. As he entered the kitchen she diverted her attention from the omelet long enough to peruse his suit slacks, dress shirt, and tie. After hanging the jacket on the back of a chair, he marched directly to the coffee Amanda had brewed.

"You're up early," he said after his first sip.

"I wanted to get an early start." If he looked wonderful in jeans, he was devastating in navy suit and print tie. "You're going out today?" she asked, as she concentrated on her omelet to slow her accelerated heartbeat.

"I have meetings at the office all day. I should be back by six tonight." He peered at her intently. She could almost imagine he referred to a date.

"Good." Her pitch was unusually high. Every time his gaze met hers, her heart turned over in response.

"Joe is an excellent trainer. He should be able to answer any of your questions. I've made a list of phone numbers for you."

Her fingers trembled as she took the paper from him.

With cup in hand, Adam leaned against the counter. He had a way of just observing and focusing that made a person believe he knew their innermost secrets.

She fervently hoped he didn't know hers. She was so ashamed of feeling like this for Brian's friend. She squeezed her eyes and cleared her throat.

"I'll hold dinner until six-thirty," she said.

After she set his plate on the table she straightened up the kitchen and joined him, with a cup of hot tea for herself, basking in the novelty of having someone to talk to in the morning.

She wondered what it would be like to have him here every morning as more than Brian's friend and partner.

"How does baked chicken sound for dinner?" she asked as he forked the last bite of omelet. Thank God he wasn't a mind reader.

"Anything you fix is delicious. If I keep eating like this, I'll gain ten pounds in no time. Then I'll have to join a health club just to keep trim."

Amanda didn't comment on that. He looked trim to her. "I usually walk three times a week, though I haven't been able to lately with the Christmas rush."

"We'll have to walk together then."

Picturing long masculine legs beside her, she knew she was too obsessed with this man. He had so many favorable qualities.

With a penchant for neatness, each morning he made his own bed and picked up after himself. Over the weekend, he'd even helped her with the cleaning and he stacked his own dishes into the dishwasher. He wasn't really that much extra work. It troubled her that she liked having him around the house. She found herself eating healthier now that she was cooking for two. Before, she would sometimes eat out to keep from preparing a meal just for herself.

"Do you need me to pick up anything for you on my way home?" he asked as he shrugged into his coat. She forgot, thoughtful.

"No, thank you. I have everything I need."

She stood at the door as he descended the steps. "I'll call before I leave the office just in case." He waved goodbye.

Surprised that he'd even asked, Amanda closed the door and retreated downstairs to work, promising herself she wouldn't think of him again.

She stopped on the last step. She was a fraud. Where was her anger at him? How could she have unconsciously forgiven him for what he did to her marriage? She knew how false he really was, and yet he had a way of making her forget or at the least feel foolish for holding onto the anger. Which is exactly what he wanted.

Amanda wondered at his offer. Was the job his way of keeping her in line? Adam wasn't above using anyone to get what he wanted. He'd used Brian. Was he using her now?

Then, she thought, her job was real. Even if he was using her for his own reasons, she could use him, too. She was half owner of the company. She had as much right to work in her company as he. Amanda vowed to learn as much about her company as possible. The contracts were an excellent start. Even if his motives were suspect, she'd do the very best job that she could. She'd be a useful component to her company. She lifted her head and marched into the office to attack the files with renewed vigor. Adam Somerville was not the sexiest man she'd seen in the last few months.

With the first snow of the season, the winter wonderland scene outside Adam's window made it almost impossible to concentrate on work. It had snowed off and on all day, and the snow and ice clinging to the sturdy tree limbs offered a picture-perfect view he'd only appreciated in photos and calendars for years.

He wanted to be out there with Amanda, to wrap his arms around her softness. He barely stopped himself before he reached for the phone to call her. He found himself preparing to search for her several times today, as he'd done when he worked in her house. He actually missed his first day away from her. Many comments Brian had made about her just didn't ring true. She didn't show a propensity to be a spendthrift. In fact, most of her entertainment seemed to be her volunteer work for the church. Thinking of the church threw a damper on his spirits as thoughts of Reverend Smart crept in. The man made it a regular duty to stop by Amanda's house for one thing or another.

"Adam," Joe Cager called from the door.

"Yes?"

"Here're the files you requested. They're all small companies that only require a minimum of services. I worked most of the day with Amanda. She's catching on pretty quickly. Next week I'm going to introduce her to some of the customers. If she wants to work, she should work with me on some of the larger accounts. She's not going to be able to do much with these." He placed the stack on Adam's desk and pushed his wire rims up on his nose.

Adam sifted through the folders giving minimum attention to Joe. "We'll let her work with those for now." His fleeting smile indicated the decision was closed, but Joe didn't take the hint.

"But, Adam, she's not going to be able to do much with them. They don't want any other services."

Adam arched a brow.

"Oh," Joe said, catching the drift at last. For such a brilliant employee, he could be slow on the uptake.

Adam stashed the folders into his briefcase. "These should keep her busy for a while."

Clearly uncomfortable with the subterfuge, Joe shoved his hands in his pockets. "She never seemed interested before."

"With Brian gone, she wants to become more involved."

"Anytime she wants real work, let me know." Joe stuck a pencil in his pocket pack, clearly affronted by the waste of time. "One good thing, you'll get an opportunity to attend the company New Year's party. She can throw a great party."

"Um." Adam looked at his watch. It was time to go home. "I'll see you in two days, Joe. Bring the rest of the files by Amanda's tomorrow."

"Will, do." He walked toward the door. "See you later."

Adam reached for the phone then and dialed Amanda's.

"Hi."

Her soft, sweet voice greeting him over the wire was like a breath of sunshine. He could imagine her bright eyes lighting up when she realized it was him. At least he hoped she was as pleased to hear him as he was to call. "I'm getting ready to leave. Do you need anything?"

"No," she said. "Your timing's perfect. Dinner's almost ready."

"I'm looking forward to it." Adam hung up with a smile on his face. Then he stopped cold reminding himself, yet again, that she was Brian's wife. Not his. Now, where did that notion come from? Thoughtfully, he gathered his coat. But even the thought of Brian didn't take away his eagerness to get home.

The Christmas season was very much in evidence as he walked out of his office. Miniature pine trees decorated several desktops. Decorative foil covered doors outlined with garlands. Colorful lights twinkled in the twilight. Immediately, he was thrown into Christmas cheer. Even the bumper-to-bumper traffic didn't throttle his spirits when it took an extra twenty minutes to reach home.

Everett's car in Amanda's yard accomplished what the rush hour traffic failed to do. Thoroughly irritated at having to put up with the man again, his good mood evaporated. Obviously the work he'd given her didn't keep her busy enough.

As he parked in his half of his garage he remembered that Brian's Land Rover should be around. Perhaps Josh had it, but it seemed an expensive vehicle for a college student.

The laundry room door led in from the garage. As Adam entered the house, he could hear Amanda laughing at something Everett had said. Her laughter was more spontaneous than with him. When he closed the door, she faced him, the laughter dying on her lips.

"Oh, Adam. Hi." Her eyes still sparkled. Adam's gut tightened. That sparkle shouldn't have been for the preacher. This must be how a man felt when he caught his woman with another man.

"Hi." He wanted to go up to Amanda and kiss her. He placed his briefcase by the counter, instead.

"You've got great timing. Everett's joining us for dinner, Adam."

"Oh? Good. Good to see you—again, Everett." Adam felt anything but. So much for his quiet evening alone with Amanda.

Everett merely gave him a smirk, as if to say he knew the score. Well so did Adam. And Adam was presently staying under the woman's roof, so to speak. Territorial rights were suddenly called to order. Besides, who better to look out for Amanda's welfare?

This had been the longest dinner Amanda had ever endured. Carrying on a silent war of wills, Adam and Everett had both gotten on her nerves. Amanda felt pulled into the middle. She was not surprised by Adam's aggressive attitude, as that was his usual nature, but Everett had always been soft spoken and— pleasant. Since Brian's death, she'd seen him as a sturdy, calming rock upon which she could lay her burdens, and yet he expected nothing in return. Through his encouragement, she'd increased her volunteer work, thus taking up the excess time for brooding and grief with Brian's death, and Josh, now away in college.

Tonight, Everett had presented a layer of steel she didn't know was there. She almost wished she hadn't invited him to stay to dinner. When he stopped by, she'd thought he'd be the perfect diversion from Adam. That wasn't fair of her, especially after all that Everett had done for her.

After the meal, the three of them sat in her living room, making small and difficult conversation until almost nine, when Everett finally excused himself to leave.

"The evening with you was pleasant as always, Amanda."

Remembering Lottie's comment, Amanda's unease grew at his comment. Then she stopped herself. This was the same Everett who'd made the same small talk for more than a year. Everett hadn't changed, only Lottie's silly imaginings and her stupid obsession with Adam—temporary obsession.

"I always enjoy your company, Everett."

"I'm glad." He pulled her to him and kissed her on the

cheek. A move he'd never made before. "I'll see you tomorrow night."

Amanda hated to admit that perhaps Lottie was on target. But a kiss on the cheek was certainly innocent. She was reading too much into it.

Adam cleared his throat and joined them at the door. They jumped apart.

"I hope you'll join us at church Sunday, Adam," Everett said, releasing her hand, scratching his head, a sign of nervousness, before stepping out into the cold.

"I wouldn't miss it," Adam responded, closing the door in his face and twisting the lock.

Amanda hugged her arms, more from frayed nerves than the cold blast of air that had entered.

"Adam, that was rude." She was sick of men in general and these two in particular. If their posturing continued, at this rate they'd keep her on tenterhooks.

"He overstayed his welcome. We both have work to do tomorrow." He stalked beside her. "Is he coming over to dinner tomorrow night, too? He's not going to make it a nightly routine, is he?"

"Everett has been very kind to me. Having him over to dinner isn't an imposition."

"For me it is."

She stopped and confronted him. He would not run roughshod over her.

"The house is half mine, remember."

"And half mine. And I need to get to bed."

"Who's keeping you? You will not control my life like you did Brian's. We had best come to that understanding immediately."

"I never ran Brian's life. What are you talking about?"

"The only thing you need to remember is that my life is my business, not yours." With hands on hips, she swung around furiously.

He almost shouted, "Maybe you should talk to Everett and

limit his visits to Sunday after church,'' his harsh voice lashed out at her.

''No one asked you to join us in the living room. You could have gone on to bed,'' she snapped and started for the stairs.

''He needs to respect the fact that you're working a full-time job now. He can't monopolize all your time.''

''This conversation has passed reasonableness.'' Suddenly, it dawned on Amanda that this idiotic conversation had nothing to do with dinner, but the sharp, banked fire that lit the brown eyes glaring at her, and her own sensual awareness of him.

At that instant, she knew he wanted her. Worse, her woman's instincts answered that male call. Before, she had deluded herself into believing her reaction was from her long abstinence. She knew it was from desire for this man. Desire for the last man she wanted anything intimate with. And as suddenly, the sharp control she knew so well replaced the fire in his eyes. Had she not been starring him in the face, she'd have never know it was even there.

''I'm going to bed.'' She gave him her back and ascended the steps.

''Just make sure he doesn't show up to dinner every evening.''

Amanda stopped on the fourth step and turned to face him. ''Well, you won't have that to worry about. Tomorrow night is our night to serve food for people in need. You get to fare for yourself.''

''What time will you be in?''

''Too late for you to wait dinner. You'll have to fix your own.''

''What time do you leave here?''

''Don't worry. I will put in a full day's work before leaving for my volunteer work.''

''That's the least of my worries. It's not safe for you to be out roaming about alone at night.''

''Don't be ridiculous. I'm not roaming. I'm always out at night.''

"Not anymore. I will take you and return to pick you up later."

"I can drive my own car, Adam. You're trying to run my life and I won't have it." Close to screaming, she counted to ten.

"Look there are high-jackings all over the place now. I don't want anything happening to you. Don't begrudge me that. I can take the time to take you out when I don't think it's safe for you."

"Adam, you can't take me every place I need to go. I've been on my own for a while now. Coming and going day and night. At my choosing. I couldn't stand for you to cramp my style that way. Thank you for your concern though." Amanda climbed the stairs.

Think again, Adam said to himself. He was going to have more to say about her life than she'd ever dreamed. And what did she mean when she said he controlled Brian's life?

What was better for her anyway? Him or someone who would take advantage of her good nature? Amanda was still vulnerable. It was his duty to protect her from men like Everett. She was so trusting and fragile. How could he help but have warm feelings for her? They were nothing more than the warm feelings any man would have for a close friend.

In her hurry to leave him, she'd forgotten to turn out the Christmas lights. Visible from the family room, the warm glow invited him to watch them for a while. He reclined on the overstuffed sofa, mesmerized by the twinkling lights, and deep into thoughts about the changes coming over him. Positive changes, he hoped.

Then he realized he was being unreasonable. Try as he might, he couldn't seem to stop himself. Amanda had a disquieting magnetic pull on him in a way he'd never thought a woman would. She conjured thoughts of family and relationships. Forever crept into his mind at an alarming rate. He didn't know if it was from the Christmas season or from being home. Perhaps this attraction was much more. He could feel his reserve cracking. This change creeping in almost frightened him.

After her shower, Amanda combed out her shoulder length hair and tied a band around it. *That impossible man.* As her hand dropped to the dressing table to arrange things in the proper order before retiring, she wondered what they'd do about this awareness between them. Or was it subterfuge? Could a man check his response that quickly, or was it really a ruse to throw her off the track of what she really should concentrate on? *Her work.*

This would all go away when he moved. Acting as though having dinner with Everett would pose a problem with her working. He had her emotions so twisted, it left her in a state of constant confusion.

Perhaps he really didn't have confidence she could do the job. Panic seized her. It was imperative that she do well on her first paying job. She simply couldn't fail. She vowed to put in more hours. Her work today went well. It was certainly interesting. She could go back downstairs for another two hours tonight.

When she crept out her door, all was quiet. Adam must have already retired to his room. She didn't want to run into him again tonight. She slipped downstairs only to find him fast asleep on the couch.

A softness stole over his features as he slept. The calculating barrier always so much in evidence was gone. Her hand was almost to his forehead before she snatched it back. She'd been alone much too long.

She went to the closet, pulled out a blanket, and covered him. He immediately snuggled deeper into the covers much as Josh did.

Too disquieted to deal with her attraction to Adam, Amanda turned the lights off and continued downstairs to her office.

Chapter 5

Two mornings later, Amanda came downstairs later than usual. Most nights now, she'd slip to the office basement, familiarizing herself with the services the company offered and her accounts. A great sense of pride overcame her at the responsibility Adam was entrusting her with. In a short while she'd learned more than she'd gathered over the last fifteen years. After putting in another five hours before retiring, she rose later than usual.

Adam had already made coffee for himself and tea for her by the time she arrived in the kitchen.

"Bless you." With only six hours sleep under her belt, she desperately needed the caffeine kick of the tea. After her first swallow, she caught her first glimpse of his breakfast.

He crunched on a spoonful of cold cereal Josh had gotten when he was home for Thanksgiving.

She eyed his bowl dubiously. "I'll fix you a more substantial breakfast," she offered while opening the cabinet for a pan.

"This is good. I can't eat lavishly every day."

It must be stale. But Amanda knew hungry men tended not

to care. Still the guilt from leaving him on his own two nights ago ate at her conscience. "Oatmeal then. It'll stick to you longer. The perfect breakfast item on cold mornings." She grabbed milk out the fridge without her usual gusto. Yawning, Amanda pulled out oatmeal and fixed bowls for them both, topping it with cinnamon and brown sugar.

Having quickly adjusted to this new lifestyle, it would be difficult when he moved out in a month and once again she'd be alone. Amanda didn't want to be too comfortable or too dependent on him.

"How is the house hunting going?" she asked.

"A few of the places looked interesting. I'm waiting until after the Holiday to make a final decision. This oatmeal is delicious."

"I need to take my car to the shop to get the oil changed and get a few other little things done. I don't want to wait for it. Could you pick me up?"

"I can change your oil. What else needs doing?"

She ran down the list.

"I can do all that this weekend. Can it wait that long?"

"Sure."

"What happened to the Land Rover?"

"I sold it in January to pay for Josh's tuition this year and put the rest away for next year's fees."

He had his coffee halfway to his mouth and checked the motion. "If you didn't have the money for Josh's schooling, why didn't you let me know?"

"Believe me, I got more than enough from the Land Rover to cover the expense. It was new." Amanda had thought it silly to pay such an exorbitant price for a car.

"Give me the tuition bill. I'll take care of it."

"No need. It's already done."

"I'll reimburse you for it. Brian and I had made a deal that we'd find a way to pay for it."

"No. And that's final." She was not depending on anyone else again. "Well, I'm ready to get to work."

"You don't have to rush off. I'll make the repairs on Saturday. In the meantime, I have to go out, but it'll be six before I return. I'll take you to the shelter."

Amanda waved a hand. "Everett's already offered. We're going to pick up the turkeys and other food for Christmas dinner for the shelter and deliver it to the church."

Silence. "What time will you be ready? I'll pick you up from church on my way home then."

She shook her head at his reluctance to give up his overprotective nature. "Seven," she said, shortly averting another argument.

It had been a very hectic day, Adam thought, as he went in search of Amanda. He found her and Everett talking almost secretively in the church kitchen. He didn't realize putting groceries away could be such an intimate experience. He was getting darned tired of catching them like this. As he stomped in, they jumped apart almost guiltily.

"Adam," Everett said, sporting a silly grin. "You didn't have to make the trip. Since she was too busy to cook today, I was planning to take Amanda out to eat before bringing her home. Care to join us?"

Again? "That won't be necessary. We'll just stop some place on our way home."

"Really, it'll only take me a moment to throw something together," Amanda cut in.

Everett grasped her hand. "I won't hear of your cooking tonight. You worked so hard today. Thanks for coming by the senior's home to help before grocery shopping."

She shrugged it off. "It was nothing. I was glad to help out."

She gathered her coat and purse.

"Really, Amanda. The Chinese restaurant down the street is quiet and the service is quick. We can relax for a while. I need to unwind, too."

"If you worked her that hard, we can pick up something on our way home," Adam cut in.

"He didn't work me hard at all."

"You deserve to be pampered," Everett insisted.

"I'll tell you what, I'll just take a taxi. I'm not in the mood for this bickering." She started toward the door.

"Amanda," Everett called out.

"I'll talk to you tomorrow, Everett."

Adam cut a hard stare at Everett, grabbed Amanda's arm and ushered her to the car.

They picked up Chinese on the way home.

After dinner and preparations for bed, Amanda wasn't ready for sleep. She'd put in long hours all week. It was Friday, a week before Christmas and she wanted a treat. A good romance would do the trick. She retrieved a new novel by her favorite author she hadn't had time to read yet. Romance had been definitely missing in her life. She settled back on plump pillows and read for an hour before she dozed off after a love scene.

Amanda was abruptly awakened by a loud crash. Groggily she got up to investigate.

"Adam?" She knocked tentatively on his door.

"It's okay," he called out.

She opened the door a few inches. When she saw the overturned coffee pot, she ran into the bathroom, grabbed the towel, and wet it. By the time she returned, Adam had righted the pot.

"I wasn't looking at what I was doing," he said dabbing at the stain. Since he'd drank several cups while working on the contract, only a little had soaked his T-shirt and spilled on the floor.

Adam set the pottery on the hamper while she mopped up the last of the liquid and hung the towel to dry.

Returning to the room, Amanda stopped short as she noticed he had discarded his damp shirt. Cold bumps gathered on his bare chest. Even more disturbing was the fact that he wore only briefs.

Adam, too, finally noticed the cotton gown outlining her pert nipples in the cool room. A thin cotton nightgown didn't hide her lacy panties at all. On her bare feet, shapely calves showed below the nightgown. She stood barely a foot away. He reached out to her and ran a hand up her arm. She stood as if rooted to the spot. Adam pulled her into his arms and did what he'd longed to do unceasingly. He kissed her, forgetting he was kissing his best friend's wife. The soft skin, sweet mouth, and drugging kiss rocked his senses. He wanted to explore her leisurely, but the blood that had boiled in his veins made that impossible. It seemed he'd been in a constant state of need forever. He pressed her tighter against himself and felt her arms encircle his neck. Inching the thin gown aside bit by bit, he strung kisses down her neck and caressed her skin.

Gathering her in his arms, he carried her to his bed and placed her in its center, shoving the papers to the side in a disheveled pile. He removed her thin lace gown and delicate panties. Feeling the heat of her desire, he touched her soft skin, urged on by her sweet moans. He took his time exploring, touching. A fine sheen of sweat enveloped him as he struggled to hold back while her soft hands eagerly scanned his body. And then he was in her tight passage. Ecstasy, sweet, sweet heaven. They moved deep, slow, then fast and slow again, feeling each centimeter of her. Enjoying her tightness, the friction, until he couldn't hold on any longer. Continuing the cadence known since the dawning of time, they erupted in a cataclysmic explosion. He held her, felt her arms and legs around him until the last tremble. Kissing her, he held onto her as they both reached for calm.

He rolled over, turned out the bedside light, and brought the covers over them. With her head on his arm, her body cupped into his, he sought and found the sleep so elusive only an hour ago.

* * *

As Adam slept peacefully beside her, Amanda slipped off the bed, gathered her discarded clothing, and escaped to her own room, locking the door for the first time since Adam arrived. Pressing one hand to her aching and racing heart, she stood there, unable to move her tense fingers from the knob. Leaning against the door for support, she wondered how could she betray Brian's memory by sleeping with his best friend? And under his very own roof?

Worst of all, how could she act so . . . wantonly? She clutched the collar of her gown, remembering her unrestrained response to his lovemaking . . . how much she enjoyed it. Heat spread throughout her body at her passionate abandon. This passion that had been tormenting her since Adam's arrival.

She and Brian had enjoyed very satisfying lovemaking. But this . . . this had been more than enjoyment. It had been another world.

Adam had to leave. Or she had to. They simply couldn't live in the same house any longer.

"Amanda?" The door knob rattled.

She jumped at hearing his voice. "Go back to bed, Adam." Apprehension swept through her.

"Not until we talk." He rattled the knob again.

"It's late . . . I can't talk tonight. Please go away," she gasped.

"Amanda. Both of us are single. We didn't . . ."

"I'm not single. I'm Brian's wife." The thought tore at her insides.

"Not any longer," he said softly, not unkindly.

"I can't deal with this . . . Please go away." Tears swam in her eyes.

"I can't leave you like this. Open the door." He showed no signs of relenting.

"No." Panic rioted within her. She wasn't ready for this.

"I'll pick the lock."

Adam heard the lock turn and the door whispered open.

"Amanda."

She turned her back to him. "You have to leave. Or I'll go. We can't live in the same house. This can't happen again."

"There are still papers I have to go through."

Business, always business. "Then I'll go."

He grabbed her and turned her to face him, angry and with guilt about her reaction. "You'll do no such thing. We're adults, we've done nothing wrong. Brian isn't here any longer."

"I know that. You were his best friend. I . . . his wife."

"You're no longer married."

"It still doesn't feel right. In his home."

"In our home, Amanda. Yours and mine," he all but shouted through gritted teeth.

She shook her head. "It shouldn't be this way. Brian and I shared this bed, this house . . . It's not . . ."

"It is right. What we did and what we felt was right. Give us a chance."

"The way you gave Brian and me a chance? Always calling him away so we had very little time together. Calling him away so we couldn't even take a honeymoon together for our twentieth anniversary?"

He dropped his arms. "What are you talking about?"

"Oh, come on." She all but sneered. "Do you think I'll involve myself with another workaholic. Someone who'd care so much about the company he won't appreciate the people around him? No, thank you," she snapped.

Looking at her dumbfounded, Adam was at a loss for words. "Amanda . . ."

"Go, just go." She tilted her head up, gathering strength. "I won't leave, and I won't insist that you go. But don't think for a second there will be a repeat performance. Now, leave my room. That much of the house is still mine."

Chapter 6

Adam wandered back to his room in a daze. She blamed him for keeping Brian away from her. Brian had been his own man. Adam never interfered in his life except on company decisions. Both of them were expected to travel. Why didn't she understand that?

She'd laid the blame for it all at his door. How was he going to handle the responsibility of her loss of the man she loved? She still loved Brian. How was he going to alienate her affections from Brian—or at least help her find a place in her heart for him?

When he'd lost his parents, Adam felt a fear incomparable with anything life ever threw him. He'd grieved, survived, and gone on with his life. Now, as his gut tightened, that same fear was beginning to swamp him again.

He didn't know whether he should leave now to give her temporary space, or stay to try to work out their relationship. Retreat wasn't in his vocabulary.

If he left now, she'd shut him out of her life completely. Now, after so many years of feeling lost, with no sense of family, he couldn't let her get away so easily. For the first time since his mother died, Adam felt like he was home. He felt the sense of completeness that he'd been searching for unconsciously . . . that now felt so right. He'd thought that work would give him all the fulfillment he needed. But dreaming about his own company and having made a success of it didn't accomplish it. What he needed was a special someone to share it with. What he needed was love.

Adam stopped short as he reached for the light.

He was in love with Amanda. And she was running, frightened, in the opposite direction.

"You're in love with him, aren't you?"

Her stricken eyes met Everett's briefly before darting away. "No, I'm just so—confused. I just don't know what's happening with me." She straightened a picture on the wall. "He's bossy and interfering. And . . . and he's a workaholic like Brian. There wouldn't be any room left in his life for a woman."

"Are you sure the intruding isn't, perhaps, concern?" He gave her a half smile. A sad smile. "It's all right you know. Brian's gone. You're a widow and Adam's single. As much as I'd like to have you for myself . . ."

"What!" came the stricken reply, her fingers going to her lips. It was one thing for Lottie, fickle Lottie, to say it, but to hear the same declaration from Everett . . .

"That shouldn't shock you. I'm a single man and you're a single woman. There's nothing wrong with the two of us together."

"Oh, Everett, I—I don't know what to say." Her voice rose with anguish.

"It's okay for you to love Adam," he said with an understanding Amanda could only cherish. Their relationship, such as it was, had crossed a barrier. The easy camaraderie and sharing wouldn't be the same. Everything in her life was changing. She just couldn't love Adam. Sure, she enjoyed his company, but. . . . Too many changes were occurring.

"Don't say that. We . . . we're not in love!" Her eyes softened with sadness. "You've been so wonderful this last year in your guidance. I don't know how I would have made it without you." She wanted her comfortable little world back. Josh's departure to college, Brian's death, Adam's moving into her house were all huge milestones in her life. Amanda wanted to know what each day would bring. She was uncomfortable with the uncertainty.

Everett advanced to her. Holding her cheeks between his hands, Everett tilted her head and kissed her. She wrapped her arms around his neck, trying to respond, trying to give him some semblance of what he'd given her.

It didn't work and they both knew it. The sparks that ignited with Adam's kisses didn't even begin to generate with Everett. Regret filled her heart as he pulled away from her and a tear slid down her smooth cheek.

He caught it with one gentle finger. He seemed to know it, too. "Just put your trust in God," he said softly. "He'll guide you in making the proper decision. Nothing will happen before its proper time." His brow puckered as if it hurt him to say the words that followed, but thank goodness he was taking it so well. "Take it one day at a time. Perhaps this is why God saw fit to send Adam back now. You weren't ready for him a few months ago, but you are now. I . . . I just had to kiss you just once," he whispered and turned, leaving the room and Amanda in a quagmire of mixed emotions.

Adam dropped the contract on his desk and looked up, squeezing the bridge of his nose. How he'd much rather be working in the office at home. The building was quiet and still. It was Saturday, and only two people were working. He wondered if Amanda was back from her volunteer project yet.

The daunting thought wandered again to the fact that she

blamed him for many of the problems in her marriage. How could she believe he chose the times Brian took trips? It was true that he'd been in constant contact and planned some of the trips that Brian took, it was part of the business. He took trips to Europe and parts of Africa. They were responsible for their respective territories. And now that Brian was dead, Adam had to make the trips and chart the course. He'd expected that as part of being a business owner. Now, they had received some long-range satellite contracts that would require less travel. Therefore, it was essential that he get a signed contract on the Scott project.

If she ever discovered the work he gave her wasn't real . . . Maybe he should have given her a legitimate assignment. But Brian had always said she was so scatterbrained.

Adam should have known better than to have believed Brian. He could see, with the volunteer work she did, that she was a hard worker. Everett relied heavily on her skills.

A nervous roiling stirred in Adam's stomach. Everett had always been true to her, respected her talents, while he, Adam, had been so sure of his own worth he hadn't taken her's seriously. According to Lottie, Everett was in love with Amanda. Given a choice, who would she prefer? Someone who trusted and believed in her? Or someone who never respected her or valued her talents? The pencil broke in his hand. Adam picked up the pieces as evidence of his emotions. He tossed them in the trash.

Then his resolve strengthened. Adam Somerville had never given up without a fight. He wouldn't now. The rev was in for the fight of his life and as soon as the New Year started, Adam was going to give her an assignment worthy of her skills.

What he didn't need now was to take a trip. Looking at every angle imaginable, trying to avoid it, he saw it was impossible. At least he could delay it until a day or two after Christmas. He thought he'd have—needed to have—more time with Amanda before leaving.

Knowing he'd be spending the day in the office, Amanda

had purposely gotten up late this morning. Every day this week, she'd been up by six. Today when she knew he couldn't linger, she hadn't made an appearance by eight. He'd been worried and knocked on her door to make sure she was all right only to get the response that she'd slept in.

Before getting to know her, he could believe that she was frivolous. Now he knew her to be a warm-hearted, kind, and very intelligent woman.

Even if she would relent enough to let him into her life, she'd more than likely compare him to Brian because, yet again, she's alone for a portion of the holidays. And according to her, they were both workaholics.

Neither did he want to leave her alone, giving Everett an opportunity to make moon eyes at his woman or sitting at her dining room table enjoying candlelight dinners. That notion was enough to make Adam change his plans. If it wasn't imperative that he lock in this contract, he *would* change his plans until their relationship was more established. It never occurred to him that perhaps Amanda wouldn't eventually come to love him.

Mere days before Christmas and he had yet to get her gift. That problem he could solve quickly, Adam thought, as he looked at his watch. Five o'clock in the afternoon so close to Christmas was not the best of times to shop, but there was no avoiding it.

While passing the Porcelain Gallery he noticed clusters of figurines in the window depicting a tender scene and remembered the knicknacks displayed prominently in Amanda's living room curio cabinet. There was space for others. He had the gift wrapped.

His next stop was a jewelry store. Once there, Adam looked at an array of diamonds and other precious gems wondering what a woman like Amanda would appreciate. The teardrop diamond earrings the salesman displayed to him would look perfect on her. In thirty minutes, Adam walked out with diamond earrings boxed and wrapped, leaving a happy sales clerk behind. Pleased with his purchases, he skirted around enthusiastic and desperate shoppers as he glided through the packed mall.

Since most of the cars were at shopping centers, the traffic was decent in the D.C. suburbs. He slowed to a snail's pace as he drove through the neighborhood, taking in the lavishly decorated homes with sleighs and other holiday scenes. How lovely it was driving through neighborhoods competing for their creativity in producing outdoor displays.

The radio commentator announced a downtown display. Suddenly he wanted to celebrate. Take an evening off. It was Saturday, after all—and Christmas.

The garage door was closing as he pulled up into the drive. Parking in the adjourning space, he soon joined Amanda in the kitchen.

"Dinner will be a little late tonight," she said stashing her purse in the closet and then noticing the blinking light on the answering machine. She punched the button. It was a message from Josh saying he'd call back tomorrow. He'd be out until late helping to birth a calf.

"Let's go out instead."

Amanda didn't look at him. "That's a good idea. You go out. I'm staying in."

Adam grasped her shoulder. "We can't ignore what happened last night. I don't want to ignore it."

"It's not that. I have to fix dinner."

"You've been working all day. Have you been to the Ellipse yet to see the decorated trees?"

"The Ellipse?" She shook her head. "No."

"I'm not really hungry right now. If you can hold off, let's go there and after, have dinner. I want to see the lights. It's been years," he said softly.

Though she knew she should, Amanda didn't have the heart to refuse him. "All right." She sighed.

"First," he started quietly, "we need to discuss last night."

"There won't be any repeat performances," Amanda declared.

He lifted a hand and pressed a feather touch to her cheek. "There's nothing wrong with two people who care for each other to make love."

"Not us," she whispered.

"Exactly us."

"I explained to you last night I wasn't ready. It's all too new." How could he understand that she'd never been with anyone other than Brian. How could she explain she didn't know how to even go about dating anymore? She married at eighteen, right out of high school. Brian had graduated from college that May and as soon as she got her diploma, they married. Brian was the only man she'd ever dated. She didn't know how to start her life over.

One day at a time, Everett had said. Amanda looked at Adam. "I'll only be a minute." She put lotion on her hands and repaired her makeup. In five minutes, they left.

Chapter 7

Hand in hand, they strolled around the sights, Amanda as lighthearted as she was at eighteen. She forced worries from her mind and concentrated on the delightful events happening for her at that moment. They wandered leisurely among trees that had been decorated for each state. Missing this year were the reindeer. Added to the celebratory cheer, the band played Christmas songs and each member of the choir, snuggled into winter coats, sang.

Children exclaimed in awe as they circled the grounds with their parents, too impatient to see the sights to relish the music from the choir, while the younger ones sat in their strollers mesmerized by the lilting voices. Amanda remembered Josh and his impatience at that age. Instead of the pain she expected, she enjoyed the memory. She was basking in many memories, experiencing more than the pain. She'd expected to spend the holidays alone and now she was with Adam, enjoying herself. Life had a way of balancing itself out.

Now Amanda was looking at this holiday as one of hope.

They ate in the Trade, an Ethiopian restaurant in Georgetown.

Pictures of Africa graced the walls. Wooden statues sat on strategically placed shelves.

A hostess soon escorted them to a table for two where one candlelight burned in the center.

Amanda's first experience with the delicious food made her wonder what took her so long to try this place. They tore pieces of the Ethiopian bread to use in place of utensils to dish up the succulent and spicy fare. Their selections were served on a silver platter that they shared.

"Um, we have to come here again," Amanda said as she popped *daro watt,* a spicy chicken dish, into her mouth.

"We'll come often." Adam tore a piece of *yebeg alitcha,* lamb cooked in herbs, and slipped it into her mouth. It turned into an intimate gesture that held unspoken possibilities before a shadow wiped the intimacy away. "I have to leave for New York shortly after the New Year. I'd hoped to hold it off longer but, I can't. I hate to leave you right now, Amanda."

She reached out across the small table to stroke his hand. "You work so hard. Have you ever heard of delegating?" Amanda struggled to keep from saying more. She was beginning to nag him as Brian often accused her of. Adam was not her husband. She had no right to tell him how to live his life. *Enjoy the moment,* she repeated to herself.

"I can't delegate everything. This is something I must do."

"All right. Adam, thank you for this evening. I've enjoyed it."

"It's not over yet," he said with a quirk of an eyebrow.

"I want to thank you again for offering me this job. I love the work I'm doing and I feel I have purpose again."

He grew quiet. Contemplating.

Some people were embarrassed by praise. Amanda guessed Adam was one of them. "I know you don't want to talk about work tonight, but I needed that in my life." She hoped she didn't look as giddy as she felt. But she couldn't let the evening go on without thanking him for offering her a purpose in life. She had a reason to get up each morning now, and security.

She had to let him know, regardless of how uncomfortable it made him.

"I'm going to add to your duties at the beginning of the year. I'm working on the Scott contract right now. You'll help me with it once we win the bid."

Amanda noticed that he said once, not if. Another indication of his intentions.

"I think the added assignments will be more rewarding for you." He cast her a fleeting smile. So serious, and cloaked with a soft heart.

"I'm already rewarded. But if you feel I need to do more, I'm more than ready."

Adam reached over and took her soft and greasy hand in his and kissed her palm. "Amanda, we need to talk about last night." He held on when she tried to retrieve it, stroking with his fingers.

"Adam . . ."

"I can't leave this hanging. Why do you blame me for problems in your marriage? You're forty. You knew that Brian had to work, just as I have to work now. And because we have to always seek out new business, we need to take trips now and then. Not too often, but they're a requirement. That doesn't mean that there can't be family time."

She seemed to freeze before his eyes. "You know nothing of my marriage. I don't want to discuss it with you."

"But you put me in the middle of this. We can't go on until this is solved. We have to talk about it, Amanda."

"What happened with Brian and me is none of your business." She grabbed a napkin and wiped her hands.

"We can't hope for any kind of future until this is cleared." Adam threw his own napkin on the table and leaned forward, elbows on the table.

Her head snapped back. "There isn't an us!"

He pinched the bridge of his nose and tried for a reasonableness. "There can be. Last night meant more to me than a one night toss. It's what I want."

She let out a low pitch laugh. "I learned a long time ago, we can't always have everything we want."

The waitress brought them warm, moist towels for their hands when she brought them the bill. Amanda made quick work of cleaning her hands, scooted back in her chair, and stood, ready to leave, thinking that was the end of it.

It was, but only until they arrived home and hung their coats in the closet. "We have to resolve this, Amanda," Adam began again. "Why do you think I'm responsible for some failure in your marriage?"

All his badgering was too much. He baited her like a dog with a bone. Amanda shoved her purse into the closet and rounded on him.

"All right. Since you want to know. Yes,"—she nodded with a taut jerk of her head—"I understood Brian had to work. I understood that we couldn't get away for a honeymoon *one* year, but I *don't* understand why we couldn't get away for *five*. Why did you always have to plan trips for Brian that time of year? I've planned five honeymoons and I've had to cancel five. We needed that time to regroup, to rejuvenate our marriage. We needed *some* time. Worldwide Satellites shouldn't have taken *all* the time."

"I don't think it should have either. Come on in the family room and take a seat so we can talk calmly about this." He grasped her shoulders to steer her.

She flinched away. "Maybe you can be calm. It wasn't your marriage. It wasn't your life. I can't be calm," she said, all but trembling.

"Sit anyway." He steered her stiff form to a couch and faced her on it, grasping both her hands. "Amanda, Brian had to take trips. And I required them. But it was up to him when he went. He should have taken time out for the important things. Maybe I am partly responsible. I've been so focused on the business that I haven't thought about his time with you and Josh. Just that there was a job that needed to be done. And as half-owner it was his responsibility."

"Right. So you can understand why I won't get involved with you and go through this again, don't you?" she huffed, pulling back from him.

Adam grasped her chin in his hand and caught her eyes, "But it was up to Brian, as a husband and father, to take care of his family's needs. There's no reason he couldn't take a honeymoon for five years. Maybe not on the exact date that you wanted to, but he could take some time away from the job. I want you in my life, Amanda. I plan to take the time to cultivate our relationship."

"Just as Brian took the time to cultivate his. In the beginning. There's more to a relationship than just getting a woman. We're here after that, too. And there's more than throwing a business party or two."

"I'm asking you to give us a chance." A look of implacable determination on his face.

"I'm not going through that a second time. It'll be even worse. Before, there was Brian to take up the slack at Worldwide. Now, there's only you." Her voice caught.

"And you. Josh is in college. You can take a major role in the business."

"Believe me, I plan to."

"There's still room for us. I'll make room, Amanda. You're important enough for me."

Having heard it all before, Amanda smiled with a bittersweet sadness. What was the purpose of continuing with this argument. "It's ten and I'm beat. I think I'll call it a night. Thank you for the evening." She stood on stiff legs.

He escorted her to her bedroom door. "It was my pleasure. Think about what I've said." The light feather touch on her cheek was unexpected. So were the warm lips that replaced it for a second. So quick Amanda didn't get the opportunity to snatch away before the muffled steps on the carpet carried him to the opposite end of the hall.

She stumbled into her own room and closed the door, holding

onto the knob, gathering strength for a full two minutes before she stumbled over to her bed and sank onto it.

So many memories, so many failures he'd bought up. Hanging by a thread, Amanda rested her face in her hands as she replayed their heated conversation. But she refused to wallow in self-pity. After Brian's death, she'd had to force herself up, to place one foot in front of the other, until the pain lessened. Now, she got up to shower.

All day she'd been busy enough to avoid concentrating on last night's lovemaking too long. Now, in the quiet of night, the house settling around her, it was impossible not to think of its implications.

Was she using Brian as an excuse to evade a new relationship? How could she love Brian's best friend, especially after he'd been a key factor in their marriage's failure. She sighed in confusion and regret, letting the hot water roll over her. It was time to resolve what had really occurred in her marriage.

Brian and she had grown apart. They shared very little in the end, an all too often sad reality. This was the main reason she was so cautious. At eighteen, they'd been so in love and they'd shared everything. Brian would come home from his job and discuss his day with her. They planned outings and projects together. They were very happy. Soon after they were blessed with Josh, they did less and less together, talked even more infrequently. And then the arguments started. He'd accuse her of nagging him, of wanting him to be everything for her, while she had wanted them to live as a family, to be part of each other's lives. For her it was more than making love, sharing a house, and raising a child. She had her own interests. She just wanted a sharing marriage. Amanda clutched the wash cloth in her tense fingers.

The time came when they couldn't agree on anything anymore. There wasn't any togetherness. The glue that bound them was gradually slipping away. What was the purpose of marriage if you didn't share—if you didn't take the time to nourish it? They'd grown apart and into their own little worlds. Brian into

Worldwide Satellite, and she into her volunteer work at church and school.

Amanda knew that Adam wasn't responsible for her marriage's failure. It was easier to lay it at his door and not with Brian and herself. Brian could have found time for Josh and her if he'd wanted to. He didn't consider their relationship important enough.

She could be blamed, too. After a while, she just gave up. Perhaps she could have tried harder to reach him and bring their marriage back to what it had been. She also knew it took two people. She couldn't do it alone.

As she dried off with a soft sunshine yellow towel, she realized her last few years had been as bleak as the dreary, cold night. It was time to get rid of the blame, to leave the past where it belonged—in the past—and start with something new. She knew she couldn't, wouldn't start with another workaholic like Brian. She also knew she wanted that special sharing relationship again. As the towel stroked her tender breasts, Amanda realized that tonight she wanted to wear something that made her feel feminine. She selected a white silk teddy that contrasted with the rich brown hues of her skin. If only she could make her body believe that, she'd be fine.

Tonight, as she pulled on her gown, she thought what a loss it was when two people lost that special something they had to offer each other.

She started at hearing a knock on her door. She donned a robe and opened the door to admit Adam. He'd showered and changed into pajama bottoms but at least he had on a robe, though he'd left it hanging open. Whether he'd keep it on was another matter. Her hands itched to touch the springy hairs on his chest.

He offered her a cup of her favorite tea as a peace offering. "Let's watch a movie together," he said leaning into the doorjamb looking devilishly carefree. "I've discovered I'm not sleepy after all."

"Nothing's playing tonight," she all but whispered.

"I have a tape." He lifted it for her to see. "Wesley Snipes. I missed a lot overseas."

Amanda wavered, and reached out to take the proffered cup. "Thanks for the tea." Her nerves tingling with awareness, they descended the stairs. She discovered that even with a paucity of sleep the previous night, she wasn't sleepy at all. They sat on the couch in the family room facing the large-screened television, at opposite sides of the couch.

As the tape rolled the previews at the beginning, Adam said, "This isn't going to work."

"What isn't?" Amanda asked.

He scooted next to her and put an arm around her shoulder. "That's better. Courting couples don't sit a mile apart."

"We aren't courting." The idea stirred around in her head. She'd almost forgotten what snuggling up was like. Perhaps she could court again. *Grow up into the nineties, Amanda. You aren't getting married. You're just enjoying the man's presence.*

"Of course, we are."

Amanda strained against his arm. "We need to settle something. I wasn't ready for what happened last night."

"I can wait until you *are* ready." As Wesley rolled into his first quagmire on the colorful screen, Adam lifted Amanda's chin with his forefinger. "Don't keep me waiting too long, baby. Once a man has tasted heaven, he can't settle for less and waiting can be pure hell."

Regardless of what he said, holding Amanda was a slice of heaven. He'd never taken time out to enjoy relationships. He remembered his mom smiling and singing to herself as she worked or sipped a cup of coffee. He'd ask what she was thinking about. She'd pat him on the cheek and say, "I'm smelling the roses, son." Many times, that was followed by a leisurely hug, and he would get a whiff of lemon and spices for perfume in her warm comforting arms.

He'd never taken the time to smell the roses. Of late that time was becoming more important to him. He hoped Amanda could come to care enough for him to smell the roses with him, and he hoped she'd forgive him for his part in her estrangement from her husband. Determined not to make the same mistake, he tightened his arm around her shoulder.

Chapter 8

Amanda spent the remainder of the time before Christmas talking to her clients and finalizing details and services they'd need for the next year. With pages of lines drawn through items listed in her Day Timer, she had concrete proof that she was making progress on her assignments. She checked one more item when she hung up from her call to Joe.

Joe hated to hear her voice on the phone because she called him often, very often, to clear up areas she wasn't familiar with and to discern if the company could provide one service or another that a client was interested in.

"Sorry I'm late, Adam, but Amanda calls me at least four times a day." Joe hurried into Adam's office, his expression harassed. "And it's not easy getting her off the phone. For busy work, she's certainly taking it seriously. Maybe you need to tell *her* it's busy work."

"Just keep her happy. She'll be getting real assignments soon. For now, we need to work on the Scott contract. I'm going to New York right after Christmas."

"Don't they lay low between the holiday like most normal

people?'' He handed Adam some papers and sank into a chair facing the desk.

"Apparently not. And since we want their business, we won't, either.'' Adam perused the papers, making mental notes.

As Joe left the office, guilt ate at Adam for the useless work Amanda was doing on the contracts. She worked night and day. Maybe not completely useless. The company needed to stay abreast of small clients' needs and it served to give her a feel for the company.

Thinking of his next encounter with her, which didn't include work, Adam couldn't wait to get home. He'd also get her to lighten up.

Amanda stood at the kitchen sink washing broccoli when Adam entered the room. She looked over her shoulder and smiled, tantalizing him.

"Hi,'' she said in that saucy voice he loved to hear.

"I hear you're working overtime on these contracts,'' he said as he placed his briefcase by the counter.

"I'm enjoying it.''

"Don't work too hard. I only gave them to you to get a feel for the company. You won't get very much out of them.'' He went up behind her, slid his hands around her waist, stroking her and nuzzled her neck.

"I beg to differ, Mr. Somerville.'' Her voice caught when his fingers slipped lower. "I've already tripled our business with them.'' Her voice was filled with pride.

Hands stilling, Adam stopped his nuzzling, turned her and looked into her eyes. "You've what?''

"I've talked with all the clients and most of them need additional services. Several of them have expanded and were thinking of going to another company for additional services because they didn't know what we provided.'' She tapped him on the shoulder. "What were you thinking of? How could you stay in business so long if you don't keep current with your clients? Most of those companies don't know what we offer.''

''Brian assured me he was on top of these small companies,'' Adam said and wondered what else had been neglected around the office while he was overseas. ''I'm glad I put you on them.''

He had been so busy training someone to take his position in the Ivory Coast and the expansion. He knew Joe worked side by side with Brian and kept things going as it had been. It seemed things hadn't been going as smoothly as he'd thought. Brian was great with large companies, but they couldn't afford to let the small ones go.

Amanda had put her hands back into the water.

He nuzzled and stroked her abdomen and slid his hands between her legs, still kissing her neck and ear.

''Adam . . . I've got my hands in water,'' she whispered. ''You want dinner . . . don't you?''

''Dinner can wait.'' He turned her around, with dripping hands unnoticed and claimed her lips. After missing her all day, he couldn't wait another minute. Without breaking contact, he shucked his jacket and pressed her against the sink.

She felt around behind her for a dishcloth and wiped her hands.

Soft hands on his shoulders and back drove his ardor to the limit. Unsnapping her jeans, he slid them down her hips. At the same time, her hands dealt with his shirt buttons slowly, seductively stroking his chest.

Her warm breath kissed his neck, leisurely explored his chest. His heart skipped a beat as her tongue traced his nipple. Lips parted, her warm breath kissed his neck, chest, nipple. He sucked in a breath in sweet anticipation as her fingers unbuckled his belt as if they had all night to explore, unzipped his pants inch by inch. The mere touch of her hand sent a warm shiver through him. He swelled in anticipation as her fingers leisurely slid inside.

''Umm, baby,'' he groaned as his hands contracted as they wrapped around her thighs just below the juncture. Her sweet moans were music to his ears as he hooked a finger around her damp panties and slid inside to feel her heat. She moved against his fingers, sliding his pants down. He turned, inched back, and lifted her onto the edge of the granite counter top, then slid her panties and jeans completely off. And impaled her. His groan mixed with her high-pitched sigh as she dropped her chin to his chest. Her trembling limbs clung to him. Her touch firm and persuasive, invited more of him.

He sank deeper into her as she wrapped her legs tighter around his waist, her hands gripping his back as she cried out. They moved together, sensations spiraling. Wanting her to reach ecstasy in time with his own, one of his large hands cupped her buttocks, the other reached and stroked her intimately. Her thighs clenched tighter as he stroked her, impaled her, touched her, engulfed her, her breath whispering against his chest. He slowed their pace savoring their passion—until he couldn't hold on any longer. As she writhed against him, the desire he held at bay broke free. He knew he touched her core as they moved urgently together reaching unnamed heights. They held each other, lost in the aftershocks, trembling, hearts pounding, muscles clenching. It all seemed to go on forever. Adam knew he could stay as he was for eternity.

He also knew he'd never give up this piece of heaven. He'd spend a lifetime trying to convince her that they belonged together . . . were made for each other.

As he absorbed the last of her trembling, for once in the last thirty-three years he wasn't an outsider looking in. He belonged.

On Christmas Eve, Adam still hadn't found the appropriate time to tell Amanda he was leaving after Christmas. She still thought he'd be with her until after New Year.

He almost felt angry for having to tiptoe around her this way. It would only give her another excuse to compare him with Brian. At this stage of their relationship, he didn't need that.

As Reverend Everett Smart spoke of the purpose of Christmas at the midnight service, Adam gripped Amanda's hand, offering up a prayer for enlightenment.

He compared his life from a year ago when he'd been shut up with paperwork, sipping a glass of wine. And his visits to church, although he was a believer, had been few. His dad was fun loving, but his mom was a staunch worshiper. She dragged him and his dad there every Sunday morning, quite often having to wear the same starched and faded dress over and over and his dad wearing the same bedraggled suit, though it was always pressed. But she was there with her Sunday hat perched on her tight curls, nodding during the sermon, giving the preacher encouragement. The sermon would put cheer in her heart to last through the week, because she'd be humming her songs day after day.

And he remembered he was in every last Christmas play, getting teased afterward by the boys who weren't required to get up in front of the church for the display. But she made sure he participated.

He'd cast those memories aside for years, the pain piercing him too sharply to remember. With Amanda beside him, he wasn't afraid to dwell on the fond times.

As Everett led them through the last prayer, he knew he had truly been blessed this Christmas season, and he rejoiced in it as they sang "Joy to the World." He felt the joy his mom carried through her week in his heart. He knew why she sang.

Christmas morning was snowy and cold. The fire Adam had made while Amanda cooked breakfast was roaring and toasty. After breakfast, Amanda opened Josh's gift first and exclaimed over the silk scarf and bracelet he bought her. Adam opened his and oohed and ahed over the Washington Redskin's sweatshirt.

Finally, they exchanged gifts.

"You shouldn't have," Amanda said as she tore the paper off to bare the delicate porcelain figurine, her eyes sparkling.

"It's so beautiful," she whispered. "Thank you. Oh, Adam, I didn't expect this." She put the delicate piece on the table and hugged him.

Adam used it as an excuse for a lingering kiss. "Had I known I'd get this response, I'd have given you more," he said huskily.

"Oh, you." She sat back and plucked up a small package. "I've got something for you, too."

"To mimic you, you shouldn't have," he said as he tore into the paper to reveal engraved gold cuff links and a snow globe with a Christmas scene inside.

Adam swallowed several times before he could say anything. The gifts he received from Brian and her were the only ones he'd received for years. His throat felt too clogged to utter a word. "I'll treasure it always." His voice cracked. He cleared his throat. "Hey, I've got another one for you." He reached into his pocket for a small package and handed it to her.

Amanda unwrapped it to reveal diamond teardrop earrings. Each was one carat. "This is too much. Oh, Adam." She looked up at him. "Why?"

"They're for a very special lady."

Tears sparkled in her eyes. He was making her believe again. She couldn't afford to do that. Love wasn't forever. But it was Christmas and the magic of it was spinning in waves around her. The fire only escalated the sentiment.

They reached for each other at the same time. The actual gifts didn't matter but the sentiment did. In the season of love, they needed to belong, they needed to love, they needed each other.

"Words can't express how much I need you," he said, pressing a kiss to her lips. She sighed in remembered pleasure as he pealed off her clothes to reveal her glistening skin inch by inch. It was a time to revel, not for haste. He brushed his chest against her nipples.

She trailed her fingertips lightly over his skin. He followed the sensuous curves and lines, covering the surface with a carpet of kisses. They stroked, squeezed each other, their arousal undulating like waves in the ocean before they were joined as one.

As the light filtered through sheer curtains covering the windows and the warm heat from the fire kissed their skin, they fragmented into a burst of flame to rival that of the brightest star.

Josh called later in the day. "Merry Christmas, Mom."

"Merry Christmas to you. How is it there?"

"It's wonderful, but," he whispered, "I miss your cooking."

Amanda laughed. "I'll freeze some for you."

"Good. How's work?"

"It's going well."

"And Adam?"

He asked a lot about Adam, Amanda thought. "He's fine. I'll let you speak to him before we hang up."

"I'd like that." An unusual silence, then, "You know, Mom, I never told you, but I always talked to Adam more than I did to Dad. I felt guilty about that after he died."

"Oh, honey."

"Adam was always easy to talk to. He would answer questions and deal with stuff Dad never seemed to have an answer for. I used to call him collect in Africa because Dad never knew what to say about certain things, or never had the time."

"Why didn't you come to me if you felt you couldn't talk to your father?"

"They were men things, Mom. I couldn't talk to you about it."

"Of course you could. I thought you knew you could come to me about anything." Amanda said, feeling hurt, and wondering what she did wrong that her own son who slept down the hall from her, couldn't come to her.

"I knew that, but you're a woman. I needed to talk to another man. It's a guy thing. I'm not telling you to upset you."

"I'm not upset. I just wanted to be there for you."

"You were. Still are. I love you, Mom."

Tears misted her eyes. "I love you, too, sweetheart," she sniffed.

"Okay, don't start crying on me now."

"I just can't help it."

"Oh, God. You okay?"

"Yes I am. I'll let you talk to Adam, now."

Amanda called Adam to the phone and went upstairs to change clothes for the dinner with Everett, Lottie, Henry, and their two sons home from college.

"Hi, Josh." Adam sat on one of the high bar chairs in the kitchen.

"How's Mom?"

"She's great."

"Good. I worry about her."

"You shouldn't. I'm keeping an eye on her."

"Good. Good. Oh, and how are you?"

"Thanks for remembering. I'm fine."

"You're always okay."

Adam wondered why he would think that. But he also needed to talk to Josh about his relationship with Amanda. How did you gracefully tell a woman's son that you had the hots for his mom? "I was wondering, Josh. How would you feel if your mom and I . . . well, if we discovered that we . . . liked each other?"

"You and Mom?"

"Your mom and me, yes." Adam held his breath waiting for the response of a lifetime.

"So you really are going to stay in Virginia."

"That's the plan."

"I think she needs someone like you. Dad was never very sensitive to her needs. And you are, at least you were there for me. You'll be a good change for her."

Adam let out a sigh of relief. "Thanks, Josh."

"Just take good care of my mom," he said as he hung up. Adam helped Amanda finish the Christmas dinner and by two o'clock, the house was busy with people. This time, however, Adam did not feel even a twinge of jealousy in Everett's presence. And he reveled in this heartwarming Christmas Day. It couldn't have been better.

Chapter 9

The day after Christmas they were snuggled in Adam's bed, warm and contented after lovemaking. Christmas had been magical, both warm and tender. It still lingered as they woke the next morning. She wanted it to last another week. Maybe— just maybe she meant more than Adam's work. Perhaps his words rang true. Their relationship was important to him. She understood that, when they started Worldwide Satellites, Brian and Adam needed to put in the long hours to establish the business. But they'd been in business for fifteen years now. It was well established and they were making great profits. There was no reason he couldn't take a week off for them. She wanted—needed—time for intimacy. Time for just the two of them.

At least Adam wouldn't have to leave before after the New Year. Then, he'd be much too busy with the company expansion for the time for them.

Adam gave her one last kiss. Leaning over her, he smoothed her brow.

"Adam, Josh told me how you were there for him. Thank you."

"It was nothing."

She reached up and touched his brow. "In a time when so many children are following the wrong path, it meant more than you'll ever realize."

"He's my godson. It's my job to be there for him."

"Not every godparent takes their responsibility that seriously."

He smiled. "You're welcome."

She reached up and kissed him.

When they came up for air, Adam said, "Amanda?"

"Yes?" Her response was soft, her eyes light.

"I have to leave tomorrow."

"So soon? You can't wait another week?" Disappointment spiraled through her.

Adam sighed. "I'm sorry Amanda, I can't. We have to settle this before the end of the year."

At least they could still be together, even if it was in New York Amanda thought, annoyed that, yet again, work intruded. Perhaps they could see a play on Broadway. She wanted the warm moments to last.

"Some of the contracts I'm working on are based in New York. This would be the perfect opportunity to meet the clients," she suggested, stroking the stubble on his chin. Being together was the important thing here. Then she hit her head with the palm of her hand. "I can't do that. The party! I don't understand why this can't wait a few days."

Adam kissed the top of her head. "I wish it could wait, but it can't."

"I knew this was going to happen," she interrupted him vehemently. "You're turning out to be just like Brian. Most of his trips were around holidays, too. Are you even going to make it back in time for the party? Or do I have to give it alone?"

Amanda didn't immediately notice the subtle stiffness in him. "Don't compare us. I'm not Brian."

"Well, you certainly act alike," she snapped.

He caught her chin in his hand. "Do you pretend you're in bed with Brian when we're together, Amanda?" Adam asked quietly through clenched teeth. Too quietly. "Do you close your eyes, when you reach your peak and think Brian's name?"

"That's cruel, crude, and undeserved . . ."

"Do you dream that you have your husband all over again in me?" He threw the cover back, stormed out of bed.

"What are you talking about? I know who you are. I know who Brian was? I'm not confusing the two of you and I don't like the implication. You need to accept the fact that both of you live and breathe Worldwide Satellites. Nothing else compares." She glowered at him and turned.

"You don't have to go to New York. Your job isn't real anyway." Too late he realized what he'd said. A sudden thin chill hung on the edge of his words. "Oh, boy!"

"The job isn't real?" Amanda scooted over and pulled the sheet up to her chin glaring at him with burning reproachful eyes. "What do you mean by that statement?"

"Nothing. Forget I said anything." He stiffened, momentarily abashed.

"Forget what, exactly?" She got up, wrapping the sheet around her sarong-style. Shock yielded quickly to fury.

Adam swiped a hand through his hair in resignation. "It was meant to get you familiar with the company and contracts. You've done a great job," he placated. "I never expected you to pull that much out of those contracts. You even plugged some holes I wasn't aware were there."

"Exactly how were these contracts going to familiarize me with the company?" She seethed with mounting rage.

"We don't have to go through this now." He sighed. "You were supposed to get familiar with the company and the services we offer by studying these contracts. I didn't expect you to actually contact them all and go over everything in detail. It's turned into more than I ever expected."

"You lied to me." Her voice trembled.

What was he to say?

"I didn't know you. I couldn't very well set you up with major client's accounts when you knew nothing about the business. I didn't know your capabilities. Especially since Brian . . ."

"Brian what?"

His breath wooshed out. ". . . said you were flighty, if the truth be told."

"Oh, so now you're telling the truth? When it comes back on me!"

"I know you're nothing like what Brian said. Actually, I've been thinking that we need a full-time person for that customer service area."

"A full-time person like whom, may I ask?" She spat out the words contemptuously.

"You. You've done a first-rate effort on them. You have a real feel for the business."

"And the little matter of asking me simply slipped your mind, I take it."

"I had to see how you handled it before I assigned you more challenging duties."

"Oh, so now it's a real job! Which is it—real or toy job, Adam? You know, if there's one thing I can't stand it's lying. If you needed to know something about me, you only had to ask. I have enough sense to know that if I couldn't do something, I needed to come to you for guidance. You aren't talking to a teenager." She patted her forehead. "But now I understand. You did this because I was ready to sell the company, didn't you?"

"Amanda. You are a very responsible woman who has done a magnificent job. I respect your capabilities."

"I asked you. Is this about the stock?"

"All right. In the beginning it was about the stock. I put my life's blood in this company and you were ready to sell it out from under me. I couldn't let that happen. I didn't know you. Now I do."

"Let me tell you something, Adam Somerville. I've changed

my mind. I'm not selling my stock, but I'm having equal say in this company. And you don't have to lie to me about trips. I overheard one of Brian's phone conversations where he admitted he didn't really need to take a trip to conduct business after he had yet again canceled one of our family outings. He could have handled it by phone and fax. I don't care about your personal life. Only Worldwide Satellites concern me. Every major decision made will go through me.'' Amanda dropped the sheet and pulled her robe on, and marched out of Adam's room.

''Like hell it will,'' he said under his breath. ''We have to talk more about it,'' he shouted after her.

She looked over her shoulder. ''I've said everything I need to say.''

Suddenly, the beauty of the holidays left and a pall fell over Amanda's heart.

She thought Adam had believed in her, trusted her.

It hit Amanda as she shed the robe and turned on the shower with an angry twist of her wrist. He was merely using her. Standing under the spray didn't have its usual soothing effect but the exact opposite. She tried very hard not to sink into despair.

Male using female stories were rampant in novels, television, and in real life. Safely tucked in marriage, Amanda had thought herself immune. Now she knew different.

At least Everett, who'd been gentle and caring, had been true, but she didn't love Everett.

''Amanda,'' Adam entreated from her office doorway, hoping to call a truce before he left, knowing his chances were slim to none.

''Yes?'' she returned, posture stiff, manner cold. She was unbending, and holding up a sheet of paper with stiff fingers.

''We'll work on us when I return.'' He advanced into the small office and rounded the desk. He admired the proud stiffness in her shoulders and winced for the hurt in her and the fact that she valiantly tried to shield herself. If he could have rescinded his decision a thousand times, he would have. If this trip didn't mean half of next year's salaries would be covered ... but it did. No one else could negotiate this contract for him.

Adam felt pulled in two. He loved this woman. Did loving mean having to choose between his work and the woman who should stand with him? It needn't be a contest. Why was she making it into one?

She gave him a cold, fleeting smile. "Sure," and dropped the paper on the desk.

If ever he was greeted with a cold shower, this was it. He glanced at his watch, knowing he had to leave now or miss his flight. He bent, grabbing her in his arms and kissed her long and hard. Surprisingly, she responded to his gesture. "I love you, Amanda," he whispered.

And then he was gone.

Such simple words that held more importance than any combination.

Amanda sat speechless and in doubt, with hope racing through her.

She wanted someone who trusted her, believed in her abilities. She couldn't, wouldn't, fight the battle with him that she fought with Brian who'd never believed in her. Adam had shown her he didn't either.

It hurt letting him go with unresolved anger between them. She understood that he had work to do. And that he had to do it now. But she didn't understand why he lied to her.

Why was life so complicated?

Chapter 10

Heart heavy, Adam deplaned. The cold send off he'd received from Amanda rivaled New York's frigid temperatures. How the hell could he have fallen in love with her?

Brian was dead. And he, Adam, was flesh and blood alive. Couldn't she see that? *Did* she think of Brian when she was in bed with him? Adam pulled his collar up. Couldn't she see the love they had to offer one another. How perfectly they fit? It was more than sex. It was a blending of spirits. He felt so much at home. He felt she belonged with him. That he had a real purpose in life other than making a living and surviving. Life was made for love, his father had said before his mom's death. Adam thought of the loving snapshot of his parents and was thinking for once he'd have that love for himself. Finally he'd found a woman he thought could give him all his wildest dreams. A woman worth taking the risk for.

Then he remembered his father's last comments while in his deepest moments of despair. *Be careful of your dreams, son. Deal with what you know. Dreams are for fools.* You weren't wrong to live your life the way you lived it, Dad, Adam thought.

His mother was one of the happiest Moms around. To be a Somerville was to be a dreamer. That was what made them so special, so loving with so very much to offer.

What were dreams if not to share? The last few weeks had emphasized how much he needed Amanda. He couldn't go back to a work-only existence.

Adam hailed a waiting taxi. Maybe it had come down to making a choice between work and Amanda. Perhaps he had to consider giving up the company. Giving up Worldwide Satellites would be tantamount to giving up part of himself. Was his love for Amanda that significant?

He'd visit Tiffany's while in New York and he'd ask Amanda to marry him as soon as he returned home. New Year's Eve at midnight. It would be the perfect time to propose.

Adam had a feeling this was going to be the biggest gamble of his life. Amanda could be as difficult to gauge as his most demanding client.

"You've been making yourself too scarce, with that new man, girlfriend," Lottie greeted Amanda with a peck on the cheek at The Little Cafe. They took their seats and the menus the hostess handed them.

"He's gone."

She dropped her menu. "For good?"

"For the week."

Lottie negligently waved a hand then resumed perusing her menu. "That's nothing. You said it like it was the end of the world. Young love." She shook her head. "I'm too old for this."

"It's over between us."

"Oh, Lord. That's horrible. What happened?"

The waitress stepped up for their selections. They quickly scanned the menu. Amanda didn't care what she ordered. Just to order something, she selected a grilled chicken and cheese sandwich. Lottie hastily ordered a ham and cheese croissant and New England clam chowder.

After the woman walked away, Lottie said, "Okay. What happened with the hunk?"

She retold the argument.

"Oh, shoot. I thought he was just the perfect one for you, too. Are you sure you can't work it out?"

"I don't know, Lottie. He swears that he loves me, but . . . I can't trust what he says."

"Well, you did say that Brian told him you were scatter-brained. He should have waited to get to know you before forming an opinion, but he trusted Brian. You know how men are." Lottie reached across and patted Amanda's hand. "Honey, he just might love you. At least give him a chance to redeem himself. Maybe he'll throw in some jewelry in the process." She smiled at her own facetious reply.

Amanda shook her head in exasperation. "How did you and Everett end up siblings? He's down to earth and you're out in left field."

She waved a hand at her. "Girl, please. He's so stodgy. That's why the two of you wouldn't do. You'd bore each other to death in no time."

Amanda ignored Lottie's assessment. "How is he? I've neglected him lately."

"Brooding over you, but he'll get over it," was her perky reply.

Adam looked out at the rush of people passing his window as he had dinner with Price Turner who had been trying to buy Worldwide for years.

"So," Price said as he sliced into his medium-rare steak. "Have you decided to sell Worldwide yet?"

The man looked up when Adam didn't respond immediately. "I'm considering it." He needed to play by ear. With the downsizings and changes occurring at astronomical speeds, an offer made a year ago wouldn't necessarily still hold true.

Price's fork clattered as it hit the plate. "I can't believe it. I thought you'd never sell that company."

"I said I'm thinking about it," Adam warned.

"Anytime you're ready, we are," Price said, a gleam in his eye rubbing his hands in anticipation.

"I need to know that you'll retain the employees. You won't find a better group."

"Hell, I'm not stupid, man. I'm not about to get rid of good workers. I'll even let you continue to manage it if you want to stay in the business."

Adam took in a deep breath. "Thanks. Give me a month to think about it, Price."

The older man looked at Adam. "I'll give you all the time you need."

Chapter 11

The warm homecoming and the exuberant kisses Adam had hoped for upon his return were at odds with the welcoming he received. Amanda was not waiting with open arms to greet him. If possible, she was even more restrained than when he'd left. He left his suitcase by the stairs.

"Oh, you're back," she managed to say as he entered the kitchen, minus the warm embracing enthusiasm he'd become accustomed to, before turning back to stirring something quite aromatic on the stove. The caterers walked briskly back and forth from the truck to the kitchen and dining room. The house was a flurry of activity. The atmosphere wasn't conducive to ironing out family squabbles.

"Could we talk upstairs?" he asked, hands in pocket.

"Now?" she questioned, wooden spoon hovering in the air.

"Yes, now, please."

"Give me a few minutes to finish this off." She resumed her stirring.

Adam skirted a woman carrying a huge punch bowl as he hauled his things to his room. Once there, to calm his jumping stomach, he unpacked. Ten minutes passed before Amanda knocked on the door before opening it. Warily, she stepped over the threshold.

As his thoughts had been centered around her since he left, he closed the door behind her and hauled her into his arms. Her startled shriek was quickly masked by his lips. He sighed when her arms reached around his neck. Instead of waiting, as soon as their lips parted, he asked, "Marry me, Amanda. I've missed you." The smile lit his eyes.

"Adam?"

"What is it, sweetheart?"

"I . . . I'm shocked. I didn't know you were thinking of marriage."

"Why not? I love you. Whatever our problems, we can work them out."

Oh, Lord. She was old and wise enough to know love didn't conquer all.

"I'm . . . I'm not ready for it. It's not as easy as it sounds. This isn't a fairy tale of happily ever after."

Adam dropped his hand from her arms, turned, and paced to the window. "You're not ready for me."

"For anyone."

Hands on his hips now, he asked, "Why not? Is it Brian again?"

"It's not a matter of comparing. I'm cautious. I don't want to make the same mistakes this time that I made with Brian. I'm a grown woman, able to accept responsibility and deserving of respect. I can't live without respect."

"I have never disrespected you. I know you're a woman."

"I'm not talking about sex."

"Don't insult my intelligence. You're not talking to a sixteen-year-old."

"You have to understand." She advanced farther in the room and sat on his bed. "Brian took care of everything. Bills, insurances, investments. Everything. I was the little stay-at-home wife who raised our son, supported Brian in his business, and did volunteer work in the church. I didn't know anything about the insurance. Everything was for the company, and that is where you are exactly the same.'' She held up a hand to forestall his comments. ''It never occurred to him that Josh and I would need something to live off of in the event that he wasn't here or that Josh needed money for his education. He left everything to Worldwide Satellites. And if it wasn't for you, for the funds coming from the company, I wouldn't have had anything to live on. That's frightening. Not to really know where my next loaf of bread is coming from. That's why it's so important that I have a career. It's why it's so important that I have some control over my life. I can't live with the uncertainty. At forty, I need stability.''

''I wouldn't dream of taking all that from you. I don't mind sharing every aspect of the business with you, or our lives. As half of this union, you have a right to know. That isn't unreasonable. Every woman should know where she stands financially. I don't have a problem with that. I prefer having a marriage of sharing.'' Adam sat beside her and grasped her hand in a possessive gesture. ''Don't substitute Brian for me. We aren't the same person. We're different men with different drives, different desires, different ultimate goals. Judge me for who I am. Not for what another man has done.''

''B . . . Adam.''

He took her face in his palms. ''I'm not Brian. You have to remember that.''

''I know you aren't Brian. I just need more time. It's too soon.''

Amanda left Adam sitting on his bed.

The door closing after Amanda sounded like a bomb in his head.

Adam had always been a strategist. He knew he had two choices. He could give up Amanda completely, or he could bide his time and convince her they belonged together.

Giving up was not an option for the woman he loved. He'd give her time. As she worked more for the company. As she got an opportunity to know him better, she'd see things his way.

By ten that evening, the first floor and basement rec room were filled with people. Adam was irresistible in his formal attire. Amanda had been itching to open that tuxedo shirt and run her fingers through that hair for hours. Now, he was talking to the Blake brothers who always managed to crash the party. They also tended to stay low-keyed, offering Worldwide's employees better positions. They lost a few, but none in the last five years. Most of the Blake brother's employees had moved on to other positions after dismantling companies. Worldwide employees liked having the security of management.

"And here is the woman who has been tormenting me for weeks now." Joe was unsteady on his feet.

"Coffee and soda for you the rest of the evening," Amanda said, disgruntled that the man had already imbibed too much so early in the evening. This was a company affair, after all, and Joe was part of management. She could never tolerate excessive drinking. His inebriated state was at odds with his work ethic. He'd done a tremendous job in training her on the contracts and he was a good addition to the company. Actually, he was tops in his position.

Joe's wife came up behind them. "Is he troubling you already, Amanda? The night's only begun." She tapped him on the arm and she and Amanda both had to balance him as he began to topple.

"I'm not tormenting her. She's tormented me!" he sputtered, outraged.

"Come on Joe," his wife said, disgusted. "Let's eat. It's a good thing I'm driving tonight." She took his hand and pulled him toward the buffet.

None of the drivers were allowed to drink at the party.

Worldwide Satellites couldn't afford to get sued for someone's drunken driving. And Amanda was very conscious of safety.

It was ten minutes before midnight and the crowd was getting geared up for the countdown. Amanda donned a coat and stepped out onto the deck for some peace and quiet before the ruckus of the New Year. She paced to the railing, leaned against it, and took a breath of the cold, refreshing air when she heard the sliding door behind her.

"You look beautiful." Amanda turned at hearing Adam's voice. She wore the tear drop earrings he'd given her with her black velvet midcalf evening dress.

"Thank you."

"What's wrong, sweetheart?" Adam asked.

"I just wanted some time alone, that's all. Nothing's wrong."

His footsteps sounded on the wooden boards as he approached her, put his hands on her shoulders, slowly turned her. "Mind if I join you?" The moonlight cast irregular shadows on her face.

"Not at all."

"I've made a decision." He tilted her chin, pressed her close to him.

She leaned her head to the side. "What decision?"

"I've decided to sell the business. I'll have less responsibility, more time . . ."

"You're selling it to the Blakes?" She leaned back in horror, pressing a hand to his chest.

"No, no. You remember Price. I don't want the business broken apart. I want it kept intact for the employees. Price is dependable. He runs a tight ship. He'll do right by the employees."

"You see, that's exactly what I meant." Shoving away from him, she paced away, then turned to face him again. "Why didn't you talk to me about it? Why did you make a decision like that on your own?"

"You know what Amanda, there's no pleasing you." His angry retort hardened his features. "You don't like the business. Now you want the business. What the hell do you want, woman?"

"I don't want you to sell it. You love that company. How could you think that I could love you and want you to give up something so important to you?"

"You love me." It was a statement, not a question. His anger evaporated, leaving only confusion.

"You haven't learned anything from all this. I want you to communicate with me."

"I am communicating with you." The shock of her announcement almost left him tongue-tied.

"No, you aren't. You're making decisions before you talk to me. You can't read my mind. I want you to talk to me before you make major decisions."

"All right, all right. What do you want? I'm all ears." He crossed his arms to keep from sweeping her off her feet and escape upstairs.

"First, judge me by your own assessment of me, not by what Brian has said."

"I . . ."

She put a finger to his lips to silence him. "Next, don't lie to me. If you have reservations about my abilities, let me know."

"You're very capable. I know that."

"And last, I want the business. I just want to make sure that there's time for us, too."

"There will always be time for us." He took her face in his hands. "I'll always *make* time for us. We got the Scott contract, and," he reached into his pocket and pulled out two plane tickets, "in a week we have tickets for a two-week vacation to Fiji. Let this trip be a new beginning for us."

She could barely control her gasp of surprise. "You can get away for . . ."

Their heads turned when they heard the countdown, sixty,

fifty-nine . . . "We have to join them." Amanda led him into the house and grabbed noise makers, party hats, and champagne to welcome in the new year. When Adams lips touched hers and he gathered her into his arms, she knew the New Year would be a new beginning for their lives together. He was willing to give up the most important part of his life for her. He was willing to contribute making their marriage work. And she loved him. What more could she ask for? When their lips parted, she said, "I'll marry you Adam Somerville."

He kissed her again and when they came up for air and were once again aware of their surroundings, Josh was beside them. "I guess you don't need mistletoe." He held a sprig above their heads.

Amanda had to blink twice to assure herself she wasn't hallucinating, that she was actually looking at her son. "Josh?" she asked.

"I couldn't miss your engagement," he said, grinning from ear to ear.

She clasped his cheeks in her hands. He grabbed her in a bear hug.

"I can't believe it!"

"Believe it," Adam said from behind.

"You told him?" Amanda asked.

"Of course. He has to give the bride away. Pardon me, is it all right for your son to give you away? You're not too independent for traditions, are you?"

"I'd love for my son to give me away." She laughed. Then she sobered. "How do you feel about Adam and me?"

"I'm happy for you, Mom. As long as you're happy, go for it. You deserve the best."

Tears filled her eyes.

"How did you grow up so fast?"

"It's a new year, Amanda. Isn't this a wonderful start?" Adam gathered the three of them together. "We're a family."

"Yes." It started with the two people she loved most with her. It couldn't have been better.

Adam slipped his hand in his pocket and brought out a three carat diamond ring and slipped it on her finger.

"Now, now," Everett said. "It's time to bless this engagement." He winked at Amanda and shook Adam's hand. "May God be with you." Everyone bowed their heads as he said a special prayer for them.

About The Authors

Bridget Anderson's first Arabesque title, SOUL MATES, won rave reviews. She lives in Atlanta, Georgia where she is busy working on her next romance for Arabesque.

Candice Poarch made the bestsellers list with her first novel *White Lightning*. She lives in Springfield, Virginia where she is busy working on her next romance for Arabesque.

Adrienne Ellis Reeves is a multipublished Arabesque author. She lives in Summerville, South Carolina with her husband. She is delighted to receive reader mail at:

975 Bacons Bridge Road,
Suite 164, Box 122,
Summerville, SC 29485.

Look for these upcoming Arabesque titles:

January 1998
WITH THIS KISS by Candice Poarch
NIGHT SECRETS by Doris Johnson
SIMPLY IRRESISTIBLE by Geri Guillaume
A NIGHT TO REMEMBER by Niqui Stanhope

February 1998
HEART OF THE FALCON by Francis Ray
A PRIVATE AFFAIR by Donna Hill
RENDEZVOUS by Bridget Anderson
I DO! A Valentine's Day Collection

March 1998
KEEPING SECRETS by Carmen Green
SILVER LOVE by Layle Giusto
PRIVATE LIES by Robyn Amos
SWEET SURRENDER by Angela Winters

TIMELESS LOVE

Look for these historical romances in the Arabesque line:

BLACK PEARL by Francine Craft (0236-0, $4.99)

CLARA'S PROMISE by Shirley Hailstock (0147-X, $4.99)

MIDNIGHT MOON by Mildred Riley (0200-X; $4.99)

SUNSHINE AND SHADOWS by Roberta Gayle (0136-4, $4.99)